In the Manor with the Millionaire

CASSIE MILES

MILLS & BOON®
Pure reading pleasure™

All th[...] characters in [...] existence [...]e the
imagin[...]on of the author, and have no relation whatsoever [...]nyone
bearin[...] the same name or names. The[...] not even distantly inspired
by any individual known or unknown [...] the author, and all the
incide[...] are pure invention.

First published in Great Britain 2009
by Harlequin Mills & Boon Limited,
Eton House, 18-24 Paradise Road, Richmond, Surrey TW9 1SR

© Harlequin Books S.A. 2008

Special thanks and acknowledgement to Cassie Miles for her
contribution to THE CURSE OF RAVEN'S CLIFF mini-series.

ISBN: 978 0 263 87281 1

46-0409

Harlequin Mills & Boon policy is to use papers that are
natural, renewable and recyclable products and made from
wood grown in sustainable forests. The logging and
manufacturing processes conform to the legal environmental
regulations of the country of origin.

Printed and bound in Spain
by Litografia Rosés S.A., Barcelona

ABOUT THE AUTHOR

For Cassie Miles, the best part about writing a story set in Eagle County near the Vail ski area is the ready-made excuse to head into the mountains for research. Though the winter snows are great for skiing, her favourite season is autumn when the aspens turn gold.

The rest of the time, Cassie lives in Denver where she takes urban hikes around Cheesman Park, reads a ton and critiques often. Her current plans include a Vespa and a road trip, despite eye-rolling objections from her adult children.

To Lee Carr, the world's greatest gothic writer.
And, as always, to Rick.

Chapter One

"One, two, three…" Duncan Monroe counted the steps as he climbed the stairs, not touching the banister or the wall. "…four, five, six."

That was how old he was. Six years old.

"Seven, eight, nine."

Here was where the staircase made a corner, and he could see to the top. Daddy had turned on the light in his bedroom, but there were shadows. Dark, scary shadows. Outside the rain came down and rattled against the windows.

Duncan shivered. Even though this was the middle of summertime, he felt cold on the inside. So cold it made his tummy hurt. Sometimes, when he touched people or things, he got creepy feelings like spider legs running up and down his arms. And he saw stuff. Bad stuff.

But he wasn't touching anything. His feet were in sneakers. He had on jeans and a long-sleeved T-shirt. He shouldn't be scared.

"Duncan." His dad called to him. "Are you getting ready for bed?"

"No." He hadn't meant to yell. His voice was too loud.

He covered his open mouth with both hands. His fingers pushed hard, holding back an even louder yell. His skin tasted like salt. Usually he wore gloves to keep from feeling things.

"Duncan, are you all right?"

His dad hated when Duncan was inappropriate. That's what his teacher used to call it. *Inappropriate behavior*. The doctors had other words for him. *Trauma. Autism. Hyper-something*. They all meant the same thing. He was a freak.

He yanked his hands down to his sides. "I'm okay."

"Get into your pajamas, buddy. I'll be there in a minute."

The shadow at the top of the stairs was as big as a T-Rex with giant, pointy teeth. Duncan wasn't going there. He turned around on the stairs and quietly counted backward. "Nine, eight, seven…"

He was at the front door of the big house they had just moved into. Though he didn't like touching doorknobs, he grabbed it and pulled.

Outside, the rain wasn't too bad. Big, fat drops splashed on the flat stones leading up to the front door. He stuck out his hand to catch them.

He walked out into it. Five steps. Then ten.

The light by the front door didn't reach very far into the dark. The thunder went boom. He heard the ocean smashing on the rocks at the bottom of the cliff.

He turned around and stared at the big house. On the first floor were four windows and one door, exactly in the middle. Five windows, all exactly the same size, on top. All exactly balanced. He liked that. What he didn't like was the big, old, wrecked-up tower that Daddy said used to be a lighthouse.

He looked toward it and saw a girl in a long dress and a red cape. She skipped toward the trees in the forest.

She giggled. Not the kind of mean laugh that kids used when they pointed at his gloves and called him Dunk the Skunk. She waved to him as though she wanted to play.

He heard her singing. "She sells seashells by the seashore."

MADELINE DOUGLAS gripped the steering wheel with both hands and squinted through her glasses at the narrow road winding through the thick Maine forest. Her headlights barely penetrated the rain and fog that had turned the summer night into a dense black shroud.

She opened her window to disperse the condensation on her windshield; the defroster in her ancient Volkswagen station wagon had quit working. This cranky old rattletrap always chose the worst possible moment to be temperamental. If the skies had been clear—the way normal weather in July ought to be—the defrost would have been fine.

How much farther? The man at the service station in Raven's Cliff where she'd spent her last ten bucks on gas told her that this road led to Beacon Manor. "Can't miss it," he'd said.

"We'll see about that," she muttered. Thus far, everything about her drive from Boston to this remote fishing village in Maine had gone wrong. An accident with a logging truck had clogged the highway. Then, she'd missed the turnoff and had to backtrack several miles. Then, her cell phone died. And now, the weather from hell.

At five minutes past eight o'clock, she was more than

half an hour late for her interview with world-famous architect Blake Monroe. Not to mention that she was a mess. Her green-patterned blouse didn't go with the bright red cardigan she'd dragged out of her suitcase when the rain started. Her khaki skirt was creased with wrinkles. Her black hair, pulled up in a knot on top of her head, had to be a frizz mop.

Somehow, she had to pull herself together and convince Blake Monroe to hire her as a tutor for his six-year-old son, Duncan, who had been diagnosed with a form of high-functioning autism. Though she had no formal training in handling kids with special needs, Madeline had been a substitute teacher for the past two years in Boston's inner-city schools. She had first-hand experience with a wide range of behaviors.

She'd convince him. *She had to.*

If Blake Monroe didn't hire her, she had a serious problem. With her meager supply of cash spent and her credit cards maxed, she couldn't even afford a cheap motel room for tonight. Sleeping in her car would be difficult; she'd crammed all her earthly belongings in here, including the potted ficus that sat beside her on the passenger seat.

The rain died down, replaced by gusts of fog that slapped against her windshield like tattered curtains. The tired old engine coughed on the verge of a breakdown as she emerged from the forest.

In the distance, perhaps a half mile away, she saw the glimmer of lights. Beacon Manor. Huge as a fortress, the mansion loomed in the foreboding darkness.

She maneuvered around a sharp curve that circled a stand of trees. On the opposite side, the shoulder of the road vanished into nothingness at the edge of a cliff. A dangerous precipice with no guard rail.

Her headlights shone on a dark-colored SUV parked smack in the middle of the road. His lights were off. There was no way around him.

She cranked the steering wheel hard left—away from the cliff—and slammed on the brake. Though she couldn't have been going more than twenty miles an hour, her tires skidded on the wet asphalt.

In slow motion, she saw the inevitable collision coming closer, inch by inch. Her brakes screeched. The fog whirled. Her headlights wavered.

Her right fender dinged the rear bumper of the SUV, and she jolted against her seat belt. Though the impact felt minor, the passenger-side airbag deployed against the ficus. Great! Her plant was protected from whiplash.

But not herself. The driver's-side airbag stayed in place. Like everything else in her life, it was broken.

She slumped over the steering wheel. A nasty, metallic stink from the engine gushed through her open window. A car wreck would have been disaster, and she ought to be grateful that her car wasn't a crumpled mass. Instead, hot tears burned the insides of her eyelids. In spite of a lifetime of careful plans and hard work, in spite of her best intentions…

A hand reached through the window and grabbed her upper arm. "What's wrong with you? Didn't you see me?"

Startled, she stared into the stark face of a smallish man with a goatee. A sheen of moisture accented the hollows beneath his eyes and his angry, distorted snarl.

He shook her. "Don't think you can run away. You'll pay for this damage."

Enough! She shoved open her door, forcing him back.

Justified rage shot through her as she leaped from the car into the drizzle. "You're the one at fault. Look where you're parked. There's no way I could get around you."

"You're trespassing." With his left hand, he pulled his collar tight around his throat. His right arm hung loosely at his side. "This is my property."

Her hopes sank. "Blake Monroe?"

"Monroe? He's the architect I hired to fix this place up." His skinny neck craned. Even so, he wasn't as tall as her own five feet, ten inches. "I own Beacon Manor. I'm Theodore Fisher. *Doctor* Fisher."

He announced himself as if she should be impressed, but she'd never heard of him. "All right, *Doctor*. Let's take a look at the damage."

The deep gouge on her fender blended with other scrapes and nicks. Dr. Fisher glanced at the scratch on his SUV, then turned his back on her. Clearly agitated, he walked wide of the two vehicles with tense, jerky steps. His brow furrowed as he peered into the darkness at the edge of the cliff. Watching for something? For someone? As he paced, he muttered under his breath. Though she couldn't make out the words, he sounded furious.

Madeline didn't want that crazy anger turned in her direction. Speaking with the measured voice she used to calm a classroom full of second-graders, she said, "We should exchange insurance information."

"Not necessary," he snapped.

"I agree." She wouldn't bother with this repair, couldn't afford to have her insurance premiums go up. "I'm willing to forget about this if you are."

His head swiveled on his neck. He focused intently on her. "Not trying to pull a fast one, are you?"

"Certainly not." She removed her rain-splattered glasses. His face blurred.

"Why are you here?" he demanded.

"I'm applying for a job as a tutor for Blake Monroe's son."

"So you'll be staying at the Manor. At my house." Very deliberately, he approached her. "I'll always know where to find you."

The wind wailed through the trees, and she heard something else. A voice? Dr. Fisher turned toward the sound. His arm raised. In his right hand, he held an automatic pistol.

SHE SELLS seashells…

In her long dress, she was the prettiest girl Duncan had ever seen. Her hair was golden. Her skin was white. She looked like the marble angel on Mama's gravestone.

"I would like to be your friend," she said. "My name is Temperance Raven."

"That's the name of this town," Duncan said. "Raven's Cliff."

"Named after my father," she said. "Captain Raven."

He knew she was telling a lie. The town was founded in 1794. He remembered that date, just as he remembered all numbers. So what if she fibbed? He liked the way she talked, like an accent. "Where are you from?"

"Dover in England."

They were standing under the trees, and his clothes were soppy. But she hardly seemed wet at all. "Come inside, Temperance. I'll show you my computer games."

Maybe he'd even let her win. Her smile was so pretty.

Seashells, seashells. By the seashore.

She held up her hand. "I brought a gift for you."

Before he could tell her that he never touched anyone or anything with his bare hands, she placed a glowing white shell on the ground before him. "It's for you, Duncan."

If he didn't pick it up, she'd think he was scared. Then she'd laugh at him and run away. So, he leaned down and grabbed the shell. It burned his hand. He couldn't let go. Shivers ran up his arm. There was a roar inside his head.

"Temperance." He gasped.

"I am here, Duncan. I will always be here for you."

His eyes closed and he fell to the ground. In his mind, he saw a whole different place. A different time: Sunset. He was at the bottom of the cliff, near the rocks that stuck out into the waves.

He moaned and tried to get up. Something very bad had happened in this place and time, something that had to do with the shell....

He saw a pretty lady with curly black hair. Sofia, her name was Sofia. She had on a long white dress, kind of like the one Temperance wore, and she was lying on the rocks. Duncan felt her fear. Inside his head, he heard her silent screams for help, but she was too weak to move. Couldn't even lift a finger.

Someone else chanted. In a low voice, he sang about the sea. The dangers of the sea. The curse of the sea.

Duncan couldn't see his face. But he knew. This man was very bad. Very strong. Very mean. He put a necklace of seashells over Sofia's head.

"No," Duncan cried out. "Stop him. No."

The bad man pulled the necklace tighter and tighter. He twisted hard. Duncan felt the shells bite into his own throat. He couldn't breathe.

Lying on the wet grasses, he shook and shook. He was crying. He heard grunts and whimpers, and he knew the sounds were coming from him.

His eyes opened.

There was a lady kneeling beside him. She wore glasses. Her hair was pulled back, but some had got loose. It was black and curly. She looked kind of like Sofia. He whispered the name. "Sofia?"

"My name is Madeline," she said, reaching toward him. "Are you—"

"Don't," he yelled. "Don't touch me. Never touch."

She held up both hands. "Okay. Whatever you say. You're Duncan, right?"

He sat up and looked around for Temperance. She was gone. But he still held the shell in his hand. It was a warning. Temperance had warned him about the bad man.

He scrambled to his feet. Where was Temperance? Where was his friend? "She sells seashells…"

"By the seashore." The lady smiled and stood beside him. She was tall for a girl. "She sells seashells."

"By the seashore," he said.

She pointed. "Do you see that light over there? I'll bet that's your father's flashlight."

"He's going to be mad. I was inappropriate."

Madeline looked down at the sopping-wet boy in his jeans and T-shirt. A terrible sadness emanated from this child. She longed to cuddle him in her arms and reassure him, but she'd promised not to touch.

"There's nothing wrong with being inappropriate," she said. "I've often been that way myself."

He stared up at her. "Are you a freak?"

"Absolutely." She took off her glasses, tried wiping the

lenses on her damp shirt and gave up, stowing them in the pocket of her skirt. "It takes someone courageous to be different. I think you're very brave, Duncan."

The hint of a smile curved his mouth. "You do?"

"Very brave indeed." She bobbed her head. "Let's find your father."

When the boy took off running toward the flashlight's beacon, Madeline had a hard time keeping up. The two-inch heels on the beige leather pumps she'd worn to create a professional appearance for her interview made divots in the rain-soaked earth.

The flashlight's beam wavered, then charged in their direction. In seconds, a tall man in a hooded rain poncho was upon them. He held out his arms to Duncan, but the boy stopped a few yards away and folded his arms across his skinny torso. "I'm okay, Daddy."

"Thank God," his father murmured. "I was worried."

"I'm okay," Duncan shouted.

Blake Monroe dropped to one knee. He reached toward his son. Without touching the boy, he caressed the air around him with such poignancy that Madeline's heart ached.

Before she'd set out on this journey, she'd taken a couple of minutes to check out Blake Monroe on the Internet. An internationally renowned architect and designer, he'd worked in Berlin, Paris and all over the United States, most notably on historic renovations and exclusive boutique hotels. His international fame was somewhat intimidating, but right now he was a frightened parent whose only concern was the safety of his child.

Blake stood, whipped off his poncho and dropped it around his son's shoulders.

When he turned toward her, a flash of lightning illuminated his high cheekbones and the sharp line of his jaw. Even without her glasses, she realized that he was one of the most handsome men she'd ever seen.

The rain started up with renewed fury, lashing against his broad shoulders, but he didn't cower the way she did. His powerful presence suggested a strength that could match the raging storm. His fiery gaze met her eyes, and a sizzle penetrated her cold, wet body.

"Who are you?"

"Madeline Douglas. I'm here about the teaching position."

"What were you doing out here with my son?"

There was an unmistakable accusation in his question. He blamed her? Did he think she'd lured Duncan out of the house in this storm?

Fumbling in her pocket, she found her glasses and stuck them onto her nose, wishing she had a ten-inch-thick shield of bulletproof glass to protect herself from his hostility. "I was driving along the road, just coming out of the forest. And I had a bit of an accident with Dr. Fisher."

"The owner of the Manor," Blake said. "Nice move."

Though Madeline had done nothing wrong, she felt defensive. "We decided that the damage was too minor to report. Then we heard something from the forest. Voices." With Duncan standing here, she decided not to mention Dr. Fisher's gun. "I followed the sound of Duncan's voice. Found him at the edge of the trees."

"She did," Duncan said. "She's pretty. I thought she was Sofia."

Blake tensed. He hunkered down so his eyes were level with his son's. "What name did you say?"

"Poor, poor Sofia. She's with Mama and the angels."

"Did you see something, Duncan?"

"No," he shouted. "No, no, no."

"Let's go inside," Blake said.

Duncan spun in a circle. "Where's Temperance? She's my friend."

"Time for bed, son. Back to the house. You can count the steps."

The boy walked toward the front door in a perfectly straight line, counting each step aloud.

Without saying another word to her, Blake walked beside him.

"Hey," she called after them. "Should I bring my car around to the front?"

"I don't give a damn what you do."

A scream of sheer frustration crawled up the back of her throat. This trip was cursed. Every instinct warned her to give up, to turn back, find another way.

But she was desperate.

Through the driving rain, she heard Duncan counting and singing. "She sells seashells…"

Chapter Two

Gathering up the remnants of her shredded self-respect, Madeline chased after Blake and his son. If she didn't follow them into the house, she was certain that the door would be locked against her. Not only did she need this job, but she wanted it. She'd connected with Duncan. In him, she saw a reflection of her own childhood. She knew what it was like to be called a freak. Always to be an outsider.

As the daughter of a drug-addicted mother and an absent father, she'd been shuffled from one foster home to another until she was finally adopted by the Douglases when she was twelve. In spite of their kindness and warmth, Madeline still hadn't fitted in with other kids. Her adopted family was poor, and she grew too fast. Her secondhand clothing never fitted properly on her long, gangly frame. And then there were the glasses she'd worn since first grade.

Most of the time, her childhood was best forgotten. But, oddly, her past had brought her here. Standing in the doorway of Beacon Manor, Madeline saw someone she had once lived with. Alma Eisen.

Eighteen years ago, Alma had been a foster parent for Madeline and her older brother, Marty. They'd stayed with her for a year—a dark and terrible year during which Alma had decided to divorce her abusive husband. Unlike the other fosters, Alma had stayed in touch with Christmas cards and birthday greetings, which Madeline had dutifully responded to.

It was Alma—now employed as Blake's housekeeper and cook—who had told Madeline about the tutoring position. At the door to the manor, she greeted Madeline with a smile but held her at arm's length, not wanting to get wet. "What on earth happened to you?"

"Long story."

The years had been kind to Alma Eisen. Her hair was still blond and elaborately styled with spit curls at the cheeks. Her makeup, including blue eye shadow, almost disguised the wrinkles. Madeline figured that this petite woman had to be in her fifties. "You look terrific."

"Thanks, hon. Wish I could say the same for you."

Blake had followed his son—who was still counting aloud—to the top of the staircase.

Madeline called to him. "Mr. Monroe?"

He glared. "What is it?"

"I came all this way, sir. At the very least, I'd like to have an interview."

"After I get my son to bed, I'll deal with you."

He turned away. Though Madeline wasn't a betting woman, she guessed that her odds of being hired were about a thousand to one. A shiver trembled through her.

"You need to get out of those wet clothes," Alma said, "before you catch your death of cold."

"I don't have anything to change into. My car is parked way down the road."

"Come with me, hon. I'll take care of you."

Though Alma had stayed in touch, Madeline didn't remember her as a particularly nurturing woman. Her phone call about this job had been a huge surprise, and Madeline couldn't help wondering about Alma's motives. What could she hope to gain from having Madeline working here?

She trailed the small woman up the grand staircase and looked back down at the graceful oval of the foyer. She couldn't see into any of the other rooms. Doors were closed, and plastic sheeting hung across the arched entry to what must have been a drawing room. Signs of disrepair marred the grandeur of the manor, but the design showed a certain civility and elegance, like a dowager duchess who had fallen on hard times.

Alma hustled her past Duncan's bedroom to the far end of the long, wainscoted hallway with wallpaper peeling in the corners. She opened the door farthest from the staircase and hustled Madeline inside.

The center light reflected off the crystals of a delicate little chandelier. With dark wood furnishings, somewhat worn, and a four-poster bed with a faded gray silk duvet, this bedroom was the essence of "shabby chic."

"Guest room," Alma said as she rummaged through the drawers of a bureau. "This is where you'll be staying after you're hired."

"Hired?" She scoffed. "I doubt it. Blake Monroe can't stand me."

"In any case, you're staying here tonight. It's not safe for you to be out." She tossed a pair of sweatpants and a T-shirt toward her. "These ought to fit. They were left behind by one of Blake's friends who spent the night."

Madeline picked up the ratty gray sweatpants. "I really appreciate this, Alma."

"Don't thank me yet." She lowered her voice. "This little town, Raven's Cliff, comes with a curse."

"Superstitions," Madeline said.

"Don't be so sure. There's a serial killer on the loose. A couple of weeks ago, he murdered two girls on the eve of their senior prom. One of them was the sister of a local cop. Sofia Lagios."

Sofia. Duncan had looked at Madeline and spoken that name. "What did she look like?"

"I've only seen photographs. But she was a bit like you. Long, curly black hair."

Duncan must have heard people talking about the serial killer. But why would a six-year-old remember the name of a murder victim?

"Get changed," Alma said. "I'll tell Blake that you're too pooped to talk tonight. In the morning, you can have a nice, professional interview."

"Great." She dropped her car keys on top of the bureau. "Nothing sounds better right now than a good night's sleep."

BLAKE LINGERED in the doorway of his son's bedroom, gazing with all the love he possessed at Duncan's angelic little face. So beautiful. So like his mother. Often, when Blake looked into his son's bright blue eyes, he saw Kathleen staring back at him. On those rare occasions when Duncan laughed, he heard echoes of her own joy, and he remembered the good times. Only three years ago, cancer had taken her away from him forever.

"Time for sleep, Duncan."

As usual, no response.

To get an answer, Blake used the rhyming repetition that his son enjoyed. "Nighty-night. Sleep tight…"

"And don't let the bedbugs bite," Duncan said.

Sometimes, the kid scared the hell out of him. Tonight, when he'd disappeared, Blake had feared disaster. A fall from the precipitous cliffs near the lighthouse. An attack by wild dogs or animals. Worse, a confrontation with a serial killer. Why had Duncan spoken the name of one of the victims? The boy must have known that Sofia Lagios was dead because he said she was with the angels. But how? How had he known?

Life would be a lot easier if Blake could ask a simple question and get a simple answer, but his son's brain didn't work that way.

Duncan stared up at the fluorescent stars Blake had attached to the ceiling in a precise geometric pattern. "I have a friend," he said. "She sells seashells."

"That's great, buddy." It had to be an imaginary friend. He hadn't been around any other children. "What's her name?"

"Temperance Raven. She wears a red cape." His tiny fingers laced together, then pulled apart. He repeated the action three times. "I like French fries."

"Where did you meet Temperance?"

"By the lighthouse. She wanted me to play with her."

Blake didn't like the sound of this. The lighthouse was under construction, dangerous. "Was Temperance outside? In the rain?"

Duncan turned to his side. "Seashells, seashells, seashells…"

"Goodnight, son."

Blake left the door to his son's bedroom ajar. Duncan wanted it that way.

Blake wanted to find out what had happened tonight,

and there was one person who could tell him. He'd seen Alma escorting that very wet young woman down the hall toward the guest room. What was her name? Madeline? She might be able to give him information about Duncan's supposed new friend. Blake tapped on her door.

"Alma?" she called out. "Come on in."

Blake strode inside. "We need to talk."

Wearing baggy sweatpants and an oversize T-shirt, she stood in front of the mirror above the antique dressing table. Her long black hair fell past her shoulders in a mass of damp tangles. As soon as she spotted him, she grabbed her black-framed glasses and stuck them on the end of her straight, patrician nose. "Mr. Monroe. I thought we might have our interview tomorrow."

He'd almost forgotten that she was here to apply for a job as his son's tutor. "I need to know what happened tonight. Duncan mentioned someone named Temperance."

"I didn't see anyone else," she said. "There aren't any other houses nearby, are there?"

"We're isolated."

"That could be a problem." She pushed the heavy mane away from her face. Her complexion was fresh, with rosy tints on her cheeks and the tip of her nose. Behind those glasses, black lashes outlined her eyes. An unusual color. Aquamarine.

"Problem?" he asked.

"Not having neighbors." She gave him a prim smile. "Surely, you'll want Duncan to have playmates."

"He doesn't do well with other children."

"I know," she said. "He told me."

Like hell he did. His son's conversations were limited to discussions of simple activities, like brushing his teeth. Or repetitions. Or numbers.

She continued, "He was worried that you'd be angry because he was…how did he say it? Inappropriate."

That sounded like Duncan. "His teachers said his behavior was inappropriate. The word stuck in his mind."

"Everybody's like that. We all tend to remember the words that hurt. To let criticism soak in."

His son wasn't like everybody else. Far from it. But he appreciated the way she phrased her comments, and Duncan seemed to like her. Maybe Madeline Douglas would be a suitable tutor, after all.

He crossed the room and took a seat in a carved wooden rocking chair, one of several handmade pieces in the manor. "Show me your résumé and recommendations."

When she gestured toward the window, the graceful motion of her wrist contrasted the baggy black T-shirt. "All my papers are in my car, which is still down the road."

"Where you ran into Teddy Fisher."

"I didn't want to mention this in front of Duncan," she said, "but Dr. Fisher had a handgun."

Not good news. He hated to hear that the local loons were armed. Fisher had tons of money and a decent reputation as a scientist with his own laboratories in Raven's Cliff. He came from a good family; his father had been a Nobel Prize winner. But Teddy's behavior went beyond eccentric into borderline insanity.

The main reason Blake had taken this job—a step down from his typically high-profile architectural assignments—was because he wanted to get Duncan out of the city into a small-town environment where the pace was slow and distractions were minimal.

"Teddy Fisher owns the Manor," he said. "But he's not supposed to visit without notifying me. I'll remind him."

She gave a brisk nod. "If you like, I can tell you about my qualifications."

"Do it."

She started by rattling off her educational achievements, special recognitions and a bachelor's degree from an undistinguished college which had taken six years because she'd been holding down a job while going to school. For two years, she'd taught second grade at a parochial school. "Then I started substitute teaching in some of Boston's inner-city schools."

He held up his hand, signaling a stop. "Why did you leave a full-time position to be a sub?"

"Alma might have mentioned that I grew up in the foster-care system."

Vaguely, he recalled some comment. "She might have."

"I was a throwaway kid. No one expected me to amount to much. But I had a teacher in third grade…a wonderful teacher. She wouldn't let me shirk on my assignments, made me work hard and kept after me to do better. She noticed me."

Behind her glasses, her eyes teared up. "She changed my life. By working in inner-city schools, I felt like I might make that kind of difference."

He liked her earnest compassion. She sure as hell had the empathy needed to work with his son. But did she have the training? Blake wasn't accustomed to settling for second best. "How much do you know about autism?"

She picked up a straight-back wooden chair and moved it close to his rocker. When she sat, she leaned forward. "What can you tell me about Duncan's behavior?"

"On the behavioral range of autism, he's considered to be high-functioning." Blake had taken his son to a cadre of doctors and therapists. "Initially, we tried drug therapy, but Duncan didn't respond well. The specialists call his condition a form of hypersensitivity."

"Which is why he doesn't like to be touched."

"When he touches someone, he says that he knows what they're thinking."

"Like a psychic."

"Don't go there," he warned. It was difficult enough to manage Duncan's illness without the extra burden of some harebrained, paranormal philosophy.

"I'm trying to understand," she said. "When I found Duncan in the woods, we had a coherent communication. More important, he reacted to me. He looked me in the eye, and he smiled. That behavior isn't consistent with what I know about autism."

Her presumption ticked him off. For the past three years, since his wife had died, he'd struggled with his son's condition. They'd gone through brain scans, blood tests, physical and psychological diagnostics…. He rose from the rocking chair. "Are you an expert?"

"No, but I can see the obvious." Instead of cowering, she stood to confront him. "Duncan is smart. And he cares about what you think. He wants you to love him."

Her words were a slap in the face. Tight-lipped, he said, "This interview is over."

WITH THE ECHO of the door slamming behind Blake still ringing in her ears, Madeline collapsed onto the bed. Disaster! She'd infuriated Blake and blown her chance at this job. Truly a shame because she thought she might work well with Duncan, and she found herself drawn to his father. What red-blooded woman wouldn't be? Blake was gorgeous and intense. Unfortunately, he despised her.

She shifted around on the bed. Before she went to sleep, she needed to use the facilities.

Since there was no adjoining bathroom with this bedroom, she had to go into the hallway. Poking her head out the door, she checked to make sure Blake was nowhere in sight. One doorway stood ajar and light spilled into the corridor. Duncan's room. She tiptoed past.

"Madeline?"

Peeking into his room, she said, "You remembered my name. Hi, Duncan."

"Will I see my friend again?"

She had no right to be here, no justifiable reason to talk with Blake's son. But she couldn't turn away from this troubled child. Slipping into his room, she pulled a rocking chair near his bed. "Is her name Temperance?"

"Temperance Raven."

"Like the town," Madeline said. "Raven's Cliff."

"Temperance lied to me about the town being named after her daddy in 1794. But I don't care. Lots of people lie. Liar, liar, pants on fire."

"Hang them up on a telephone wire," she responded. "You like rhymes."

"Temperance gave me a present." He rolled over on his bed and picked up a smooth, white shell.

Madeline grinned. "She sells seashells."

"By the seashore," Duncan concluded.

Though their conversation scattered in several directions, they were communicating. Instead of telling him that she liked his room, she pointed up at the ceiling and recited, "Starlight, star bright. First star I see tonight."

He watched her with an intensity that reminded her of his father. "Finish the rhyme."

"Wish I may, wish I might, have the wish I wish tonight."

He parroted the rhyme back to her perfectly. Not once, but three times. Then he laughed.

Hearing a sound near the door, she glanced over her shoulder and saw Blake standing in the hallway. He stepped away too quickly for her to decide if he was angry about her talking to Duncan. And, frankly, she didn't care. This wasn't about him.

"Duncan," she said, "I know a very long rhyme. A poem about baseball."

He nodded for her to continue.

"You'd like baseball. It's all about numbers." She drew a diamond in the air as she talked about the bases and the pitcher and the batter. "Four balls and three strikes."

"Three strikes and you're out," he said.

"You're right," she said. "This poem is called 'Casey at the Bat.'"

He lay back on his pillow to listen while she recited the poem she'd memorized in fifth grade. The rhyming cadence lulled him, and Duncan's eyelids began to droop.

When she had finished, he roused himself. "Again."

She started over. By the time she finished, he was sound asleep.

Leaving his door ajar, exactly the way she'd found it, she went down the hallway to the bathroom. Like every other part of the house she'd seen, the room was sorely in need of fresh paint. But it seemed clean and had an old-fashioned claw-footed tub. Fantastic! One of her favorite pastimes was a long, hot soak. And why not? It wasn't as if she could make Blake Monroe dislike her even more. Besides, she didn't know when or if she'd ever have the chance to luxuriate in a tub again.

As she filled the tub, fears about her uncertain future arose. No money. No job. No home. She had only enough gas to get back to Raven's Cliff. That would have to be where she started her new life, maybe working as a waitress or a short-order cook. She had experience at both from when she was putting herself through college.

Stripping off the sweatpants and T-shirt, she eased into the hot, steamy water.

Damn it, Marty. This is all your fault. Her brother had popped back into her life just long enough to wreck everything. When he'd showed up, she should have thrown him out on his handsome butt. Should have, but didn't. Water under the bridge.

After a nice, long soak, she climbed out of the tub, somewhat refreshed, and padded down the hallway to her "shabby chic" room.

The door was open, just the way she'd left it. But something was different. At the foot of her bed was the canvas suitcase that had been in the back of her car. Had Alma trudged all the way down the road to get it? She opened the flap and took out a nightgown.

"Madeline Douglas."

She turned and saw Blake standing in the doorway. He tossed the keys to her car to the center of the bed. "You shouldn't leave these lying around."

"I didn't." The keys had been on top of the bureau in her room. *Inside her room!* Even if the door was open, he shouldn't have barged in uninvited.

"You're hired," he said without smiling. "We'll talk in the morning."

The door closed behind him.

Chapter Three

The next morning, the skies outside Madeline's bedroom window were clear, washed clean by the rain. And she tried to focus on the sunny side. She had a job and a place to live. Working with Duncan provided an interesting challenge. For now, she was safe.

The dark cloud on her emotional horizon was Blake Monroe. A volatile man. She didn't know why he had changed his mind about hiring her and decided it was best not to ask too many questions. He didn't seem like the type of man who bothered to explain himself.

Entering the high-ceilinged kitchen, she smiled at Alma, who sat at the table, drinking coffee and keeping company with a morning television chat program on a small flat-screen.

"I'm hired," Madeline announced. "I can't thank you enough for telling me about this job."

"Congrats." Using the remote, Alma turned down the volume. "How about lending me a hand with breakfast?"

"Sure."

She turned and confronted a mountain of dirty dishes, glasses, pots and crusted skillets that spread across the countertop like a culinary apocalypse. It appeared that Alma hadn't wiped a single plate since they'd moved into this house.

How could anyone stand such a mess! Madeline rolled up the sleeves of her daisy-patterned cotton shirt, grabbed an apron that was wadded in the corner of the counter and dug in.

"You haven't changed a bit," Alma said. "Even as a kid, you were good about cleaning up."

Maybe even a teensy bit compulsive. "Is that why you thought of me for this job?"

"I don't mind having a helper." Alma shuffled toward the butcher-block island and leaned against it. Though she was completely dressed with hair and makeup done, she wore fuzzy pink slippers. "Did you sleep well?"

"Took me a while to get accustomed to the creaks and groans in this old house." Once during the night, she'd startled awake, certain that someone had been in the room with her. She'd even imagined that she saw the door closing, which made her wonder. "Does Duncan ever sleepwalk?"

"Not as far as I know, but I wouldn't be surprised by anything that kid does. Or his father, for that matter."

"Is Blake difficult to work for?"

"A real pain in the rear."

Yet, he put up with the mess in the kitchen. "How so?"

"In the past year, he went through two other housekeepers and four nannies."

"Why?"

"His lordship is one of those dark, brooding, artistic types. Real moody. Gets caught up in a project and nothing else matters. He forgets to eat, then blames you for not feeding him." She patted her sculpted blond curls. "It's not part of my job description to keep track of his phone calls, and most of the business contacts go through his office in New York. But if I forget a phone call, he blows a gasket."

"He yells at you?" Madeline was beginning to feel more and more trepidation about this job.

"Never raises his voice," Alma said. "He growls. Real low. Like an angry lion."

With Blake's overgrown dark blond mane and intense hazel eyes, a lion was an apt comparison. As Madeline rinsed glasses and loaded them into the dishwasher, she said, "I looked Blake up on the Internet. He does amazing restorations. There were interior photos of this gorgeous hotel in Paris."

"Paris." Alma sighed. "That's what I expected when I signed on as a housekeeper four months ago. Trips to Europe. Fancy places. Fancy people. La-di-dah."

"Sounds like a lovely adventure."

"So far, I've been at the brownstone in Manhattan and here—Maine. I mean, Maine? The whole state is about as glamorous as a lumberjack's plaid shirt." She paused to sip her coffee. "Let's hear about you, hon. How's your big brother, Marty?"

At the mention of her brother's name, Madeline almost dropped the plate she was scrubbing in the sink. "We've kind of lost touch."

"Good-looking kid. A bit devilish, though. Didn't he get into some kind of trouble with the law?"

She heard Duncan counting his steps as he came down the hall to the kitchen and assumed his father wasn't far behind. "I'd rather not talk about Marty."

"It's okay." Alma patted her arm. "I won't say a word."

Duncan preceded his father into the kitchen. His clothing was the same as last night: a long-sleeved, striped
T-shirt and jeans. At the table, he climbed into his chair and
sat, staring straight ahead.

Alma went into action. She measured oat-bran cereal
into a clear glass bowl, then measured the milk. She placed
them in front of Duncan, then fetched a pre-chilled glass
of OJ from the fridge.

Neither she nor Blake said a word.

Madeline assumed this was some sort of ritual and
didn't interfere until Duncan had taken his first bite of
cereal. Then she took a seat opposite him and watched as
he chewed carefully before swallowing. She smiled.
"Good morning, Duncan."

He said nothing, didn't acknowledge her presence in any
way.

Blake cleared his throat. When she looked at him, he shook
his head, warning her not to rock the boat. She rose from her
seat and went toward him. Seeing him in the morning light,
she noticed the lightly etched crow's feet at the corners of his
eyes and the unshaven stubble on his chin. He dragged his
fingers through his unruly dark blond hair. His careless
grooming and apparent disarray reminded her of an unmade
bed that had been torn apart in a night of wild, sexual abandon.

She intended to discuss her plans for Duncan's lessons.
After his interest in the "Casey at the Bat" poem, she'd
decided to use baseball as a learning tool. There were other
things she needed to ask Blake about, such as her salary,
rules of the household and teaching supplies. But being
near him left her tongue-tied.

She pushed her glasses up on her nose and said, "Do you
have a baseball?"

"I can find one."

Her cheeks were warm with embarrassment. Seldom was she so inarticulate. "Other supplies? Pencils and paper?"

"Everything you'll need is in a room at the end of this hallway. It was once a conservatory so there's a whole wall of windows. Until the renovations are done, we're using it as a family room. Alma can show you."

She stammered. "I-is there, um, some kind of schedule?"

He lifted an eyebrow; his expression changed from arrogant to vaguely amused. He stretched out his arm and pointed to the wall beside her. "How's this?"

Right in front of her nose was a three-foot-by-two-foot poster board with a heading in letters five inches high: Duncan's Schedule. The entire day was plotted in detail.

"I've found," he said, "that Duncan does best when we stick to a consistent routine."

She pointed to the slot after breakfast. "Quiet Time in Family Room. What does that mean?"

"Exactly what it says. Duncan likes to spend time by himself, and all his toys are in the family room. Usually he plays computer games."

The next slot said Lessons. "How do I know where to start?"

"Duncan's last tutor left a log that detailed her teaching plans and Duncan's progress. She wasn't a live-in, and I can't say that I was happy with her results." He glanced toward the housekeeper. "Is that coffee hot?"

"Piping."

He went to the coffeemaker and filled a mug. "Well, Alma, it's nice to see that you're finally cleaning up in here."

"I aim to please," she said. "Breakfast in your studio?"

"Eggs over easy, wheat toast and bacon."

With a nod to Madeline, he left the kitchen.

Though his back was turned, she made a "bye-bye" motion with her hand. Oh, good grief. Could she possibly be more of a dork?

Alma chuckled. "Got a little crush on his lordship?"

"Of course not."

"He's a handsome thing. And he's even taller than you are. Probably six foot two or three."

"I hadn't noticed."

She returned to the sink and dug into the stack of dirty dishes with renewed vigor. After she'd cleaned up the kitchen and grabbed an energy bar for breakfast, she trailed Duncan into the family room. He spoke not a word, went directly to his computer and turned it on.

Like the kitchen, this room was a mess. Sunlight gushed through a wall of windows, illuminating a cluttered worktable where Duncan sat at his computer. Though the wall had a neat row of storage bins and shelves, everything had been heaped on the floor—played with and then discarded.

The chaos didn't make sense. Every hour of Duncan's day was regimented, but here—in the place where he was supposed to learn—he was surrounded by disarray.

Obviously, she needed to put things in order. One of the earliest lessons taught in grade school was "Putting Things Away." Getting Duncan to participate in the clean-up would have been good, but she didn't want to disrupt his schedule. This hour was for quiet time.

While he fiddled with his computer, she picked up a plush blue pony and placed it on the shelf labeled Stuffed Animals. Then another stuffed toy. Blocks in the bin.

Crayons back in their box. Trucks and cars on another labeled shelf.

Eventually, she found a place for everything. "All done," she said. "I'm going out to my car to bring a few things inside."

He didn't even glance in her direction. No communication whatsoever. A cone of isolation surrounded him. No one was allowed to touch.

After running up to her bedroom to grab her car keys, she stepped outside into the sunny warmth of a July day. Her beat-up Volkswagen station wagon with the brand-new dent from her collision with Dr. Fisher was parked just outside the front door. When she unlocked the back, she noticed that the flaps on a couple of boxes were open. She hadn't put them in here like that. Everything had been sealed with tape or had the flaps tucked in. Had someone been tampering with her things? When Blake got her suitcase, did he also search her belongings?

Before she built up a full-blown anger at him about his callous intrusion into her privacy, a more ominous thought occurred. What if it was someone else?

Last night, she'd sensed that someone was in her bedroom. She hadn't actually seen anyone; it was just a fleeting impression. But what if it were true? Dr. Fisher had said that he'd "always know where to find her." He owned this house. Surely he had a key. But why would he look through her things?

"Need some help?" Alma called from the doorway.

Madeline slammed the rear door. "I'll worry about this stuff later. But I need to get the ficus out of the front seat before it wilts."

She unlocked the passenger-side door and liberated

the plant. The ficus itself wasn't anything special, but the fluted porcelain pot painted with rosebuds was one of her favorite things.

"Heavy," she muttered as she kicked the car door closed and lurched toward the house, not stopping until she reached her second-floor bedroom where she set the plant near the window. The delicately painted pot looked as though it belonged here—more than she did.

Had someone crept into her room last night? There was no way to prove she'd had an intruder unless she contacted the police and had them take fingerprints. Even then, Dr. Fisher had a right to be in the house; he owned the place. If not Fisher, who? The serial killer. His last victim, Sofia, had looked like her.

Madeline plucked off her glasses and wiped the lenses. She didn't want to raise an alarm about a prowler unless she had tangible evidence. Tonight, before she went to bed, she'd push the ficus against the door so no one could enter without making a lot of noise.

She hurried down the staircase toward the family room. In the doorway, she came to an abrupt halt. The room she had so carefully cleaned was ransacked. Stuffed animals had been flung in every direction. Books spilled across the floor. The toy trucks and cars looked like a major highway collision. Little Duncan stood in the midst of it, oblivious to her presence.

Either she could laugh or cry. She chose the former, letting out her frustration in a chuckle. Now she knew why the room had been a mess.

Duncan paced toward her. When he held out his hand, she saw that he was wearing latex gloves. In the center of his palm was the white seashell he'd shown her last night.

"Temperance," she said.

He marched past her into the corridor that led to the front door. His clear intention was to go outside. And how could she stop him? From the information she had on autistic kids, she knew that corporal punishment often led to tantrums. Arguments were futile.

The key, she decided, was to gain his trust. Maybe she could impart a few bits of knowledge along the way.

At the front door, she stepped ahead of him, blocking his way and creating the illusion that she was in control. "We're going to take a walk. Across the yard to the forest. And we'll gather pinecones. Six pinecones."

"Ten," he said.

"Ten is good."

Outside, he started counting his steps. "One, two, three…"

"*Uno, dos, tres.* Those are Spanish numbers."

He repeated the words back to her. She took him up to ten in Spanish, then started over. At least he was learning something.

Halfway across the grassy stretch leading to the forested area, Blake jogged up beside them.

"It's such a beautiful day," she said. "We decided to do our lesson outdoors."

"Couldn't stand the mess in the family room?"

"I might be a bit of a neat freak," she admitted. "Anyway, we're learning numbers in Spanish."

He fell into step beside her, and she surreptitiously peeked up at him. Definitely taller than she, he moved with a casual, athletic grace.

Near the woods, Duncan scampered ahead of them.

"It's good for him to be outside," Blake said. "Gives him a chance to work on his coordination."

"His fine motor skills are okay. He didn't seem to be having any problem with the computer."

"It's the big stuff that gives him problems. Running, skipping, playing catch."

Duncan had entered the trees but was still clearly visible. She glanced over her shoulder at the house. In daylight, the two-story, beige-brick building with four tall chimneys looked elegant and imposing. "What are your plans for the Manor?"

He was taken aback by her question. "How much do you know about historic restoration?"

"Very little. But I looked up some of your other architectural projects on the Web. Many seemed more modern than traditional."

"That's one reason why this project appealed to me. I plan to restore the American Federalist style while totally updating with new wiring, plumbing and insulation. I want to go green—make it ecological."

"Solar panels?"

"Too clumsy," he said. "The challenge in this project," he said, "is to maintain the original exterior design and restore the decorative flourishes of the interior. At the same time, I'm planning modern upgrades. Maybe a sauna and gym in the basement."

As he talked about architecture, she caught a glimpse of a different Blake Monroe—a man who was passionate about his work. Still intense, but focused. And eager to have an adult conversation.

She liked this side of his personality. Liked him a lot.

"She sells seashells…" Duncan repeated the rhyme again and again. "Temperance, where are you?"

"Here I am."

She stood with her back against a tree. He could see her, but his daddy and Madeline couldn't. And that was good. He didn't want to share his new friend.

He held out the shell. "You gave me this to warn me about the bad man."

She bent down and picked up a pinecone. Her shiny golden hair fell across her face. "There is something dangerous in the Manor."

"What?"

"Perhaps the basement. I cannot enter the Manor."

"You don't have to be scared, Temperance. I won't let anybody hurt you."

She placed a pinecone into his gloved hand. "You need ten of these. For your teacher."

He was happy to have a friend who didn't tease about his gloves. "I'm very brave. Madeline said so."

"Duncan, you must not forget the danger."

"Danger," he repeated.

Chapter Four

Half an hour before the scheduled time for lunch, Madeline was pleased with their progress. She and Duncan had arranged the ten pinecones for an afternoon art project. And they'd read an entire book about trains.

Her initial assessment of his skills matched the reports from his previous tutor. Exceptional mathematic ability. Reading and writing skills were poor.

Duncan jumped to his feet. "I want to explore."

"So do I," she said. "We could get your father to give us a tour. He knows a lot about the Manor."

"No," he shouted. "No."

His loud, strident voice had an edge to it. She hadn't figured out how to deal with disagreements, but it couldn't be good to continually back down to his demands. She replied with a statement, not a question. "We'll explore one room."

"Basement," he said.

Not what she was hoping for. She should have been more specific, should have told him that they would explore his father's studio, which would give her a chance to spend a bit more time with Blake. Unfortunately, she hadn't specified a room, and she needed to be unambiguous with Duncan. "The basement it is."

The door leading to the basement was off the kitchen where Alma should have been preparing lunch. She was nowhere in sight.

Madeline turned on the light, revealing a wooden staircase that descended straight down. "I'll go first," she said. "You need to hold tight to the railing."

Duncan followed behind her, counting each step aloud.

A series of bare bulbs lit the huge space that was divided with heavy support pillars and walls. The ceiling was only eight feet high. Like most unfinished basements, it was used for storage. There were stacks of old boxes, discarded furniture and tools. A series of notched shelves suggested that the basement had at one time been a wine cellar.

A damp, musty smell coiled around them, and she shuddered, thinking of rats and spiders. As far as she could tell, there were no windows.

"I've seen enough," she said.

Duncan reached out and touched a concrete wall with his gloved hand. "Danger," he said.

The word startled her.

He zigzagged from the walls to the stairs and back. In spite of her rising trepidation, Madeline noticed a geometric pattern in his movements. If she could have traced his steps, the pattern would form a perfect isosceles triangle. Under his breath, Duncan repeated, "Danger."

She took the warning to heart; his father said that he sensed things. And Alma had mentioned a curse on the town. "Danger means we should leave. Right now."

He ran away from her and disappeared behind a concrete wall.

She started after him. "Duncan, listen to me."

"Danger," came a louder shout.

The door at the top of the stairs slammed with a heavy thud. Fear shot through her. She spun around, staring toward the stairs. Though she saw no one, her sense of being stalked became palpable. That door hadn't blown shut by accident.

The lights blinked out. Darkness consumed her. Not the faintest glimmer penetrated this windowless tomb. Trapped. She thought of Teddy Fisher. Of the serial killer who liked women with long black hair.

Terror stole her breath. Where were the stairs? To her right? Her left? Her hands thrust forward, groping in empty space.

If she'd been here by herself, Madeline would have screamed for help. But Duncan was with her, and she didn't want to frighten him. "Duncan? Where are you?"

"Right here." He didn't sound scared. "Thirty-six steps from the stairs."

"Don't move." She listened hard, trying to discern if anyone else was here with them. The silence filled with dark portent. She moved forward with hesitant steps. Her shin bumped against a cardboard box. Her outstretched hands felt the cold that emanated from the walls. She pivoted and took another step. Was she going the wrong way? "Duncan, can you find the stairs?"

Instead of answering, he started counting backward from thirty-six. His strange habit came in handy; the boy seemed to know his exact location while she was utterly disoriented.

She bit back a sob. Even with her eyes accustomed to the dark, she couldn't see a thing.

"I'm at the stairs," Duncan announced.

She took a step toward his voice and stumbled. Falling forward to her hands and knees, she let out a yip.

"I'm okay," she said, though Duncan hadn't inquired. The only way she'd find the stairs was for him to keep talking. "Can you say the poem about starlight?"

Instead, he chanted, "She sells seashells…"

Crouched low, she inched toward the sound. When her hand connected with the stair rail, she latched on, desperately needing an anchor, something solid in the dark.

"Danger," he shouted

Shivers chased up and down her spine. She had to get a grip, had to get them to safety. "I'm going up the stairs, Duncan. I'll open the door so we have enough light to see. Then I'll come back down for you."

"I can go. I'm very brave."

"Yes, you are." But she didn't want to take a chance on having him slip and fall on the stairs. "That's why you can stay right here. Very still."

As she stumbled up the steps in the pitch-dark, the staircase seemed ten miles long. By the time she reached the door, a clammy sweat coated her forehead. Her fingers closed around the round brass doorknob. It didn't move.

She jiggled and twisted. It was locked.

Panic flashed inside her head. A faint shimmer of daylight came around the edge of the door, and she clawed at the light as if she could pry this heavy door open.

Drawing back her fists, she hammered against the door. "Alma. Help. We're trapped in the basement. Help."

Behind her, she heard Duncan start up the stairs. She couldn't allow him to climb. In the darkness, balance was precarious, and Duncan wasn't like other kids. She couldn't hold his arm and keep him from falling, couldn't touch him at all.

"Wait," she said, "I'm coming back down."

Quickly, she descended. They'd just have to wait until they were found. Not much of a plan, but it was all she had. She sat beside Duncan on the second step from the bottom. "Here's what we're going to do. I'll count to five and you call for help. Then you count for me. Start now."

He yelled at the top of his lungs.

Then it was her turn. Screaming felt good. Her tension loosened. After she caught her breath, she said, "Now, we wait. Somebody will find us."

"My mama is already here," he said quietly. "She takes care of me. Whenever I get in trouble, my mama is close. She promised. She's always close."

His childlike faith touched her heart. "Your mama must be a very good woman. Can you tell me about her?"

"Soft and pretty. Even when she was crying, she smiled at me."

"She loved you," Madeline said. "And your daddy loves you, too."

"So do you," he said confidently. "From the first time you saw me."

In spite of her fear, Madeline breathed more easily. She should have been the one comforting him. Instead, this young boy lightened the weight of the terrible darkness with his surprising optimism. "You're very lovable."

"And brave."

"Let's yell again. Go."

At the end of his five seconds of shouting, the door at the top of the staircase opened. Daylight poured down with blinding, wonderful brilliance. Silhouetted in that light was the powerful masculine form of Blake Monroe.

"What the hell is going on?" he growled.

"Danger," Duncan yelled.

She heard Blake flick the light switch. "What's wrong with the lights?"

Duncan scrambled up the wooden staircase, and she followed. Stepping into the kitchen, she inhaled the light and warmth. This must be how it felt to escape from being buried alive. As she stepped away from the basement door, she wiped the clammy sweat from her forehead with the back of her hand. She and Duncan were free. No harm done.

When she saw the expression on Blake's face, her sense of relief vanished like seeds on the wind. The friendly camaraderie of this morning had been replaced by tight-lipped anger. "I want an explanation," he said.

She pushed her glasses up on her nose and cleared her throat. "Duncan and I decided to explore one room of the house before lunchtime."

"And you chose the basement." His hazel eyes flared. "There's all kinds of crap down there. Damn it, Madeline. What the hell were you thinking?"

She wouldn't blame this dreadful excursion on Duncan's insistence that they go to the basement. She was the person in charge. "We were fine until the door slammed shut. It was locked."

His brows arched in disbelief. He went down a step to test the doorknob, and the horrible darkness crawled up his leg. She was tempted, like Duncan, to warn him. To shout the word *danger* until her lungs burst.

Blake jiggled the knob. "It's sticking but not locked. You must have twisted it the wrong way."

She hadn't turned the knob wrong. That door had been locked. "Then the lights went out."

"There's a rational explanation. I have a crew of electricians working today."

She glanced toward Duncan, who stood silently, staring down at the toes of his sneakers. She didn't want to frighten the boy with her suspicions about Dr. Fisher or being stalked by the serial killer, but they hadn't been trapped by accident.

Blake yanked the door shut with a resounding slam and took a step toward her. Anger rolled off him in hot, turbulent waves.

Frankly, she couldn't blame him. It appeared that she'd made an irresponsible decision. When he spoke, his voice was low and ominous, like the rumble of an approaching freight train. And she was tied to the tracks. "You're supposed to be teaching my son. Not leading him into a potentially dangerous situation."

"All of life is potentially risky," she said in her defense. "Children need to explore and grow. New experiences are—"

"Stop." He held up a hand to halt her flow of words. "I don't need a lecture."

"Perhaps I'm not explaining well."

"You're fired, Madeline."

"What?" She took a step backward. Perhaps she deserved a reprimand, but not this.

He reached into his back pocket and pulled out a wallet. Peeling off a hundred-dollar bill, he slapped it down on the counter. "This should cover your expenses. Pack your things and get out."

Looking past his right shoulder, she saw Alma enter

through the back door with a couple of grocery bags in her arms. The housekeeper wouldn't be happy about Madeline being fired. Nor would Duncan.

But Blake was the boss. And his attitude showed no willingness to negotiate.

Though she would have liked to refuse his money, pride was not an option. She was too broke. With a weak sigh, she reached for the bill.

"Daddy, no." Duncan rushed across the kitchen and wrapped his skinny arms around his father's waist. "I like Madeline. I want her to stay."

Blake's eyes widened in surprise, and she knew that her own expression mirrored his. They were both stunned by this minor miracle. Duncan was touching his father, clinging to him.

As Blake stroked his son's shoulders with an amazing tenderness, she wondered how long it had been since Duncan had allowed him to come close.

The boy looked up at him. "Please, Daddy."

Blake squatted down to his son's level. Though Duncan's eyes were bright blue and his hair was a lighter shade of blond, the physical resemblance between father and son resonated.

Blake asked, "Do you want Madeline to stay?"

The hint of a smile touched Duncan's mouth. He reached toward his father's face with his gloved hand and patted Blake's cheek. "I like her."

With the slow, careful, deliberate motions used to approach a feral creature, Blake enclosed his son in a yearning embrace. A moment ago, he'd been all arrogance and hostility. Now, he exuded pure love.

Empathy brought Madeline close to tears. Her hand

covered her mouth. Staying at Beacon Manor was like riding an emotional roller coaster. In the basement, she'd been terrified. Facing Blake's rage, she was defensive and intimidated. As she watched the tenderness between father and son, her heart swelled.

The front doorbell rang.

"Get the door," Blake said to her.

Hadn't she just been fired? "I don't—"

"You're not fired. You're still Duncan's teacher. Now, answer the door."

Not much of an apology, but she'd take it. She needed this job. Straightening her shoulders, she walked down the corridor to the front door.

Standing at the entryway were two women. A cheerful smile fitted naturally on the attractive face of a slender lady in a stylish ivory suit with gray-blue piping that matched the color of her eyes. Her short, tawny hair whisked neatly in the breeze. Confidently, she introduced herself. "I'm Beatrice Wells, the mayor's wife."

Madeline opened the door wider to invite them inside. "I'm Madeline Douglas. Duncan's teacher."

When she held out her hand, she noticed the smears of dirt from crawling around in the basement and quickly pulled her hand back. "I should wait to shake your hand until I've had a chance to wash up."

"It's not a problem, dear." Beatrice gave her hand a squeeze, then turned toward her companion. "I'd like you to meet Helen Fisher."

As in Teddy Fisher? Madeline couldn't imagine that creep had a wife. "Are you related to Dr. Fisher?"

The frowning, angular woman gave a disgusted snort. "Teddy is my brother."

She stalked through the open door in her practical oxblood loafers. Her nostrils pinched and the frown deepened as she set a battered briefcase on the floor. She folded her arms below her chest, causing a wrinkle in her midcalf dress and brown cardigan. Though the month was July and the weather was sunny, Helen Fisher reminded Madeline of the drab days at the end of autumn. Everything about her said "old maid." Madeline suppressed a shudder. For the past couple of years, she'd feared that "old maid" would be her own destiny. If she stayed at this job long enough to put some money aside, she really ought to invest in something pretty and sexy. A red dress.

Beatrice Wells twinkled as if to counterbalance her companion's grumpy attitude. "Helen is our town librarian, and we're here to talk with Blake about the renovations."

"Beacon Manor is a historic landmark," Helen said. "The designs have to be approved by the historical committee."

"I really don't know anything about the house. My job is Duncan." She looked toward Beatrice. "I wondered if there was a baseball team in town. Something I could take Duncan to watch."

"We have an excellent parks and recreation program. There's even a T-ball program for the children."

Though Madeline wasn't sure if Duncan could handle a team sport, T-ball might be worth a try. "I'll certainly look into it."

When Blake came down the corridor toward them, he seemed like a different man. An easy grin lightened his features. He looked five years younger…and incredibly handsome. Even Helen was not immune to his masculine charms. She perked up when he warmly shook her hand. A girlish giggle twisted through her dour lips.

Given half a chance, Blake Monroe could charm the fish from the sea.

Chapter Five

As Blake escorted Beatrice Wells and Helen Fisher into the formal dining room with the ornate ceiling mural, he listened with half an ear to their commentary about the historical significance of Beacon Manor. In their eyes, the painting of cherubs and harvest vegetables rivaled the Sistine Chapel.

His thoughts were elsewhere. When he'd held Duncan in his arms, his blood had stirred. His son had smiled, actually smiled, and responded to a direct question. For the first time in years, Blake had seen a spark in his son's eyes.

Then Duncan had turned away from him and marched to his seat at the kitchen table for his usual silent lunch.

For today, one hug was enough. Maybe tomorrow…

Helen placed her fat leather briefcase on the dropcloth covering the carved cherrywood table and pulled out a stack of photographs. "These pictures were taken in the 1940s during an earlier restoration. Perhaps they'll be useful in recreating the ceiling mural."

"I've already ordered the paint," Blake said, "including the gold leaf. There's an artist in New York who specializes in historical restorations."

"Sounds expensive," Helen said archly. "I don't suppose my brother has set any sort of prudent financial limits."

Blake had submitted a detailed budget. Not that the expenditure was any of Helen's business. "You'll have to talk to Teddy about that."

As they moved to another room, he heard Madeline talking to Alma in the kitchen. How had she made such a difference with Duncan in such a short time? She lacked the expertise of the autism specialists he'd consulted. She wasn't a psychologist or a behaviorist. Just a schoolteacher.

For some unknown reason, his son connected with her. Was it her appearance? At first glance, he hadn't noticed anything remarkable about her, except for those incredibly long legs. When she took her glasses off, her aquamarine eyes glowed like the mysterious depths below the ocean waves. Was she magical? Hell, no. Madeline was down-to-earth. Definitely not an enchantress. And yet there was something about her that even he had to admit was intriguing.

He climbed the sweeping front staircase behind the two ladies from town. At the landing, Beatrice paused to catch her breath and said, "Duncan's teacher mentioned that you might be interested in signing your son up for one of the T-ball teams."

"Did she?" A baseball team? What was she thinking?

"Raven's Cliff might not have all the cultural advantages of a big city, but there's nowhere like a small town for raising children."

If Duncan did well here, Blake was ready to move in a heartbeat. "How's the real estate market?"

"Quite good." Beatrice warmed to him. "In fact, my husband and I are considering selling a lovely three-bedroom on the waterfront. Should I have Perry talk to you about it?"

"Sure."

He imagined himself living in this Maine backwater, planting a vegetable garden while Duncan played in the yard behind a white picket fence. Maybe his son could find friends his own age. Maybe a dog. Blake imagined a two-story slate-blue house with white shutters. The back door would open, and Madeline would step through, carrying a plate of cookies. Yeah, sure. Then they could all travel in their time machine back to the 1950s when life seemed pure and simple.

After he showed the ladies the one bedroom that had been repainted and refurbished with velvet drapes, they went back down the staircase to the first floor. Without being rude, he guided them toward the exit.

Standing at the doorway, Beatrice said, "Be sure to tell that nice young woman, Madeline, that the person to contact about the T-ball team is Grant Bridges. He's an assistant District Attorney. A fine young man."

He noticed a tremor in her voice. "Are you feeling all right, Beatrice?"

"Grant was almost my son-in-law," she said softly. "It's difficult to think of him without remembering my beautiful daughter. Camille."

He'd heard this tragic story before. It was part of the curse of Raven's Cliff. "I'm sorry for your loss."

They stepped onto the porch below the Palladian window just as Teddy Fisher's forest-green SUV screeched to a halt at the entrance. Blake remembered what Madeline had said about Fisher carrying a handgun and stepped protectively in front of the women.

Teddy sprang from the driver's-side door like a Jack-in-the-box with a goatee. With a fastidious twitch, he straightened the lapels of his tweed jacket. Every time Blake had dealt with Teddy, he'd been well-mannered, but he seemed distracted, unhinged. His small face twisted with strong emotion that might be anger. Or it might be fear.

Helen shoved past Blake and confronted her brother with fists on her skinny hips. "Well, well. If it isn't the mad scientist."

"We haven't spoken in months, Helen. At least try to be civil."

"Don't bother holding out an olive branch to me," she snapped. "You don't deserve my forgiveness."

"Your forgiveness?" His eyebrows arched. "I don't recall apologizing to you."

When he lifted his chin, Blake noticed that Teddy's shirt collar was loose. He'd been losing weight, had been under stress. Blake had heard stories about how Teddy's latest "scientific breakthrough"—a nutrient for fish—had caused a recent epidemic in Raven's Cliff.

"Bastard!" Oddly, Helen's facial expression mirrored that of her brother. "You ought to be in jail."

"At least I'm trying to do something with my life, working to enhance the Fisher name, like our grandfather."

"Grandfather won the Nobel Prize for science." Her voice rang with pride. "You're the booby prize."

"And I suppose it's better to play it safe like you? The town librarian? A manless crone who grows older and more dried up every day?"

"How dare you." She turned toward Beatrice, who watched with horrified eyes. "Your husband never should have allowed Teddy to buy the Manor."

Beatrice shifted uncomfortably. "There wasn't much choice, Helen. The abandoned property belonged to the town. After the hurricane, Raven's Cliff needed the revenue from the sale."

Frankly, Blake was glad that the Manor had only one owner. If he'd been forced to get approval from some kind of township committee, the restoration of the Manor and lighthouse would have been impossible.

Helen went on the attack again. "Damn you, Teddy. You hoarded your share of the family inheritance."

"And you frittered yours away."

"I invested in you," she said with hoarse loathing.

He gave a smug little grin. "Someday you'll get your investment back. I'm on the verge of a discovery."

She poked at him with a long finger. "The only way I'll ever be paid back is when you're dead."

Blake stepped in before this brother-and-sister reunion erupted into a physical fight. He grasped Teddy's arm and guided him away from Helen with a brisk, "Please excuse us, ladies."

Teddy walked a few paces before he shook Blake's hand off. "I'm sorry you had to witness that outburst. My sister has always been hot-tempered."

Blake glanced over his shoulder at the plain, thin woman whose angular face had gone white with rage. "Yeah, she's a real spitfire."

"She never believed in me. Not really."

"Was there something you wanted to talk to me about, Teddy?"

"I saw Beatrice and Helen arrive, and I just wanted to remind you that you're working for me. Not some idiotic historical society."

"I'm clear on who's paying the tab," Blake said.

"Well, good."

In his architectural redesign business, Blake came into contact with a number of eccentrics. He had to draw clear boundaries and didn't like the idea that Teddy had been watching the manor. "You know, Teddy, anytime you want to see the progress on the restoration, I'll try to accommodate you."

"Of course." The little man pulled a white handkerchief from his jacket pocket and dabbed nervously at his forehead. His beady little eyes darted. "It's my house, after all."

"However," Blake said, "while my family is in residence, you need an appointment to set foot inside. Otherwise, you're trespassing. And I don't deal kindly with trespassers."

"Is that a threat?"

"A friendly warning," Blake said.

Beacon Manor was only a job. Duncan's safety took precedence.

THAT NIGHT, after Duncan had gone to bed, Madeline finished unpacking in her bedroom. She'd found a place for all her clothing, set up her laptop and placed a few precious knickknacks around the room. There wasn't space for her books, so she'd left three full boxes in the back of her station wagon. All her other belongings had either been sold or given to charity, which was no great loss. Her apartment had been mostly furnished with hand-me-downs and inexpensive necessities.

At least, that was what she told herself. She ought to be glad to get rid of that worthless clutter, but her foster-home upbringing made her into a bit of a security junkie. She tended to hoard things for no other reason than to have them. That had to change. She needed to embrace the fact that she was unencumbered, free to pick up and leave at a moment's notice…the next time Blake fired her.

That man was an enigma. At times, he seemed to be the archetype of a dark, brooding genius who was passionate about his work. But he was also a loving father who clearly adored his son. When he was around Duncan, his barriers dropped, and she saw genuine warmth. Otherwise, he was arrogant, demanding. Sophisticated, but not much of a conversationalist.

Earlier this afternoon, he'd pulled her aside to offer a rational explanation for what had happened when she and Duncan were trapped in the basement. The door at the top of the staircase must have blown shut in a gust of wind. He pointed out that several windows had been left open to let in the warm July weather. One of the electricians working on the renovations had tripped the breaker switch, causing the lights to go out. Blake had insisted that the basement door wasn't locked.

She wanted to believe him, to accept the possibility that being trapped in the basement was nothing more than an unfortunate accident. Yet, she had sensed the danger that Duncan identified in shouts, and she fully intended to shove her potted ficus in front of the bedroom door before she fell asleep.

When she heard a tap on her bedroom door, she pulled it open. Blake stood there. He was dressed for the outdoors in a denim jacket and jeans. No matter what else she thought of him, Madeline couldn't deny the obvious. He was intensely handsome.

However, seeing him at her door, she assumed the worst. "Is something wrong? Does Duncan need something?"

"He fell asleep as soon as his head hit the pillow." A tender smile lit his features. "He let me kiss his forehead and tuck him in."

She couldn't take credit for his son's change of habit. The workings of Duncan's mind were a mystery to her. "He truly cares about you."

"It occurred to me," he said, "that it's a pleasant night. Would you like to take a walk on the grounds?"

"In the dark?"

"It might be better to do this while Duncan is asleep. There are several places I'd prefer he didn't explore."

His rationale made sense; she ought to be aware of the boundaries. "Let me grab a jacket."

She pulled a lightweight blue sweatshirt over her cotton blouse and khaki slacks. Since she was already wearing sneakers, she was appropriately dressed for a trek. Stepping into the hallway, she said, "Lead the way."

Outside, in the moonlight, she appreciated the pristine isolation and beauty of their surroundings. In last night's storm, the rugged forests had loomed and threatened. Tonight, the tall pines formed a protective boundary at the western edge of the property. A sea-scented breeze whispered through the high branches as they stretched toward the canopy of stars.

With his hands clasped behind his back, Blake walked along the road leading toward the lighthouse ruins. Moonlight cast mysterious shadows on the charred, tumbled-down tower.

"How was the lighthouse destroyed?" she asked.

"A fire and a freak category-five hurricane. It was about five years ago. That storm also did a lot of damage to the Manor that was never properly repaired."

"I can understand why someone would want to restore the Manor. It's a beautiful house. But why bother with the lighthouse? With GPS satellite navigational systems, nobody needs these old lighthouses anymore."

"Both the Manor and lighthouse are part of the legacy of the town. If you're interested, Helen Fisher dropped off a booklet about the history of Raven's Cliff."

"And the curse?"

"A legend that started when the town was founded. It's good for tourists. Everybody loves a ghost story."

"I suppose so."

"By the way, the lighthouse is off-limits to Duncan. Especially after the scaffolding goes up and reconstruction gets under way."

Obviously, a construction site was no place for a child. Nor was a basement. She never should have allowed Duncan to go down there. The echo of his voice rang in her mind. *Danger. Danger. Danger.* "What about the serial killer? The Seaside Strangler. Is he part of the curse?"

"He's real. Abducts young women, dresses them in white gowns, like brides, and drapes them in seaweed before he kills them."

A shiver ripped down her spine. The first time Duncan had seen her, he'd identified her with one of the victims. "That doesn't seem like a story that would draw visitors."

"Which is why the locals play it down. Tourism is the second most important industry in Raven's Cliff. Mostly, this is a fishing village."

He directed her toward the rocky edge of the cliff. Across the bay, the lights of the town glimmered. Fishing boats and other sailing crafts bobbed in the harbor. She saw the spire of a church and a few other tall buildings but nothing that resembled a skyscraper. Though she'd expected to find average dwellings and stores in Raven's Cliff, this picturesque view could have come from another century. "When was Raven's Cliff founded?"

"Late 1700s." He glanced down at her. "You're going to keep asking questions until I tell you the whole story, aren't you?"

She couldn't tell if he was irritated or amused. "I'll read Helen Fisher's booklet later. Just give me the short version."

"Captain Earl Raven owned the land. When he brought his wife and two small children over from England, his boat was shipwrecked on those rocks." He pointed toward a treacherous shoal. Even in this pleasant July night, the dark waves crashed and plumed against the rugged outcropping. "His wife and children were washed away and their bodies never found."

"Sounds like the town started with a curse."

"Could be. Captain Raven was involved in some shady dealings," he said. "Stricken with grief, he settled here and commissioned the building of the lighthouse with a powerful beacon. One night a year, on the anniversary of his family's death, he focused the beam on those rocks. His apprentice claimed that on that dark and scary night he saw Raven take a sailboat out to the rocks where he was joined by the ghosts of his family."

Pushing her glasses up on her nose, she peered down at the rugged coastline. Relentless waves crashed against the dark, jagged rocks. "A family of ghosts. What happened next?"

"After Raven passed away, the apprentice inherited the Manor. The town prospered and grew."

He went silent, and she turned toward him. His expression was utterly unreadable. She wondered if he was thinking of his personal ghost—his wife who had passed away only a few years ago.

"The townsfolk kept up the old traditions," he said. "Even after the lighthouse was no longer in use, the lighthouse keeper fired up the beacon every year on the anniversary. Until five years ago."

"The start of the curse."

He nodded. "The beacon wasn't lit at the appointed time. Somebody screwed up. Then came the fire that claimed the lives of the elderly lighthouse keeper and his grandson, Nicholas Sterling. The hurricane not only damaged the manor but destroyed a lot of other property in the town. Since then, Raven's Cliff has been plagued by bad luck."

"More than the serial killer?"

"Deaths at sea. Fishermen losing their boats. Strange disappearances. Recently there was a weird genetic mutation in the fish that caused an epidemic. And a couple of months ago, the daughter of the mayor was swept off the edge of the cliff in a gale-force wind. It happened on her wedding day."

"The daughter of Beatrice Wells?" Madeline remembered the determinedly perky smile of the mayor's wife. Beatrice didn't look like someone who had lost her daughter so recently. Either she was amazingly resilient or firmly in denial.

"There are rumors that the daughter, Camille, is still alive." He raised a skeptical eyebrow. "That ought to be enough story-telling to satisfy your curiosity."

"Perhaps."

When he started walking at the edge of the cliff, she chose the inward side to walk beside him. Though not afraid of heights, she was thinking about the bride who was whisked over the edge by a gust of wind. "These local legends are interesting. I could make the history of Raven's Cliff into a lesson for Duncan."

"I'd rather you didn't. I don't want him worrying about the curse. He's already picked up something he must have heard about Sofia Lagios."

"Which indicates an interest," she said. "Something I could use to focus his reading and writing skills."

"No serial killers," he repeated firmly. "Duncan has already had enough tragedy in his life."

She pressed her lips together to keep from arguing, but she didn't agree. Blake couldn't pretend that the death of Duncan's mother had never happened, especially since the boy talked to her ghost every day.

Chapter Six

Following the moonlit path at the edge of the cliff, Blake led her to the weathered, wooden staircase that descended forty feet to the rugged private beach. He hadn't decided how he felt about Duncan being allowed to explore in this hazard-filled area. Swimming was, of course, out of the question in these frigid northern Atlantic waters. Not to mention these treacherous currents.

He paused at the top of the staircase and watched as Madeline tentatively stepped onto the landing and peeked over the railing. Tendrils of her black hair had escaped the tight ponytail on top of her head and formed delicate curls against her pale cheeks.

The real reason he'd wanted to take this walk with her was to express his gratitude for whatever she'd done to cause Duncan to open up. Her work impressed him, but he didn't want to give the impression that she had free rein with her lesson plans. Left to her own devices, she'd probably be teaching his six-year-old son how to spell *homicide* and *strangulation*.

He needed to get a handle on this tall, slender school-teacher who had made such a huge impression on his son.

Who was Madeline Douglas? Her reticent nature made her almost invisible. She seemed organized, almost fastidious. And yet—by her own admission—she'd shown up on his doorstep without a penny to her name.

It shouldn't be so hard for him to figure her out. She was only an employee—another in the seemingly endless parade of tutors, teachers and nannies. But he knew she was different. Duncan cared about her; that made her special.

As she leaned out over the railing, he noticed the flare of her hips and the rounded curve of her bottom. She sure as hell didn't dress to show off her shape. Not in those prim little cotton blouses and baggy sweatshirts. Right now, the only skin visible was that on her trim ankles above her sneakers. His gaze swept the length of her legs. Too easily, he could imagine those legs entwined with his.

When she faced him, her eyes widened behind her glasses. "Where do the stairs lead?"

"To a private beach and several caves." He stepped in front of her. "I'll go first. If you slip, I can catch you. Hang on tight to the railing."

The wood-plank staircase, firmly anchored to the wall of the cliff, zigzagged like a fire escape. At the bottom was a cove of jagged rock that surrounded less than a mile of dark, wet sand. Moonlight shone on the churning waves, and the roar of the surf echoed against rock walls. Even on a temperate night like this, the rugged beach was lashed by wind and sea. The power of these untamed elements aroused his artistic nature, reminding him of life's fragility. The buildings he designed and restored—even skyscrapers and cathedrals—were frail shells compared to the timeless ocean.

She walked across the sand, leaving footprints, until she

stood at the edge of the foaming surf. "The water looks cold."

"And the undertow is deadly."

"I wonder," she said, "if there's any way I could bring Duncan down here. It's so beautiful."

"The problem with introducing Duncan to this area is that he might try to come here alone. Sometimes, he sticks to the rules. And other times…"

"He's headstrong," she said.

Her plain-spoken description amused him. His son's autistic behavior had been studied by teams of specialists who stated their theories in polysyllabic profusion: *Pervasive developmental disorder. Hypersensitivity. Asperger's Syndrome.*

She called it headstrong. If only life were so simple.

"For now," Blake said, "let's keep this area off-limits to Duncan."

"For now."

As she nodded, he studied the sharp outline of her jaw. Her features were too angular to be pretty, but her face had character. An interesting face. Appealing.

When she met his gaze, she seemed startled to find him watching her. Quickly, she looked down. Shyness? Or was she hiding something?

"Madeline, there's something I need to tell you."

"You're not going to fire me again, are you?"

"Hell, no. Why would you think that?"

"Because I've only been at the Manor for twenty-four hours, and you've already ordered me to get out twice."

Damn it, she made him sound like a total bastard. He pushed away his irritation. "I wanted to thank you. It's been months since Duncan has allowed me to hold him in my arms, to kiss his forehead, to tuck him under the covers. Thank you for this precious gift."

She darted a glance in his direction. "You're welcome."

"I want to build on this foundation. Tell me how you got my son to open up?"

She shrugged. "I haven't been following any special program. Mostly, I just treat him like a regular kid."

Not what he wanted to hear. In the back of his mind, Blake had been hoping for a teaching technique—a set of rules he could follow.

He strode across the sand. "This way to the caves."

"Of course," Madeline said, though she wasn't sure she wanted to go spelunking in the dark.

Carefully picking her way across the narrow strip of dark sand toward the wild shrubs near the cliff wall, she followed his lead. His expression of gratitude surprised her. Though he'd been visibly moved when he held Duncan in his arms, she never thought he'd attribute his son's openness to her.

At the inward side of the cove, craggy granite formations sloped down to the sea, like the arms of a giant reaching for the surf. Blake stepped onto the ledge and held out his hand to assist her. When her fingers linked with his, a powerful surge raced up her arm. His intensity frightened her while his strength drew her closer.

He helped her onto the ledge and steadied her by holding her other arm. Their position was almost an embrace. She met his gaze and saw starlight reflected in his hazel eyes. On this rocky promontory jutting into the sea, Blake was in his element, braced firmly against the wind and salt spray from crashing waves.

For a moment, she wished his touch meant something

more intimate. She wished for his affection, wished that this dynamic, talented man could care for her.

Releasing her arm, he pointed upward. "There's a shallow cave there. We'll have to climb."

"I see the opening." She had no desire to test her balance on these slippery rocks. "But let's not go there."

"I thought you were curious, ready for an adventure."

"Not if it means breaking my leg when I slip and fall." If she hadn't been firmly anchored to his hand, she might have stumbled right here. "Let me get my bearings. Where are we in terms of the lighthouse and the manor?"

He looked skyward as if he could discern their location by the position of the stars. "Do you see the trees up there? We're almost directly across from the entrance to the manor."

She hadn't realized that the cliff's edge was so close to the forest. No wonder he insisted on having Duncan accompanied on his outdoor excursions.

"The largest cavern is back on the beach."

"No climbing?"

"Not a bit."

"Let's check it out."

He helped her down from the ledge and crossed the sand to a gaping maw the size of a double-wide garage. A few standing rocks, taller than her head, shielded the entrance from view. "I can't believe I didn't see this giant hole before."

"It's the shape of the rocks and the shadows," he said. "Even in daylight, you might not notice the cave."

As soon as she stepped inside, the cold stone walls shielded her from the wind. An impermeable curtain of darkness hung before her. They had entered a place of eerie secrets. A dragon's lair.

"It's huge." Her voice dropped to a whisper. "Did smugglers and pirates once use these caves?"

"You'll have to read Helen Fisher's history of the town to learn the local superstitions."

Though she didn't consider herself psychic, she felt a deep foreboding. Bad things had happened in this cave—murders and intrigues by seafaring renegades. Or perhaps something had happened not too long ago. The curse of Raven's Cliff.

After a few steps into the darkness, she scooted back into the moonlight. Her memory of being trapped in the windowless basement was still too fresh. She had no desire to go deeper. "This is enough for me."

"Scared of the ghosts?" he teased.

"Not all ghosts are frightening, you know." Though she hated to risk making him angry, she felt it was important for him to know about Duncan's connection to his deceased mother. "Duncan has spoken to me about his mother."

"Kathleen."

When he whispered her name, a pall of sadness slipped over him. In the moonlight, she saw a haunted expression in his eyes. "Can you tell me about her?"

He raked his fingers through his dark blond hair. A nervous habit. "She was beautiful. Blond hair. Laughing eyes. She loved to dance. And she was a gourmet chef."

The combination of wistful sorrow in his voice and the strange atmosphere of the cave was almost too heavy for her to bear. Still, she wanted to know more. "Why did you and your wife choose to name your son Duncan?"

"Family name. I used to tease Kathleen that she'd named our boy after the cake mix."

"A major insult for someone who cooked from scratch."

"I guess so." He shook his head as if to clear the cobwebs on these buried memories. "When she didn't like one of my architectural designs, she called me Frank Lloyd Wrong."

"She had a good sense of humor."

"Kathleen was good at everything."

It was obvious that he still treasured her memory, still loved her. She doubted anyone would ever measure up to his deceased wife. "Before she passed away, was she aware of Duncan's disability?"

"She was spared that pain. Duncan was only three, almost four, when she died. He was always a goofy kid. A trickster. Loved to play games." His eyebrows lifted. "I never thought of this before. It was Kathleen who started his habit of counting his steps. When they came out the door of our brownstone, they counted the stairs. Up and down. Up and down the stairs."

Madeline wondered if the boy heard the echo of his mother's voice when he measured his steps. "She sounds like a good mother."

"A lot better at parenting than I was." He winced as if in physical pain. "I was building my career. Spent a lot of time away from home on different restoration projects. Always thought there'd be more time with Kathleen. Then, the cancer. I didn't know our days were limited."

Acting on an instinct to comfort him, she placed her hand on his arm. His muscles tensed, hard as granite. "You couldn't predict the future, Blake."

"After she died, I was even more of a workaholic. Couldn't stand being in the house where we'd been so happy. I sold it. We moved. I took every project that came my way. I was running day and night, running away from my sorrow, so caught up in my own pain that I lost track of Duncan. I was a damn selfish fool. I should have been there for Duncan. Should have…"

His voice trailed off in the wind.

There was nothing she could say to heal his grief and soothe his regrets. Her concern was his son. For his sake, she had to speak. "When Duncan and I were trapped in the basement, he told me that I didn't need to be afraid because his mother was watching over us. She's always there for him. He talks to her. She's a very real presence in his life."

"Like a ghost?" he asked angrily.

"An angel."

Anguish deepened the lines in his face. For a moment, she thought he might erupt. By poking into the past, she might have overstepped the bounds of propriety. He had a right to his privacy, his personal hell.

"An angel," he whispered. "I like that."

His tension seemed to ebb as he strode across the wind-swept sands. At the foot of the weathered wooden staircase, he turned toward her.

Nervously, she met his gaze, preparing herself for the worst. The man was so mercurial that she didn't know what to expect. He was capable of ferocious anger. And even greater love, like the abiding love for his wife.

The merest hint of a smile played at the corner of his mouth. "I'm glad you told me."

"Oh." She exhaled in a whoosh. "Not fired?"

His smile spread. When he rested his hand on her shoulder, she felt the warmth of connection. A warmth that sent her heart soaring. What would it be like to experience the force of his passion? To be swept away?

"You'll always have a place with me, Madeline."

This was where she belonged. With him. And Duncan.

Chapter Seven

After a few days with no major disasters, Madeline began
to believe that she really was part of this odd little family.
Duncan's carefully charted daily routine gave a rhythm to
each day in spite of the arrival of roofers and bricklayers who
were repairing the chimneys. The workmen kept Blake busy;
she'd hardly been alone with him since their walk on the
beach.

He'd been friendly—at least, what passed for friendly
with this brooding architectural genius—and she couldn't
complain about the way he treated her. Still, Madeline had
hopes for something more. A real friendship, perhaps. Who
was she kidding? Her fantasies about Blake skipped down
a far more sensual path—one that was totally inappropriate.

While Duncan ate his solitary lunch, counting each
chew before he swallowed, she delivered a lunch tray to
Blake's studio on the first floor. Originally, this room had
been a formal library, and one wall was still floor-to-ceiling
books. The antiques that would one day occupy this space
had been removed for expert refinishing, and Blake used
a purely functional, L-shaped desk and black metal file

cabinets. His computer, phones and fax machine rested amid stacks of papers, invoices and research materials.

His back was toward her as he stared at blueprints taped onto a slanted drafting table near the west-facing window. Without turning, he said, "Just leave the lunch on the table. Thanks, Alma."

"It's me," she said quietly, not wanting to disturb his concentration but wanting him to notice her.

He pivoted. His unguarded gaze sent a bolt of heat in her direction. "Hello, Madeline."

Those two simple words unleashed an earthquake of awareness through her body. She placed the lunch tray on his desk before she dropped it. He'd shaved today. The sharp line of his jaw was softened by a dimple at the left corner of his mouth.

Pushing her glasses up on her nose, she broached the topic she'd wanted to discuss. "I was wondering if I could possibly get an advance on my paycheck. There were a few things I wanted to purchase. For Duncan."

"I'd be happy to pay for anything my son needs."

"These aren't teaching supplies." His prior teachers had compiled an excellent selection of books, educational materials and computer programs. "It's other stuff."

He came around the desk. "What kind of stuff?"

She hated asking for money, even though she had a good reason. Avoiding his direct gaze, she mumbled, "Baseball equipment. Duncan and I have been playing catch in the afternoon and I—"

"Catch? You and Duncan?"

"After his regular lessons are finished," she assured him. "We've gotten to the point where we can throw the ball back and forth five times without either of us dropping it."

"Five catches? That's better than Duncan has ever done before. Why didn't you tell me?"

"You've been so busy with the work crews arriving."

"I'm never too busy for my son. I made that mistake once already, and I won't make it again. Duncan is my number-one concern. The whole reason I took this job in Raven's Cliff was so I could spend more time with him in a relaxed, stress-free atmosphere."

She couldn't imagine a situation involving Blake that would be without stress. The air surrounding him crackled with electricity. "Of course, you're welcome to join us."

He sat on the edge of his desk with his arms folded across his broad chest. "I've tried physical activities with Duncan before. It's never turned out well."

"Playing with me is no challenge because—as Duncan is delighted to point out—I'm just a girl. There's more pressure with you."

"Why?"

She shrugged. "He doesn't want to disappoint you. He can play catch, but he's no Roger Clemens or Wade Boggs."

"Clemens and Boggs. Legendary Red Sox players."

"I'm from Boston."

"Uh-huh." He nodded slowly. "It's high time for me to get involved in this baseball teaching plan of yours. Can't have you raising my boy to be a Sox fan. This family roots for the Cubs."

She drew the obvious conclusion. "You're from Chicago."

"Born and bred in the 'burbs. One sister, one brother and a German shepherd named Rex." He went behind his desk, opened a drawer and pulled out a checkbook. "No problem with an advance, Madeline. You've made excellent progress with Duncan. He's still letting me hug him and touch him."

The boy hadn't yet extended that invitation to her. Nor had his father, she thought ruefully.

Blake handed the check to her. Reading the amount, her eyes popped. Five hundred dollars. "This is too much."

"And I'll be paying for his sports equipment out of my own pocket. Getting my son his own glove, his own bat. Damn. That's every father's dream. Give me an hour to make sure everything here is running smoothly. Then we'll all go into town. You and me and Duncan."

"We'll be ready." A trip into Raven's Cliff sounded like an adventure. She hadn't left the Manor since she'd arrived and was beginning to feel cloistered.

She returned to the kitchen just as Duncan set down his spoon. Without a word, he hopped down from his chair and marched toward the family room. His schedule called for quiet time, which usually meant he sat at his computer.

Since Alma was nowhere in sight, Madeline cleaned up the dishes and loaded them in the dishwasher. For the past couple of days, she'd been using this after-lunch lull as her own personal time to read or fiddle around on her laptop. Today, she was too excited to sit still.

She climbed the staircase to her bedroom and tucked Blake's check into her wallet. With this money, she'd open a bank account and start rebuilding the chaos of her life. As if to underline her thoughts of reconstruction, she heard hammering from the roofers overhead. Progress, she thought. Progress in many directions.

With a bounce in her step, she returned to the family room where Duncan sat on the floor amid a clutter of toy trucks. Instead of following her regular pattern of relentlessly tidying up the mess, she pushed aside a couple of books on the large sectional sofa, grabbed the remote from the top of the television and sat facing the screen.

Duncan cast a curious glance in her direction. He seldom asked what she was doing. Planning ahead wasn't part of his behavior, and she was careful not to make that sort of demand. Instead, she announced, "I'm going to watch a baseball game on TV. You're welcome to join me."

She tuned in to a Boston station on cable. The game hadn't yet started, and a local news program was on. The smoothly coiffed anchorman glanced down at his notes, and she caught the words *diamond heist* and *estimated loss of over seven hundred thousand dollars.* Quite a haul. She couldn't even imagine what seven hundred thousand dollars' worth of diamonds looked like.

A mug shot of her brother appeared on the screen. "A suspect is in custody."

Oh my God, Marty. What have you done?

The anchorman's words hit her like a hail of bullets. "The jewels have not been recovered. Police are looking for an accomplice."

Her thumb hit the off button and the TV went blank.

"Where's the game?" Duncan looked up at her. "I want to watch the baseball."

"In a minute."

Her gut clenched. The ache spread through her body. She wanted to bury her face in her hands and sob, but she didn't want Duncan to be alarmed. Or, even worse, to start asking questions. *Damn it.* She'd known that Marty was up to no good.

A few months ago, he'd shown up on her doorstep. Miserable and broke, he'd told her that he wanted to go straight but owed a lot of money. He had to pay it back or he'd be hurt, maybe even killed. How could she turn him away? He was her brother.

Fearing the worst, she'd emptied her bank account and savings to give him the cash he needed. Instead of thanks, he ran her credit card up to the max. She had no way to pay rent or any of her other bills.

Maybe she could have worked things out, but Marty got into a knock-down, drag-out argument with her landlord. She had to move. There was always the option of going home to live with the Douglases, but she'd been too humiliated. They'd always told her she couldn't trust Marty. Even as a child, he'd been a liar and a thief. But pulling off a diamond heist?

Damn you, Marty. Two weeks ago when she'd confronted him, he put on a cool, smug attitude and told her not to worry because he was coming into a lot of money. From a debt that was owed to him. Hah! She should have suspected the worst. But she'd purposely closed her eyes, wanting to believe that maybe, just maybe, her brother was telling the truth.

When she got the call from Alma about the teaching position with Duncan, it had seemed like a godsend. At least Madeline would have employment and a place to live. Being far away from Marty in Maine seemed prudent.

The night before she left, he'd showed up at her apartment. Instead of his usual smooth talk, he'd been agitated and sweaty. Had he just stolen those diamonds? He'd collapsed on the floor in her empty apartment and slept like a log. The next morning, he was gone but had left a note that said: "The police might come around asking about me. Don't tell them anything."

That should have been her cue to go directly to the police. But she didn't have anything to tell them. She didn't know what her brother had done. Until now.

Looking up, she saw Duncan standing only a few feet away from her, watching her curiously, almost as though he could read all the dark thoughts swirling inside her head.

Were the Boston police looking for her? The TV anchorman had mentioned an accomplice. Would the authorities think she'd aided and abetted in the jewel heist? Would she end up in jail for no other reason than her brother was a criminal?

No, she wouldn't allow Marty to destroy her life any more than he had already.

No, she wouldn't talk to the police. She had no useful information for an investigator.

No, no, no. This wasn't happening.

If she kept her mouth shut, she'd be safe. *Don't make trouble. Stay in the background.* As a child in foster care, she'd learned those lessons well.

Forcing a smile, she looked at Duncan. "The baseball game should be on now."

He climbed onto the sofa, and she turned on the television. A wide-angle shot of Fenway Park appeared on the screen.

Duncan pointed and said, "Ninety feet from base to base. It's a square."

"But they call it a diamond," she said, cringing at the word. Over seventy thousand dollars' worth of diamonds.

When the national anthem was played, she stood on shaky legs. "Every game starts with that song about our country. We stand and place our hand over our heart to show respect."

Duncan pointed to the flag on the screen. "Fifty stars for fifty states."

She looked down at his smooth blond hair as he stood at attention. The innocence of this troubled boy soothed her own fears. If she concentrated solely on Duncan, she might be able to forget her own problems.

As the Red Sox took the field, she ran through all the numbers that would appeal to him. First base, second and third. Nine players on a team. Distance from the pitcher's mound to home plate was sixty and a half feet.

"When we play catch," he asked, "how far apart are we?"

"I don't know. We'll have to measure."

"Good."

Duncan leaned forward. He seemed to be completely caught up in the game. As they counted balls and strikes together, her fears lessened. The symmetry of the game comforted her. All of life was about balance. Ups and downs. She and her brother had always been at opposite ends of the spectrum.

Suddenly, Duncan jumped off the sofa. He ran close to the television, then back to the sofa. He was breathing fast, almost hyperventilating.

"You want to show me something," she guessed. "Something on the television. What is it?"

At that moment, Blake sauntered into the room.

Duncan's skinny arm pumped back and forth like a metronome at the television screen. "Gloves," he said.

"That's right," his father said. "Baseball players in the field need to wear a glove to catch the ball."

"Not them." Duncan shook his head. "The man with the bat. The batter. He has gloves."

And so he did. The man at the plate wore leather gloves on both hands. Madeline hadn't even thought of this advantage. When Duncan played baseball with other kids, he could wear gloves and not be considered strange at all.

"Batting gloves," Blake said with a wide smile. "Do you want to get some batting gloves?"

"Yes." Duncan's blue eyes actually seemed to sparkle. "I want to be a baseball player when I grow up."

Wearing gloves was a simple solution, allowing him to be around other children without touching. She wished that her own problems could be so easily solved.

Chapter Eight

The central business district in Raven's Cliff clung desperately to its heritage as a historic New England village. Tourists enjoyed the ambience. Blake didn't.

As a general rule, he disdained any shop with "Ye Olde" in the name. Still, he preferred shopping in the village to visiting a superstore with drab neutral walls and overstuffed rows of undifferentiated merchandise. He appreciated that most of these businesses—even those that were self-consciously cutesy—were mom-and-pop operations that had been in the family for years.

He parked on the street opposite the Cliffside Inn, a three-story bed-and-breakfast with genuinely interesting features, including a two-story tower with cornice and a cone-shaped roof.

"Charming," Madeline said as she peered through the windshield at the house. "Look at the roses. Those gardens are brilliant."

"I stayed at the Inn on my first visit to Raven's Cliff," he said. "The interior has nicely maintained Victorian antiques and some very good art, but the real draw is the proprietor, Hazel Baker. She's a character."

When he stepped out of the SUV and held the back door open for Duncan, he spotted Hazel in the front yard with a garden hose. Her long, rainbow-colored skirt caught the July breeze and swirled around her sturdy legs as she waved vigorously and called out, "Good afternoon, Blake. Lovely weather, eh?"

"Nice to see you, Hazel."

He liked that they knew each other's name. This sort of small-town atmosphere was exactly what he wanted for Duncan. In a place where people looked out for each other, a kid like Duncan had a shot at being accepted.

Though he would have liked to cross the street and introduce Madeline to kooky Hazel, who declared herself to be Wiccan, Duncan was tugging on his arm. "Hurry, Daddy. We have to get my gloves."

"Sure thing, buddy."

He linked his hand with his son's. Though he knew from experience that Duncan could, at any moment, pitch a tantrum or go stiff as a board, he savored this moment. Having a kid who was excited about baseball was so damn normal. Once again, he had Madeline to thank for this phenomenon.

As she strolled along the wide sidewalk on the other side of Duncan, she smiled at every person they met—tourists and residents alike. Straightforward and direct, this woman had nothing to hide. Behind her glasses, her gaze scanned constantly, taking in all the details of the neatly painted storefronts and the various eateries, most of which were off-limits to Duncan because of his dietary restrictions. No sugar. No wheat. No salt.

Madeline was quick to point out a sign in the bakery window. "Gluten-free, sugar-free muffins."

"This is where Alma picks up our bread."

"Maybe later, we could get a treat."

Duncan yanked his hand. "First, my gloves."

They crossed the street to enter the general store—a large, high-ceilinged space with an array of tourist products up front. A tall, barrel-chested man with curly red hair and a beard to match approached them. "Hey, now. Aren't you that architect fella working up at the Manor?"

"That's me." Blake shook his hand. "I'm Blake Monroe. This is my son, Duncan. And his teacher, Madeline Douglas."

"I'm Stuart Chapman. What can I do you for?"

"Sporting equipment," Blake said.

When Stuart reached up to scratch his head, Blake noticed the tattoos on his forearms. Inside a heart with bluebirds on each side was the name *Dorothy.* "I don't have a whole lot of stock, but I can order anything you need."

"It's for Duncan," Madeline explained. "He'd like to start playing T-ball."

"You're in luck," Stuart boomed as he lumbered toward the rear of the store. "We've got a T-ball league for the youngsters, and I carry all the equipment. Hats, balls, gloves."

"Gloves," Duncan said loudly.

Blake knew that tone of voice. A signal of tension building inside his son. A warning.

Hoping to avoid an outburst, Blake went directly to the batting gloves and selected one that ought to fit his son. Opening the package, he held it out. "Try this."

As soon as Duncan slipped the leather-backed glove onto his right hand, he beamed. Finally, this was a glove he could wear without being teased.

"The other hand," he said.

"Well, now," Stuart said. "Most batters just use the one. No need for two."

"Not really," Madeline said. "All the major leaguers wear gloves on both hands."

"Eh, yup. You're right about that." Stuart chuckled. "Duncan could be the next Wade Boggs."

"Boggs," Blake muttered. "Another Red Sox fan."

They picked out another glove, which Duncan insisted on wearing, then selected mitts for each of them, bats and a tee for practicing. All things considered, this was one of the most blissfully normal shopping trips he'd ever had with his son.

He eyed the bases. "I'm thinking we might go all the way and set up our own practice field at the Manor."

Stuart chuckled again. "I'd like to see the look on Helen Fisher's face if you do."

"True," Madeline said. "I doubt they ever had a baseball field at the Manor."

Stuart shrugged his heavy shoulders. "That Helen. She's a stickler for historical accuracy."

The hell with Helen Fisher and the good folks of Raven's Cliff Historical Preservation Committee. This was his son. "We'll take the bases. And a couple of duffel bags to carry everything."

"Good for you." Stuart clapped Blake on the shoulder. "When my four boys were young, I'd have chosen them over historical accuracy any day of the week. Building the athletes of tomorrow. Ain't that right, Duncan?"

"Yes."

Before Blake could stop him, Stuart reached down and ruffled the hair on Duncan's head. Then he turned away to gather up their equipment.

Duncan's reaction to physical contact with a stranger was immediate. His lips pressed together in a tight, white line. His eyes went blank. He seemed to stop breathing.

Dreading the worst, Blake squatted down to his son's eye level. "Are you okay, buddy?"

Madeline was also leaning down. She whispered, "Tell your daddy what you saw."

Duncan's chest jerked as he inhaled. "That man is very sad. Dorothy is sick. His wife. Must be brave. Must hope for the best."

"Thank you for telling us," Madeline said.

Duncan's eyes flickered to his father's face. His breathing returned to a more normal rhythm. He licked his lips, blinked, then he held up both hands. "Gloves."

Blake studied his son's face. The signs of tension had already faded. He ran to the front of the store where Stuart was ringing up their total expenditure on an old-fashioned cash register.

Crisis averted.

Madeline stepped up beside him. "Do you think Duncan really saw something? That he sensed what Stuart was feeling?"

"No," he said curtly. Dealing with an autistic child was difficult enough. He damn well refused to start worrying about his son being a psychic weirdo. Leave that nonsense to the kooks like Hazel at the Cliffside Inn.

While Stuart was tallying up their haul, Blake thought he recognized the mayor walking past the front window. "Is that Perry Wells?"

"Yup." Stuart frowned. "I'm surprised he's got the nerve to show his face."

"Why?" Madeline asked.

"There's been letters in the newspaper about corruption in the mayor's office." He ran the back of his fingers across his beard. "Anonymous letters."

"A cowardly way to make accusations," Madeline said. "How can you believe someone who won't sign their—"

"Excuse me," Blake said. He handed his wallet to Madeline. "Pay for this. I'll be right back."

His reason for talking to Mayor Perry Wells had nothing to do with accusations or political corruption. A few days ago, when the mayor's wife had come to the Manor, she'd mentioned the possibility of a house for sale. A beachfront three-bedroom. It was worth taking a look.

On the sidewalk, he called out, "Mayor Wells."

The tall man in a khaki-colored suit came to an abrupt halt and darted a nervous glance over his shoulder as if expecting someone to throw a pie in his face.

Blake strode toward him. "Good afternoon, sir. I'm not sure if you remember me. Blake Monroe."

"Of course. Call me Perry." His practiced politician's smile lifted the corners of his mouth.

When he shook Blake's hand, his fingers trembled. Those anonymous letters must be having an effect, which made Blake wonder about the validity of the charges. "I'm enjoying my time in Raven's Cliff."

"And you're doing important work at the Manor. Vital to our town."

"Nice to be appreciated," Blake said, "but I'm just doing my job. Teddy Fisher is paying me very well."

At the mention of Teddy's name, the mayor's elegant features tensed, but he was quick to recover his poise and launch into what sounded like a prepared speech. "When the restoration of the Manor and the lighthouse are complete, when the beacon shines forth across the sea, it will signal a new era of prosperity for Raven's Cliff. A full recovery from our tragedies. A lifting of the curse."

Blake couldn't let that remark pass. "Surely a man such as yourself doesn't believe in a curse."

"It's symbolic. On that dark day when the lighthouse was destroyed, the hearts and minds of the citizens in Raven's Cliff were poisoned."

"You must be pleased that Teddy has taken on the responsibility of restoring the lighthouse."

"Why do you keep mentioning him? Teddy isn't..." He paused, visibly shaken. What had Teddy Fisher done to this man to provoke such a response?

Blake dropped the topic, which was really none of his concern. "A few days ago, your wife visited the Manor and mentioned a house you might have for sale."

"Are you thinking of settling in our town?"

"Considering it."

Perry reached into his tailored jacket and took out a polished gold case. He handed his card to Blake. "Call my office, and we'll make an appointment. I'd be happy to have you as one of my constituents."

Pocketing the card, Blake returned to the general store to gather up their purchases. Two duffel bags full.

After they'd dragged the baseball equipment back to the car, he was ready to head back to the Manor. So far, this had been a pleasant outing. He didn't want to push their luck.

When he unlocked his driver's-side door, Madeline objected. "Wait. I had a few things I wanted to do. A stop at the bank. And I noticed a dress in one of the store windows."

He glanced over at Duncan, who paced in a circle around a streetlamp. "What do you think, buddy? I say we hang around while Madeline goes shopping."

Duncan stopped in front of his father. With an expression typical of any other six-year-old, he rolled his eyes. "I guess."

"We can watch the fishing boats."

"Yes," he shouted.

"It's settled," Blake said. "We'll wait for you at the docks. On the bench outside the Coastal Fish Shop."

"Thanks, boys."

As she hurried down the street ahead of them, he was struck by the feline gracefulness of her walk. Most of the time, she looked like a drab little house cat, but when she moved with a purpose, her long legs stretched and strode like a more exotic creature. Maybe a cheetah.

He and Duncan took their time going back into town. They stopped in the bakery for a gluten-free, sugar-free cookie and a couple of bottled waters. Then they went to watch the boats.

Beyond the end of the commercial district, the street sloped down to the fishing docks. Not many tourists came to this fishy-smelling area where hardworking crews off loaded the day's catch from boats that had been battered by years at sea. They were coarse men, scarred and weathered from their heavy, sometimes dangerous labor. Blake admired their grit and determination.

Drinking their bottled water, he and Duncan sat on a bench outside Coastal Fish—a business that had almost gone under during the recent epidemic that had been traced to genetically altered fish.

Across the cove, the ruins of the lighthouse seemed picturesque. He pointed it out to Duncan. "There's where we live."

"I don't see our house."

"It's behind the trees. But there's the lighthouse."

He stood and craned forward for a better view. "I'm not supposed to go to the lighthouse."

"You got that right."

He counted four steps forward, then four steps back, then forward again. His gaze stuck on a group of fishermen. Two grizzled older men smoked and laughed. The third was younger, more refined in his features. He turned toward Duncan and stared for a long moment.

"Four, three, two, one." Duncan was back at his side. He pressed his face against Blake's arm. Under his breath, he mumbled unintelligible words.

"I can't hear you," Blake said.

"She sells seashells," Duncan said. "Seashells by the seashore. Seashells."

He was tired. After a full afternoon, he needed to get back to the Manor. They needed to go. Now.

Fortunately, Madeline appeared on the docks with a bag from the dress shop hanging from her arm.

When Blake looked back toward the fishermen, the younger man had vanished.

Chapter Nine

After they returned to the Manor, Madeline left Blake and Duncan to sort out the new baseball equipment while she went up to her room. Kicking off her sneakers and socks, she stretched out on the duvet. A sea-scented breeze through the open window stirred the dangling teardrop crystals on the quaint little chandelier, causing bits of reflected light to dance against the walls like a swarm of fireflies.

She closed her eyes, thinking she might catch a nap, but there were too many other worries. At the bank in Raven's Cliff, she'd cashed the check from Blake but hadn't opened an account, fearing that her location might be traced by the Boston police. As if withholding her name from a bank account would hide her whereabouts. She had to file a change of address form to make sure her creditors knew her location. She couldn't just disappear. If the police wanted to find her, they would.

And she couldn't keep her brother's crime a secret, certainly not from Blake. Alma knew Marty. It was only a matter of time before Alma heard about the diamond heist and said something. It would be a hundred times better if Blake heard about Marty from her own lips.

She left the downy-soft bed and went to the window overlooking the grounds at the front of the house. It was after five o'clock; the roofers and other workmen had knocked off for the day. The scheduled dinnertime was in less than an hour. For now, Blake and Duncan were playing catch.

Her own games with Duncan had been casual, tossing the ball and reciting rhymes while pausing to pick wildflowers. With his father in charge, catch took on the aspect of a male-bonding ritual. Not only did he throw the ball back and forth, but also straight up in the air and bouncing wildly across the grass. Blake chased after one of those grounders, scooped it up and rolled across the ground in a somersault and lay there. Duncan ran to him and pounced on his chest. Both were laughing.

So normal. So sweet.

Stepping away from the window, she took the red dress from the bag and prepared to hang it in her closet. The silky fabric glided through her fingers. Never in her life had she purchased anything so blatantly flirty.

She tore off her everyday outfit and slipped the dress over her head. The sleeveless bodice criss-crossed over her breasts and nipped in at the waist, giving her an hourglass shape. The skirt floated gracefully over her hips and ended at her knees. The clerk in the store had complimented the hem length, which would have been too long on a shorter woman.

The clerk had also given her another bit of information that she needed to share with Blake, even though he probably wouldn't want to hear it.

On tiptoe, she twirled in front of the antique mirror above the dressing table. A red dress. Definitely not the sort of outfit for an old-maid schoolteacher.

A bit of jewelry at the throat might be nice. She tried on various lockets and pearls. None of her accessories seemed chic enough for the dress. The same was true for her clunky, practical shoes.

She reached up on top of her head and unfastened the clip holding her hair in place. The heavy black curls tumbled around her neck and shoulders. Still watching herself in the mirror, she went to the bed and sat on the edge, crossing her legs. When she leaned forward, the plunging neckline showed a nice bit of cleavage.

Tonight she would tell Blake about Marty and the diamond heist. Why shouldn't she? Her brother might be a crook, but she had nothing to hide.

A tap on her bedroom door startled her, and she bolted to her feet. "Who is it?"

"Blake."

She snatched her other outfit from the bed where she'd discarded it. She ought to change clothes, slip back into her teacher persona. But why? If she ever intended to wear this red dress outside the confines of her own bedroom, she ought to get a second opinion from Blake.

Tossing her other clothes into the closet, she straightened her shoulders. "Come in."

The instant he saw her, his eyes lit up. "Wow."

His appreciative grin was worth every penny she'd paid for the dress. "I wanted to try it on," she said. "To see if it looked as good here as in the shop."

He came forward, took her hand and raised it to his lips for a light kiss that sent a tingle up her arm. He murmured, "You're beautiful."

"Thank you." She dropped a small curtsy and reclaimed her hand. Unaccustomed to such outright admiration from the opposite sex, she experienced a nervous flutter in her tummy. He wasn't lying. He really liked the dress.

"Turn around," he said.

She twirled on her bare toes, and the fabric floated away from her legs.

"I need shoes," she said. "I don't have a single pair that looks right with the dress."

"I like your bare feet," he said as he came closer.

She was about to complain about the size of her feet, something that made her nearly as self-conscious as her height, but the glow from his hazel eyes mesmerized her. She froze where she stood, watching with almost detached curiosity as he reached toward her.

His fingers glided through her hair as he removed her glasses. "The color of your eyes is striking. Aquamarine."

He stood close enough that she could see him clearly without her glasses. His lips parted.

She tilted her chin upward, waiting to accept whatever he offered. Gently, he kissed her forehead just above her eyes. She wanted so much more.

When his hand clasped her waist, she responded. Leaning toward him, the tips of her breasts grazed his broad chest. She reached up and caressed the firm line of his clean-shaven jaw.

Then he kissed her for real. His mouth pressed hard against hers. A fierce heat blazed in her chest, stealing her breath. She clung to him, caught up in this magical moment, lost in a red-dress fantasy. The most handsome man she'd ever seen was kissing her. Her? Tall, gawky Madeline? It didn't seem possible. Somehow, in a moment, she'd transformed into a swan.

His tongue slid across the surface of her teeth and

plunged into her mouth. She responded with a passion she'd never known existed within the boundaries of her humdrum life. She was spinning and dizzy, yet utterly aware of every incredible sensation.

When they separated, she was gasping. She wanted him close where she could see him. Wanted many more kisses. A thousand or so.

AFTER DINNER, Duncan knew he shouldn't be outside. But there was still a little bit of sun in the sky, and the stars weren't out. He wanted to set up the bases so he and Daddy could play real baseball.

He carried one of the flat, white rubber bases into the yard and dropped it. "Home plate," he said.

First base was ninety feet away. How many steps was that? He picked up another base from the duffel bag and turned toward the forest. He counted his steps all the way to fifty, then fifty again, then backward ten. This wasn't right. Too far.

Then he heard her voice, high and pretty, singing the seashell song.

"Temperance," he called out.

He dropped the base and ran toward the sound. He wanted to show her his new batting gloves and tell her about the trip to Raven's Cliff.

Where was she? He looked around the tree trunks but didn't see her white dress and long gold hair.

"Don't play hide-and-seek." He turned around in a circle, looking everywhere. "That's a baby game."

There were so many shadows in the forest. He heard the waves at the bottom of the cliff. He was never, ever supposed to go near the cliff alone. But he wasn't by himself. Temperance was here.

She stepped out from behind a tree trunk. "Hide-and-seek is not a baby game."

"I play baseball." He reached into his pocket and pulled out his new gloves. "This is what baseball players wear."

She turned up her nose. "Can girls play?"

"Mostly not. Madeline tries, but she's not as good as my daddy."

"I dislike baseball." Temperance stamped her foot. "How should I like a game I cannot play?"

"Don't be mad." He hid his gloves behind his back. "You're my friend, Temperance. I'll teach you how to play."

"Really?"

"I'm making a diamond." He remembered how she said she could never go into the Manor. "It's outdoors."

She wrinkled her brow. "There is danger in the Manor. In the basement."

Danger. The basement was dark and scary, but nobody had hurt him when he got trapped with Madeline. "I'm not afraid."

"Come with me." She laughed. "There is something I must show you."

He followed her through the trees to the very edge of the cliff. She was standing way too close. The wind blew her dress and her red cape. "Come back, Temperance."

She pointed along the ledge. "Do you see that man?"

He squinted through the gloom. The sun was gone. Night was coming. "I can't see him."

"Step out here by me."

This was wrong. His daddy would be very angry if he found out. Taking very careful baby steps, he left the shelter of the trees. The wind blew right in his face, but he didn't run away. He wasn't a scaredy-cat.

Take a look at what's on offer at
www.millsandboon.co.uk

☜

ⓇMILLS & BOON™
Pure reading pleasure

My Account / Offer of the Month / Our Authors / Book Club / Contact us

All of the latest books are there PLUS

Ⓜ Free Online reads

Ⓜ **Exclusive** offers and competitions

Ⓜ At least **15% discount** on our huge back list

Ⓜ Sign up to our **free** monthly eNewsletter

Ⓜ More info on your **favourite authors**

Ⓜ **Browse the Book** to try before you buy

Ⓜ **eBooks** available for most titles

Ⓜ Join the M&B community and **discuss your favourite books** with other readers

Far away along the cliffside, he saw the man. "Who is he?"

"The lighthouse keeper's grandson. Nicholas."

"Is he the bad man? The one who hurt Sofia?"

"Goodness, no." Her mouth made a pretty little bow. "He is very unhappy, as well he should be. He caused the fire in the lighthouse and brought the curse on Raven's Cliff."

Duncan didn't know much about curses. But starting a fire was bad. "I want to go back to the yard."

"Come play with me." She twirled on her tiptoes at the edge. "You are my best friend."

He had never been anybody's best friend. He wanted to please Temperance. He took one more step forward. The waves roared. The noise filled up his head and made him dizzy.

Temperance sang, "She sells seashells."

"By the seashore," he responded. "I want to go back."

"And so we shall." She darted into the forest.

Duncan turned to follow, but he couldn't move. His feet seemed to be stuck at the rocky edge of the cliff. He looked out at the waves and saw a boat coming. Danger. The boat could run into the rocks. Danger.

The wind pushed him closer to the edge.

Someone grabbed him. He couldn't see the person, but he felt skeleton fingers close tightly around his arm and shake him until his teeth rattled.

Black darkness rolled over him. Hate-filled darkness.

Chapter Ten

"Alma, have you seen Duncan?"

"Sorry, boss."

Blake left the kitchen and headed upstairs. He'd only left Duncan alone for a moment while he went into his studio to tidy up the details of the day's work. Now he couldn't find the boy. He checked the bedroom. The bathroom. Maybe he was with Madeline.

Blake paused outside her bedroom door. Only a few hours ago, a simple knock on this door had introduced him to a vision in red and the most incredible kisses. Her slender body had fitted so perfectly in his arms that she seemed to be made for him—created to fulfill his exact specifications. The subtle fragrance of her hair had enticed him. Her lips had been soft and sweet. He hadn't wanted to stop. His instincts told him to seize the moment, to make love to her—this amazing, feminine creature with the mesmerizing eyes, cascading black hair and long legs.

A thin leash of propriety had held him back. She was Duncan's teacher and doing a damn good job with his son. Blake would be a fool to jeopardize that relationship by taking Madeline to bed.

He tapped on the door.

She opened. Her glasses were perched on her nose. Her hair was twisted up on top of her head, and she wore loose-fitting jeans and a baggy T-shirt. In reverse metamorphosis, she'd gone from a butterfly to a plain caterpillar.

"What's wrong?" she asked.

"I can't find Duncan."

Twin frown lines furrowed her brow. "Do you think he went outside?"

"I sure as hell hope not. I've told him a hundred times that he's not to go outside after dark." Apparently, a hundred wasn't enough. "Damn it. Every time I start thinking that he's like other kids, he pulls something."

"Seems to me that a little boy wanting to play outside is the least strange thing in the world." She stepped into the hallway and closed the door behind her. "Let's go find him."

She made everything sound so simple. As they descended the staircase, he said, "You understand, don't you? Duncan isn't like other kids?"

"He's special." In the foyer, she turned to him. "When I was in town, buying my dress—"

"Your red dress." He couldn't help grinning as he thought of that silky fabric sliding over her body.

Behind her glasses, she gave him a wink. "I talked to the clerk about Dorothy. Do you remember Dorothy? She's the wife of Stuart, the man who owns the general store. When Stuart touched Duncan, he said Dorothy was sick."

Blake remembered. He'd seen the Dorothy tattoo on Stuart's beefy forearm. "And?"

"Dorothy is battling MS. Duncan sensed that from touching her husband."

He didn't like where this conversation was headed. "Let's not get started on the psychic crap."

"Duncan might be an empath. Someone who can sense the emotions of others with just a touch. Don't you see, Blake? That's good news."

He didn't see anything positive about having his son take on yet another abnormality. "Why good?"

"I'm not an expert," she said, "but empathy seems to be somewhat the opposite of autism. Instead of being trapped in his own little world, Duncan might be supersensitive to the moods and feelings of others."

"And that's good?"

"Difficult," she admitted. "Can you imagine what it must be like to know what other people are feeling?"

If anyone but Madeline had suggested this theory, he would have scoffed. But she'd been right before.

And his beloved Kathleen had been sensitive. Always talking about feelings, she seemed to know who he could trust and who he should avoid. Her first impressions were always on target. Autism was supposed to have a basis in genetics. What if the same were true for empathy? What if Duncan inherited that ability from his mother?

Blake's gaze dropped to the patterned tile floor in the foyer. Near the door were the duffel bags holding the baseball equipment. One was missing. Duncan must have taken it.

He was probably outside right now, setting up the baseball diamond. "Let's go find my son."

Outside, the dusk had settled into night. He strode across the unkempt grassy area until he saw the glow of moonlight on home plate. Duncan had been out here.

Madeline pointed to another base that was nearer the trees. His son was nowhere in sight.

"Duncan," he called out. "Duncan, where are you?"

Anxiously, he looked toward the lighthouse. The charred, jagged tower held a dark foreboding. For a young boy, danger was everywhere. Climbing around on that lighthouse presented formidable hazards. Not to mention the cliffs with their fierce winds and uncertain footing.

Even more than the natural perils, Blake feared the human danger. Until now, the Seaside Strangler had only attacked young women. But Duncan had known the name of Sofia Lagios. He might have witnessed something suspicious, might be a threat to this predator.

From the corner of his eye, Blake caught a flash of movement. Heart pounding, he raced toward the trees. "Duncan."

Madeline was close beside him. When he looked into her face, he saw a reflection of his own panic. They were near the cliffs. The wind howling through the branches sounded like a cry for help.

As he stepped closer to the edge, he looked down and saw the gloves on the ground. Duncan's batting gloves. Oh God, no. He knelt and picked up the limp little gloves.

How could this be happening? Blake couldn't lose Duncan. He couldn't. Not his son. Not his precious child.

Fear paralyzed him. His heart stopped.

He couldn't bring himself to look over the edge, couldn't bear the thought of seeing Duncan's small body crumpled on the rocks below, his blue eyes staring sightless into the dark.

"Back this way," Madeline said. She tugged on his arm. "Come on, Blake."

"What?"

"I heard something. A shout. Back toward the house."

Desperately hoping that she was right, he fought his way through the low-hanging branches until they were back at the yard.

He saw Duncan stumbling toward the house.

Frantic, Blake dashed toward him, gathered the child up in his arms and held on tightly. "Are you all right? Are you hurt?"

Duncan's small body trembled. Over and over, he mumbled, "Danger, danger, danger."

"It's okay," Blake assured him. Waves of relief rushed through him. His cheeks were wet with tears. "It's okay, Duncan. I've got you. You're safe."

He carried the boy back to the manor. Inside, in the light, he could examine his son for possible injuries. In the kitchen, he sat Duncan on the countertop.

Alma poked her head around the corner. "Heavens, what's going on?"

"Get the first-aid kit," Blake ordered. He stared into his son's pale face. There was a smear of mud on his cheek, but Blake didn't see blood, thank God. "Duncan, can you hear me?"

"Yes."

"Are you hurt?"

The boy grabbed his own arm below the shoulder. "He held on to me here. And he shook me. He hates everybody. They don't treat him right."

"Who did this to you?" Blake immediately thought of Dr. Fisher and how he was always lurking around the grounds. If that bastard had laid a hand on his son…

"What did he look like?"

Duncan's eyelids drooped. His shoulders sagged forward. "Danger. Don't go in the basement. Danger."

Alma placed the first-aid kit on the countertop beside Blake and stepped back. Madeline stood on the other side. Blake was only marginally aware of their presence. His entire focus was on his son. "Who shook you, Duncan?"

"I don't know." He leaned forward, almost toppling from the counter. "Bedtime."

"He's exhausted," Madeline said. "Maybe in the morning, he'll remember more."

Not likely. Duncan's attention span was short-lived. By tomorrow, he would have forgotten this entire incident. "Why were you near the cliff? I've told you again and again how dangerous that is. You're not ever to go—"

A sharp jab in his ribs stopped his tirade. Madeline glared at him. "Bedtime," she said.

Duncan had scared him half to death with this escapade, and the boy knew better. "He needs to hear this."

"He needs you."

Her steady gaze grounded him. Blake had every right to be angry, but more than that, he was thankful and relieved. Now wasn't the time for scolding. He kissed the boy on the top of his head. "I love you, Duncan. I'm so glad. So glad that you're safe."

"Nicholas," Duncan said. "I saw Nicholas."

"Is that who grabbed your arm?"

Duncan frowned. "Nicholas. The lighthouse keeper's grandson."

That wasn't the answer Blake wanted to hear. Nicholas Sterling the Third had died five years ago when the lighthouse was destroyed.

AFTER DUNCAN went to bed, Madeline joined Blake in the studio downstairs. They needed to discuss what had happened to his son. Someone had frightened Duncan. A predator. "In my opinion," she said, "we should report this Nicholas person to the police."

"I don't think so."

"Why not?"

"Nicholas Sterling is dead."

She sank into the chair opposite the desk. "But Duncan saw him. Was he a ghost?"

"Obviously not." Blake stood in front of his drafting table where several blueprints were taped. "The only way my son would know that name and the fact that Nicholas Sterling was the lighthouse keeper's grandson is if someone told him. That same person must have mentioned the name of Sofia Lagios."

She couldn't imagine anyone so depraved. Telling stories about curses and murder victims to an innocent child? "Who would do that? Why?"

Blake picked up a T-square and held it against the blueprint. "Could be Helen Fisher, who is obsessed with the history of Raven's Cliff. Could be her nutball brother."

"Teddy." She'd despised that nasty little man since she'd bumped his car. "Sometimes he wanders around on the grounds."

"It's his property."

"That certainly doesn't excuse him. Why would he grab Duncan and scare him?"

Blake stared intently at the blueprints. "Both times when Duncan got himself lost in the night, he was warned about danger in the basement. Whoever keeps frightening him doesn't want him to go down there."

When she and Duncan had disobeyed that warning, they'd been trapped. No matter how many times Blake gave her a logical explanation for what had happened, she knew better. Maybe someone had been trying to scare them. "You might be onto something."

He tapped his forefinger against the blueprints. "I've noticed anomalies in the structural measurements regarding the basement. We need to check it out."

Fear rippled around the edges of her consciousness. Go back into that overwhelming darkness? "Maybe we should call the police."

"And tell them what? My son saw a ghost who told him not to go into the basement?"

A little boy's nightmare vision wouldn't be taken seriously. "You're right."

"We should explore now. While Duncan's asleep." He lightly stroked her cheek. "If you want to stay here, it's okay. I'll understand."

Now was her chance to back down. She had nothing to prove, had never claimed to be courageous. But he needed her, and she liked the feeling of being able to help. "I want flashlights. Several flashlights."

The appreciative light from his hazel eyes warmed her heart. "Don't worry, Madeline. I won't let anyone—human or ghost—hurt you."

He crossed the studio to the closet near the door. From the top shelf, he took down a locked box which he placed on the desk while he flipped through a set of keys in the top drawer.

Unlocked, the box revealed an automatic handgun and a holster—lethal protection against any threat that might live in the basement. Knowing they would be armed should have made her feel safer. Instead, her blood ran cold.

Chapter Eleven

They left Alma in Duncan's room, keeping watch over him while he slept. Madeline had a cell phone to call the house-keeper in case of trouble. She stashed the cell in the left back pocket of her jeans. In the other back pocket was a small penlight. In her right hand was a heavy-duty metal flashlight—just in case the electricity malfunctioned again.

Together, she and Blake descended the wooden stair-case.

With the lights on, the musty concrete basement didn't appear too frightening, yet the word *danger* echoed inside her head. *Danger, danger, danger.* She looked for spiders on the dusty, broken shelving that leaned drunkenly against one wall. The creaks and groans of the old house made her think of ghosts walking across the floorboards above their head. Oh, she hoped not. There was enough to worry about without bringing in threats from the supernatural.

She followed Blake as he picked his way through the fat, heavy support beams and framed walls that divided the space into haphazard rooms.

Shaking off her sense of foreboding, she asked, "Why aren't there any windows down here?"

"This house was built in the late 1700s. A long time before finished basements." Blake adjusted the blueprints in his hand and turned to his left. "Originally, this was probably a pantry for preserves. Then a wine cellar. In later years, there was a coal chute for the furnace."

"Which means there must be another way out."

"There was." He pointed to the blueprint. "When the furnace and water heater were upgraded, the chute was plastered over."

Despite the lack of windows and doors, the musty air stirred as they walked through it. Motes of dust that hadn't been disturbed for years swirled near her feet. The cold seeped through her sweatshirt to her bones, and she shivered. "Doesn't seem safe to have only one way out."

"I'll need to add another exit if I do upgrades down here."

She followed Blake behind one of the walls. The current furnace and water heater were fairly modern, probably only ten or fifteen years old, housed in the cleanest part of the basement. Behind the next wall was a filthy pen of heavy wood.

"Coal bin," Blake said as he kept moving.

Stacked haphazardly in corners of the makeshift rooms were cardboard cartons, old furniture and discarded odds and ends. Paint cans. A rolled-up sheet of linoleum. Several sheets of paneling.

"Junk," Blake said. "Unfortunately, I can't trash this stuff until I sort through it. There could be something of value."

"Maybe that's why someone warned Duncan to stay away from the basement. A hidden treasure."

"Maybe."

He went around another wall, then pivoted and came back in the opposite direction. His intense concentration on the blueprints reminded her of Duncan's single-mindedness, but Blake wasn't the least bit boyish. Not with those muscular shoulders. Not with the holster fastened to his belt.

She tiptoed behind him. "Could there really be a treasure?"

"Beacon Manor is the real deal, full of valuable antiques. Anything could be stashed down here." At the far eastern end of the basement, he ran his hand along the concrete. "There could be a hidden room."

"Is that why you keep checking the blueprints?"

"There are several discrepancies in the measurements," he said. "Most notable is a difference of eighteen inches between the upstairs floor plan and the basement, which could be explained by poor draftsmanship."

"Or a secret room."

A rising excitement replaced her cold dread. They had embarked on a real-life treasure hunt. She imagined rare artworks, priceless antique silver, a pirate's chest full of gold doubloons.

He pulled a sheet of plywood away from the wall, revealing nothing but more concrete. A daunting pile of clutter stood between them and the last bit of wall. Moving all that junk would be filthy work.

"I have another idea," Blake said.

She followed him as he retraced his steps to the coal bin. Blake climbed over the heavy boards blackened by ancient soot. With some trepidation, she followed. "Now what?"

"When you said the coal bin provided another way out, it got me thinking. All the outer walls are concrete, except for here. This could be a door. A crude door that was built over two hundred years ago."

"I don't see it."

"Look hard." He felt along the rough-hewn boards at the rear wall. His hands were immediately covered with thick black grime. "Do you feel that, Madeline? A breeze."

She heard the anticipation in his voice, but she didn't feel the breeze, didn't see the door. "I don't—"

"Got it." His fingers closed around a ridge in the wood. "A hinge."

In a moment, he'd found the latch and opened the secret door. A whisper of chill air swept over her. Beyond the entrance was nothing but darkness.

She turned on her flashlight and shone the beam into the open space—an earthen tunnel that led straight down. "A secret passageway."

Beaming as though he'd unearthed the treasures of King Tut's tomb, he turned to her. "This is a first for me. I've worked on some really old properties. Ancient. Mysterious. A villa in Milan. A small castle in Tuscany. And I've never discovered a secret passageway before."

She didn't share his enthusiasm. A passageway leading out meant that other people could secretly enter the house, which might explain how some nefarious person could have been sneaking into her room. That person could be lurking down there right now, hidden in the darkness. "Where do you think it goes?"

"There's only one way to know for sure. Bring the flashlight closer."

Instead, she drew back. Her feet rooted to the filthy floor of the coal bin. "What if someone's down there?"

"Then we've found what we're looking for." He drew

his automatic pistol from the holster. "I can carry this if it makes you feel better."

It didn't. The idea of a shoot-out in a dark cave terrified her. "I don't think we should do this. We should come back tomorrow with plenty of lights. And a police escort."

"How many times in your life will you discover a secret passageway? Come on, Madeline. Take a chance."

She'd never been a risk-taker. Those few times in her life when she'd acted against her cautious instincts—like when she'd trusted her brother—had resulted in disaster. But Blake's eyes enticed her. His eagerness to explore would not be denied. "You go first."

"I'll need the flashlight."

Reluctantly, she handed it over while keeping the smaller one for herself. "I'll be right behind you."

He stepped into the darkness. Slowly, he walked through the tunnel that appeared to be carved from the stone. The earth floor slanted down at a steep angle; they descended through bedrock.

The beams of their flashlights barely cut into the thick darkness—so heavy that she felt as though she was suffocating. The sound of her own breathing echoed in her ears. She shivered as an icy draft brushed her cheeks. God, it was cold.

The only way she could keep going forward was to concentrate on Blake's back. She followed him as closely as a shadow.

"The floor seems to be leveling out," he said. "There's a curve ahead. An intersection with another tunnel."

What if this tunnel turned into another? And another. What if they'd entered a labyrinth? She wished Duncan were here to count their steps. They could be lost forever.

When Blake halted, she bumped into him. "What is it?"

"A cave."

Peeking around his shoulder, she watched the beam of his flashlight as it played across a high, craggy ceiling. Massive boulders clumped on the floor like the crude furniture of a giant. His flashlight beam reflected on a small, opaque puddle of water, reminding her that they were near the shore. "Do you think this cave reaches all the way to the beach?"

"Oh, yeah. The tunnel we came through was man-made. This is natural." He pointed his flashlight to the right. "This way. Watch your step. There are lots of loose rocks."

She stumbled along behind him, trying to guess the distance from the manor to the shore. Half a mile? It felt like more, seemed like they were walking forever. Climbing over piles of rock, slipping through odd-shaped spaces as the cave widened and narrowed.

"I can hear the ocean," Blake said.

She heard it, too. The crashing of waves outside the cave. The darkness thinned. The air freshened. Excited that they were almost out, she dodged around him. Then slipped. Then fell.

She landed hard on her backside.

Blake was immediately attentive. He took her hand and pulled her to her feet. "Are you okay?"

"More embarrassed than hurt." She reached into her back pocket and took out the smashed cell phone. "Which is more than I can say for the phone."

He played his flashlight over her hands, then lifted the beam to her face. "We're almost out."

And she was proud of herself for taking the risk. "This isn't like anything I've ever done before. I'm glad I'm here."

"So am I."

He pushed stray wisps of hair off her forehead and gently kissed her lips—a reminder of their passion when she was wearing the red dress.

As they moved forward again, his flashlight shone on a plain, rectangular structure about the size of a trailer. Was someone living down here?

They approached the door, found it unlocked and entered. A switch turned on overhead lights, illuminating an open space with tables lining the walls, two large refrigerators and a desk. The generator that powered the lights must have also activated a fan because she heard the hum of a ventilation system. Stacked near the door were several wooden crates and packing materials. Resting on the tables were microscopes and laboratory equipment.

She examined a large centrifuge and read the label on the side, "Fisher Laboratories."

"Son of a bitch." Blake rummaged through the desk. "Teddy Fisher moved his lab down here."

"No wonder he's always creeping around the Manor."

"Technically, this property belongs to him. The private beach is part of the estate."

"But why? Why would anybody put a laboratory here?" She wished that they had stumbled across a chest of pirate's gold. Nothing good would result from this discovery. "This is all wrong."

INSIDE THE makeshift lab, Blake slammed a desk drawer. He was tempted to rake his arm across the surface of the lab tables, sending beakers and instruments flying. What the hell was Teddy trying to pull? His motive had to be criminal. "The only reason to put a lab here is to keep it secret."

"You said something about Teddy's experiments and an epidemic."

"He was looking for a nutrient to make fish bigger and more prolific."

"Not a bad idea," she said. "Bigger fish. More fish. That sounds like an economic boon for the town."

"Teddy's plan was a hell of a lot bigger than Raven's Cliff." The first time Blake had met the little scientist, Teddy had been bubbling with excitement, patting himself on the back so vigorously that he could have dislocated a shoulder. "The fish experiment was supposed to be his claim to fame. A cure for world hunger."

"But it backfired."

"In a big way." He tried to remember details of the stories he'd heard secondhand. "The fish weren't hurt. But people who ate them fell ill. Some died."

"That's murder," she said. "Why is Teddy walking around free? Why isn't he in jail?"

He'd wondered the same thing. "I looked into the situation. I had to."

"Of course you did. You wouldn't want to be hired by a murderer."

Actually, Blake's ethical concerns were secondary. Most of the wealthy, powerful people he'd worked for weren't Boy Scouts. If he started turning down projects because his clients weren't entirely innocent, he'd soon be left with nothing better to do than charity work for churches.

His main reason for wanting to know about the charges against Teddy was monetary; he didn't want to move to Raven's Cliff if the guy paying the bills was going to prison. "Teddy wasn't charged."

"Why not?"

"The curse."

The corner of her delectable mouth pulled into a frown, and he could tell that she didn't like what she was hearing. Primly, she said, "Please continue."

"A lot of the townspeople and the fishermen themselves blamed the epidemic on the curse. The gods of the sea are angry, and the spirit of Captain Raven is offended." A load of superstitious crap. "The only way to lift the curse is to rebuild the lighthouse and shine the beacon."

"Which made them anxious to have you get started."

He'd been welcomed with open arms. "I was assured that Teddy was in the clear. He voluntarily closed down his laboratory operation."

"Apparently not." She took the damaged cell phone from her pocket and punched the keys. "It's definitely broken."

"What are you doing?"

"We need to inform the proper authorities about Teddy's secret lab. He was clearly up to no good."

If he had ever felt the need for a moral compass, he need look no further. Madeline had the earnest eyes and determined chin of a crusader—a defender of underdogs, losers and endangered species. He usually found those traits to be tedious and incompatible with his creativity. Rules were made to be broken.

After Kathleen died, he'd preferred women who were free and easy, who left before breakfast, who wanted nothing but a one-night stand. Madeline was the opposite; she'd always expect him to do the right thing. "I'll bet you never break the rules."

"I try not to," she said.

"You use the turn signal even when there aren't other cars behind you."

"Yes," she said.

"If a clerk gives you change for a twenty when you gave them a ten, you return the extra."

"And I tip twenty percent, even if the waitress is surly. I don't cheat on my taxes. Don't jaywalk. I follow the recipes exactly when I cook."

"No risks. No adventures."

"I like order." She took a step toward him. Her voice softened to a whisper that made those solid values resonate with a purely sensual undertone. "I'm not a risk-taker. Sorry if that disappoints you."

His arm slipped around her slender waist and pulled her snug against him. "Who says I'm disappointed?"

"Most men are."

He nuzzled her ear and felt her body respond with a quiver. At this moment, he wanted to give her all the stability her heart desired. "I'm not most men."

She kissed him with a passion that seemed at odds with her need for order. Messy and wild. He didn't try to make sense of it. Just leaned into the kiss and enjoyed.

Breaking away from him, she said, "We should get back to the Manor."

To his bed. Making love to her was becoming more and more inevitable. Damn, he was ready.

As they stepped out of Teddy's secret lab, they were blinded by the darkness of the cave. Taking charge, Blake aimed the beam of his flashlight toward the secret passage, then in the opposite direction. "Let's keep heading toward the shore."

"Agreed. I don't want to go back through that passage unless I have to."

He led the way, circling an outcropping of stone that

kept the location of the lab hidden. Through another chamber, then into the final cave where the stone walls were damp with salt spray and the bright moonlight beckoned them toward the roaring surf.

"Wait," she said. Her flashlight pointed at the rocks near the edge of the cave, and she picked up a necklace made of shells. "Duncan has a shell like this."

Before he could respond, he heard a moan. A weak cry for help. Just outside the cave, something was moving. Blake handed his flashlight to Madeline and drew his handgun. "Stay back."

On the rocks outside the cave, Blake saw him. Teddy Fisher. Or what was left of him.

Struggling for every inch, Teddy crawled—dragging himself across the rocks. One of his legs was bent at an unnatural angle. His head was bloody. His eyes swollen shut. His dapper gray suit was torn and smeared with blood.

He'd been beaten by someone who knew how to make it hurt.

Chapter Twelve

Instinct drove Madeline forward. No matter how much she disliked Teddy Fisher, the man was seriously injured and needed help.

Blake caught hold of her arm. "No closer," he warned. "He might be armed."

She shone her flashlight back toward the cave. The person who had beaten Teddy might still be nearby. Might have been following them. Might be biding his time before he lashed out at them. What if there was more than one attacker? What if they were facing an army?

Blake handed her the gun. The heft of it surprised her. She'd never held a firearm before, hated when the kids in her classes pretended to shoot each other. Guns weren't toys.

Blake knelt on the rocks beside the injured man, rolled him onto his back and frisked his clothing.

Teddy's face was grotesque. Inside the neat circle of his goatee, his lips were bruised and bloody. Dark crimson blood streaked across his forehead. Each breath he drew caused him to wince.

He was trying to speak.

"What is it?" Blake asked. "Teddy, who did this?"

The swollen lips moved, but the only sound he made was a guttural moan. He convulsed. His body went limp.

Blake tore open Teddy's shirt.

"What are you doing?" she asked.

"Looking for other wounds. Shine the flashlight down here." He pushed aside the blood-stained white shirt. Using his fingers, he gently probed the harsh, red welts that criss-crossed Teddy's rib cage. "The blood seems to be coming from his head and other abrasions. He wasn't stabbed or shot."

But beaten to within an inch of his life. She turned away, couldn't stand to look. What kind of person could possibly inflict so much damage on another? To what purpose?

Blake stood. "There's got to be internal bleeding. He needs a doctor. Madeline, do you know CPR?"

In a couple of teacher-training sessions, she'd taken lessons. But she had never practiced life-saving techniques on another human being. "Not well enough."

"One of us needs to stay with Teddy. The other has to go to the house and call an ambulance."

Both alternatives sounded equally terrible. Facing un-known dangers on the way to the house? Staying here with the crashing waves and dark cave, watching over a dying man? She didn't know how she could manage to do either. Never in her life had she been heroic.

Blake stood and peeled off his jacket. "We need to move fast. He's fighting for his life."

"You're right." She swallowed hard. "Of course, you're right."

"Stay or go?"

Though she might encounter danger on the way to the

house, she'd be better at running than staying here to help Teddy. If he died under her watch, she couldn't live with that guilt. "I'll go."

"Take the gun," Blake said. "If anyone comes near you, shoot. Don't worry about aiming. The noise should keep them back."

"Okay."

"If I hear a gunshot, I'll come running." He squeezed her shoulder. "You can do this."

Though she didn't share his confidence, she turned on her heel and ran. In one hand, she clutched the flashlight. The other held the gun. Neither comforted her.

Scrambling across the uneven rocks on the shore, she moved faster than she would have thought possible. In minutes, she had reached the staircase. Moonlight shimmered on each stair, but she only saw shadows—formless shapes, threatening outlines.

Her heart pounded against her rib cage. In spite of the night breeze, sweat beaded across her forehead. As she climbed, the muscles in her legs throbbed, more from tension than exertion. Common sense held her back, warned her to be careful. But she had to get to the house, to summon the police. They needed the help of the authorities, and Teddy desperately needed a doctor.

At the top of the staircase, she drew huge gulps of air into her aching lungs. The beam of her flashlight slashed across the tree trunks of the forest that separated her from the Manor. Fierce gusts of wind chased over the edge of the cliff.

Before her fears took solid form, she plunged into the trees and fought her way through, shoving tree branches out of her way, stumbling, falling and rising again. She emerged on the other side. Across the yard, she could see the house. Only one light shone from the windows. The light from her own bedroom.

That could not be. She'd left the light off.

Though she couldn't see clearly from this distance, a shadow passed behind her bedroom curtains. Was it him? The person who attacked Teddy Fisher? He could be in her bedroom. Only a few steps away from Duncan.

The fear she felt for herself was nothing compared to her need to protect the child. She ran full out with her legs churning and arms pumping. She would not, could not, allow anyone to hurt Duncan.

At the front door, she stabbed her key into the lock. Barely pausing, she charged up the staircase and down the hall. Into Duncan's room. In the faint glow of a night-light, she saw him sleeping. His lips parted as he breathed steadily, peacefully. A sweet, innocent boy. Protected by his mother, an angel.

Madeline turned back toward the corridor. She leveled the gun. If anyone came near Duncan, she'd have no trouble pulling the trigger.

The hall light went on, and she blinked. Standing near the bathroom was Alma. In her hand, she held a gun. "What's going on?" she demanded.

"Why do you have a gun?"

"Why do you?"

Her chin thrust out. Though Alma's face without her usual makeup showed her age, Madeline caught a hint of a younger woman. A woman she'd known many years ago. Her foster mother. Always yelling, thriving on conflict. Alma hadn't been mean, but angry. So very angry.

She shook away the memory; Madeline wasn't a help-less child. "What were you doing in my room?"

"I heard a noise." Alma looked down at the gun and seemed almost surprised that she was holding it. Immediately, she lowered the muzzle. "Sorry, honey. I was a little scared."

As well she should be. The vicious attack on Teddy Fisher gave validity to all of Madeline's vague fears. It was time to call the police.

As SOON AS the ambulance and paramedics arrived, Blake raced back to the house where he was greeted by Alma. Though a fresh coat of makeup smeared across her face, she couldn't disguise the tension at the corners of her eyes.

"Is he dead?" she asked.

"Hanging on by a thread." Teddy had never regained consciousness. Every ragged breath he inhaled seemed like his last. The external injuries were horrific, but Blake suspected worse damage had been done to his insides. Ruptured organs. Internal bleeding. "Where's Duncan? Where's Madeline?"

"Family room," Alma said. "Should I make coffee?"

"I'd say so. In a couple of minutes, we'll have a house full of cops."

He ran upstairs to wash the blood from his hands and change into a clean shirt. No need to scare Duncan by looking as though he'd been through a war. The circumstances would be traumatic enough for his overly sensitive son.

The police would have questions for the boy, namely who had grabbed him earlier tonight? If Duncan started talking about the ghost of Nicholas Sterling, things could get complicated.

In the family room, he found Madeline reading a book of rhymes to Duncan, who was still wearing his flannel pajamas. Her voice was low and soothing. Though her hair was a mass of tangles, she managed to appear calm.

Not the way she'd been when they'd found Teddy outside the cave. Then she'd been terror-stricken. Her delicate face had turned as white as ivory. Every muscle in her body had trembled, and she'd looked as if she was on the verge of fainting. It had taken a lot of courage for her to make it back to the house and call 911.

Duncan looked up, saw Blake and vaulted off the sofa. He ran to his father, who hoisted him into his arms and held him close.

"It's going to be okay, buddy." Blake stroked his son's fine blond hair. "Everything is going to be okay."

"What happened, Daddy? Madeline said you'd tell me."

"A man was badly hurt." The fewer details, the better. "Pretty soon, the police are going to come here and ask us some questions."

Duncan pulled back so he could look into his father's face. "Real policemen?"

"That's right."

The boy considered for a moment, digesting this information. Then he shrugged. "Okay."

"When we talk to the real policemen, we have to tell the truth. Isn't that right, Madeline?"

"You bet." The color had returned to her cheeks. The smudges of soot on her chin and forehead would have been cute if the expression in her aquamarine eyes hadn't been so solemn and serious.

His own feelings were more akin to euphoria. They'd been in a dire situation and had escaped intact. He'd been lucky as hell that whoever attacked Teddy hadn't stayed around to finish the job.

Apparently, Madeline took the wider view. A man had been brutally beaten. There was a dangerous person on the loose. Primly, she said, "Before the police arrive, I should change clothes."

Still holding his son, he held out his other arm toward her, pulled her close and gave her a hug. "You did good," he said.

"The night isn't over yet."

As she left the family room, he carried Duncan into the kitchen where he smelled the aroma of fresh brewed coffee. Alma had also laid out mugs, plates and napkins. She slid a tray of frozen baked goods into the oven.

Blake made a mental note. If he wanted Alma to perform in the kitchen, all he needed to do was to promise a houseful of handsome young cops.

The short end of the rectangular kitchen table fitted up against the wall, and Blake seated Duncan in the chair nearest the wall where he'd be protected from accidental touches from the police. After providing his son with bottled water to drink and a coloring book to keep him occupied, he left Alma watching Duncan as he went to answer the doorbell.

Two uniformed cops arrived first. The taller officer had red hair like the proprietor of the general store, and the metal name tag pinned above his front pocket said Chapman.

Blake shook hands. "Is Stuart Chapman your father?"

"That's right. All four of us Chapman boys are on the force." His proud grin and the sprinkle of freckles across his nose made him look more like a choirboy than an officer of the law. His eyes widened as he scanned the entryway. "I haven't been inside Beacon Manor since I was a kid singing Christmas carols."

"Most of the rooms are under construction. You'll need to watch your step."

"I'll do that, sir." He cleared his throat and tried to look official. "Can you tell me how many people are currently living at the house?"

"Myself, the housekeeper, my six-year-old son and his teacher." Blake glanced down the hallway toward the kitchen and lowered his voice so Duncan couldn't possibly overhear. "We never saw the person who attacked Dr. Fisher. In case he's still hanging around, I'd appreciate it if your officers could search the house and the grounds."

"He was found at the bottom of the cliff. What makes you think his attacker might be in the house?"

"In the basement, there's a passage that leads down to the caves by the shore."

"A secret passageway?" Chapman nudged his partner. "We gotta check that out."

Another squad car pulled up with lights flashing. Then two more unmarked vehicles. Though Blake hadn't expected such a large response, he was glad to see the cops converging on his front door. He'd meant what he said about a thorough search.

The man in charge wore a dark suit, white shirt and dark necktie. His hair was jet-black and curly. His ebony eyes held the haunted sadness of someone who had experienced recent tragedy. After he conferred briefly with Chapman, he introduced the plainclothes cop who was with him. "This is Detective Joe Curtis. I understand you have some concerns about an intruder."

"Yeah, I'm concerned." Blake shook hands with Curtis, a thick-necked man with a short-cropped, military haircut and shoulders like a bull. "I'm worried that whoever attacked Dr. Fisher is still here."

"Detective Curtis will be in charge of organizing a sweep of the house and the grounds." He held out his hand. "I'm Detective Andrei Lagios. Homicide."

Blake winced. "Is Dr. Fisher dead?"

"DOA at the nearest hospital."

"I'm sorry to hear that."

"Were you a close friend?"

Blake shook his head. "Hardly knew the man."

Teddy Fisher was, however, the person paying the bills for this restoration. Though Blake drew his necessary funds from an escrow account, Teddy's death would have an impact on what happened to the Manor and the lighthouse. Those were worries for tomorrow. For right now, Blake had something else on his mind. He pulled Lagios aside. "Before you start taking statements, I need you to be aware of one thing. My son, Duncan, is autistic. I'm never sure how he'll react to strangers."

"I'll keep that in mind." His gaze sharpened. "Is there a reason I should talk to the boy?"

Blake considered lying to protect his son, but he was fairly sure that Lagios would see through any deception. Unlike the boyish Chapman, the homicide detective was intense. Tough. Professional. Though Andrei Lagios worked on a small-town police force, he sure as hell wasn't a hick.

"Earlier tonight," Blake said, "Duncan was outside playing. He was upset. Said a man grabbed his arm."

"The man who attacked Dr. Fisher?"

"Could be." That was truth. "Duncan said he didn't get a good look at the guy. Sometimes, he imagines things."

The detective gave a quick nod. "I'll try not to upset the boy. Why don't I talk to him first so he can go to bed?"

As if Duncan would fall asleep with all this commotion in the house. Blake led the way to the kitchen where he sat beside Duncan at the table, shielding him. His son concentrated intently on the coloring book, staying precisely within the lines.

When Lagios sat opposite them, Blake said, "Duncan, this is Detective Lagios."

Without looking up, Duncan said, "We tell the truth to the policemen."

Blake prompted, "Earlier today, you went outside to measure the yard for a baseball diamond. Then something happened. Tell us about it."

"Temperance was in the forest. She's my very, very best friend. She went close to the cliff. I'm not supposed to go there. Inappropriate behavior." He fell silent. The crayon in his hand poised above the page.

Blake guessed that Duncan had also gone to the edge of the cliff when he knew damn well he shouldn't. "It's okay, buddy. I'm not angry."

"I understand," Lagios said in a voice so gentle that it was almost musical. "Temperance went near the cliff. Then what?"

Duncan threw down the crayon. His fingers balled into tight little fists. "He grabbed me. And shook me. A bad man. He's very bad."

"What did he look like?"

"I don't know."

"It's okay," Lagios soothed. "Does he have a name?"

Duncan shouted. "Don't know."

Blake recognized the signs of an oncoming tantrum and

was glad when Madeline joined them. Her presence seemed to brighten the room and defuse the rising tension. She was so blessedly normal and grounded.

She introduced a clean-cut guy wearing a polo shirt and a sweater knotted around his neck, preppy-style. He looked familiar. "This is Grant Bridges, Assistant District Attorney. He's in charge of the T-ball program for the kids in town."

Bridges offered an affable grin as he shook hands with Blake. "I believe we've met. When you were staying at the Cliffside Inn."

"Of course." Blake recalled that Grant Bridges lived at the Inn. "Are you here in an official capacity?"

"I like to get in early on the investigation. This is going to be a high-profile homicide."

Blake recognized ambition when he saw it. Bridges was hoping to be assigned as prosecutor on this crime. "The detective had a few questions for my son."

"Madeline tells me that Duncan is interested in playing T-ball." He leaned toward the boy. "Is that right?"

Through pinched lips, Duncan said, "Yes."

"We'd be happy to have you on the team."

"I have gloves," Duncan said, too loudly.

"That's terrific." He glanced at Blake. "I'll make sure Madeline has our schedule."

When he looked back at her, his smile was warm and appreciative…too appreciative. His eyes twinkled.

Blake was pretty sure he didn't like Grant Bridges, and he had the sense that Lagios felt the same antipathy. Though the detective had acknowledged Bridges's presence, he retreated into stoic silence, waiting for the assistant DA to move aside so his investigation could proceed.

It was Madeline who provided the next distraction. To Duncan, she said, "Hey, I have a surprise for you."

He looked up at her. "Why?"

"Because I like you." She pulled her hand out of her pocket. Dangling from her fingertips was the shell necklace she'd found. "I thought you'd like this."

Lagios reacted. He stood so quickly that his chair crashed backward onto the floor. "Where did you find that?"

"In the caves." Her gaze stayed on Duncan. "You have that other shell that's exactly like these."

"From Temperance." Instead of reaching for the necklace, he plunged his hands into his lap. "Don't want to touch it."

"May I?" Lagios took the necklace from Madeline, handling it carefully by the string as if he didn't want to leave fingerprints.

"What is it?" Blake asked.

Instead of answering, Lagios spoke to Duncan. "Do you have another shell like these?"

The boy nodded.

"I'd like to see it."

"Fine," Madeline said. "Duncan, we'll go to your bedroom and find the shell."

Duncan climbed down from his chair. He walked close to Madeline without touching her. Under his breath, he counted every step as they left the kitchen.

As soon as they were gone, Blake confronted Lagios. "What is it? What's the deal with that necklace?"

"I've seen another exactly like this." His dark eyes turned as hard as anthracite. "The Seaside Strangler uses these necklaces to kill his victims."

Chapter Thirteen

Duncan went to find his seashell for the policeman with the sad, dark eyes. Madeline came with him, and he stayed close to her. Up the stairs to his bedroom. "One, two, three…"

These policemen were very loud. Some of them were mean. "…seven, eight…"

He put his hands over his ears so he couldn't hear the noise. He stared at the floor so he couldn't see, but the inside of his tummy hurt. There was something bad in the house. Something that could hurt him.

Inside his bedroom, Madeline closed the door. "They're making a lot of noise. Even more than the workmen on the roof. Does it bother you?"

"Some."

"They're searching the whole house to make sure we're safe. They're on this floor right now. With those heavy boots, it sounds like there are fifty of them."

"Not fifty." Fifty was half a hundred. Really a lot.

"Maybe five," she said.

In here with Madeline, he felt safe. Duncan ran across the floor and jumped into the center of his bed. The covers were soft and puffy. He wanted everybody to go away.

Madeline sat in the rocking chair beside his bed. "It's lucky that Mr. Bridges came here. He could be your baseball coach."

"I'm going to be a baseball player. Like Wade Boggs."

"Exactly like Wade Boggs." She rocked back and forth. He counted six times before she talked again. "Detective Lagios really wants to see your shell."

"He misses Sofia." Pretty Sofia in her long white dress. "He's unhappy."

"He might want to take the shell with him."

Inside his head, Duncan heard Temperance's voice. *She sells seashells…* "Danger."

"Where is the danger?"

"Basement." Like Temperance always said.

"Anywhere else?"

"Don't know." But he could feel it. All creepy and dark, it was coming closer. "I want my daddy."

"We can go back downstairs."

"No." His voice wasn't too loud. "I want him here."

Madeline frowned, but he knew she wasn't mad at him. She made that face when she was thinking. "I can get him, but I'd have to leave you here by yourself."

"Yes. I want him here. Here, here, here."

"Okay, I'll take the shell."

"No." He was louder. "I want Daddy."

"Stay right here. I'll be back in a flash."

When she left the room, he dove under the covers and curled up in a ball. Outside his room, he heard lots of feet walking. Policeman feet.

He couldn't hide under a blanket. That was dumb. And he didn't want to be a scaredy-cat. He was a baseball player. And he was brave.

He ran to his bedroom door and pulled it open. He charged into the hallway and ran smack into a big man in a suit.

"Hey, kid. Watch where you're going."

"You watch."

"Careful there. You're going to fall down."

Duncan turned away. He slipped.

The big man grabbed his hand. His skin was rough like a tree trunk. His breath was cold. Ice-cold.

"No." Duncan gasped. He couldn't breathe.

The big face came closer and closer. He had sharp, pointy teeth, and they were dripping with blood. Instead of arms, he had big heavy hammers.

They were in a dark, wet place. The hammer came down hard. "Don't hit me," he yelled.

He felt as if his bones were cracking.

Another thud from the hammer. He pulled his arms up over his head. "No, no, no. Help. Danger."

"What the hell is wrong with you, kid?"

He was a bully. A bad man.

Duncan fell to his knees. Thud, thud, thud. His eyes squeezed shut.

BLAKE HEARD his son's frantic cries and raced up the stairs to find Duncan curled up on the floor with Detective Curtis kneeling beside him. His beefy hand rested at Duncan's throat, feeling for a pulse.

He was touching Duncan. Damn it! Blake should have been more specific when he informed Lagios about his son's autism, should have warned him about touching.

He shoved Curtis's shoulder. "Get back."

The big cop looked up and shook his head in confusion.

"I don't know what happened. The kid came busting out of his room and ran right into me. I tried to steady him so he wouldn't fall down."

"Get away from him," Blake snapped.

He scooped Duncan off the floor and carried his limp body into his bedroom. Sitting on the bed, he held his son close. Duncan coughed. A sob convulsed his skinny chest and he clung tightly to his father.

"The bad man." Duncan choked out the words. "Hammer arms. And blood."

Blake looked past Duncan's shoulder to the doorway where Joe Curtis stood, watching and waiting. Though obviously nervous about what had happened, there was something menacing about the man. The way his fingers flexed then tightened into fists. The set of his heavy shoulders.

When Madeline touched Curtis's arm, he pivoted so quickly to face her that she took a step backward. He wasn't much taller than she, but his bulk loomed over her as she said, "It's best if you leave."

"What's wrong with the kid?" he asked.

Madeline stiffened her shoulders. As Blake well knew, she hated any suggestion that there was something wrong with his son. "Forget it, Detective. You wouldn't understand."

"I didn't do anything." He looked out toward the hall where a couple of other uniformed cops had gathered. "I swear. I didn't do a damn thing. The kid was just—"

"Frightened." Madeline's voice took on an authoritative teacherly tone as she defended his son. "Quite frankly, I can't blame Duncan. Not a bit. You're a big, rough man, Detective Curtis. In the eyes of a little boy, you must look as terrifying as a T-Rex."

There were guffaws from the cops in the hall.

Madeline silenced them with a glare. "Step back, gentlemen. We'll handle this."

When she again touched Curtis's arm to push him out of the way, he balked. In that physical contact, Blake saw a battle of wills. A stare-down. Behind her glasses, Madeline's eyes flared with determination.

Curtis met her gaze with an instant of unguarded hostility. Then he shrugged and stepped aside as Madeline closed the door to Duncan's bedroom and came toward them.

If Blake hadn't already been attracted to her, this moment would have convinced him that she was the right woman for him. She'd defended his son fiercely.

HOURS LATER, Madeline kicked off her slippers and dove under the bedcovers. The coolness of the sheets did little to quench her rising anxiety. Her mind raced. She remembered the impenetrable dark of the cave, the mangled body of Dr. Fisher, the clawing branches of trees as she ran through the forest toward the house. Most of all, she thought of Duncan.

The boy had been terrified after his encounter with Detective Curtis, and she knew in her heart that Duncan had sensed something. What was it? What did he see?

After Duncan had calmed down, Blake had stayed with him in his room, leaving her and Alma to deal with the herd of cops who centered their search on the passageway which definitely wasn't a secret anymore.

The police were reassuring, especially Detective Lagios. He seemed certain that the murder of Teddy Fisher was unrelated to the Manor. Teddy had a lot of enemies—one of whom he had driven over the edge.

Supposedly, they were safe. Madeline wasn't sure that she believed that logic. Any person capable of murder was dangerous. They might strike again.

She took off her glasses and reached to turn off her bedside lamp, then hesitated. Sleep wouldn't come easily tonight, not while her nerves vibrated with tension. Even though the Manor was locked up tightly, including the door from the basement leading into the house, and she had shoved her potted ficus against her bedroom door, she was still afraid.

She glanced at the novel on her bedside table—a thriller with a tough heroine who pulverized evil-doers with karate kicks. Nothing could be further from Madeline's reality. In her own way, she was tough. Growing up in foster care meant learning survival skills. But she'd never been a fighter.

There was a tap on the door. Blake whispered, "Madeline, are you awake?"

"Just a minute."

She leaped from the bed, dragged the ficus away from the door and opened it.

Exhaustion deepened the lines at the corners of his lips, but his hazel eyes burned with intensity. His gaze skimmed the outline of her body under her blue cotton nightgown. "I wanted to make sure you were all right," he said.

"I'm fine," she lied. "How's Duncan?"

"He seems okay. I'll never understand what goes on in that little head of his." He exhaled a weary sigh. "I've been watching him sleep for the past half hour."

Feeling exposed, she folded her arms across her breasts. For a moment, she considered grabbing her robe from the closet and covering up. Then she remembered his kiss, and she purposely lowered her arms to her sides. *Let him look. Let him come closer.* A night in his strong arms would be the perfect antidote to her fears.

She cleared her throat and asked, "Did Duncan tell you what he saw when he touched Detective Curtis?"

"A big, bad man with bloody teeth and hammer fists. Then, being Duncan, he started counting in Spanish and showed me how the hands on a clock move." He stepped inside her room, closed the door and glanced at the ficus. "Odd place to put a plant."

Not wanting to tell him that she'd been using her ficus to barricade the door, she ignored his observation. "I know you don't believe in psychic abilities, but we really must consider the possibility that Duncan sensed danger from Detective Curtis."

"Must we?" He raised an eyebrow. "Why?"

"Because Teddy Fisher was beaten to death."

"You think Curtis killed him?" He considered for a moment, then shook his head. "He's a cop, Madeline. His job involves danger. I'm not surprised that he gives off that vibe."

"Nobody knows Curtis well. Detective Lagios said he recently transferred here from Los Angeles."

"The LAPD? That's a tough place to work. A violent place. That's got to be what Duncan sensed."

She wasn't willing to dismiss Duncan's premonition so quickly. The boy had been right when Stuart Chapman had touched him and he had sensed that Stuart's wife was gravely ill. "What if Duncan is right? What if Curtis is dangerous?"

A smile curved his lips. "I get it, Madeline. You believe in Duncan."

"Of course I do."

"I appreciated the way you defended him when Curtis said there was something wrong with the kid." He reached toward her. With the back of his hand, he stroked the line of her chin. "But facts are facts. Duncan is autistic. He sometimes says things that don't make sense. He isn't like other kids."

In her mind, that was a positive attribute. Duncan was smarter than most. And more sensitive. "Being normal is highly overrated."

He came closer to her. "Are you speaking from experience?"

His voice had dropped to a low, intimate level. Even without her glasses, she could clearly see his intentions and she welcomed them. "I know what it's like to be an outsider."

"So do I."

She didn't believe for a moment that this tall, gorgeous, confident man had ever been the butt of jokes. Yet, he was diffident and cool. "Were you a bit of a lone wolf?"

"Even as a kid, I spent a lot of time by myself, imagining castles in the air."

She leaned toward him. The tips of her breasts were inches from his chest. "As an architect, you've been able to turn your daydreams into reality."

His arm slipped around her waist and pulled her close. "I usually get what I want."

Apparently, he wanted her. And she was glad, truly glad, because she wanted him, too. Willingly, she allowed herself to be overwhelmed by the force of his embrace and the wonderful pressure of his lips against hers. Joyfully, she savored the taste of him.

Behind her closed eyelids, starbursts exploded. Sensation flooded her body, rushing through her veins as his hand closed over her breast. His hard body pressed against hers. His thigh parted her legs.

An excited gasp escaped her lips. In her admittedly limited experience of lovemaking there had usually been a great deal of fumbling around. Not with Blake. He knew what he wanted. Even better, he knew what *she* wanted. Every murmur, every kiss, every caress aroused her more.

He was a fierce lover. Strong and demanding. How could she ever resist him? Why would she? Swept away by a roaring passion, she disregarded the small, logical voice in the back of her mind that told her this could never work, could never be a real relationship. They had no future. They were from different worlds. He was her employer. The bottom line she couldn't ignore: he was still in love with his late wife.

This might be a one-night stand. But what a night!

She tore at the buttons on his shirt. In a frenzy, their clothing peeled away. Naked, their bodies joined, and the impact stunned her. Her skin was on fire.

Every cell in her body throbbed with aching desire as he lowered her to the bed. His fingers tangled in her long hair, and he kissed her hard.

She clawed at his back, pulling him closer, needing him inside her. In the momentary pause while he sheathed himself in a condom, she couldn't keep her hands off him. His muscular arms. The crisp hair on his chest. The sharp angle of his jaw.

His gaze became tender. With an expression she'd never seen from him before, he looked deep, seeing her in a different way. Momentarily gentle, he stroked her cheek. "Your eyes are the most amazing color. Aquamarine."

He lightly tasted her lips. "I love your long hair."

He arranged her curls on the pillow, framing her face. Then he leaned down and kissed her again. The time for talk was over.

Chapter Fourteen

The next morning, Blake got out of his bed at the same time as usual. He followed his regular routine, got Duncan up and dressed. All the while, he knew that today was different—not because of the secret passageway in the basement or the police investigation or even the murder of Teddy Fisher. Today was different because of Madeline.

As he followed his son down the staircase, Blake had a bounce in his step. He couldn't wait to see her. His fingers twitched as he recalled the feel of her curly, silky black hair and the satin-softness of her ivory skin. The amazing color of her eyes made him think of deep, clear waters.

The intensity of her passion had surprised the hell out of him. Last night, Madeline had been a wild woman—an untamed, tempestuous force of nature. When he saw her this morning, he halfway expected her to growl. Or pounce. Oh yeah, that would be good.

As he stepped into the kitchen, his gaze went directly to her. Washing dishes at the sink, she had her back to him. Her luxurious hair was pulled into a tidy knot at the top of her head. Not one single, flirty tendril escaped. She'd covered her pastel-patterned cotton blouse and loose-fitting khaki slacks with a blue apron. On her feet were practical loafers, a little worn down at the heel. Definitely not the type of outfit worn by a wild woman. He'd been hoping for a topless sarong.

When she turned and faced him, her expression behind her black-rimmed glasses showed nothing more than the usual friendliness. Likewise, her smile was annoyingly calm.

"Good morning, Blake." She nodded to his son. "Hi, Duncan."

"Good morning," Blake said as Duncan climbed into his seat and began his silent breakfast-eating procedure.

Alma stalked toward him on four-inch heels. "Here's the deal, Blake. I know you hate when I make plans for you, but I had to set this appointment." With her pouffy hair, tight slacks and makeup, she was making ten times the effort to be attractive that Madeline put forth. She continued, "Detective Lagios will be here in about half an hour. He wants to finish the conversation you started last night."

"Fine," Blake said. His gaze returned to Madeline. Oddly enough, her prim exterior aroused him even more than if she'd been flaunting herself.

"I'll make fresh coffee for the detective," Alma said. "Maybe some sweet rolls. Would that be okay for your breakfast, Blake?"

"Whatever." Food was the last thing on his mind.

Alma turned to Madeline. "Did you know that Detective Lagios is single?"

"I wasn't aware," Madeline said.

"So is Grant Bridges. He's not a bad-looking guy and seems to have recovered from the tragedy of losing his bride on their wedding day."

"Must have been terrible," Madeline said.

Blake realized that she was avoiding his gaze, keeping herself so tightly wrapped that not even Alma suspected what had happened last night.

"I'll take breakfast in my studio," he said as he grabbed a mug of coffee. He needed to put some distance between himself and Madeline before he lost control.

In the studio, he sank into the chair behind his desk and quickly sorted through the progress reports of various crews and today's schedule. Concentrating on his work usually provided an orderly solution for life's other problems. No matter what else happened, he could see real progress in the completion of tasks.

Not today. He was distracted by Madeline's transformation. Today, she gave every appearance of propriety. Cool and distant. Nothing wanton about her. Was she playing games with him? Acting out a role? Was this prissy-proper attitude supposed to be a variation on the naughty-secretary fantasy?

He didn't think so. She wasn't a gamer. Madeline was just being herself, keeping her passions in check. But if he teased her, how would she react? Blake sipped his coffee. If he kissed her?

Lagios arrived before Blake's breakfast. After a brisk handshake, he took the chair opposite the desk. From his inner jacket pocket, he produced a small notebook. "I have a few more questions," he said.

"So do I." This conversation didn't need to be a confrontation; they were both on the same page. All the same, he would have appreciated an apology from Lagios for upsetting Duncan. "Starting with Detective Joe Curtis. I understand he's new in town."

"He's from LA. His experience has been useful on the Seaside Strangler investigation."

Blake thought of Madeline's concerns last night and her belief that Duncan had sensed a threat from Curtis. That suspicion could be easily erased if Curtis had an alibi for last night.

Blake tried to be subtle. "My son thought he recognized Curtis, but I don't recall meeting him. Has he ever been at the Manor before?"

"I don't know."

"What about last night? Was Curtis at the Manor last night or was he on duty?"

Lagios frowned. "What are you implying?"

So much for subtlety. "Does he have an alibi for the time of the murder?"

The detective's dark eyes flared with temper. "I don't keep track of the men I work with. When they're off duty, their time is their own. If you have questions about Curtis, I suggest you talk directly to him."

"I'll do that."

The door to the study opened, and Alma minced across the hardwood floor on her high heels. She carried a tray piled high with sweet rolls, bagels and a mug of coffee for Lagios. Her attempt at flirting with the detective fell flat as a water balloon dropped from a ten-story balcony.

Lagios didn't waste time with small-town charm. As soon as Alma left the room, he asked, "Have you noticed anyone unusual on the grounds of the Manor?"

"You'll have to be more specific," Blake said.

"You know what I mean."

Blake matched the detective's brusque manner with his own sarcasm. "If you're asking if I've seen obvious homicidal maniacs, the answer is no. But there are lots of people on the grounds, every day. I have several crews of workmen. Roofers. Carpenters. Painters."

"I'll need a list of names."

"Everything is taken care of through subcontractors. They hire their own men and pay them." He took a duplicate sheet from a folder inside his desk drawer. "These are the companies I'm working with."

"Did anyone have contact with Dr. Fisher?"

"I don't keep track of my crew." Blake lobbed Lagios's comment about Curtis back at him. "Off duty, their time is their own."

"How was your relationship with Fisher?"

"You suspect me? Seriously?" Blake's mood was moving rapidly from irritated to angry. "I have no motive for hurting Teddy Fisher. He's the guy who hired me—the man with the wallet. Plus, I have an alibi for last night."

"I had to ask." Without backing down, Lagios reached into his pocket and placed Duncan's shell on the desktop. "Your son can have this back."

"Did it match the necklace?"

Lagios nodded. "Necklaces similar to the one Madeline found were used by the Seaside Strangler."

The detective's sister, Sofia, had been one of the Strangler's victims. As Blake retrieved the shell and slipped it into his pocket, he adjusted his attitude and cut Lagios some slack. It must be hell to investigate the murder of a close family member. "Do you have any leads on the Strangler?"

"Not much." He glanced down at the notebook in his hand. "I brought my family here from New York to escape violence. I thought we'd be safe. Secure."

When he looked up, his abrupt manner was replaced by a haunted expression that Blake knew well. They had both suffered the loss of a loved one. They shared that pain.

"I feel the same way about Raven's Cliff," Blake said. "It seems like a good place for my son. Maybe here, in a small town, he won't be teased. The pace is slower. There's room to grow."

"Instead, you have a murder on your doorstep." Lagios frowned. "Then somebody like Curtis implies that there's something wrong with your boy. I'm sorry."

"Thanks." The air between them cleared. "The best way I can help your investigation is through Duncan. The person who grabbed him last night on the cliffs might be your murderer. Do you think it was the Strangler?"

"Not likely. The profile for Teddy's murder and the others is completely different."

"Unfortunately, Duncan doesn't respond to direct questions. And he has an active imagination." He decided against telling Lagios about his son's mention of Sofia. "Last night, he said that he saw Nicholas Sterling."

"The lighthouse keeper's grandson." Lagios sat up straighter. "Sterling has been dead for years."

And Blake sure as hell didn't want to start a rumor that his boy saw dead people. "I thought Duncan might have identified Nicholas Sterling from family portraits in the Manor. He might have noticed a resemblance."

"This is helpful. Gives us a starting place for a physical description." Lagios made a note. "Is there anything else Duncan mentioned?"

"Hammer hands," Blake said. "He kept talking about a man with pointy teeth and arms that were hammers."

The detective reached for his coffee mug and raised it

to his lips. He seemed to be struggling with a decision about how much to say and how much to leave blank. "I want to be able to trust you."

"We both want the same thing, Detective Lagios. To keep our families safe."

"I have the preliminary autopsy results." He looked directly into Blake's eyes, hiding nothing. "Teddy Fisher was beaten to death with a hammer."

DURING THE morning lessons with Duncan, Madeline tried to get him to open up about what he'd seen after touching Detective Joe Curtis, but the boy's thoughts scattered in a wild flurry, jumping from numbers to rhymes to simple re- petitive motions. Nothing held his interest.

For the first time since she'd been at the Manor, she understood why Duncan had been diagnosed as autistic. He made no connection with her or anything she said. While she measured out geometrical shapes that usually fasci- nated him, Duncan hummed to himself and kicked his heel against the leg of his chair. He seemed lost in his own little world, unwilling to communicate.

She dropped her pencil. "It's much too nice a day to stay inside. Let's set out that baseball diamond."

He snapped to attention. "Outside."

"Yes, Duncan. We'll go outside. On the grass."

He whipped his baseball gloves from his pocket and made a beeline for the front door, counting every step.

Before leaving the house, she grabbed the duffel bag holding the bases and the measuring tape that Blake had provided for setting up a proper baseball field. As she trailed behind the small, determined boy, she couldn't help worrying about how she'd control him. If Duncan marched into the forest and approached the dangerous cliffs, she couldn't force him to stop, couldn't even touch him.

She dropped the duffel bag and loudly proclaimed, "Here is where we start with home plate."

Duncan halted, still facing the forest. In a singsong voice, he said, "She sells seashells."

"By the seashore," Madeline responded, hoping he'd turn around and come back toward her. "Duncan, come here. I need your help."

Slowly, he walked backward until he was beside her. "I want to play baseball."

"Let's set up the diamond."

"Really a square," he said.

For the next half hour, they measured and placed the bases, more or less in the right position. As long as she kept focus on the task, Duncan cooperated. But she was glad when Blake joined them.

Hearing his deep voice and seeing him stride toward them provoked a response much deeper than relief. Her stomach clenched. Her heartbeat accelerated. Though she was doing her best to maintain a proper attitude—as Duncan would say, appropriate behavior—she could barely control her raging hormones. She was willing to accept their lovemaking as a one-night stand, but she wanted so much more.

But she couldn't let her passion show. Not until she had a better idea of what their relationship—if it could even be called a relationship—entailed. Fortunately, she had a lifetime of experience in practicing restraint, never saying what she wanted, never complaining.

She was happy for the respite when he took control of their outdoor project, allowing her to step aside and watch as he and Duncan set up the bases and walked around them. First. Second. Third. Home.

"Again," Duncan shouted.

They walked again. Then jogged. Duncan's motor skills had improved tremendously.

Sitting on the duffel bag so she wouldn't get grass stains on her beige slacks, she admired Blake's easygoing attitude with his son. Male bonding, she thought. Athletics seemed to be a natural arena for fathers and sons.

With no tasks of her own, she was free to admire Blake himself. His long-legged gait. His masculine shoulders. His habit of pushing his overlong hair off his forehead. So incredibly handsome, he wasn't the type of man who usually gave her a second glance. She could hardly believe they'd made love last night with a passion as fiery as a supernova. Just thinking about it made her perspire.

Flapping her hand by her cheek, she fanned herself as she gazed up into the clear July sky. It was a warm day with the sun beating down. Several of the workmen hammering away at the Manor's rooftop had taken off their shirts.

Blake did the same. The sight of his bare chest and lean torso took her breath away. She had to make love to him again. There had to be at least one more night.

Her passionate reverie was interrupted by a car pulling up to the front door of the Manor. When she saw Detective Curtis emerge from the driver's side, she rose quickly and hurried toward him, hoping that she could handle this situation without disturbing Duncan and Blake.

Grant Bridges—dressed in a nicely tailored suit with a striped silk tie—stepped out of the passenger side and waved to her. "Hello, Madeline. Beautiful weather today."

She returned his friendly greeting. "How can I help you gentlemen?"

Curtis scowled, giving the impression that he was here under duress. "I wanted to check on the kid. Make sure he was okay."

"As well as can be expected," she said. "It's rather disruptive to have a murder so close to home."

His thick neck swiveled as he squinted toward the baseball diamond. He wore a blazer, probably to cover his shoulder holster, and a tie. Too many clothes for such a warm day. His forehead glistened with sweat. "Did the boy ever say anything? About why he got so freaked out?"

"What would you expect him to say?"

"Don't know." He stared at the field. "I should talk to him. Let him know that policemen aren't scary."

"Not today." She planted herself in front of him, ready to tackle him if he made a move toward Duncan. "Leave him alone."

"Good advice," Grant said. "Duncan seems to be doing okay. I hope you'll bring him to T-ball practice tomorrow. It'd be good for him to have other kids to play with."

"I couldn't agree more," Madeline said.

The smooth, charming Grant Bridges was the direct opposite of the thuggish policeman. With an easy grin, he asked, "Will you be coming with Duncan to T-ball practice?"

"Of course."

"Maybe afterward, we could get a cup of coffee."

He was asking her for a date? Amazing! There had been times in her adult life when she'd gone months without any man noticing she existed. Now, she had two very eligible bachelors who were both interested. Obviously, she should have moved to Maine a lot sooner.

But it wasn't right to lead him on. "I'm sorry, Grant. My responsibilities with Duncan are keeping me so busy that I can't make other plans."

"I'd like to be friends." A hint of sadness tugged at his smile. "Sometimes it's hard for me to talk to the locals. They look at me, and they remember the tragedy."

"You have my deepest sympathy." She remembered stories about the accident, in which Grant's bride was swept off the cliff on their wedding day. How could anyone get over such a terrible tragedy? He probably wasn't even asking for a date. Just companionship.

"They never found her. Camille could still be alive." He straightened his shoulders. "I want to move on, but I can't."

She changed the topic. "How's the murder investigation going?"

"I hate to say this, but suspicion seems to be centered on Mayor Wells. He was the last person to see Dr. Fisher alive. And he had motive."

Curtis cleared his throat. "We shouldn't talk about the ongoing investigation."

"No point in trying to keep this a secret. Everybody in town knows what's going on. Perry Wells hated Fisher."

"Why?" she asked.

"You might have heard about anonymous letters to the press about corruption in the mayor's office. Those accusations were written by Teddy Fisher."

She found it hard to believe that the mayor was capable of the violence that had killed Dr. Fisher. His injuries had been brutal. "Political accusations come with the territory for any elected official. They don't seem like a motive for murder."

"The mayor has been under a lot of pressure. He's falling apart. I hardly know him anymore." The smile slipped from his face. "A damned shame. Perry Wells was almost my father-in-law."

Again, she said, "I'm so sorry, Grant."

"Camille was an amazing woman. I miss her. I miss the family we could have had together." His gaze returned to the grassy field. "A son. Like Duncan."

As if sensing Grant's scrutiny, Duncan waved.

"Excuse me," Grant said. "I need to see what the newest member of my T-ball team wants."

He jogged toward Duncan and Blake, leaving her alone with Joe Curtis. When the policeman took a step to follow, she snapped, "Don't."

"Why not? Give me a reason."

Because she didn't want Duncan to be frightened again and she'd lay down her life to protect him. "I don't want you near him."

When he confronted her directly, she realized just how big he was. His shoulders looked massive enough to haul a Volkswagen.

His mouth curled in a sneer. "Why the hell shouldn't I talk to the kid?"

"Because you frighten him." She remembered his earlier question; Curtis was afraid that Duncan had said something about him.

She had no intention of explaining Duncan's abilities to this man. All she wanted was to deflect his focus from the boy. "The boy doesn't know anything, but I do."

She saw a flicker of wariness in his eyes. "Yeah? And what do you know?"

Though she'd never been a good liar, she summoned up all her confidence and nerve. This lie was for a good cause. To protect Duncan.

"I'm a little bit psychic," she said. "I can see your aura. So much violence. So much rage."

Though he scoffed, she could tell that her words made an impact. "You're a violent man, Joe Curtis." Possibly that was why he'd left the LAPD. She continued, "I know why you're here in Raven's Cliff. I'm warning you. Stay away from Duncan. Or I'll tell everything."

"You're bluffing."

"Maybe." She refused to break eye contact. "Maybe not."

Grant jogged up beside her. His earlier sadness vanished behind a brilliant smile. "Duncan is definitely on the team."

Abruptly, Joe Curtis pivoted, ending their face-to-face confrontation. He lumbered around the car to the driver's side and opened the door. Before he got behind the wheel, he cocked his fingers like a gun and aimed it at her. "I'll be seeing you, Madeline."

She wasn't looking forward to the next time.

Chapter Fifteen

Madeline went to bed early that night. During the course of the day, she and Blake had exchanged only a few words. Neither of them had mentioned their previous night of passion. Nor did they speak of what would happen next.

A few times, she'd caught him watching her with what she hoped was longing. Or perhaps, curiosity. She couldn't tell what was going on inside his head. Just like his son, Blake revealed very little of himself. The only thing he'd been adamant about was a restoration project he'd started in one of the upstairs bedrooms that involved some delicate handiwork. Repeatedly, he'd told them that no one was allowed to enter that room.

Though he'd given her no real reason to believe that he might show up at her bedroom door, she dressed in her best pink satin nightshirt with matching panties—a gift to herself from one of the better lingerie shops in Boston. With her long hair brushed to a glossy sheen, she slipped between the sheets and waited.

Duncan had been tucked in half an hour ago, plenty of time for him to be sound asleep. If Blake intended to join her in bed, there should be nothing stopping him.

A glance at the bedside clock told her that it was exactly four minutes since the last time she'd checked the time. She ought to take matters into her own hands. Trot down the hall to his room.

Their passion last night had been spectacular. Of that, she had no doubt. But he might not want a repeat. He might have decided that it was inappropriate to seduce his son's tutor. Or he might be remembering his beloved Kathleen. An angel. How could anyone compete with such a perfect memory?

Another ten minutes ticked slowly by. She exhaled a frustrated sigh. *He wasn't coming.* Might as well shove the ficus against the door and try to sleep.

Then she heard a rap on her bedroom door. She bolted to a sitting posture on the bed and called out, "Come in."

"You come out," Blake responded.

In the ensuing silence, the pounding of her heart was louder than the drum and bugle corps in the St. Patrick's Day Parade. *He wanted her to come to him.*

She floated from the bed to the mirror, put on her glasses to check her reflection, then took them off. Her hazy vision matched her dreamlike mood as she wafted to the door and opened it.

A trail of colorful wildflowers—daisies and bluebells—led down the hallway, marking the way from her bedroom to his. Never had she expected such a sweet gesture. Step by step, she gathered her bouquet, pausing at the slightly opened door to Duncan's bedroom and peeking inside at the soundly sleeping child.

Like a bride to the altar, holding her colorful bouquet, she walked the few paces. No matter what else happened between them, she would always remember this moment. More than passion, he had given her romance.

When she pushed open the door to Blake's room, she found him waiting. He scooped her off her feet and into his arms, neatly closing his door at the same time.

Her flowers scattered across the sheets as he deposited her on his bed. Unlike last night's wild frenzy of passion, tonight was slow. Deliberate. Divine.

She savored his kisses. Pushing aside his unbuttoned shirt, she traced the muscles on his chest. His strong but gentle caresses pulled her so close that they breathed as one being. Their hearts synchronized in perfect harmony.

Through her swirling senses, she heard a cry.

It was Duncan. "Danger," he shouted. "Danger."

INSTANTLY, Blake responded to his son's voice. He leaped from the bed and charged down the hall to Duncan's room. The door was shut when it should have been open. He yanked the knob, flung it open and stormed inside.

His son stood on his bed, cowering against the headboard. As Blake approached, Duncan jumped toward him, into his arms. He was cold, shivering.

"What happened?" Blake asked. "Bad dream?"

"Bad dream. Bad man. Bad dream."

Blake stroked Duncan's fine blond hair. "It's okay, buddy. Nobody is going to hurt you."

"I saw his shadow. Hammer hands."

It had been several months, nearly a year, since Duncan had last been yanked awake by a nightmare. After his mother died, these bad dreams came almost every night, but that behavior was history. Until now.

Blake glanced toward Madeline as she entered the room, wearing that sexy satin nightshirt that showed off her long, curvy legs. Her flushed complexion and disheveled hair contrasted with her calm voice as she asked, "What should I do? Duncan, do you want a glass of water?"

"No," Duncan shouted. "He'll get you. Stay."

Blake sat on the edge of the bed with Duncan on his lap. "The nightmare is gone. We're all safe."

When Madeline sat beside them—carefully not touching his son—her presence felt right. They were a unit. Together, they faced the dark fears in Duncan's mind.

She urged, "Tell us what happened, Duncan. Everything you can remember."

"Noise," he said.

"You heard a noise," she prompted.

"Thump. Big feet. The door opened up. Opened up. Opened up wide. Shadows came inside. A big shadow." He shook his head. "Danger."

"But your door was closed," Blake said.

"He shut it." His shoulders slumped as he began to calm down. "All gone now. All gone."

Blake cradled his son against his bare chest. This sure as hell wasn't the way he had planned to spend this night, but Duncan came first. And he knew Madeline would agree with him. "You've got nothing to worry about, buddy."

Duncan pulled away and looked into his eyes. It was unusual for the boy to make such direct contact. His voice was normal without a hint of agitation. "Daddy, I saw him. I really saw him."

"Who? Who did you see?"

"The man."

"What did he look like?"

"He smelled like the ocean."

Had this been more than a nightmare? It was possible that someone had crept up the staircase and into his son's room. Blake needed to know. "Concentrate, buddy. Tell me about the man. Was he tall?"

Duncan frowned and looked down at his hands. He laced his fingers together, then pulled them apart. After three repetitions of this gesture, he murmured, "She sells seashells."

Last night, Duncan had been approached on the cliff by a stranger—someone had grabbed his shoulder. Duncan was a witness. He might have seen the man who murdered Teddy Fisher. "Duncan, look at me."

The boy clapped his hands together. "All gone."

Damn, this was frustrating. All Blake wanted was an answer to a simple question. "Does the man have a name?"

"Time for sleep, Daddy." He wriggled out of Blake's arms and dove under his covers. "Nighty-night, Madeline. Don't let the bedbugs bite."

Duncan's fears—having been expressed—seemed to disappear. He closed his eyelids. With each calm breath, his skinny chest rose and fell in an untroubled, steady rhythm.

Blake was nowhere near so calm. He whispered to Madeline. "I'm staying here until he's asleep."

"Of course." She left the room.

Settling into the rocking chair beside the bed, Blake fastened the buttons on his shirt. He hoped Duncan's vision had only been a nightmare, but feared otherwise.

What the hell should be done? Trust the cops to take care of things? Though Detective Lagios seemed like a competent officer, his abilities were limited. The only clue Duncan could offer was to say he'd seen a bad man. Or Nicholas Sterling, who had been dead for years.

The Raven's Cliff police force didn't have enough manpower to stand guard over the Manor day and night.

Even if they could, there was no sure protection against a determined assailant. There were dozens of ways into this sprawling house. Windows that were being replaced. Doors that were off the hinges. Installing a security system was a waste of time with all the workmen coming and going. Not to mention the secret passageway that led from the caves into the basement.

If Duncan truly was in danger, they should pack up and leave Raven's Cliff. But Duncan was doing well in this place. Just this afternoon, they'd played baseball like a regular father and son.

Moving carefully so he wouldn't wake Duncan, Blake slipped out of the room into the hallway.

Madeline popped through her bedroom door where she'd obviously been waiting. Wearing her flannel bathrobe with her glasses perched on her nose and her hair tied back at her nape, she gave the clear signal that she wasn't interested in sex.

"Is Duncan okay?" she whispered.

He nodded and pointed toward the staircase. Together, they descended and went into the kitchen.

She went to the cabinets by the sink. "I could really use a cup of tea."

"I was thinking of something stronger." From a top shelf, he took down a bottle of bourbon and poured a couple of shots into a tumbler. "You?"

"I'll stick to chamomile." She placed the teakettle on the burner and turned up the flame.

He took a sip and savored the burn. "Duncan hasn't had a nightmare like this in months."

"I can't blame him for being upset. It's been a rough couple of days." Her gaze rested on the poster board—

Duncan's Schedule. "Being lost in the woods. The murder. His reaction to Joe Curtis."

"He's agitated. Overexcited."

"Of course."

Blake really wanted to believe that his son's nightmare was nothing more than imagination—a disturbing sleep experience. He sank into a chair and took another drink. "What if he really saw someone?"

"It's possible. Very possible." She dove into the chair opposite him and leaned forward on her elbows. Her robe gaped open, giving a glimpse of the pink satin. "Someone could have come into his room."

Fear struck him hard. "A killer in the same room with my son."

Behind her glasses, her eyes shone with purpose and hope. "It's up to us, Blake. We have to find out what Duncan saw."

He agreed, but trying to figure out what was going on in Duncan's brain was like entering a maze. "Got any ideas?"

"There's got to be a way we can get Duncan to identify the person who grabbed him on the cliff."

"Then what?" He inhaled another gulp of bourbon, hoping to deaden the fear that writhed inside his chest. "I won't put my son through the ordeal of testifying. He can hardly stand to be in the same room with other people much less face a judge and jury. Damn it, he's only six years old."

"We need to know the truth, Blake."

"Here's what I need, Madeline. To keep my child safe. I should cancel all the work crews and bar the doors. Better yet, we should leave. Get the hell away from this cursed little town."

On the stove, the teakettle whistled, and she went to prepare her drink. "Is that what you want, Blake? To leave?"

"No." His response was immediate and definite. He was enjoying the restoration of this American Federalist estate, especially the project he'd started in the upstairs bedroom this afternoon. Even more important, Duncan's behavior improved every day by leaps and bounds. "I want my son to have a normal life, to play baseball. I want him to have a chance to be like other kids."

She returned to her seat opposite Blake and placed the flower-sprigged cup and saucer on the tabletop. "That's not too much to hope for."

Ever since the first diagnosis of autism, Blake's life with Duncan had been a series of disappointments. He'd learned not to expect too much. A normal life? "It's an impossible dream."

Reaching across the table, she laced her fingers with his. Her hand was soft and warm from holding her teacup. "Sometimes," she said, "the impossible comes true."

Her sincerity struck a chord inside him. Through his anger and frustration, he felt an echo of her hope. Sometime. Somehow. Someday. His son would be all right.

"I want to believe that."

"You can."

He liked the way her common sense cut through all the complications. She made all things seem possible. In so many ways, she amazed him. Being with Madeline was part of the reason he wanted to stay in Raven's Cliff. Their relationship was still in the early, delicate stages. He needed time to nurture his feelings for her, to see if his heart could ever blossom again.

But Duncan came first. "I've got to protect my son. If he's in danger, we can't stay here."

"As you well know," she said, "I'm Duncan's biggest

advocate. I think he sees things that the rest of us don't. But what happened tonight might have been nothing more than a bad dream."

"True." He could be making too much of a nightmare. "If we stay, we can't leave him alone. Not for a minute."

"But we can't lock him up in his room. Tomorrow, we should go to the T-ball practice in town."

"That's dangerous on so many levels. First, there's the basic problem of having Duncan interact with other kids. Leaving the house. Changing his schedule." A worse thought occurred. "What if he sees the killer?"

"A good thing," she said firmly. "If he identifies the killer, Lagios can arrest him. Duncan will be safe."

She made the process of putting his son in close proximity to a murderer sound rational. "The next thing you'll suggest is that we arrange for a police lineup of the main suspects."

"Probably not," she conceded. "That's too much pressure. I wouldn't want to put Duncan in the position of coming face-to-face with his nightmare man."

With a final squeeze, she withdrew her hand and concentrated on her tea. Her ladylike manner when she lifted the cup to her lips was a definite turn-on. He was tempted to sweep everything off the kitchen table and take her right here.

"Perhaps," she said, "there's a way for Duncan to see the suspects without facing them. We could arrange our own lineup."

"How?"

"Using your cell phone, you could take photos of the various suspects. I believe the police are concentrating on the mayor, Perry Wells."

"I still don't understand what you're talking about."

"We can make it a game. Like a lesson plan. Show Duncan all the photos and watch his reaction."

Once again, she'd come up with a simple solution for a complex problem. Using cell-phone photos, they could create their own photo array for Duncan to use in identification. In that way, his son wouldn't have to face the police. If he recognized the killer, they'd be right there beside him.

Blake turned the idea over in his head, looked at it from several angles. He couldn't find a flaw.

He raised his tumbler to her in toast. "We'll do it. It's a good plan."

"Thank you." She clinked her dainty teacup with his bourbon tumbler.

A very good plan. Maybe even brilliant. If grade-school teachers were running Homeland Security, the terrorists wouldn't stand a chance.

Chapter Sixteen

"First base, second base…" In the back of the car, Duncan counted to himself and punched his batting glove into the big catcher's mitt. Yesterday, Daddy had showed him how to do a high five. "…third base. Home plate. Home run."

He was on a team. A T-ball team. And he knew all the numbers. He leaned forward against his seat belt and stuck out his catching glove toward the front seat. "Madeline. High five."

She turned around and slapped the glove. "High five."

She looked funny in her Red Sox baseball cap with her ponytail hanging out the back. But her teeth were pretty and white, and she smiled a lot. That made him think of his best friend, Temperance, and how it sounded when she laughed. He wished Temperance could see him play baseball.

His Daddy parked and turned around. He smiled, too.

"Hey, buddy."

"Hey, Daddy."

"I'm proud of you, Duncan. Let's play ball."

He jumped out of the car. There was a fence and a green field with bases. Lots of kids. Lots of parents.

Duncan wasn't scared. He knew all the numbers.

STEPPING OUT of the car into a sunny summer day, Madeline tensed. The possibility of running into the person who killed Teddy Fisher was secondary to her concerns for Duncan. More than anything, she wanted him to have a positive experience this afternoon. She walked stiffly at Blake's side—as apprehensive as if she herself were approaching the batter's box in Fenway Park.

The baseball diamond where the kids—aged five to seven—played T-ball was in a park across the street from the high school. A tall chain-link fence formed the backstop. The grass was cut short in the infield, and the paths for base running were marked off with white chalk lines. A simple setup with no dugouts or bleachers. She noticed that some of the other adults had brought along their own lawn chairs.

Grant Bridges sauntered toward them. His casual shorts and T-shirt didn't flatter him nearly as much as his suit and tie. Though he seemed fit, he lacked the athletic grace that came so naturally to Blake.

"Glad you're here," Grant said as he shook hands with Blake and twinkled a grin at Madeline. "With Duncan playing we've got enough kids for two full teams."

"Nine players on a team," Duncan said quickly.

"That's right," Grant said. "Come with me and we'll meet the other kids."

With a wave of his gloved hand, Duncan went forward.

Madeline held her breath. Since she'd never seen Duncan with other children, she didn't really know what to expect. But Blake did. With arms folded across his chest and every muscle in his body clenched, he radiated nervous energy.

They were close enough to overhear the other kids greet

Duncan. He was quickly surrounded by four boys and two girls, all wearing baseball caps.

A stocky, redheaded boy who looked as if he might belong to the Chapman clan said, "You live in that big place near the lighthouse."

"Yes," Duncan said.

"There was a murder there."

The other kids jostled closer, obviously curious. There were comments about scary murders and the curse. One of the boys spat into the dirt.

Madeline noticed that Blake's arms had dropped to his sides and he leaned forward on the balls of his feet as if ready to immediately sprint to his son's aid.

The redheaded kid spoke to Duncan again. "Did you see him? Did you see the dead guy?"

"No."

A skinny little girl with long blond braids started to tremble. "Don't talk about it. I'm scared."

"Geez, Annie," said the other girl. "You're such a big crybaby."

"Am not!"

With his gloved hand, Duncan reached toward Annie and patted her shoulder. "It's okay. The bad man isn't here."

"Aren't you scared?"

"Sometimes." He shrugged. "I don't like T-Rex dinosaurs."

"Me, too," piped up the shortest boy in the group. "And sharks. I hate sharks. They can eat you up in one bite."

Grant stepped in to break up the conversation, assigning them places in the field for practice. Duncan ran to second base and stood on the bag. Though his lips were tight, Madeline detected the beginning of a grin. She beamed back at him. A sense of real pride bubbled up inside her. When Grant lobbed a ball toward him, Duncan managed to scoop it up and throw in the general direction of first base. His playing skills seemed to be no better and no worse than most of the other kids'.

She touched Blake's arm. "He's going to be okay."

"Thanks to you." When he looked at her, his eyes held a special tenderness and intimacy. "You've done so much. Our little family is coming together."

Our family? He seemed to be including her in that unit. "We're a good team."

"You, me and Duncan," he said. "I never imagined my son being able to play baseball."

She held his gaze, not wanting to make too much of the casual way he lumped them together. Being accepted as part of a family—his family—was deeply important to her. She'd always yearned for a family of her own. Not her adoptive parents. Not her addict mother who'd tossed her into the foster-care system. Certainly not her genetic sibling, Marty. Which reminded her that she still hadn't found the right time to tell Blake about the diamond theft. Now was certainly not that moment.

She turned toward the sidelines where the other parents had gathered. "We should introduce ourselves to the parents of Duncan's new friends."

"Friends," he said with obvious satisfaction. "Duncan's friends. That's a hell of a concept."

"Maybe we can set up a couple of playdates."

He took his cell phone from his pocket. "Or snap a

couple of pictures. I'm going to include Grant Bridges in our photo array."

She didn't understand why he'd taken such a dislike to Grant. "Okay."

None of the people they met seemed the least bit suspicious. Average people. Very pleasant. Like the kids on the field, they were all buzzing about the murder of Teddy Fisher. The general opinion seemed to be that Dr. Fisher was an obnoxious person, too rich for his own good, a genuine eccentric.

"And dangerous," said Lucy Tucker in a conspiratorial tone. Her trinket shop—Tidal Treasures—was in the center of town, and Lucy seemed to have her finger on the pulse of Raven's Cliff.

"Why dangerous?" Madeline asked.

The petite strawberry blonde pulled her aside. "You didn't hear this from me, but Dr. Fisher's experiments at his lab caused the epidemic. You know, the dark-line disease that killed people? If it hadn't been for Dr. Peterson, we'd all be dead."

With no encouragement, Lucy rattled on about the lady doctor who had apparently hooked up with a sexy toxicologist and they were getting married. "I mean, he's a babe magnet. And a doctor."

Madeline had never been fond of gossip but wanted to bond with Lucy, who was the aunt of Annie—the little girl with braids whom Duncan had comforted. "About the epidemic," she said. "Weren't there anonymous letters in the paper saying that Mayor Wells was to blame?"

"Lower your voice," Lucy warned as she nodded toward her left. "That skinny guy in the suit is Rick Simpson, the mayor's top aide."

Rick Simpson appeared to be deep in conversation with two other men who looked as if they'd just stepped out of their offices. "Who's with him?"

"A couple of guys who work in the D.A.'s office. You know, lawyers."

Madeline glanced toward the baseball diamond where Grant Bridges was organizing the kids into two teams, then turned back to Lucy. "There are a lot of high-powered people here. Are they all parents?"

"Mostly," Lucy said. "Some of them are here because the mayor's wife supports the baseball program."

Apparently, showing up at a T-ball game was a good way to impress the powers that be. Now Madeline understood why Grant Bridges—a single man with no children of his own—had volunteered to coach the team. This was his way of making contacts. "Why is Beatrice Wells so involved?"

"Raven's Cliff baseball is a whole program—from these little ones to middle school. According to Beatrice, sports are a good way to keep the kids off the street."

These teams of five- to seven-year-olds hardly looked like budding juvenile delinquents, but Madeline liked the idea of children being involved in group sports, especially during the summer when they tended to lose focus. From her years of teaching, she remembered how dreadful the first weeks of school could be.

But she wasn't here to discuss her educational philosophy with Lucy. Madeline returned to the pertinent gossip about the murder. "I've heard that Mayor Wells is a suspect."

"If he killed Teddy Fisher, I say good for him. Fisher was a menace." Her blue eyes brightened as she caught sight of two tough-looking fishermen approaching. "That's my boyfriend, Alex Gibson. Got to run."

Madeline turned her gaze toward the field where Duncan's team sat in a row on the sideline, waiting for their turn to bat. The rules in T-ball were different than regular baseball. Though one of the kids stood on the mound, the pitcher didn't really throw the ball. He just pantomimed the motion. The actual ball rested on a stand, and the batter had unlimited swings in trying to hit it. An inning came to an end when every kid on the team had had a turn at bat.

The theory was to give the kids an idea of how to run bases and field without really keeping score. The atmosphere should have been low-pressure, but Blake was tense as he came up beside her. "Duncan is next."

"He'll do fine," she assured him.

"We haven't practiced much on batting. I showed him how to swing, but that's about it."

The batter before Duncan wound up and unleashed a monster swing that spun him around like a top. He did, however, miss the ball standing on the tee.

"Strike one," his teammates yelled.

His second swing connected for a dribbling little hit that was enough for the boy to run to first base.

It was Duncan's turn. As he walked to the plate, his lips were moving. Madeline knew he was silently counting his steps. His small gloved hands wrapped around the bat, and he took his stance. With serious concentration, he swung. A hit!

"Yes," Blake said with a quiet fist pump. "Okay, son. Now run. Run to first."

Duncan went to first. Then second. That was where he

stopped. Breathing hard, he gave a high five to the second baseman for the other team. Then he waved to his father.

"That's my boy. He hit a double."

While Duncan was on base, Blake concentrated on the field with a mixture of pride and incredulity. He couldn't believe how well Duncan was doing. No outbursts. No signs of rising panic. The batting gloves kept him shielded from unwanted touches, and the mechanics of the game kept his attention occupied. When he crossed home plate, he jumped on it with both feet.

Even more satisfying for Blake was the way Duncan interacted with his teammates. Though his son never laughed, a tiny grin played around the corners of his mouth. Blake overheard Duncan volunteering information, citing statistics about Madeline's beloved Red Sox.

Even that jerk, Grant Bridges, took notice of Duncan's expertise. "You're quite a Sox fan," he said.

"Yes," Duncan replied. "And the Cubbies."

That's my boy!

Blake's paternal reverie ended abruptly when he saw Helen Fisher charging toward him from the street. She was dressed in black from head to toe in apparent mourning for her dead brother. She'd topped the outfit with a big-brimmed straw hat that made her look like a walking lampshade.

She planted her feet in front of him and glared. "I want an accounting of every penny you spend on the restoration of the Manor. And I want it now."

Blake had no intention of being drawn into a business discussion at his son's T-ball game. "My condolences on the loss of your brother."

"Right. Thanks." She spat the words. "Teddy died without a will and has no heirs. That means Beacon Manor now belongs to me."

"That's for the probate courts to decide."

"Don't you dare put me off." Her voice rose to a finger-nails-on-chalkboard vibrato. "I own it."

Madeline stepped in to defuse the situation. "Perhaps we could talk about this another time."

Helen's furious glare swept past her and encompassed the rest of the people gathered at the sidelines. "I own the Manor and the lighthouse. I might just decide to move in and shut down the renovations entirely."

A tough-looking guy growled at her. "You can't do that."

"Don't tell me what I can't do, Alex Gibson."

"The lighthouse has to be repaired," he said. "It's the only way to lift the curse."

"All of you fishermen are so superstitious." Her mouth puckered. "The Manor is a historic landmark. The curse isn't real."

As Alex Gibson rose to his feet, Blake recognized him. He was the fisherman whom Duncan had seen at the docks and reacted to—definitely someone Blake should have in his photo array of suspects.

"Never deny the curse," Alex said darkly.

The little strawberry blonde who owned the trinket shop backed him up. "Helen, please. We're on the right track with repairing the lighthouse."

"How can you say that? Teddy was killed." Amid the crowd who were mostly dressed in summery clothing, her black dress marked her as a harbinger of bad luck. "You'd all better get used to treating me with more respect. I'm a wealthy woman now."

Which sounded to Blake like a damn good motive for

murder. Did Helen have the strength to beat her brother to death with a hammer?

Beatrice Wells hurried toward them, covering the last few yards across the grass with surprising speed for a small, short-legged woman. Gasping for breath, she said, "Helen, dear, you simply must lower your voice. You're upsetting the children."

Was she? Blake glanced back toward the field. None of the kids were watching. Even Duncan appeared to be undisturbed as he stared across the baseball diamond at the far edge of the outfield.

"Of all people," Helen said to Beatrice, "I'd expect you to understand. The money my brother threw away by hiring a world-famous designer could have gone to charity."

Beatrice tossed an apologetic smile toward Blake while Helen continued, "My brother got rich, and I spent my whole life struggling to get by."

"Not much of a struggle," said the trinket-shop owner. "The way I've heard it, you own your house and your bills are paid by a family trust."

Mayor Perry Wells had followed his wife to the sidelines. Though he was obviously ragged around the edges and stressed, his voice rang with the authority of his office. "Everyone calm down. You're distraught, Helen. Which is understandable under the circumstances. But you need to take it easy."

"Or what? What are you going to do, Perry?" She sneered. "Are you going to kill me, too?"

Beatrice gasped. Her small hand flew to cover her mouth. A murmur ripped through the people at the sidelines.

Helen took no notice. She turned on her heel and stalked off.

To his credit, Perry Wells didn't react to Helen's accusation. He pasted a smile on his face. "It's a beautiful day. Beautiful! Play ball."

Though Blake took out his cell phone and started snapping picture of possible suspects, he had to agree with the mayor. A beautiful day!

Raven's Cliff was one hell of a weird little town, but his son was thriving. This T-ball game was as close to normal as Duncan had been in years.

Madeline came up beside him. "How are you doing?"

"Normal." He savored the word. Nothing in the world seemed more beautiful than an ordinary day, watching Duncan at play with other kids. No tantrums. No hysterics. No inappropriate behavior.

"Helen Fisher didn't get to you?"

"Not at all."

It would take more than wild-eyed demands and accusations from Helen Fisher to drive him away. This little town was where Blake intended to stay. In spite of the curse.

Chapter Seventeen

During the four innings of T-Ball, Blake had collected a series of photos on his cell phone which he printed out in his office and spread across his desktop. None of these faces struck him as the visage of a murderer. He glided his hands above the pictures, trying to pick up a vibe, an idea of who among them might be dangerous. He closed his eyes and did it again. Nothing. Not even a tremor.

How did Duncan feel when he sensed danger? Did his pulse accelerate? Were there images? The boy talked about sounds. The thud of a hammer. The slam of the door.

In the past, Blake had dismissed his son's reactions, considering them to be imaginary. Preparing this photo array was the closest he'd come to acknowledging the possibility that his son had some kind of psychic ability. Though Blake wanted to tell himself that the pictures were only a police lineup to jog Duncan's memory, he knew it was more. Duncan saw more than other people; he sensed moods and the past history of people he touched. Was that better or worse than a diagnosis of autism?

Blake sprawled in his desk chair. Tilting back, he stared at the ceiling. A couple of the roofers were still hammering, though it was after five o'clock. Time for Duncan's dinner.

The T-ball game had thrown their schedule off. By damn, that disruption was worth it. The couple of hours they'd spent on the baseball diamond would always be a treasured memory. Duncan's first hit. His first time around the bases. In his batting gloves, Duncan had been part of the group—just like any normal six-year-old. It didn't matter if he was psychic or hypersensitive or autistic. He was happy.

Madeline came through the open door of his office. Her cheeks were slightly sunburned from being outside this afternoon, and she looked particularly vivacious as she scanned the photo array. "This doesn't exactly look like murderer's row, does it?"

"They all seem pretty average," he said. "Where's Duncan?"

"In the kitchen with Alma, having dinner." She picked up the photo of the mayor. "Perry Wells. I hope it's not him. The poor man has gone through enough tragedy. He didn't have time to get over losing his daughter on her wedding day before the epidemic hit Raven's Cliff. Now, he has to deal with anonymous letters to the newspaper, accusations and gossip."

"All of which might have driven him over the edge, turning a basically decent man into a killer."

"Do you think that's possible?" Behind her glasses, her eyes were troubled. "Can a truly good person be driven to commit a terrible crime?"

"There's plenty of times when I've been angry enough or frustrated enough to consider murder."

"But you didn't act on that impulse," she pointed out.

"Thinking violent thoughts is different from carrying them out. I've always been puzzled by the nature versus nurture issue."

"Genetics," he said.

"Is behavior predetermined by DNA?" She frowned. "Is someone born to be bad? Or is that a learned behavior?"

"It sounds like you're thinking of someone specific."

"My brother, Marty."

It was the first time she'd spoken of her family, and he sensed that this was important to her. "Younger brother or older?"

"About two years older than me. He was always very handsome. We don't look much alike, expect that we're both tall and have big, gawky feet."

"There's nothing wrong with your feet." His gaze scanned from her ponytail to the tips of her sneakers. "I like *everything* about your body. Your long legs. Your slim torso. Your—"

"I get it," she said, interrupting his listing of her attributes before he got to the interesting parts. She still insisted on a proper atmosphere during the day. At night, she was a different creature. "We were talking about my brother."

"Go ahead."

"When we were growing up, Marty was always in trouble. He got in fights and stole things. It almost seemed that he preferred lies to the truth. And he was a huge tease."

"Did he steal your Barbie dolls?"

"Worse. He hid my books before I was done reading them."

He imagined her as an adorable little girl with curly black hair and incredible aquamarine eyes. "I bet you were a shy kid."

Her eyebrows arched. "We aren't talking about me."

He couldn't resist teasing. "With your cute little nose always buried in a book."

"After I was adopted," she continued, "I lost touch with Marty. We didn't go to the same schools. I hardly ever saw him."

"Did you miss him?"

"Sometimes." She exhaled a ragged sigh. "I can't help wondering what would have happened if Marty had been the one to be adopted. If he'd been with caring, nurturing parents, he might have turned out better."

Her insistence on talking about her brother made him think that there was more to this story—something more pertinent to her life right now. "Where's Marty now?"

"In jail."

"I'm sorry, Madeline."

"That isn't the worst part." Her slender fingers knotted together. "Marty came to me a couple of weeks ago, needing money. I couldn't refuse. I gave him everything I had, even ran up my credit cards to the max."

Which explained why she'd turned up on his doorstep flat broke and desperate for a job. He had wondered about her circumstances, about how a supposedly well-organized, intelligent woman didn't have a savings account.

Trusting her ne'er-do-well brother might have been foolish, but Blake knew all about family loyalty. He rose from his chair and went toward her. "I understand."

She held up her hand, warding off his approach. "There's more I need to tell you."

What the hell was this about? "Go on."

"I knew Marty was up to something, even when he promised to pay me back with interest. He said that if the police ever came looking for him, I should keep my mouth shut." Her eyes filled with pain. "I swear to you, Blake. I swear. I never suspected that he was talking about a major crime."

"Not murder."

"No, thank God. I didn't know what Marty had done until I got here and saw it on the news from Boston. He's in jail because he's suspected of stealing diamonds worth seven hundred thousand dollars."

"You think he's guilty."

"I don't know. The diamonds still haven't been recovered, and I hope the police will find that someone else is responsible." She clenched her fingers again in an attitude that was almost like prayer. "He's my brother. How could he do this?"

Blake hated this situation. Unwittingly, he'd hired the sister of a major felon to work with his son, to teach Duncan. Damn it. What if Marty's partners in crime came after her? What if she'd brought another form of danger into his house?

"If you'd told me this when you arrived, I wouldn't have hired you."

"You almost didn't hire me," she reminded him. "When I first arrived here, I didn't know what my brother had done. Only that he was in trouble again. That's something I've had to live with since birth."

"Does he know you're here?"

"No. I haven't heard anything from him."

He believed her. Madeline was the most honest person he'd ever known. "I don't blame you for your brother's crime. I'm glad you're here, glad you're part of our family now."

When she stepped into his embrace and rested her head against his shoulder, he realized that this was the first time they'd touched outside the bedroom. Her nearness felt right to him. Part of the family. His family.

He inhaled the fragrance of her thick, curly hair and whispered, "You're a good person, Madeline. You just got caught up in a bad situation."

She swiped the corner of her eye. A relieved smile curved her lips and brightened her face. "Thank you, Blake, for understanding. Being with you and Duncan means everything to me."

Before her gratitude took on an uncomfortable weight, he changed the topic. Gesturing to the photos, he said, "What do you think?"

She leaned over the photos. "You don't have Helen Fisher. According to Lucy Tucker, Helen ought to be considered a suspect in her brother's murder."

Though Blake agreed that Helen's hate-filled attitude could turn violent, he didn't consider her a possibility. "Duncan was clear about one thing. The person who grabbed him was male. A bad man."

Madeline looked up at him. "And you don't have Joe Curtis."

"I didn't see him this afternoon." And he couldn't think of a good excuse to stop by the police station and snap photos. "But I have an idea of how I can get his mug shot."

She cocked her head to one side. "How?"

"I did a restoration project for a Washington, D.C., client who's a hotshot in Homeland Security. He's got access to photos from police departments, and he owes me a favor. He can fax it to me."

"Maybe he can do a background check on Joe Curtis.

Maybe there's something in his past with LAPD that would explain why Duncan had such a strong reaction to him."

"I'll make the call," Blake said. "Tomorrow, we'll do this photo array. Right now, he's too tired."

"He did so well at the T-ball game. Today was wonderful."

And tonight, Blake thought, would be even better.

WITH A clear conscience, Madeline prepared for bed. Telling Blake about Marty had been difficult, but his response had warmed her heart. He thought of her as family, as part of his life. She couldn't hope for more.

She'd barely had a chance to brush her hair when she heard the tap on her bedroom door. "Blake?"

Just like last night, he told her to come out. This time, she opened the door confidently. A trail of votive candles lit her way down the hall to his bed. As she followed the flickering lights, she paused and blew each one out.

Tonight, she noticed, the door to Duncan's room was closed. As soon as she entered Blake's room, he swept her into his arms for a long, deep kiss.

With her senses reeling, she leaned back in his arms and gazed at his oh-so-sexy smile. "Are you worried about leaving Duncan alone?"

"He agreed to have his door locked tonight. He'll be safe." He leaned close and kissed the tip of her nose. "Why did you blow the candles out?"

"Fire hazard," she said.

His low chuckle resonated inside his chest. "Safety first."

"I *am* a schoolteacher."

His hands slid down her back and cupped her bottom,

positioning her firmly against him. "It's a good thing that I never had a teacher as pretty as you. I wouldn't have learned a thing."

"I know your type." She reached up to run her fingers through his disheveled hair. "The second-grade boy who gives me love notes and shares half of his candy bar."

"I'm not the first to have a crush on the teacher."

"Actually," she said, "I was hoping there might be something you could teach me."

"About what?"

"You seem to be an expert in here." Boldly, she gestured toward the bed. In these intimate moments with Blake, her normal inhibitions evaporated like dew on a hot summer morning. "Teach me."

He needed no further encouragement. In seconds, he had her on the bed. Stretched out on his sheets, she experienced a crash course in sensuality. His expert touch aroused her in ways she'd never imagined possible. His kisses left her breathless. Gasping, she asked, "How on earth do you do that thing with your tongue?"

"First lesson," he murmured. "Don't analyze."

"But how will I learn if I don't ask questions?"

"Number two." He nibbled below her earlobe. "Accept the experience."

Trembling sensations raised goose bumps on her arms. "How many lessons are there?"

"Only one more." He straddled her thighs, looked directly into her eyes and said, "Enjoy."

"That," she said, "I can do."

Willingly, she gave herself over to a surging tide of pleasure as he fondled and nibbled and caressed. A clever student, she found her own creative ways of giving back to him. When he finally entered her, her level of excitement was such that she felt as if she might expire from an overdose of sheer ecstasy.

Afterward, she lay beside him on the bed, fully satisfied and blissful. The word *love* popped into her mind. Did she love him?

With a shake of her head on his pillow, she chased that idea away. For now, it was more than enough to make love…rather than *being* in love.

Chapter Eighteen

The next morning, Madeline woke early, still sorting out her emotions and wishing it were as easy as pulling petals from a daisy. *I love him…I love him not.* Not an easy decision.

Instead of pondering all the complications of their relationship, she decided it was time to completely erase her guilt about Marty. Talking to Blake had been the hard part. Now she needed to come clean with Alma.

As usual, the housekeeper sat at the kitchen table, already dressed and coiffed with the puffy blond hairdo that hadn't changed in twenty years. Madeline's typical procedure was to start off the day by wiping down the countertops and sweeping crumbs off the floor. Instead, she poured herself a mug of coffee and took the chair opposite Alma. "There's something I need to tell you."

Using the remote, Alma clicked off the small television she'd been watching. "It's about Marty, isn't it?"

She nodded. "He's gotten himself into a lot of trouble back in Boston."

"I saw it on the news. He stole seven hundred thousand dollars' worth of diamonds." She hoisted a penciled eyebrow. "And the loot still hasn't been recovered."

Madeline eyed her curiously. "You knew but you didn't say anything?"

"I didn't want to mess up this thing you've got going with Blake. You turned out okay, Madeline. I'm proud of you. Twenty-three kids passed through my home, and most of them are doing just fine. But you? You're special."

Though Alma's compliment had the ring of sincerity, Madeline didn't quite trust her. "You stay in touch with all your former fosters?"

"I do my best, hon. It doesn't take much to send a Christmas card or an occasional note."

"I remember those notes." Most of which related to a "great new project" that Alma was selling, like mail-order detergent, homemade jewelry or hypoallergenic makeup. Madeline had purchased some of these things, which undoubtedly kept her on Alma's list.

Her former foster mother had a mercenary side and generally put her own self-interest above all other concerns. But she wasn't a bad person.

"I never had any kids of my own." Her brassy voice softened with a sigh. "Sometimes I think that was a big mistake. I like kids."

"Even Duncan?"

"He's a dickens. But he's not mean, and he's got his father's good looks. Duncan can be as cute as a little angel."

Though this was the first time she'd heard Alma say anything nice about Duncan, the housekeeper was always gentle with Blake's son. The only household chore she took seriously was the preparation of Duncan's meals.

Alma continued, "If your fling with Blake goes anywhere, I want you to remember who's responsible for getting you this job."

Not quite ready to say thank you, Madeline asked, "Did you stay in contact with Marty?"

"I always liked your brother. He's a rogue. But such a handsome young man."

"You've seen him? Recently?"

In her fuzzy slippers, Alma shuffled to the coffee machine for a refill. "Marty always had your best interests at heart."

Madeline seriously doubted that. "Why do you think so?"

"Here's the thing. You weren't topmost in my mind when Blake started looking for a tutor. The real reason I got in touch with you was that Marty called me and said that you needed a job."

Her explanation sounded innocent. Perhaps too innocent. "Why didn't you tell me this before?"

"Must have slipped my mind."

Not likely. Alma had a reason for keeping her conversation with Marty a secret. She was covering something up. *Like what? Like his plan to steal the diamonds?*

That had to be the answer. Alma and Marty were working together. "Oh my God, you're his accomplice."

"Don't be silly, Madeline. I was here in Maine when Marty was robbing that safe."

Her statement was as good as a confession. "How do you know when he was committing the robbery?"

"Just guessing." Her shoulders twitched in another shrug.

"How do you know he robbed a safe?"

"Calm down." She returned to the table and sat. "Let's just take it easy, okay?"

Her eyes darted as if searching for a plausible lie, but it

was too late. Madeline already had a pretty good idea of what had happened. "You knew what Marty was planning."

"I tried to talk him out of it. I warned him. Told him that he'd probably get caught. And he did, didn't he?"

Madeline was all too familiar with her brother's machinations and his persuasive skills. "He talked to you because he wanted something. What was it?"

"He asked me to take care of you. He wanted you to get out of town and asked me if I could invite you to stay with me. Since Blake was already looking for a tutor, it seemed like a perfect fit."

"What did you ask for in return? What was your payoff?"

"He promised that he'd make it worth my while. After the heat died down in Boston, he was going to come up here and join us."

"Why?"

Her gaze sharpened. "In the last call I had from Marty, he said the diamonds were with you."

Shocked, Madeline sat back in her chair. "With me?"

"At first, I thought you knew about the jewels, that you were hiding them." Her tongue slid across her lower lip as if tasting the sweetness of promised wealth. "If I found them, I figured that I'd get a reward."

"You searched my things."

"I'm not proud of myself," Alma admitted. "I should have known that you'd never do anything illegal. You've always been a good girl."

"It was you." Incredulous, Madeline glared. "You were the one who kept sneaking into my room and going through my stuff."

"But no harm done. Now that I've explained, we can

forget about it. There's no need to tell Blake." She tried a smile. "Am I right?"

Anger surged through Madeline, driving her to her feet. "What about the basement? Did you lock me and Duncan in the dark basement so you could search?"

"I needed time to go through all your things."

"How could you?"

"I wasn't thinking straight." Alma stood on the opposite side of the table. She was at least six inches shorter than Madeline. "I didn't plan to trap you down there. But when I saw you both go into the basement, I took advantage of the situation."

"I was scared half to death. Duncan could have been traumatized."

Alma spread her small hands, holding out an invisible olive branch. "I'm sorry. Truly, I'm sorry."

"Why should I believe you?"

"I'd never do anything to hurt that little boy. I might not be the best housekeeper in the world. Or the most upright, honest human being. But I like kids. I really do." Once again, her voice muted. "Poor little Duncan. He's had it rough. I want the best for him."

Though still furious, Madeline believed that voice, that tone as soothing as a lullaby. Though Alma pretended to be tough, she liked kids, wished she had some of her own. But that didn't excuse what she'd done. "What about Marty's accomplice? Is there somebody else coming after these jewels that I don't have?"

"No," Alma said simply. "Marty planned the heist by himself. He'd been working construction at the home of these rich people and somehow got the combination to their safe. He was working alone."

"You believe him?"

"Your brother has never lied to me."

Unlike the way he'd treated her. Marty had looked her straight in the eye and told one lie after another. He'd used her to get what he wanted, what he needed.

"There's one lie," Madeline said. "He never gave the jewels to me."

"I guess not." The air went out of her, and she sank back into her chair. "Are you going to tell Blake?"

"I haven't decided," Madeline said. "But I promise you this. From now on, you're washing the dishes and scrubbing the floors. You're going to do the job you were hired for."

Unable to stand being in the kitchen with Alma for one more second, she stalked down the hallway to the front door and went outside. A misty rain was falling. Through the hazy sky, the morning light spread lightly on the treetops and the grassy yard. From the cliff beyond the forest, she heard the echo of the surf pounding against the rocky shore.

Madeline should have been relieved to know that Alma had been the one who pawed through her things when she first arrived at the Manor. No other person had been entering the house through the secret passageway. It was only Alma. A confused and deceptive woman. But not a murderer.

Through the mist, she saw a shadow moving through the trees. A glimpse of darkness.

And Madeline knew the danger was not yet over.

THE RAINY WEATHER meant Blake's construction crew wouldn't be working today, and he was glad for the break.

He needed some creative time for himself to complete the project he'd been working on in the upstairs front bedroom. He stepped back from the wall mural he'd just completed. A damn fine job, if he said so himself.

The four-poster bed was made, and the curtains were hung. Only a few more details needed to be added. Though the bold color in this design scheme didn't match the American Federalist decor in the rest of the house, he knew that Madeline would love this room.

The only other project on his schedule for the day was the photo array, and he was prepared. His former client at Homeland Security had already faxed a mug shot for Joe Curtis and promised to check further into Curtis's background with LAPD.

He and Madeline planned the photo array for midafternoon—about an hour from now. If Duncan was upset by what he saw or what he sensed, they'd have plenty of time to get him calmed down before bed.

As he adjusted the red velvet curtains, Blake looked through the window and saw headlights cutting through the steady rain. A jolt of tension went down his spine. Who the hell was coming here? He had a bad feeling about this unscheduled visitor.

Leaving the bedroom, he went downstairs and opened the door for Perry Wells. Stepping inside, the mayor brushed droplets from the sleeves of his trench coat. He took off his rain hat and dragged his fingers through his salt-and-pepper hair. The man looked like hell. His complexion was pasty white. "That's a nasty little storm," he said. "I trust you're all well."

"The heating system in the Manor leaves a lot to be desired," Blake said. "The furnace is relatively new, but a lot of ducts are clogged, and the windows aren't properly sealed."

"Your renovations will take care of those problems."

"Hope so." He didn't really think Mayor Wells had come here for an update on the progress of the restoration. "What can I do for you, Perry?"

"You mentioned that you might be interested in purchasing a property I own. I'm willing to drop my asking price to expedite the deal."

"But I haven't even looked at the house."

"We could go right now," he offered.

Blake was tempted. His experience in the housing market told him that the best bargains came when the seller was desperate. And that word described everything about Perry. Desperate.

As a businessman, he ought to take advantage. But he'd be a rotten human being if he exploited this man's fear. "Let me take your coat, Perry. We need to talk."

When Blake entered his office, he turned on the over head light. On a sunny day, the windows provided enough illumination to see clearly. Today was gray and murky.

He sat behind his desk. "Tell me why you're so anxious to get rid of this property."

"There's nothing wrong with the house. It's a fine little place." Instead of sitting, he paced behind the chair. "I need to improve my cash flow. Immediately."

"To hire a lawyer?" Blake cut to the chase. There was no point in dancing around the issue. "You'll need an experienced attorney to defend you if you're charged with murder."

"What have you heard?"

"I know the evidence against you is mounting."

He braced both hands on the back of the chair opposite Blake's desk. His fingers clenched, white-knuckled. "The police are at my house right now, executing a search warrant."

"What are they going to find?"

"Documents." He peered at Blake through red-rimmed eyes. "Teddy and I had a business arrangement. He needed political favors, and I complied with his wishes. I'm sure you understand. You're a man of the world, a businessman. Sometimes it's necessary to make a deal with the devil."

"What kind of deal?"

"Rebuilding Raven's Cliff after the hurricane has been expensive. Our coffers ran dry months ago. That's when Teddy Fisher stepped up with a supposedly philanthropic offer to help repair the damages. A supposedly generous offer." His tone was bitter. "In exchange for this philanthropy, he asked me to keep the inspectors away from his lab and to issue necessary permits for the purchase of raw materials. It all seemed innocent enough. Just a matter of expediency."

"Then you learned that Teddy's experiments caused the genetically mutated fish, which, in turn, started the epidemic."

"People died." He circled the chair and sat heavily. "With better oversight, those experiments would never have gone forward. I blame myself. For each and every one of those tragic deaths, I blame myself."

His shoulders bowed under the burden of his guilt. Though the mayor's political skills undoubtedly included the ability to look contrite, he wasn't faking this emotion. His grief was too raw.

Blake almost felt sorry for him. Almost. "Why didn't you expose Teddy?"

"I should have. I'm sorry. So terribly sorry."

It was all too easy for politicians to make their heartfelt apologies and throw themselves on the mercy of public opinion. "Don't look to me for forgiveness," Blake said. "Even after you knew what Teddy was doing, you continued to grant him favors. You worked your political magic and made it possible for him to purchase the Manor and to hire me."

"I stand behind that decision." He straightened in the chair. "Teddy promised to restore the lighthouse. To end the curse."

"Come on, Perry. You're a man of the world. You don't believe in superstitions." Blake was losing sympathy fast. "You couldn't turn Teddy over to the police because it made you look bad. You went along with him to save your own hide."

"That's not the only reason."

Perry's face twisted as if he were in physical pain, but Blake wasn't buying these crocodile tears. The mayor had sold his soul to the devilish Teddy Fisher, and now he was reaping the consequences. "Did you know about the lab Teddy set up in the caves? It's likely he was continuing his experiments."

"I didn't know."

"But maybe you figured it out." Blake sensed that he might be treading on dangerous ground. As he continued to talk, he unlocked his desk. His gun was in the lower left drawer within easy reach. "Maybe you knew exactly what Teddy had in mind, and you couldn't let him do it again. You couldn't let other innocent people die."

Perry rose to his feet. "You've got it all wrong."

"Do I?" Blake eased the lower drawer open. If he needed

the gun it was within reach. "I think you finally realized that the only way you could stop Teddy was to kill him."

Perry slammed his fist down hard on the desktop. "I'm not a murderer. Teddy deserved to die, but I couldn't do it. I couldn't."

"Why not?"

"Camille."

His daughter? What did any of this have to do with his daughter? "She's dead, Perry."

"Her body was never found. Teddy said she'd survived. He knew where she was. If I didn't help him, I'd never see Camille again."

Surprised, Blake jolted back in his chair. He sure as hell hadn't seen this coming. "Did you tell the police?"

"I was afraid." He trembled. "If there was any chance that Camille was still alive…"

Blake doubted that possibility. From what he'd heard, the whole town had witnessed Camille's death. More likely, Teddy had been clever enough to use the one threat that he knew would be effective in tying Perry's hands. His love for his daughter.

From down the hallway, he heard voices and the clamor of footsteps. Detective Lagios entered the study.

After a nod to Blake, he confronted the mayor and said, "Perry Wells, you're under arrest for the murder of Teddy Fisher. You have the right to remain silent…"

Chapter Nineteen

"Rain, rain, go away. Come again another day." Duncan stared through the window in the family room. He wanted to be outside. "Rain, rain, go away…"

"Hey, buddy." His daddy picked him up off his feet and spun around in a circle. "Madeline and I have a new game for you."

"Don't want a new game. I want baseball."

"We can't do that in the house. There's not enough room for the bases."

"Ninety feet from home to first." Duncan shook his head. "Not enough room."

Daddy set him down, and they went to the table where he did art projects. This morning, he'd drawn a picture of a baseball diamond and his new friend Annie. She was funny. Some of the other kids called her Annie Banana, but he didn't.

"Here's what I want you to do," Daddy said. "I want you to try to remember the man who grabbed you on the cliff."

"Geez Louise." He slapped his forehead the way he'd seen kids do at T-ball. "I told you before, Daddy. I didn't see his face."

"I know. But maybe if we show you some pictures, you'll remember."

"How many pictures?"

"Seven," Madeline said. "You take a look, then tell us if you remember anything. Let's start with this one."

She set a picture down on the table.

"That's Coach Grant." He whisked the picture off the table onto the floor. "Ready for number two."

Two, three and four were men he had seen. But they didn't mean anything. He shoved their pictures away. Number five was different. He looked real close with his nose right down by the paper. "This man came to our house today. And he left with the policeman."

He shoved the picture aside, but his Daddy put it back in front of him. "I want you to pay attention, Duncan. Is this the man from the cliff?"

"No." This game was dumb. He didn't want to play anymore. "Number six. Number six."

Madeline slid another piece of paper onto the table. It was only a picture. But kind of scary. He didn't want to touch it. "He's a fisherman."

His face was not very nice. He looked dirty. At the same time, he made Duncan think about Temperance. She could tell him if this man meant danger. Under his breath, he hummed, "She sells seashells by the…"

"Duncan?" Daddy touched his arm. "Is this the man?"

"No, no, no." With the tip of his finger, he pushed the picture away. "Number seven."

A mean face stared up at him from the table. "A bad man. He's very bad."

"Is he the one?"

In the back of his head, he heard a loud thud. A hammer. "He hurts people. Sharks eat little kids. Don't go near the seashore."

He saw big waves splash on the rocks. *Danger.* He needed to get away.

"It's okay, buddy." Daddy patted his back. "Did this man grab you?"

"Upstairs." He nodded. "In my bedroom."

Danger. He jumped off his chair and ran toward the kitchen. Alma was standing in front of him. He ran right into her.

She held him so he wouldn't fall down. She hugged him, and he felt warm inside. She didn't say anything, but he knew what she was thinking.

He patted her cheek. "I can't be your little boy, Alma. I already have a mommy."

"I know."

He liked her puffy hair. "We can be friends."

"I'd like that, Duncan." He stepped away from her and turned around. Daddy was right behind him. "We're all friends."

"You did good," Daddy said.

Duncan raised his hand. "High five."

There was only one person in this room who he hadn't hugged. Madeline. He could tell that she felt left out, and that made him sad.

He marched over to her, and she squatted down so her eyes were even with his. Pretty eyes.

He kissed her forehead above her glasses. She smelled like flowers. "I like you best of all."

"Thank you, Duncan."

He hugged her for a long time. She was cozy. They would be friends forever and ever and ever and ever.

But he felt something else. A shiver. He stepped back. "You must be very careful."

"I will."

"Danger, Madeline. Danger."

LATER THAT NIGHT while Blake was putting Duncan to bed, Madeline sat behind his desk in his studio. She still felt a pleasant glow from when Duncan had hugged her. His sweet little kiss on her forehead ranked as one of the most precious moments in her life. She had been waiting for such a long time for him to allow her to touch him and cuddle him. Now, she truly felt like a member of the family.

Yet, Duncan's warning about danger wasn't a message she wanted to hear. Flipping through their collection of mug shots, she tried to decide which of these men presented a threat. Duncan hadn't sensed any danger from his T-ball coach. He'd paused on the photo of Perry Wells. Something about Perry worried him but didn't frighten him.

The next photo was Lucy's boyfriend, Alex Gibson—a handsome, rugged man. When Duncan had looked at his face, he seemed disturbed then started humming the seashell song. In a way, that made sense because Alex was a fisherman. At the T-ball game, Alex had argued with Helen Fisher. He wanted the lighthouse to be rebuilt so the curse would be ended. A superstitious man. But was he dangerous?

Certainly not as scary as Joe Curtis. Duncan's negative reaction to the cop was unmistakably clear. Perhaps Curtis hadn't touched the boy when he stood on the cliffs, but he seemed to represent the greatest danger. She hadn't seen him since she'd warned him off with a bluff. Was that enough to keep him away from the Manor?

When Blake entered the studio, he came around the

desk and lightly kissed her cheek. "Let's go upstairs. I have something to show you."

A combination of instinct and passion told her to follow him up the stairs to the bedroom. To follow anywhere he wanted to go. But she couldn't let go of her suspicions. Holding up the photo of Curtis, she said, "This is the bad guy. Duncan thought so."

"Duncan didn't directly identify Curtis as the man who grabbed him." He unfastened the clip holding her hair up in a high ponytail. Her thick, heavy curls cascaded around her shoulders. "Let it go, Madeline. There's nothing we can do."

She looked away from him, remembering the big, muscle-bound cop aiming at her with his cocked finger. "I can't forget. He's dangerous."

"But he's not the one under arrest." He pulled out the photo of Perry Wells. "Duncan might have a psychic feeling. And you might have a hunch. But Lagios needed evidence to take the mayor into custody."

"What kind of evidence?" she asked.

"He practically confessed to me, and there are other people he could have talked to. Plus, there are the facts— Perry admitted to being the last person to see Teddy alive. The police found incriminating papers at his house."

What if the police were wrong? It wouldn't be the first time an innocent man had been accused of murder. "Wasn't your Homeland Security contact going to send you more information about Curtis?"

He went around the desk to the fax machine near the door and picked up a single sheet of paper. For a moment, Blake read in silence. "Damn."

"What is it?"

"The photograph of Joe Curtis on file with the Raven's

Cliff police department doesn't match the records from the LAPD. He faked his credentials."

Though wary, she asked, "Who is he?"

"My contact at Homeland Security ran his real photo through a system designed to recognize facial features. He found a match with a man who's on the official terrorist watch list. He works for an organization called the GFF, Global Freedom Front." When he met her gaze, his jaw was tense. "The man we know as Joe Curtis is an assassin."

Icy dread shivered down her spine as she thought of an assassin walking among them, passing as a policeman, someone to be trusted and accepted. A perfect disguise. "What should we do?"

"It's out of our hands. Homeland Security already got in touch with the local cops. And they're sending federal agents." He reached for the phone. "I'm calling Lagios."

She fidgeted behind the desk while Blake made his phone call. A professional assassin? It didn't make sense. What was a terrorist doing in Raven's Cliff? What could possibly have drawn him to this quiet little fishing village? Madeline was fairly sure that he didn't come here for the ambience or the trinkets.

Blake hung up the phone and turned to her. From his worried expression, she deduced that he didn't have good news. "Curtis is still at large."

"Maybe he's making a run for it," she said hopefully. "I hope he's running fast and far away from us."

"For now, Lagios is keeping his identity a secret, hoping they can find him before he bolts."

"So Curtis doesn't know the police are after him."

"Not yet."

"What if he comes here?"

Blake nodded. "I mentioned that possibility to Lagios, and he promised to send a couple of cops out here to keep an eye on things."

She shook her head. "I can't believe this is happening."

"It's all under control."

As she leaned her cheek against his shoulder, Madeline did her best to believe him. The danger would pass, and they'd be free from fear. Soon, she hoped. "Why would a terrorist come to Raven's Cliff?"

"Fisher Labs," he murmured. "That seems to be the only link with this little town and the wider world. Fisher Labs and Teddy's research."

"That formula he created."

"A nutrient that mutated the fish and caused an epidemic," Blake said. "In the hands of terrorists, Teddy's formula could cause a global outbreak."

That outcome was too horrifying to imagine. Though she nuzzled more tightly in his arms, her stomach plummeted. "It feels like I'm on a roller coaster. Every time I start feeling happy, I go into a tailspin."

"Come upstairs with me, Madeline. I have something to show you that will make you feel better."

The only thing to soothe her jangled nerves would be to see Joe Curtis being dragged off in handcuffs. But she appreciated Blake's effort.

At the top of the staircase, he led her past Duncan's room where the door was carefully locked. He stopped outside the forbidden room where he'd been working for the past couple of days.

"Your secret project," she said.

"Curious?"

"A bit."

He pushed open the door and turned on the light. "I call it the Madeline Room."

The red velvet curtains were the first thing to catch her eye. Then the antique white four-poster, also with red bedcovers. "It's red, like my dress."

"Scarlet is your color."

Beneath the crown moldings, an incredible mural decorated the wall nearest the closet. The style matched the other formal landscape paintings in the house, paying great attention to detail. But the colors for this painting were vivid—the strong blues and greens of a forest splashed with brilliant yellow and purple wildflowers. In their midst stood a woman in a crimson dress with long black hair flowing down her back. "Is that me?"

"It's why I call it the Madeline Room."

"You painted this?"

He shrugged. "I studied art before I got into architecture."

The breadth of his talent awed and amazed her. Reaching toward the wall, she traced the branches of the trees and each petal of the flowers. His painting made her feel as beautiful as a work of art. "This is the best present anyone has ever given me."

Stepping up behind her, he wrapped his arms around her waist. "Nothing I give you could ever equal what you've done for me. And for Duncan."

She rested in his embrace, almost forgetting the danger that swirled around them. An assassin. A terrorist. She hoped their police guards would get here soon.

Turning, she kissed his cheek and smiled. "Much as I adore being in your arms, I want to take a closer look at the Madeline Room."

Slowly, she paced around the perimeter, exploring the

exquisite details. All of the furniture was antique white, painted with a delicate primrose pattern that looked charmingly old-fashioned and very familiar.

"My ficus." She recognized the design. "This is the same design that's on the pot holding my ficus."

"Your family heirloom."

"Not that it's worth anything, but it's special to me. Let's bring it in here."

"My thought exactly."

They hurried down the hall, treading quietly so they wouldn't wake Duncan. Blake lifted the plant in its pretty container and carried it.

Anxious to see this finishing touch, she crowded through the door beside him. She bumped his elbow. He tripped. Before either of them could catch their balance, the urn holding the ficus crashed to the floor.

The primrose pottery broke into shards.

She knelt and picked one up. "It's lucky you painted a duplicate so I won't forget what this looked like."

"Sorry," he said. "This urn was important to you."

"A reminder of the past." Her regrets were minimal. The time had come to forget about her childhood in foster care—to break with her lingering sadness and repression. "I'd rather think about the future."

Picking through the shards and dirt, Blake found a zippered satchel. "What's this?"

"I have no idea."

He unfastened the zipper and poured a glittering array of cut diamonds into his hand. The sparkle took her breath away. Seven hundred thousand dollars' worth of jewels.

Marty must have stashed them in the pot, knowing that she'd never leave it behind.

When she reached toward the shimmering jewels, Blake pulled his hand back. His hazel eyes darkened with rage. "How could you do this to me? To Duncan?"

"Do what?"

"I trusted you. I accepted your teary-eyed confession about how your black-sheep brother used you."

"It was the truth."

"I'm not naive, Madeline. I can see what you are. Your brother's accomplice. You came here to hide out from the Boston police."

Shocked by his accusation, she sat back on her heels. "I knew nothing about this."

"You showed up here with nothing but your clothes, a couple of boxes and this ficus. Don't expect me to believe that was a coincidence."

"I didn't know. Really, Blake. Marty told Alma that the jewels were with me, but I had no—"

"Alma was in on this?"

He stood abruptly. His passion for her had turned to cold rage—the same outraged, overprotective fury she'd seen in him when she first arrived at the Manor. From experience, she knew there was no reasoning with him when he was in this mood. "Think what you want."

"I'll be turning this loot over to the police as soon as they get here. You might want to work on your story."

Unfolding herself from the floor, she stood tall. "I'll tell the truth."

"That your brother stole the jewels and they just happened to end up in your possession?" He scoffed. "I want you out of here. Tomorrow morning. And Alma, too."

He strode from the room, leaving her alone.

How could he be so quick to judge? Yes, the circumstances looked bad, but he ought to know by now that she wasn't a bad person.

A sob caught in her throat as she looked at the mural he'd painted for her. Another dip on the emotional roller coaster. With Blake, she experienced the highest highs and the most abject lows.

She trudged down the hall to her bedroom and closed the door. Pain washed over her. And remorse. Even though she hadn't done anything wrong, she felt guilty.

Perhaps it was better to find out now that his affections were fickle. A simple twist of fate had transformed Blake from a romantic lover into a tyrant. How could she have ever thought she was in love with him?

Then she heard the tap on her door.

He'd changed his mind.

He was coming to apologize.

She threw open the door. A cloth covered her mouth. She couldn't breathe. Everything went black.

Chapter Twenty

Behind the closed door of his studio office, Blakc stared through the window into the night. Raindrops rattled against the windowpanes in a furious staccato. How could he have been so wrong about Madeline? He had believed her, trusted her. Maybe even loved her.

And she had used him. Used his home as a hideout. Everything about her was a lie. Her sweetness. Her common sense. Her passion. All lies.

Anger surged through him. How could she have done this to him? He'd opened his heart to Madeline. For the first time since Kathleen's death, he felt like there was a reason to get out of bed in the morning. With Madeline, he'd found hope—a reason to start looking forward instead of living in the past. She'd changed him…and betrayed him.

How could she have done this to Duncan? His son would be brokenhearted when she left. Somehow, Blake had to find a way to explain to Duncan that his beloved teacher was nothing but a thief, a criminal. It didn't seem possible.

But it was true.

Returning to his desk, he unzipped the pouch and spilled the diamonds across the surface. Here was proof, undeniable proof.

Where the hell were those cops Lagios promised to send? As soon as they got here, Blake intended to turn over the diamonds and point them toward Madeline. They could take her into custody, ship her back to Boston. She'd get what she deserved.

Pain cut through his anger. How could he do this to her? How could he stand by and watch while she was arrested, marched off in handcuffs? Not Madeline. Not the woman he loved. He wanted to shelter and protect her, wanted a future with her.

That hope was dead.

He gathered the gems in his hand. As he closed his fist, a strange heat shot up his arm, igniting a stream of fire that pulsed through his veins and arteries. He was consumed by sensation. Inside his rib cage, his heart pounded. Each heavy beat echoed louder than the last.

What was happening to him? He had to fight. Be strong. But he couldn't resist.

His knees folded and he dropped into his desk chair, too weak to stand. The room began to whirl. The light from his desk lamp blurred into jagged lightning bolts outside the window. Spinning faster and faster, he couldn't breathe.

He closed his eyes. Everything went still, as if he'd entered the eye of a hurricane. He was floating, detached, unaware of bodily sensation.

Behind his eyelids, he saw a scene being played out. It was unreal, dreamlike. Yet every detail came through with crystal clarity. A clock on the wall. A purse on the table. Madeline's purse. A man he didn't recognize held the pouch. As if from far away, he heard Madeline's voice. "Marty, is that you?"

The stranger replied, "Be right there, sis."

He dug into the dirt beside the ficus, buried the pouch. Blake could hear his thoughts. *She'll never leave this pot behind. I'll get the stones later.*

In a jolt, Blake returned to his studio. Everything was exactly as it had been. The rain still slashed at the window. The desk lamp shone on the gems.

There was no rational explanation for what had just occurred, but he knew that he had seen the truth. He'd seen the past. Marty had hidden the gems without telling Madeline.

Blake had experienced a vision. The realization stunned him. Just like his son, he'd been thrown into an altered state of consciousness. All these years, he'd denied the possibility of psychic awareness. He hadn't understood why Duncan wore gloves to ward off these feelings.

Now he knew. He and his son were alike. Hypersensitive. They saw things that other people didn't know about.

Slowly, Blake rose from his chair. His legs were still weak, but his heartbeat had steadied. His breathing was normal. He felt a lightness—a purity of thought he'd never known.

Madeline was innocent. She'd been duped by her conniving brother.

Blake never should have doubted her, should have trusted the inherent instinct that told him she was a good person, worthy of trust, worthy of love.

At the edge of his desk, he saw the barrette she used to clip her hair into a high ponytail. Earlier tonight, he'd unfastened the tortoiseshell barrette, allowing her curly black hair to cascade. *I'm sorry, Madeline.*

He picked it up. In an instant, his head was spinning. Another vision crashed into his mind.

He felt her terror. She was unable to move. Her wrists and ankles were bound with rope.

Through her eyes, he saw the dark walls of the cave.

Through her ears, he heard the roaring surf.

A necklace of shells lay on the sand beside her.

She had only minutes left before that necklace was placed around her neck and tightened, choking off her breath.

LYING ON her back on the cold wet sand, Madeline blinked slowly. The insides of her eyelids felt scratchy and crusted as if she'd been crying for days. She could barely see. Her glasses were gone. But she knew where she was. The caves. She could smell the ocean and hear the waves. Must be close to the mouth of the cave.

Another blink. Her vision cleared. The dim light of an electric torch glowed against the stone walls.

How had she gotten here? She struggled to sit up but couldn't. *I can't move.* Her lungs ached as if a huge, heavy hand pressed down upon her chest.

Concentrating, she tried to lift her arm. Only a slight twitch. Looking down, she saw that her wrists were tied together. She had to get up. Had to get away.

Another effort. Nothing. She was paralyzed.

"You're awake."

The face of Joe Curtis swam into focus. She struggled to speak but could only manage a groan.

"It would have been better," he said, "if you'd stayed unconscious."

Why? What was he going to do?

"When they autopsy your body, they'll find the same

mix of drugs that were in the other victims. I've got all the details right." His heavy shoulders shrugged. A casual gesture. "That's the good thing about using a cop's identity. I know the details of the Seaside Strangler's procedure. There's no way I'll be blamed for this murder."

He didn't know his cover had been blown. He didn't know that Lagios and the rest of the Raven's Cliff police force were searching for him.

If she'd been able to speak, she could have told him. There was no need to murder her. His time would be better spent running away.

He unfastened the rope binding her ankles. "I knew you were bluffing about being psychic. But that kid? When he looked at me, it was like he saw inside. I can't take the chance that he told you. Did he?"

He looked into her eyes. There was no way she could respond.

"Doesn't matter," he said. "After you're out of the way, it won't be hard to get to the kid. Maybe he'll have a tragic fall from the cliffs."

Desperately, she tried to shake her head, to signal to Curtis that he didn't need to go after Duncan.

She managed a tiny movement. The resulting pain caused her to wince. It was as though her entire body had fallen asleep. She had to wake up.

He stood, looming over her. "Your legs are untied. Go ahead. Try to run."

She exerted a fierce effort. Couldn't move. Not an inch. Her toes tingled painfully, like a thousand needles being stabbed into her feet.

Sensation was returning to her body. If she could feel, she could move. And she had to get away, had to protect Duncan.

"Nothing personal," Curtis said as he untied her hands. "But I have to strip you. The Strangler dresses his victims in white. Like virgins. That's not you. Is it, Madeline?"

She tried to protest but could only make an unintelligible noise.

"I know about you and Blake," he said. "I've been keeping an eye on the Manor. It's easy to slip in and out through an unlocked window. Tonight, I went through that secret passage. Pretty nifty."

He unbuttoned her shirt.

Hoping to distract him, she managed to blurt a single word. "Teddy."

"You want to know if I killed Teddy?" Roughly, he pushed the fabric off her shoulders. "Hell, yes. The little traitor deserved to die. He was supposed to be manufacturing that fish nutrient, the one that caused the epidemic. Hell of a thing, huh? That prissy little scientist was trying to cure world hunger. Instead, he came up with an efficient weapon for biological warfare. In the right hands—our hands—that weapon can control the world."

As he lifted her torso and took off her shirt, the prickling beneath her skin became an aching throb. A shudder went through her.

He dropped her back onto the sand. There was nothing sexual about the way he removed her clothing. Stripping her was just part of his job.

"Assassin," she said.

He eyed her curiously. "Did you say assassin?"

She blinked her eyes as if to nod.

"You're wrong about that, lady. I believe in what I'm doing. I'm a soldier for the cause."

Madeline knew she'd struck a chord. Forcing the breath through her lips, she repeated the word. "Assassin."

"You don't get it. The people I work for paid hundreds of thousands of dollars to Teddy Fisher. He was supposed to deliver. All of a sudden, he grew a conscience. He didn't want us to poison the world's food supply. Not that we were going to kill everybody."

"Why?"

"Some populations would have to go. Those who are a drain on the world's resources. The poor. The sick." Another shrug. "For most of those people, death is a welcome cure."

In his voice, she heard the insane logic of a fanatic. Joe Curtis was a true believer. What was the name of his group? Global Freedom Front. GFF.

"When I saw that Teddy had destroyed every speck of the nutrient, I tried to get him to tell me the formula, tried to beat it out of him with a hammer. He wouldn't talk."

In the end, she thought, Teddy Fisher had been a hero. He'd stood up to Joe Curtis. And he'd died in the effort.

She couldn't allow that same fate to befall her. She had to find the strength to move.

Efficiently, Curtis unbuttoned her jeans and tugged the wet fabric down her legs.

Sprawled on the sand in her bra and panties, she'd never been more vulnerable. Or more determined. She wasn't going to die. Not here. Not now.

She had to survive. All her life, she'd kept quiet, never stood up for herself. She hid behind her glasses, faded into the background like a quiet little wallflower. Not anymore. She was a woman who could wear a red dress. A fighter.

She wouldn't give up. *It's not my time to die.* She had

to live, to convince Blake of her innocence. She would have a life with him. And with Duncan.

Clumsily, Curtis pulled the flowing white gown over her head and down her body. The muscles in her shoulder tightened.

With every second that passed, she grew stronger. Her hand flexed. She made a fist.

ON THE BEACH, Blake saw the glow from the mouth of the cave. He knew Madeline was in there. *He knew.* His senses were heightened as never before.

Though he could have waited until the cops arrived, he didn't have that much time. He'd grabbed his handgun, told Alma where he was headed and instructed her to send the reinforcements in this direction.

The rush of the surf against the rocky shore covered the sound of his footsteps as he approached. A small dinghy had been pulled onto the sand. A garland of flowers draped across the bow. A signature of the Seaside Strangler.

His heart wrenched when he saw Madeline lying on the sand in a white dress. The huge form of Joe Curtis leaned over her. He placed the seashell necklace around her throat.

No time left. Blake stepped around the edge of the cave and aimed his gun. He was only ten feet away from them. "Back off."

Curtis looked up. "Come to rescue your girlfriend?"

"Get away from her. I'll shoot."

"Here's your problem," Curtis said. "I could snap her neck in one second."

Not as fast as a bullet. Blake aimed at the center of his

chest. A massive target. "Give it up, Curtis. The cops are on the way. They know all about you and the GFF."

"What?"

"Information from Homeland Security. They identified you from the terrorist watch list."

Curtis stood. He yanked Madeline's limp body in front of him, using her as a shield. There was no chance for Blake to get a clear shot; he couldn't take the chance of hitting Madeline.

Curtis pulled his own gun. Before he could take aim, Madeline reacted. Her arm flung wildly. She stabbed at the big man's face, clawed his eyes.

With a cry, Curtis dropped her.

Blake fired. Three shots in rapid succession. At least two were direct hits.

Curtis staggered backward but didn't go down. He lowered his gun, aimed at Madeline.

Blake lunged. Before Curtis could pull the trigger, he tackled the big man and they both went down. Blood poured from the wounds in his chest, soaking them both.

Blake grabbed for his arm, slammed his wrist against the rocks. Curtis dropped the gun. For an instant, he lay still, and Blake thought he'd won.

Then Curtis surged to his feet. He threw Blake off him and staggered toward the dinghy. With the strength of a wounded beast, he shoved the boat into the surf. The waves churned against his calves.

Blake didn't give a damn if he got away. As long as Madeline was safe, he didn't care.

Curtis whirled. From inside his jacket, he pulled another gun. His huge hand shook as he took aim.

From behind his back, Blake heard a shot. Then another.

Curtis fell.

Blake turned and saw Madeline with his gun in her hand. Unsteady on her feet, she wavered.

He ran to her, enclosed her in his arms. She was ice-cold, nearly frozen. All the strength left her body as she collapsed against him.

From down the beach, he heard the police arriving.

"You're going to be all right," he said, as much to reassure himself as her. "It's over."

She murmured, "How did you find me?"

"I saw what was happening. It was a vision. Like Duncan has."

One corner of her mouth twitched as if she was trying to smile. "Runs in the family."

They were all a little bit psychic, a little bit crazy. "I had another vision about you and Marty and the diamonds. I know you were telling me the truth. I never should have doubted you."

Her luminous eyes gazed into his face. Her wet hair streamed across her forehead. The murderous shell necklace encircled her slender throat, a reminder of how close he'd come to losing her forever. "I love you, Madeline."

Her lips moved. She struggled to speak.

"Does this mean…" she gasped for breath "…that I'm not fired?"

She would never leave his side again. Madeline was the woman he meant to spend the rest of his life with.

SEVERAL DAYS LATER, Madeline stood in the yard outside the Manor and kept an eye on Duncan, who practiced hitting balls off the tee. His friend Annie would be here any minute for a playdate.

When Duncan connected with the ball for a solid hit, she waved to him and called out, "Good one."

Sunlight glittered on the huge sapphire in her engagement ring. The stone was spectacular, as blue as the sea. After Marty's crime, it didn't seem right to have a diamond. Poor Marty! After she'd turned in the stolen gems to the police and Alma gave her statement, he couldn't deny his guilt. With good behavior, he might be paroled from prison in eight years.

Though Alma had been charged for withholding evidence, she got off with a fine and probation, partly because both Blake and Madeline had testified as character witnesses. Alma was still with them in Raven's Cliff, doing her job as a housekeeper with renewed commitment.

Blake came through the front door and joined her. His arm fit so neatly around her waist. His kiss on her cheek was sweet and sexy at the same time.

"I just got off the phone with Perry Wells," he said.

Though Perry had been acquitted of murder charges when Joe Curtis had confessed to killing Teddy Fisher, the scandals hadn't gone away. Perry resigned his office in disgrace because of the sleazy agreements he'd made with Teddy. The only point that the good people of Raven's Cliff agreed upon was for renovations on Beacon Manor and the lighthouse to continue, using the money Teddy left in escrow.

"How's Perry?" she asked.

"Desperate for cash. He reduced the price on that house he owns. He wants to sell for about half of what it's worth."

"I like the house." More specifically, she liked the idea of having a residence in Raven's Cliff—a place they could always come back to after Blake's assignments took them to more exotic locales. "But it would be wrong to take advantage of Perry's distress."

He gave her a squeeze. "Don't worry, I'm not going to cheat anybody. Even though it would be a solid fiscal move."

"Good business," she said. "Bad karma."

"He started babbling about how there's a new lead on his daughter. He still thinks Camille is alive."

"Could be. After she blew off the cliff, her body was never found." Glancing toward the yard, she saw Duncan marching toward the trees.

"Hey, buddy," his father called out. "Don't go far."

"Okay." Duncan waved. "Only to the trees and back."

Blake whispered in her ear, "While Duncan is busy with his little friend, we could have a playdate of our own."

Delighted, she whispered back, "I'll meet you in the Madeline Room."

"Wear your red dress."

And nothing else but a lacy thong and a sapphire engagement ring. She grinned. Every day with Blake was a playdate.

Duncan looked back over his shoulder. Daddy was right next to Madeline, hugging her. He was always hugging her and kissing her. They were in love.

Duncan was glad. He liked Madeline.

Counting every step, he walked across the grass to the trees. Real quiet, he said, "She sells seashells."

"Here I am," Temperance said.

"I have another friend," he said. "I don't want you to be jealous. Her name is Annie."

"Very well," she said. "If ever you wish to speak with me, I shall be here."

He had a question for her. The big scary man with hammer hands was gone, but Duncan knew he wasn't the person who'd grabbed his shoulder on the cliff. "Is there more danger?"

"Not for you. Not for the moment."

"Who was the man on the cliff?"

She rolled her eyes. "I told you before. Nicholas Sterling, the lighthouse keeper's grandson. And he never meant to hurt you. He was pulling you away from the edge."

"But everybody says Nicholas Sterling is dead."

"Is he?"

He heard a car honk and heard it pull up in the driveway. Annie hopped out. He waved to her, then turned back. "Goodbye, Temperance."

She was already gone.

* * * * *

The danger still lurks in this quaint fishing village.
Next month, Elle James presents
Under Suspicion, With Child
THE CURSE OF RAVEN'S CLIFF
continues, only in Mills & Boon® Intrigue.

Mills & Boon® Intrigue
brings you a sneak preview of…

Marie Ferrarella's Secret Agent Affair

CIA agent Kane Donnelly thinks posing as an orderly to monitor rumours of terrorist activity will be easy. Then he runs into Dr Maria Pulaski, the woman who saved his life only days prior. As the investigation progresses he finds himself entangled with the feisty resident, risking his heart – and possibly his mission.

Don't miss this thrilling new story available next month in Mills & Boon® Intrigue.

Secret Agent Affair
by
Marie Ferrarella

She knew better.

Of all people, Dr. Marja Pulaski knew to be alert when she was sitting behind the wheel of a moving vehicle.

It really didn't matter that the vehicle in question, a car she shared with her sister, Tania, was going at a pace that, in comparison, would have made the tortoise of "the Tortoise and the Hare" fame change his name to Lightning. A car was a dangerous weapon, an accident waiting to happen unless it was parked in a garage.

Hadn't she seen more than her share of auto accident victims in the E.R.? Marja was well versed in the kind of damage just the barest distraction could render.

Her excuse, that she'd just come off a grueling double shift at Patience Memorial Hospital, wouldn't have held water with her if someone else had offered it. And everyone knew that the cheerful, outgoing Dr. Marja Pulaski, the youngest of the five Pulaski physicians, was harder on herself than she was on anyone else.

Other than being somewhat vulnerable and all too human, there was no real reason for Marja to have glanced over at the radio just as one of her favorite songs came on. Looking at the radio hadn't made the volume louder, or crisper. And it certainly wouldn't restart the song. It was just an automatic reflex on her part.

The song had been hers and Jack's. Before Jack had decided that he was just too young to settle down, especially with a woman who'd let him know that, although she loved him, she wasn't going to make him the center of her universe.

Trouble was, for a while, Jack *had* been the center of her universe—until she'd forced herself to take stock of the situation and pull back. Pull back and refocus. Being a doctor was not something she knew she could take lightly, especially not after all the effort that had been put forth to get her to that point.

Her parents were naturalized citizens. Both had risked their lives to come to the United States from their native country of Poland. At the time, it was still bowed beneath communist domination. They'd come so that their future children could grow up free to be whatever they wanted to be.

Once those children began coming—five girls in all—the goal of having them all become doctors had somehow materialized. Her father, Josef, and her mother, Magda, worked hard to put their firstborn through medical school. Once Sasha graduated, any money she could spare went toward helping Natalya become a doctor. Natalya, in turn, helped Kady, who then helped Tania. And it all culminated in everyone working together so that she, Marja, could follow in the firm footsteps that her sisters had laid down before her.

She didn't do it because this was the way things were, she did it because, like her sisters before her, she really *wanted* to become a physician. Looking back, Marja couldn't remember a day when she *hadn't* wanted to be a doctor.

But there were moments, like tonight, that got the better of her. She'd spent her time trying to put together the broken pieces of two young souls, barely into their permanent teeth, who'd decided to wipe one another out because one had stepped onto the other one's territory.

So when the song came on, reminding her of more carefree times, she let the memories take over and momentarily distract her.

Just long enough to glance away.

Just long enough to hit whoever she hit.

The weary smile on her lips vanished instantly as the realization of what had just happened broke through. The sickening thud resounded in the August night, causing the pit of her stomach to tighten into a huge, unmanageable knot and making her soul recoil in horror. Perspiration popped out all over her brow, all but pasting her golden-brown hair against her forehead—not because the night air was so damp and clammy with humidity but because the flash of fear had made her sweat.

Her vow, to first do no harm, exploded in her head,

mocking her even before Marja brought the vehicle to a jarring stop, threw open her door and sprang out of her car.

She worked in the city that boasted never to sleep, but at two o'clock in the morning, the number of Manhattan residents milling about on any given block had considerably diminished. When she'd turned down the side street, determined to make better time getting back to the apartment she shared with Tania, her last remaining unmarried sister, there hadn't been a soul in view. Just a few trash cans pockmarking the darkened area and one lone Dumpster in the middle of the block.

You are knowing better than to go down streets like that.

Marja could all but hear her father's heavily Polish-encrusted voice gently reprimanding her. He'd been on the police force over twenty-eight years when he finally retired, much to her mother's relief. Now he was the head of a security company that had once belonged to his best friend and was no less vigilant when it came to the female members of his family.

He was especially so with her because she was the last of his daughters—through no fault of her own, she often pointed out. He always ignored the comment, saying that the fact remained that she was the youngest and as such, in need of guidance. Stubborn mules had nothing on her father.

Marja's legs felt as if they were made out of rubber and her heart pounded harder than a marching band as she rounded her vehicle. She hoped against hope that her ears were playing tricks on her. That the thud she'd both heard and—she swore—felt along every inch of her body was all just a trick being played by her over-tired imagination.

But the moment she approached the front of her car, she knew it wasn't her imagination. Her imagination didn't use the kind of words she heard emerging from just before the front of the grille.

And then the next second, she saw him.

He was lying on the ground. A blond, lean, wiry man wearing a work shirt rolled up at the sleeves and exposing forearms that could have been carved out of granite they looked so hard. The work shirt was unbuttoned. Beneath it was a black T-shirt, adhering to more muscles.

Had the man's shirt and pants been as dark as his T-shirt, she might have missed it. But they weren't. They were both light-colored. Which was how she was able to see the blood.

What had she done?

"Oh God, I'm so sorry," Marja cried, horrified as she crouched down to the man's level to take a closer look. "I didn't see you." The words sounded so lame to her ears.

The man responded with an unintelligible growl and at first she thought he was speaking to her in another language. New York City was every bit as much of a melting pot now as it had been a century ago. The only difference was that now there were different countries sending over their tired, their poor, their huddled masses yearning to be free.

But the next moment she realized that the man spoke English, just growled the words at a lowered decibel. Maybe he was trying to mask the real words out of politeness.

No, she decided in the next moment, he didn't look like the type to tiptoe around that way.

"Are you hurt?"

It was a rhetorical question, but she was flustered. Her parents thought of her as the flighty one, but that description only applied to her social life—post-Jack. Professionally, Marja was completely serious, completely dedicated. She needed one to balance out the other.

"Of course you're hurt," she chided herself for the thoughtless question. "Can you stand?" she asked. Marja held her breath as she waited hopefully for a positive answer.

Rather than reply, the bleeding stranger continued glaring at her. She could almost feel the steely, angry green gaze, as if it were physical.

It wasn't bad enough that he'd just been shot, Kane Donnelly thought. Now they were trying to finish him off with a car.

At least, that was what he'd thought when his body had felt the initial impact of the vehicle's grille against his torso, knocking him down. But now, one look at the woman's face and the sound of her breathless voice told him that she wasn't part of the little scenario that had sent him sprinting down dark alleys, holding on to his wounded side with one hand, his gun with the other.

Damn it, he was supposed to be more on top of his game than this.

Aggie breathed, taken with the creamy yellow stone and the perfectly proportioned leaded windows.

'Sorry?' Luiz wondered whether they were looking at the same building.

'I would rather not be here with *you*,' Aggie emphasised, 'but it's beautiful. Especially with the snow on the ground and on the roof... Gosh, the snow is really deep as well!'

On that tantalising statement she flung open the car door and stepped outside, holding her arms out wide and her head tilted up so that the snow could fall directly onto her face.

In the act of reaching behind him to extract their cases, Luiz paused to stare at her. She had pulled some fingerless gloves out of her coat pocket and stuck them on, and standing like that, arms outstretched, she looked young and vulnerable and achingly innocent—like a child reacting to the thrill of being out in the snow.

What she looks like, he told himself, breaking the momentary spell to get their bags, *is beside the point*. He had a job to do, and he had no intention of having his attention diverted—least of all by a wo..... .... gold-digging intentions he had.....

Cathy Williams is originally from Trinidad, but has lived in England for a number of years. She currently has a house in Warwickshire, which she shares with her husband Richard, her three daughters, Charlotte, Olivia and Emma, and their pet cat, Salem. She adores writing romantic fiction, and would love one of her girls to become a writer—although at the moment she is happy enough if they do their homework and agree not to bicker with one another!

Recent titles by the same author:

THE GIRL HE'D OVERLOOKED
THE TRUTH BEHIND HIS TOUCH
THE SECRET SINCLAIR
HER IMPOSSIBLE BOSS

A TEMPESTUOUS TEMPTATION

BY
CATHY WILLIAMS

First published in Great Britain 2012
by Mills & Boon, an imprint of Harlequin (UK) Limited.
Harlequin (UK) Limited, Eton House, 18-24 Paradise Road,
Richmond, Surrey TW9 1SR

© Cathy Williams 2012

ISBN: 978 0 263 89127 0

Harlequin (UK) policy is to use papers that are natural, renewable and recyclable products and made from wood grown in sustainable forests. The logging and manufacturing process conform to the legal environmental regulations of the country of origin.

Printed and bound in Spain
by Blackprint CPI, Barcelona

A TEMPESTUOUS
TEMPTATION

CHAPTER ONE

Luiz Carlos Montes looked down at the slip of paper in his hand, reconfirmed that he was at the correct address and then, from the comfort of his sleek, black sports car, he briefly scanned the house and its surroundings. His immediate thought was that this was not what he had been expecting. His second thought was that it had been a mistake to drive his car here. The impression he was getting was that this was the sort of place where anything of any value that could be stolen, damaged or vandalised just for the hell of it would be.

The small terraced house, lit by the street lamp, fought a losing battle to maintain some level of attractiveness next to its less palatable neighbours. The tidy pocket-sized front garden was flanked on its left side by a cement square on which dustbins were laid out in no particular order, and on its right by a similar cement square where a rusted car languished on blocks, awaiting attention. Further along was a parade of shops comprised of a Chinese takeaway, a sub-post office, a hairdresser, an off-licence and a newsagent which seemed to be a meeting point for just the sort of youths whom Luiz suspected would not hesitate to zero in on his car the second he left it.

Fortunately he felt no apprehension as he glanced at the group of hooded teenagers smoking in a group outside the off-licence. He was six-foot-three with a muscled body that was honed to perfection thanks to a rigorous routine of exercise and sport when he could find the time. He was more than capable of putting the fear of God into any group of indolent cigarette-smoking teenagers.

But, hell, this was still the last thing he needed. On a Friday evening. In December. With the threat of snow in the air and a shedload of emails needing his attention before the whole world went to sleep for the Christmas period.

But family duty was, in the end, family duty and what choice had he had? Having seen this dump for himself, he also had to concede that his mission, inconvenient though it might be, was a necessary one.

He exhaled impatiently and swung out of the car. It was a bitterly cold night, even in London. The past week had been characterised by hard overnight frosts that had barely thawed during the day. There was a glittery coating over the rusting car in the garden next to the house and on the lids of the bins in the garden to the other side. The smell of Chinese food wafted towards him and he frowned with distaste.

This was the sort of district into which Luiz never ventured. He had no need to. The faster he could sort this whole mess out and clear out of the place, the better, as far as he was concerned.

With that in mind, he pressed the doorbell and kept his finger on it until he could hear the sound of footsteps scurrying towards the front door.

On the verge of digging into her dinner, Aggie heard the sound of the doorbell and was tempted to ignore it, not least because she had an inkling of an idea as to whose finger was on it. Mr Cholmsey, her landlord, had been making warning noises about the rent, which was overdue.

'But I always pay on time!' Aggie had protested when he had telephoned her the day before. 'And I'm only over-due by *two days*. It's not my fault that there's a postal strike!'

Apparently, though, it was. He had been kind enough to 'do her the favour' of letting her pay by cheque when *all his other tenants* paid by direct debit... And *look where it got him*...it just *wasn't good enough*... People were queu-ing for that house...he could rent it to a more reliable ten-ant *in a minute*...

If the cheque wasn't with him *by the following day*, he would have to have cash from her.

She had never actually met Mr Cholmsey. Eighteen months ago, she had found the house through an agency and everything had been absolutely fine—until Mr Cholmsey had decided that he could cut out the middle man and handle his own properties. Since then, Alfred Cholmsey had been an ongoing headache, prone to ignor-ing requests for things to be fixed and fond of reminding her how scarce rentable properties were in London.

If she ignored the summons at the door, she had no doubt that he would find some way of breaking the lease and chucking her out.

Keeping the latch on, she cautiously opened the door a crack and peered out into the darkness.

'I'm really sorry, Mr Cholmsey...' She burst into speech, determined to get her point of view across before her disagreeable, hateful landlord could launch his verbal attack. 'The cheque should have arrived by now. I'll cancel it and make sure that I have the cash for you tomorrow. I promise.' She wished the wretched man would do her the courtesy of at least standing in her very reduced line of vision instead of skulking to the side, but there was no way that she was going to pull open the door. You could never be too careful in this neighbourhood.

'Who the hell is Mr Cholmsey, and what are you talking about? Just open the door, Agatha!'

That voice, that distinctive, *loathsome* voice, was so unexpected that Aggie suddenly felt the need to pass out. What was Luiz Montes doing here? On her doorstep? *Invading her privacy?* Wasn't it bad enough that she and her brother had been held up for inspection by him over the past eight months? Verbally poked and prodded under the very thin guise of hospitality and 'just getting to know my niece's boyfriend and his family'. Asked intrusive questions which they had been forced to skirt around and generally treated with the sort of suspicion reserved for criminals out on parole.

'What are *you* doing here?'

'Just open the door! I'm not having a conversation with you on your doorstep!' Luiz didn't have to struggle to imagine what her expression would be. He had met her sufficient times with her brother and his niece to realise that she disapproved of everything he stood for and everything he said. She'd challenged him on every point he made. She was defensive, argumentative and pretty much everything he would have made an effort to avoid in a woman.

As he had told himself on numerous occasions, there was no way he would ever have subjected himself to her company had he not been placed, by his sister who lived in Brazil, in the unenviable position of having to take an interest in his niece and the man she had decided to take up with. The Montes family was worth an untold fortune. Checking out the guy his niece was dating was a simple precaution, Luisa had stressed. And, while Luiz couldn't see the point because the relationship was certain to crash and burn in due course, his sister had insisted. Knowing his sister as well as he did, he had taken the path of least resistance and agreed to keep a watchful eye on Mark Collins, and his sister, who appeared to come as part of the package.

'So who's Mr Cholmsey?' was the first thing he said as he strode past her into the house.

Aggie folded her arms and glared resentfully at him as he looked around at his surroundings with the sort of cool contempt she had come to associate with him.

Yes, he was good-looking, all tall and powerful and darkly sexy. But from the very second she had met him, she had been chilled to the bone by his arrogance, his casual contempt for both her and Mark—which he barely bothered to hide—and his thinly veiled threat that he was watching them both and they'd better not overstep the mark.

'Mr Cholmsey's the landlord—and how did you get this address? Why are you here?'

'I had no idea you rented. Stupid me. I was under the impression that you owned your own house jointly. Now, where did I get that from, I wonder?'

He rested cool, dark eyes on Aggie. 'I was also under the impression that you lived somewhere…slightly less unsavoury. A crashing misconception on my part as well.' However far removed Agatha Collins was from the sort of women Luiz preferred—tall brunettes with legs up to their armpits and amenable, yielding natures—he couldn't deny that she was startlingly pretty. Five-four tops, with pale, curly hair the colour of buttermilk and skin that was satiny smooth. Her eyes were purest aquamarine, offset by dark lashes, as though her creator had been determined to make sure that she stood out from the crowd and had taken one little detail and made it strikingly different.

Aggie flushed and mentally cursed herself for falling in

with her brother and Maria. When Luiz had made his first, unwelcome appearance in their lives, she had agreed that she would downplay their financial circumstances, that she would economise harmlessly on the unadorned truth.

'My mum's insisted that Uncle Luiz check Mark out,' Maria had explained tightly. 'And Uncle Luiz is horribly black-and-white. It'd be better if he thinks that you're… okay… Not exactly rich, but not completely broke either.'

'You still haven't told me what you're doing here,' Aggie dodged.

'Where's your brother?'

'He isn't here and neither is Maria. And when are you going to stop *spying* on us?'

'I'm beginning to think that my *spying* is starting to pay dividends,' Luiz murmured. 'Which one of you told me that you lived in Richmond?' He leaned against the wall and looked down at her with those bottomless dark eyes that always managed to send her nervous system into instant freefall.

'I didn't say that we *lived* in Richmond,' Aggie prevaricated guiltily. 'I probably told you that we go cycling there quite a bit. In the park. It's not my fault that you might have got hold of the wrong end of the stick.'

'I *never* get hold of the wrong end of the stick.' The casual interest which he had seen as an unnecessary chore now blossomed into rampant suspicion. She and her brother had lied about their financial circumstances and had probably persuaded his niece to go along for the ride and back them up. And that, to Luiz, was pointing in only one direction. 'When I got the address of this place, I had to double check because it didn't tally with what I'd been told.' He began removing his coat while Aggie watched in growing dismay.

Every single time she had met Luiz, it had been in one

of London's upmarket restaurants. She, Mark and Maria
had been treated over time to the finest Italian food money
could buy, the best Thai to be found in the country, the
most expensive French in the most exclusive area. Pre-
warned by Maria that it was her uncle's way of keeping
tabs on them, they had been unforthcoming on personal
detail and expansive on polite chitchat.

Aggie had bristled at the mere thought that they were
being sized up, and she had bristled even more at the nagging suspicion that they had both been found wanting. But
restaurants were one thing. Descending on them here was
taking it one step too far.

And now his coat was off, which implied that he wasn't
about to do the disappearing act she desperately wanted.
Something about him unsettled her and here, in this small
space, she was even more unsettled.

'Maybe you could get me something to drink,' he inserted smoothly. 'And we can explore what other little lies
might come out in the wash while I wait for your brother
to show up.'

'Why is it suddenly so important that you talk to Mark?'
Aggie asked uneasily. 'I mean, couldn't you have waited?
Maybe invited him out for dinner with Maria so that you
could try and get to the bottom of his intentions? Again?'

'Things have moved up a gear, regrettably. But I'll come
back to that.' He strolled past her through the open door
and into the sitting room. The decor here was no more
tasteful than it was in the hall. The walls were the colour
of off-cheese, depressing despite the old movie posters
that had been tacked on. The furniture was an unappealing mix of old and used and tacky, snap-together modern. In one corner, an old television set was propped on a
cheap pine unit.

'What do you mean that *things have moved up a gear*?'

Aggie demanded as he sat on one of the chairs and looked at her with unhurried thoroughness.

'I guess you know why I've been keeping tabs on your brother.'

'Maria mentioned that her mother can be a little over-protective,' Aggie mumbled. She resigned herself to the fact that Luiz wasn't leaving in a hurry and reluctantly sat down on the chair facing him.

As always, she felt dowdy and underdressed. On the occasions when she had been dragged along to those fancy restaurants—none of which she would ever have sampled had it not been for him—she had rooted out the dressiest clothes in her wardrobe and had still managed to feel cheap and mousey. Now, in baggy, thick jogging bottoms and Mark's jumper, several sizes too big, she felt screamingly, ridiculously frumpy. Which made her resent him even more.

Luiz gave an elegant shrug. 'It pays to be careful. Naturally, when my sister asked me to check your brother out, I tried to talk her out of it.'

'You did?'

'Sure. Maria's a kid and kids have relationships that fall by the wayside. It's life. I was convinced that this relationship would be no different but I eventually agreed that I would keep an eye on things.'

'By which,' Aggie inserted bitterly, 'you meant that you would quiz us on every aspect of our lives and try and trip us up.'

'Congratulations. You both provided a touchingly united front. I find that I barely know a single personal thing about either of you and it's dawning on me that the few details you've imparted have probably been a tissue of lies—starting with where you live. It would have saved

time and effort if I'd employed a detective to ferret out
whatever background information was necessary.'

'Maria thought that—'

'Do me a favour. Keep my niece out of this. You live
in a dump, which you rent from an unscrupulous landlord. You can barely afford the rent. Tell me, do either of
you hold down jobs, or were those fabrications as well?'

'I resent you barging into my house.'

'Mr Cholmsey's house—if you can call it a house.'

'Fine! I still resent you barging in here and insulting
me.'

'Tough.'

'In fact, I'm asking you to leave!'

At that, Luiz burst out laughing. 'Do you really think
that I've come all the way here so that I can leave the second the questioning gets a little too uncomfortable for
you?'

'Well, I don't see the point of you hanging around. Mark
and Maria aren't here.'

'I've come because, like I said, things have moved up
a gear. It seems that there's now talk of marriage. It's not
going to do.'

'Talk of marriage?' Aggie parroted incredulously.
'There's no talk of marriage.'

'At least, none that your brother's told you about. Maybe
the touching united front isn't quite as united as you'd like
it to be.'

'You…you are just the most *awful* human being I've
ever met!'

'I think you've made that glaringly clear on all the occasions that we've met,' Luiz remarked coolly. 'You're en-
titled to your opinions.'

'So you came here to…what? Warn my brother off?

Warn Maria off? They might be young but they're not under age.'

'Maria comes from one of the richest families in Latin America.'

'I beg your pardon?' Aggie looked at him in confusion. Yes, of course she had known that Maria was not the usual hand-to-mouth starving student working the tills on the weekend to help pay for her tuition fees. But *one of the richest families in Latin America?* No wonder she had not been in favour of either of them letting on that they were just normal people struggling to get by on a day-to-day basis!

'You're kidding, right?'

'When it comes to money, I lose my sense of humour.' Luiz abruptly sat forward, elbows resting on his thighs, and looked at her unsmilingly. 'I hadn't planned on taking a hard line, but I'm beginning to do the maths and I don't like the results I'm coming up with.'

Aggie tried and failed to meet his dark, intimidating stare. Why was it that whenever she was in this man's company her usual unflappability was scattered to the four corners? She was reduced to feeling too tight in her skin, too defensive and too self-conscious. Which meant that she could barely think straight.

'I have no idea what you're talking about,' she muttered, staring at her linked fingers while her heart rate sped up and her mouth went dry.

'Wealthy people are often targets,' Luiz gritted, spelling it out in clear syllables just in case she chose to miss the message. 'My niece is extremely wealthy and will be even wealthier when she turns twenty-one. Now it appears that the dalliance I thought would peter out after a couple of months has turned into a marriage proposal.'

'I still can't believe that. You've got your facts wrong.'

'Believe it! And what I'm seeing are a couple of fortune hunters who have lied about their circumstances to try and throw me off course.'

Aggie blanched and stared at him miserably. Those small white fibs had assumed the proportions of mountains. Her brain felt sluggish but already she could see why he would have arrived at the conclusion that he had.

Honest people didn't lie.

'Tell me…is your brother really a musician? Because I've looked him up online and, strangely enough, I can't find him anywhere.'

'Of course he's a musician! He…he plays in a band.'

'And I'm guessing this band hasn't made it big yet… hence his lack of presence on the Internet.'

'Okay! I give up! So we may have…have…'

'Tampered with the truth? Stretched it? Twisted it to the point where it became unrecognisable?'

'Maria said that you're very black-and-white.' Aggie stuck her chin up and met his frowning stare. Now, as had happened before, she marvelled that such sinful physical beauty, the sort of beauty that made people think of putting paint to canvas, could conceal such a cold, ruthless, brutally dispassionate streak.

'Me? Black-and-white?' Luiz was outraged at this preposterous assumption. 'I've never heard anything so ridiculous in my entire life!'

'She said that you form your opinions and you stick to them. You never look outside the box and allow yourself to be persuaded into another direction.'

'That's called strength of character!'

'Well, that's why we weren't inclined to be one hundred percent truthful. Not that we *lied*…'

'We just didn't reveal as much as we could have.'

'Such as you live in a rented dump, your brother sings

in pubs now and again and you are a teacher—or was that another one of those creative exaggerations?'

'Of course I'm a teacher. I teach primary school. You can check up on me if you like!'

'Well that's now by the by. The fact is, I cannot allow any marriage to take place between my niece and your brother.'

'So you're going to do what, exactly?' Aggie was genuinely bewildered. It was one thing to disapprove of someone else's choices. It was quite another to force them into accepting what you chose to cram down their throat. Luiz, Maria's mother, every single member of their super-wealthy family, for that matter, could rant, storm, wring their hands and deliver threatening lectures—but at the end of the day Maria was her own person and would make up her own mind.

She tactfully decided not to impart that point of view. He claimed that he wasn't black-and-white but she had seen enough evidence of that to convince her that he was. He also had no knowledge whatsoever of how the other half lived. In fact, she doubted that he had ever even come into contact with people who weren't exactly like him, until she and Mark had come along.

'Look.' She relented slightly as another point of view pushed its way through her self-righteous anger. 'I can understand that you might harbour one or two reservations about my brother...'

'Can you?' Luiz asked with biting sarcasm.

Right now he was kicking himself for not having taken a harder look at the pair of them. He was usually as sharp as they came when other people and their motivations were involved. He had had to be. So how had they managed to slip through the net?

Her brother was disingenuous, engaging, apparently

open. He looked like the kind of guy who could hold his own with anyone—tall, muscular, with the same shade of blonde hair as his sister but tied back in a ponytail; when he spoke, his voice was low and gentle.

And Agatha—so stunningly pretty that anyone could be forgiven for staring. But, alongside that, she had also been forthright and opinionated. Was that what had taken him in—the combination of two very different personalities? Had they cunningly worked off each other to throw him off-guard? Or had he just failed to take the situation seriously because he hadn't thought the boy's relationship with his niece would ever come to anything? Luisa was famously protective of Maria. Had he just assumed that her request for him to keep an eye out had been more of the same?

At any rate, they had now been caught out in a tangle of lies and that, to his mind, could mean only one thing.

The fact that he'd been a fool for whatever reason was something he would have to live with, but it stuck in his throat.

'And I know how it must look...that we weren't completely open with you. But you have to believe me when I tell you that you have nothing to fear.'

'Point one—fear is an emotion that's alien to me. Point two—I don't have to believe anything you say, which brings me to your question.'

'My question?'

'You wondered what I intended to do about this mess.'

Aggie felt her hackles rise, as they invariably did on the occasions when she had met him, and she made a valiant effort to keep them in check.

'So you intend to warn my brother off,' she said on a sigh.

'Oh, I intend to do much better than that,' Luiz drawled,

watching the faint colour in her cheeks and thinking that she was a damn good actress. 'You look as though you could use some money, and I suspect your brother could as well. You have a landlord baying down your neck for unpaid rent.'

'I paid!' Aggie insisted vigorously. 'It's not my fault that there's a postal strike!'

'And whatever you earn as a teacher,' Luiz continued, not bothering to give her protest house room, 'It obviously isn't enough to scrape by. Face it, if you can't afford the rent for a dump like this, then it's pretty obvious that neither of you has a penny to rub together. So my offer to get your brother off the scene and out of my niece's life should put a big smile on your face. In fact, I would go so far as to say that it should make your Christmas.'

'I don't know what you're talking about.'

Those big blue eyes, Luiz thought sourly. They had done a damn good job of throwing him off the scent.

'I'm going to give you and your brother enough money to clear out of this place. You'll each be able to afford to buy somewhere of your own, live the high life, if that's what takes your fancy. And I suspect it probably is…'

'You're going to *pay us off*? To make us *disappear*?'

'Name your price. And naturally your brother can name his. No one has ever accused me of not being a generous man. And on the subject of your brother…when exactly is he due back?' He looked pointedly at his watch and then raised his eyes to her flushed, angry face. She was perched on the very edge of her chair, ramrod-erect, and her knuckles were white where her fingers were biting into the padded seat. She was the very picture of outrage.

'I can't believe I'm hearing this.'

'I'm sure you'll find it remarkably easy to adjust to the thought.'

'You can't just *buy people off*!'

'No? Care to take a small bet on that?' His eyes were as hard and as cold as the frost gathering outside. 'Doubtless your brother wishes to further his career, if he's even interested in a career. Maybe he'd just like to blow some money on life's little luxuries. Doubtless he ascertained my niece's financial status early on in the relationship and between the two of you you decided that she was your passport to a more lucrative lifestyle. It now appears that he intends to marry her and thereby get his foot through the door, so to speak, but that's not going to happen in a million years. So when you say that I can't *buy people off*? Well, I think you'll find that I can.'

Aggie stared at him open-mouthed. She felt as though she was in the presence of someone from another planet. Was this how the wealthy behaved, as though they owned everything and everyone? As though people were pieces on a chess board to be moved around on a whim and disposed of without scruple? And why was she so surprised when she had always known that he was ruthless, cold-hearted and single-minded?

'Mark and Maria love each other! That must have been obvious to you.'

'I'm sure Maria imagines herself in love. She's young. She doesn't realise that love is an illusion. And we can sit around chatting all evening, but I still need to know when he'll be here. I want to get this situation sorted as soon as possible.'

'He won't.'

'Come again?'

'I mean,' Aggie ventured weakly, because she knew that the bloodless, heartless man in front of her wasn't going to warm to what she was about to tell him, 'he and Maria decided to have a few days away. A spur-of-the-moment thing. A little pre-Christmas break...'

'Tell me I'm not hearing this.'

'They left yesterday morning.'

She started as he vaulted upright without warning and began pacing the room, his movements restless and menacing.

'Left to go where?' It was a question phrased more like a demand. 'And don't even think of using your looks to pull a fast one.'

'Using my looks?' Aggie felt hot colour crawl into her face. While she had been sitting there in those various restaurants, feeling as awkward and as colourless as a sparrow caught up in a parade of peacocks, had he been looking at her, assessing what she looked like? That thought made her feel weirdly unsteady.

'Where have they gone?' He paused to stand in front of her and Aggie's eyes travelled up—up along that magnificent body sheathed in clothes that looked far too expensive and far too hand-made for their surroundings—until they settled on the forbidding angles of his face. She had never met someone who exuded threat and power the way he did, and who used that to his advantage.

'I don't have to give you that information,' she said stoutly and tried not to quail as his expression darkened.

'I really wouldn't play that game with me if I were you, Agatha.'

'Or else what?'

'Or else I'll make sure that your brother finds himself without a job in the foreseeable future. And the money angle? Off the cards.'

'You can't do that. I mean, you can't do anything to ruin his musical career.'

'Oh no? Please don't put that to the test.'

Aggie hesitated. There was such cool certainty in his voice that she had no doubt that he really would make sure her brother lost his job if she didn't comply and tell him what he wanted.

'Okay. They've gone to a little country hotel in the Lake District,' she imparted reluctantly. 'They wanted a romantic, snowed-in few days, and that part of the world has a lot of sentimental significance for us.' Her bag was on the ground next to her. She reached in, rummaged around and extracted a sheet of paper, confirmation of their booking. 'He gave me this, because it's got all the details in case I wanted to get in touch with him.'

'The Lake District. They've gone to the *Lake District*.' He raked his fingers through his hair, snatched the paper from her and wondered if things could get any worse. The Lake District was not exactly a hop and skip away. Nor was it a plane-ride away. He contemplated the prospect of spending hours behind the wheel of his car in bad driving conditions on a search-and-rescue mission for his sister— because if they were thinking of getting married on the sly, what better time or place? Or else doing battle with the public transport system which was breaking under the weight of the bad weather. He eliminated the public-transport option without hesitation. Which brought him back to the prospect of hours behind the wheel of his car.

'You make it sound as though they've taken a trip to the moon. Well, I guess you'll want to give Maria a call... I'm not sure there's any mobile-phone service there, though. In fact, there isn't. You'll have to phone through to the hotel and get them to transfer you. She can reassure you that they're not about to take a walk down the aisle.' Aggie wondered how her brother was going to deal with Luiz when Luiz waved a wad of notes in front of him and told him to clear off or else. Mark, stupidly, actually liked the man, and stuck up for him whenever Aggie happened to mention how much he got on her nerves.

Not her problem. She struggled to squash her instinctive urge to look out for him. She and Mark had been a tight unit since they were children, when their mother had died and, in the absence of any father, or any relatives for that matter, they had been put into care. Younger by four years, he had been a sickly child, debilitated by frequent asthma attacks. Like a surrogate mother hen, she had learnt to take care of him and to put his needs ahead of her own. She had gained strength, allowing him the freedom to be the gentle, dreamy child who had matured into a gentle, dreamy adult—despite his long hair, his earring and the tattoo on his shoulder which seemed to announce a different kind of person.

'Well, now that you know where they are, I guess you'll be leaving.'

Luiz, looking at her down-bent head, pondered this sequence of events. Missing niece. Missing boyfriend. Long trip to locate them.

'I don't know why I didn't see this coming,' he mused. 'Having a few days away would be the perfect opportunity for your brother to seal the deal. Maybe my presence on the scene alerted him to the fact that time wouldn't be on his side when it came to marrying my niece. Maybe he figured that the courtship would have to be curtailed and the main event brought forward…a winter wedding. Very romantic.'

'That's the most ridiculous thing I've ever heard!'

'I'd be surprised if you didn't say that. Well, it's not going to happen. We'll just have to make sure that we get to that romantic hideaway and surprise them before they have time to do anything regrettable.'

'We?'

Luiz looked at her with raised eyebrows. 'Well, you don't imagine that I'm going to go there on my own and leave you behind so that you can get on the phone and warn your brother of my impending arrival, do you?'

'You're crazy! I'm not going anywhere with you, Luiz Montes!'

'It's not ideal timing, and I can't say that I haven't got better things to do on a Friday evening, but I can't see a way out of it. I anticipate we'll be there by tomorrow lunchtime, so you'll have to pack enough for a weekend and make it quick. I'll need to get back to my place so that I can throw some things in a bag.'

'You're not hearing what I'm saying!'

'Correction. I am hearing. I'm just choosing to ignore what you're saying because none of it will make any difference to what I intend to do.'

'I refuse to go along with this!'

'Here's the choice. We go, I chat to your brother, I dangle my financial inducement in front of him... A few tears all round to start with but in the end everyone's happy. Plan B is I send my men up to physically bring him back to London, where he'll find that life can be very uncomfortable when all avenues of work are dried up. I'll put the word out in the music industry that he's not to be touched with a barge pole. You'd be surprised if you knew the extent of my connections. One word—*vast*. I'm guessing that as his loyal, devoted sister, option two might be tough to swallow.'

'You are...are...'

'Yes, yes, yes. I know what you think of me. I'll give you ten minutes to be at the front door. If you're not there, I'm coming in to get you. And look on the bright side, Agatha. I'm not even asking you to take time off from your job. You'll be delivered safely back here by Monday morning, in one piece and with a bank account that's stuffed to the rafters. And we'll never have to lay eyes on each other again!'

CHAPTER TWO

'I just can't believe that you would blackmail me into this,' was the first thing she said as she joined him at the front door, bag reluctantly in hand.

'Blackmail? I prefer to call it *persuasion*.' Luiz pushed himself off the wall against which he had been lounging, calculating how much work he would be missing and also working out that his date for the following night wasn't going to be overjoyed at this sudden road trip. Not that that unduly bothered him. In fact, to call it a *date* was wildly inappropriate. He had had four dates with Chloe Bern and on the fifth he had broken it gently to her that things between them weren't working out. She hadn't taken it well. This was the sixth time he would be seeing her and it would be to repeat what he had already told her on date five.

Aggie snorted derisively. She had feverishly tried to find a way of backing out, but all exits seemed to have been barred. Luiz was in hunting mode and she knew that the threats he had made hadn't been empty ones. For the sake of her brother, she had no choice but to agree to this trip and she felt like exploding with anger.

Outside, the weather was grimly uninviting, freezing cold and with an ominous stillness in the atmosphere.

She followed him to his fancy car, incongruous between

the battered, old run-arounds on either side, and made another inarticulate noise as he beeped it open.

'You're going to tell me,' Luiz said, settling into the driver's seat and waiting for her as she strapped herself in, 'that this is a pointless toy belonging to someone with more money than sense. Am I right?'

'You must be a mind reader,' Aggie said acidly.

'Not a mind reader. Just astute when it comes to remembering conversations we've had in the past.' He started the engine and the sports car purred to life.

'You can't have remembered everything I've said to you,' Aggie muttered uncomfortably.

'Everything. How do you think I'm so sure that you never mentioned renting this dump here?' He threw her a sidelong glance. 'I'm thinking that your brother doesn't contribute greatly to the family finances?' Which in turn made him wonder who would be footing the bill for the romantic getaway. If Aggie barely earned enough to keep the roof over her head, then it stood to reason that Mark earned even less, singing songs in a pub. His jaw tightened at the certainty that Maria was already the goose laying the golden eggs.

'He can't,' Aggie admitted reluctantly. 'Not that I mind, because I don't.'

'That's big of you. Most people would resent having to take care of their kid brother when he's capable of taking care of himself.' They had both been sketchy on the details of Mark's job and Luiz, impatient with a task that had been foisted onto his shoulders, had not delved deeply enough. He had been content enough to ascertain that his niece wasn't going out with a potential axe-murderer, junkie or criminal on the run. 'So…he works in a bar and plays now and then in a band. You might as well tell me the truth,

Agatha. Considering there's no longer any point in keeping secrets.'

Aggie shrugged. 'Yes, he works in a bar and gets a gig once every few weeks. But his talent is really with songwriting. You'll probably think that I'm spinning you a fairy story, because you're suspicious of everything I say...'

'With good reason, as it turns out.'

'But he's pretty amazing at composing. Often in the evenings, while I'm reading or else going through some of the homework from the kids or preparing for classes, he'll sit on the sofa playing his guitar and working on his latest song over and over until he thinks he's got it just right.'

'And you never thought to mention that to me because...?'

'I'm sure Mark told you that he enjoyed songwriting.'

'He told me that he was a musician. He may have mentioned that he knew people in the entertainment business. The general impression was that he was an established musician with an established career. I don't believe I ever heard you contradict him.'

The guy was charming but broke, and his state of penury was no passing inconvenience. He was broke because he lived in a dreamworld of strumming guitars and dabbling about with music sheets.

Thinking about it now, Luiz could see why Maria had fallen for the guy. She was the product of a fabulously wealthy background. The boys she had met had always had plentiful supplies of money. Many of them either worked in family businesses or were destined to. A musician, with a notebook and a guitar slung over his shoulder, rustling up cocktails in a bar by night? On every level he had been her accident waiting to happen. No wonder they had all seen fit to play around with the truth! Maria was sharp enough to have known that a whiff of the truth would have had alarm bells ringing in his head.

'I happen to be very proud of my brother,' Aggie said stiffly. 'It's important that people find their own way. I know you probably don't have much time for that.'

'I have a lot of time for that, provided it doesn't impact my family.'

The traffic was horrendous but eventually they cleared it and, after a series of back roads, emerged at a square of elegant red-bricked Victorian houses in the centre of which was a gated, private park.

There had been meals out but neither she nor her brother had ever actually been asked over to Luiz's house.

This was evidence of wealth on a shocking scale. Aside from Maria's expensive bags, which she'd laughingly claimed she couldn't resist and could afford because her family was 'not badly off', there had been nothing to suggest that not badly off had actually meant staggeringly rich.

Even though the restaurants had been grand and expensive, Aggie had never envisioned the actual lifestyle that Luiz enjoyed to accompany them. She had no passing acquaintance with money. Lifestyles of the rich and famous were things she occasionally read about in magazines and dismissed without giving it much thought. Getting out of the car, she realised that, between her and her brother and Luiz and his family, there was a chasm so vast that the thought of even daring to cross it gave her a headache.

Once again she was reluctantly forced to see why Maria's mother had asked Luiz to watch the situation.

Once again she backtracked over their glossing over of their circumstances and understood why Luiz was now reacting the way he was. He was so wrong about them both

but he was trapped in his own circumstances and had probably been weaned on suspicion from a very young age.

'Are you going to come out?' Luiz bent down to peer at
her through the open car door. 'Or are you going to stay
there all night gawping?'

'I wasn't gawping!' Aggie slammed the car door behind
her and followed him into a house, a four-storey house that
took her breath away, from the pale marble flooring to the
dramatic paintings on the walls to the sweeping banister
that led up to yet more impeccable elegance.

He strode into a room to the right and after a few seconds of dithering Aggie followed him inside. He hadn't
glanced at her once. Just shed his coat and headed straight
for his answer machine, which he flicked on while loos-
ening his tie.

She took the opportunity to look round her: stately proportions and the same pale marbled flooring, with softly
faded silk rugs to break the expanse. The furniture was
light leather and the floor-to-ceiling curtains thick velvet,
a shade deeper in colour than the light pinks of the rugs.

She was vaguely aware that he was listening to what
seemed to be an interminable series of business calls, until
the last message, when the breathy voice of a woman reminded him that she would be seeing him tomorrow and
that she couldn't wait.

At that, Aggie's ears pricked up. He might very well
have accused her of being shady when it came to her and
her brother's private lives. She now realised that she actually knew precious little about *him*.

He wasn't married; that much she knew for sure because Maria had confided that the whole family was waiting for him to tie the knot and settle down. Beyond that, of
course, he *would* have a girlfriend. No one as eligible as
Luiz Montes would be without one. She looked at him sur-

reptitiously and wondered what the owner of that breathy, sexy voice looked like.

'I'm going to have a quick shower. I'll be back down in ten minutes and then we'll get going. No point hanging around.'

Aggie snapped back to the present. She was blushing. She could feel it. Blushing as she speculated on his private life.

'Make yourself at home,' Luiz told her drily. 'Feel free to explore.'

'I'm fine here, thank you very much.' She perched awkwardly on the edge of one of the pristine leather sofas and rested her hands primly on her lap.

'Suit yourself.'

But as soon as he had left the room, she began exploring like a kid in a toyshop, touching some of the clearly priceless *objets d'art* he had randomly scattered around: a beautiful bronze figurine of two cheetahs on the long, low sideboard against the wall; a pair of vases that looked very much like the real thing from a Chinese dynasty; she gazed at the abstract on the wall and tried to decipher the signature.

'Do you like what you see?' Luiz asked from behind her and she started and went bright red.

'I've never been in a place like this before,' Aggie said defensively.

Her mouth went dry as she looked at him. He was dressed in a pair of black jeans and a grey-and-black-striped woollen jumper. She could see the collar of his shirt underneath, soft grey flannel. All the other times she had seen him he had been formally dressed, almost as though he had left work to meet them at whatever mega-expensive restaurant he had booked. But this was casual and he was really and truly drop-dead sexy.

'It's a house, not a museum. Shall we go?' He flicked off the light as she left the sitting room and pulled out his mobile phone to instruct his driver to bring the four-by-four round.

'*My* house is a house.' Aggie was momentarily distracted from her anger at his accusations as she stared back at the mansion behind her and waited with him for the car to be delivered.

'Correction. Your house is a hovel. Your landlord deserves to be shot for charging a tenant for a place like that. You probably haven't noticed, but in the brief time I was there I spotted the kind of cracks that advertise a problem with damp—plaster falling from the walls and patches on the ceiling that probably mean you'll have a leak sooner rather than later.'

The four-by-four, shiny and black, slowed and Luiz's driver got out.

'There's nothing I can do about that,' Aggie huffed, climbing into the passenger seat. 'Anyway, you live in a different world to me...to us. It's almost impossible to find somewhere cheap to rent in London.'

'There's a difference between cheap and hazardous. Just think of what you could buy if you had the money in your bank account...' He manoeuvred the big car away from the kerb. 'Nice house in a smart postcode... Quaint little garden at the back... You like gardening, don't you? I believe it's one of those things you mentioned...although it's open to debate whether you were telling the truth or lying to give the right impression.'

'I wasn't lying! I love gardening.'

'London gardens are generally small but you'd be surprised to discover what you can get for the right price.'

'I would never accept a penny from you, Luiz Montes!'

'You don't mean that.'

That tone of comfortable disbelief enraged her. 'I'm not interested in money!' She turned to him, looked at his aristocratic dark profile, and felt that familiar giddy feeling.

'Call me cynical, but I have yet to meet someone who isn't interested in money. They might make noises about money not being able to buy happiness and the good things in life being free, but they like the things money can do and the freebies go through the window when more expensive ways of being happy enter the equation. Tell me seriously that you didn't enjoy those meals you had out.'

'Yes, I *enjoyed* them, but I wouldn't miss them if they weren't there.'

'And what about your brother? Is he as noble minded as you?'

'Neither of us are materialistic, if that's what you mean. You met him. Did he strike you as the sort of person who... who would lead Maria on because of what he thought he could get out of her? I mean, didn't you like him at all?'

'I liked him, but that's not the point.'

'You mean the point is that Maria can go out with someone from a different background, just so long as there's no danger of getting serious, because the only person she would be allowed to settle down with would be someone of the same social standing as her.'

'You say that as though there's something wrong with it.'

'I don't want to talk about this. It's not going to get us anywhere.' She fell silent and watched the slow-moving traffic around her, a sea of headlights illuminating late-night shoppers, people hurrying towards the tube or to catch a bus. At this rate, it would be midnight before they cleared London.

'Would you tell me something?' she asked to break the silence.

'I'm listening.'

'Why didn't you try and put an end to their relationship from the start? I mean, why did you bother taking us out for all those meals?'

'Not my place to interfere. Not at that point, at any rate. I'd been asked to keep an eye on things, to meet your brother and, as it turns out, you too, because the two of you seem to be joined at the hip.' He didn't add that, having not had very much to do with his niece in the past, he had found that he rather enjoyed their company. He had liked listening to Mark and Maria entertain him with their chat about movies and music. And even more he had liked the way Aggie had argued with him, had liked the way it had challenged him into making an effort to get her to laugh. It had all made a change from the extravagant social events to which he was invited, usually in a bid by a company to impress him.

'We're not joined at the hip! We're close because...' Because of their background of foster care, but that was definitely something they had kept to themselves.

'Because you lost your parents?'

'That's right.' She had told him in passing, almost the first time she had met him, that their parents were dead and had swiftly changed the subject. Just another muddled half-truth that would further make him suspicious of their motives.

'Apart from which, I thought that my sister had been overreacting to the whole thing. Maria is an only child without a father. Luisa is prone to pointless worrying.'

'I can't imagine you taking orders from your sister.'

'You haven't met Luisa or any of my five sisters. If you had, you wouldn't make that observation.' He laughed and Aggie felt the breath catch in her throat because, for once, his laughter stemmed from genuine amusement.

'What are they like?'

'All older than me and all bossy.' He grinned sideways at her. 'It's easier to surrender than to cross them. In a family of six women, my father and I know better than to try and argue. It would be easier staging a land war in Asia.'

That glimpse of his humanity unsettled Aggie. But she had had glimpses of it before, she recalled uneasily. Times when he had managed to make her forget how dislikeable he was, when he had recounted something with such dry wit that she had caught herself trying hard to stifle a laugh. He might be hateful, judgemental and unfair, he might represent a lot of things she disliked, but there was no denying that he was one of the most intelligent men she had ever met—and, when it suited him, one of the most entertaining. She had contrived to forget all of that but, stuck here with him, it was coming back to her fast and she had to fumble her way out of her momentary distraction.

'I couldn't help overhearing those messages earlier on at the house,' she said politely.

'Messages? What are you talking about?'

'Lots of business calls. I guess you're having to sacrifice working time for this…unless you don't work on a weekend.'

'If you're thinking of using a few messages you overheard as a way of trying to talk me out of this trip, then you can forget it.'

'I wasn't thinking of doing that. I was just being polite.'

'In that case, you can rest assured that there's nothing that can't wait until Monday when I'm back in London. I have my mobile and if anything urgent comes up, then I can deal with it on the move. Nice try, though.'

'What about that other message? I gather you'll be missing a date with someone tomorrow night?'

Luiz stiffened. 'Again, nothing that can't be handled.'

'Because I would feel very guilty otherwise.'

'Don't concern yourself with my private life, Aggie.'

'Why not?' Aggie risked. 'You're concerning yourself with mine.'

'Slightly different scenario, wouldn't you agree? To the best of my knowledge, I haven't been caught trying to con anyone recently. My private life isn't the one under the spotlight.'

'You're impossible! You're so...*blinkered*! Did you know that Maria was the one who pursued Mark?'

'Do me a favour.'

'She was,' Aggie persisted. 'Mark was playing at one of the pubs and she and her friends went to hear them. She went to meet him after the gig and she gave him her mobile number, told him to get in touch.'

'I'm finding that hard to believe, but let's suppose you're telling the truth. I don't see what that has to do with anything. Whether she chased your brother or your brother chased her, the end result is the same. An heiress is an extremely lucrative proposition for someone in his position.' He switched on the radio and turned it to the traffic news.

London was crawling. The weather forecasters had been making a big deal of snow to come. There was nothing at the moment but people were still rushing to get back home and the roads were gridlocked.

Aggie wearily closed her eyes and leaned back. She was hungry and exhausted and trying to get through to Luiz was like beating her head against a brick wall.

She came to suddenly to the sound of Luiz's low, urgent voice and she blinked herself out of sleep. She had no idea how long she had been dozing, or even how she could manage to doze at all when her thoughts were all over the place.

He was on his phone, and from the sounds of it not enjoying the conversation he was having.

In fact, sitting up and stifling a yawn, it dawned on her that the voice on the other end of the mobile was the same smoky voice that had left a message on his answer machine earlier on, and the reason Aggie knew that was because the smoky voice had become high-pitched and shrill. Not only could *she* hear every word the other woman was saying, she guessed that if she rolled down her window the people in the car behind them would be able to as well.

'This is not the right time for this conversation…' Luiz was saying in a harried, urgent voice.

'Don't you dare hang up on me! I'll just keep calling! I deserve better than this!'

'Which is why you should be thanking me for putting an end to our relationship, Chloe. You do deserve a hell of a lot better than me.'

Aggie rolled her eyes. Wasn't that the oldest trick in the book? The one men used when they wanted to exit a relationship with their consciences intact? Take the blame for everything, manage to convince their hapless girlfriend that breaking up is all for her own good and then walk away feeling as though they've done their good deed for the day.

She listened while Luiz, obviously resigning himself to a conversation he hadn't initiated and didn't want, explained in various ways why they weren't working as a couple.

She had never seen him other than calm, self-assured, in complete control of himself and everything around him. People jumped to attention when he spoke and he had always had that air of command that was afforded to people of influence and power.

He was not that man when he finally ended the call to the sound of virulent abuse on the other end of the line.

'Well?' he demanded grittily. 'I am sure you have an opinion on the conversation you unfortunately had to over-hear.'

When she had asked him about his private life, this was not what she had been expecting. He had quizzed her about hers, about her brother's; a little retaliation had seemed only fair. But that conversation had been intensely personal.

'You've broken up with someone and I'm sorry about that,' Aggie said quietly. 'I know that it's wretched when a relationship comes to an end, especially if you've invested in it, and of course I don't want to talk about that. It's your business.'

'I like that.'

'What?'

'Your kind words of sympathy. Believe me when I tell you that there's nothing that could have snapped me out of my mood as efficiently as that.'

'What are you talking about?' Aggie asked, confused. She looked at him to see him smiling with amusement and when he flicked her a sideways glance his smile broadened.

'I'm not dying of a broken heart,' he assured her. 'In fact, if you'd been listening, I'm the one who instigated the break-up.'

'Yes,' Aggie agreed smartly. 'Which doesn't mean that it didn't hurt.'

'Are you speaking from experience?'

'Well, yes, as a matter of fact!'

'I'm inclined to believe you,' Luiz drawled. 'So why did you dump him? Wasn't he man enough to deal with your wilful, argumentative nature?'

'I'm neither of those things!' Aggie reddened and glared at his averted profile.

'On that point, we're going to have to differ.'

'I'm only argumentative with *you*, Luiz Montes! And perhaps that's because you've accused me of being a liar and an opportunist, plotting with my brother to take advantage of your niece!'

'Give it a rest. You have done nothing but argue with me since the second you met me. You've made telling comments about every restaurant, about the value of money, about people who think they can rule the world from a chequebook… You've covered all the ground when it comes to letting me know that you disapprove of wealth. Course, how was I to know that those were just cleverly positioned comments to downplay what you were all about? But let's leave that aside for the moment. Why did you dump the poor guy?'

'If you must know,' Aggie said, partly because constant arguing was tiring and partly because she wanted to let him know that Stu had not found her in the least bit argumentative, 'he became too jealous and too possessive, and I don't like those traits.'

'Amazing. I think we've discovered common ground.'

'Meaning?'

'Chloe went from obliging to demanding in record time.' They had finally cleared London and Luiz realised that unless they continued driving through the night they would have to take a break at some point along the route. It was also beginning to snow. For the moment, though, that was something he would keep to himself.

'Never a good trait as far as I am concerned.' He glanced at Aggie and was struck again by the extreme ultra-femininity of her looks. He imagined that guys could get sucked in by those looks only to discover a wildcat be-

hind the angelic front. Whatever scam she and her brother
had concocted between them, she had definitely been the
brains behind it. Hell, he could almost appreciate the sharp,
outspoken intelligence there. Under the low-level sniping,
she was a woman a guy could have a conversation with
and that, Luiz conceded, was something. He didn't have
much use for conversation with women, not when there
were always so many more entertaining ways of spending time with them.

Generally speaking, the women he had gone out with
had never sparked curiosity. Why would they? They had
always been a known quantity, wealthy socialites with
impeccable pedigrees. He was thirty-three years old and
could honestly say that he had never deviated from the
expected.

With work always centre-stage, it had been very easy
to slide in and out of relationships with women who were
socially acceptable. In a world where greed and avarice
lurked around every corner, it made sense to eliminate
the opportunist by making sure never to date anyone who
could fall into that category. He had never questioned it.
If none of the women in his past had ever succeeded in
capturing his attention for longer than ten seconds, then
he wasn't bothered. His sisters, bar two, had all done their
duty and reproduced, leaving him free to live his life the
way he saw fit.

'So…what do you mean? That the minute a woman
wants something committed you back away? Was that
what your ex-girlfriend was guilty of?'

'I make it my duty never to make promises I can't keep,'
Luiz informed her coolly. 'I'm always straight with women.
I'm not in it for the long run. Chloe, unfortunately, began
thinking that the rules of the game could be changed
somewhere along the line. I should have seen the signs,

of course,' he continued half to himself. 'The minute a woman starts making noises about wanting to spend a night in and play happy families is the minute the warning bells should start going off.'

'And they didn't?' Aggie was thinking that wanting to spend the odd night in didn't sound like an impossible dream or an undercover marriage proposal.

'She *was* very beautiful,' Luiz conceded with a laugh.

'Was that why you went out with her? Because of the way she looked?'

'I'm a great believer in the power of sexual attraction.'

'That's very shallow.'

Luiz laughed again and slanted an amused look at her. 'You're not into sex?'

Aggie reddened and her heart started pounding like a drum beat inside her. 'That's none of your business!'

'Some women aren't.' Luiz pushed the boundaries. Unlike the other times he had seen her, he now had her all to himself, undiluted by the presence of Mark and his niece. Naturally he would use the time to find out everything he could about her and her brother, all the better to prepare him for when they finally made it to the Lake District. But for now it was no hardship trying to prise underneath her prickly exterior to find out what made her tick. They were cooped up together in a car. What else was there to do? 'Are you one of those women?' he asked silkily.

'I happen to think that sex isn't the most important thing in a relationship!'

'That's probably because you haven't experienced good sex.'

'That's the most ridiculous thing I've ever heard in my life!' But her face was hot and flushed and she was finding it difficult to breathe properly.

'I hope I'm not embarrassing you...'

'I'm not *embarrassed*. I just think that this is an inappropriate conversation.'

'Because...?'

'Because I don't want to be here. Because you're dragging me off on a trek to find my brother so that you can accuse him of being an opportunist and fling money at him so that he goes away. Because you think that we can be bought off.'

'That aside...' He switched on his wipers as the first flurries of snow began to cloud the glass. 'We're here and we can't maintain hostilities indefinitely. And I hate to break this to you, but it looks as though our trip might end up taking a little longer than originally anticipated.'

'What do you mean?'

'Look ahead of you. The traffic is crawling and the snow's started to fall. I can keep driving for another hour or so but then we're probably going to have to pull in somewhere for the night. In fact, keep your eyes open. I'm going to divert to the nearest town and we're going to find somewhere overnight.'

CHAPTER THREE

IN THE end, she had to look up somewhere on his phone because they appeared to have entered hotel-free territory.

'It's just one reason why I try to never leave London,' Luiz muttered in frustration. 'Wide, empty open spaces with nothing inside them. Not even a halfway decent hotel, from the looks of it.'

'That's what most people love about getting out of London.'

'Repeat—different strokes for different folks. What have you found?' They had left the grinding traffic behind them. Now he had to contend with dangerously icy roads and thickly falling snow that limited his vision. He glanced across but couldn't see her face because of the fall of soft, finely spun golden hair across it.

'You're going to be disappointed because there are no fancy hotels, although there *is* a B and B about five miles away and it's rated very highly. It's a bit of a detour but it's the only thing I've been able to locate.'

'Address.' He punched it into his guidance system and relaxed at the thought that he would be able to take a break. 'Read me what it says about this place.'

'I don't suppose anyone's ever told you this but you talk to people as though they're your servants. You just expect people to do what you want them to do without question.'

'I would be inclined to agree with that,' Luiz drawled. 'But for the fact that you don't slot into that category, so there goes your argument. I ask you to simply tell me about this bed and breakfast, which you'll do but not until you let me know that you resent the request, and you resent the request for no other reason that I happen to be the one making it. The down side of accusing someone of being black-and-white is that you should be very sure that you don't fall into the same category yourself.'

Aggie flushed and scowled. 'Five bedrooms, two *en suite*, a sitting room. And the price includes a full English breakfast. There's also a charming garden area but I don't suppose that's relevant considering the weather. And I'm the least prejudiced person I know. I'm extremely open minded!'

'Five bedrooms. Two *en suite*. Is there nothing a little less basic in the vicinity?'

'We're in the country now,' Aggie informed him tersely, half-annoyed because he hadn't taken her up on what she had said. 'There are no five-star hotels, if that's what you mean.'

'You know,' Luiz murmured softly, straining to see his way forward when the wipers could barely handle the fall of snow on the windscreen, 'I can understand your hostility towards me, but what I find a little more difficult to understand is your hostility towards all displays of wealth. The first time I met you, you made it clear that expensive restaurants were a waste of money when all over the world people were going without food... But hell, I don't want to get into this. It's hard enough trying to concentrate on not going off the road without launching into yet another pointless exchange of words. You're going to have to look out for a sign.'

Of course, he had no interest in her personally, not be-

yond wanting to protect his family and their wealth from
her, so she should be able to disregard everything he said.
But he had still managed to make her feel like a hypocrite
and Aggie shifted uncomfortably.

'I'm sorry I can't offer to share the driving,' she muttered, to smooth over her sudden confusion at the way he
had managed to turn her notions about herself on their
head. 'But I don't have my driving licence.'

'I wouldn't ask you to drive even if you did,' Luiz informed her.

'Because women need protecting?' But she was half-
smiling when she said that.

'Because I would have a nervous breakdown.'

Aggie stifled a giggle. He had a talent for making her
want to laugh when she knew she should be on the defensive. 'That's very chauvinistic.'

'I think you've got the measure of me. I don't make a
good back-seat driver.'

'That's probably because you feel that you always have
to be in control,' Aggie pointed out. 'And I suppose you
really are always in control, aren't you?'

'I like to be.' Luiz had slowed the car right down. Even
though it was a powerful four-wheel drive, he knew that
the road was treacherous and ungritted. 'Are you going to
waste a few minutes trying to analyse me now?'

'I wouldn't dream of it!' But she was feverishly ana-
lysing him in her head, eaten up with curiosity as to what
made this complex man tick. She didn't care, of course. It
was a game generated by the fact that they were in close
proximity, but she caught herself wondering whether his
need for absolute control wasn't an inherited obligation.
He was an only son of a Latin American magnate. Had
he been trained to see himself as ruler of all he surveyed?
It occurred to her that this wasn't the first time she had

found herself wondering about him, and that was an uneasy thought.

'Anyway, we're here.' They were now in a village and she could see that it barely encompassed a handful of shops, in between and around which radiated small houses, the sort of houses found in books depicting the perfect English country village. The bed and breakfast was a tiny semi-detached house, very easily bypassed were it not for the sign swinging outside, barely visible under the snow.

It was very late and the roads were completely deserted. Even the bed and breakfast was plunged in darkness, except for two outside lights which just about managed to illuminate the front of the house and a metre or two of garden in front.

With barely contained resignation, Luiz pulled up outside and killed the engine.

'It looks wonderful,' Aggie breathed, taken with the creamy yellow stone and the perfectly proportioned leaded windows. She could picture the riot of colour in summer with all manner of flowers ablaze in the front garden and the soporific sound of the bees buzzing between them.

'Sorry?' Luiz wondered whether they were looking at the same house.

' 'Course, I would rather not be here with *you*,' Aggie emphasised. 'But it's beautiful. Especially with the snow on the ground and on the roof. Gosh, it's really deep as well! That's the one thing I really miss about living in the south. Snow.'

On that tantalising statement, she flung open the car door and stepped outside, holding her arms out wide and her head tilted up so that the snow could fall directly onto her face.

In the act of reaching behind him to extract their cases, Luiz paused to stare at her. She had pulled some fingerless gloves out of her coat pocket and stuck them on and standing like that, arms outstretched, she looked young, vulnerable and achingly innocent, a child reacting to the thrill of being out in the snow.

Beside the point what she looks like, he told himself, breaking the momentary spell to get their bags. She was pretty. He knew that. He had known that from the very first second he had set eyes on her. The world was full of pretty women, especially *his* world, which was not only full of pretty women but pretty women willing to throw themselves at him.

Aggie began walking towards the house, her feet sinking into the snow, and only turned to look around when he had slammed shut the car door and was standing in front of it, a bag in either hand—his mega-expensive bag, her forlorn and cheaply made one which had been her companion from the age of fourteen when she had spent her first night at a friend's house.

He looked just so incongruous. She couldn't see his expression because it was dark but she imagined that he would be bewildered, removed from his precious creature comforts and thrown into a world far removed from the expensive one he occupied. A bed and breakfast with just five bedrooms, only two of which were *en suite*! What a horror story for him! Not to mention the fact that he would have to force himself to carry on being polite to the sister of an unscrupulous opportunist who was plotting to milk his niece for her millions. He was lead actor in the middle of his very worst nightmare and as he stood there, watching her, she reached down to scoop up a handful of snow, cold and crisp and begging to be moulded into a ball.

All her anger and frustration towards him and towards herself for reacting to him when she should be able to be cool and dismissive went into that throw, and she held her breath as the snowball arched upwards and travelled with deadly accuracy towards him, hitting him right in the middle of that broad, muscled, arrogant chest.

She didn't know who was more surprised. Her, for having thrown it in the first place, or him for being hit for the first time in his life by a snowball. Before he could react, she turned her back and began plodding to the front door.

He deserved that, she told herself nervously. He was insulting, offensive and dismissive. He had accused her and her brother in the worst possible way of the worst possible things and had not been prepared to nurture any doubts that he might be wrong. Plus he had had the cheek to make her question herself when she hadn't done anything wrong!

Nevertheless, she didn't want to look back over her shoulder for fear of seeing what his reaction might be at her small act of resentful rebellion.

'Nice shot!' she heard him shout, at which she began to turn around when she felt the cold, wet compacted blow of his retaliation. She had launched her missile at his chest and he had done the same, and his shot was even more faultless than hers had been.

Aggie's mouth dropped open and she looked at him incredulously as he began walking towards her.

'Good shot. Bull's eye.' He grinned at her and he was transformed, the harsh, unforgiving lines of his face replaced by a sex appeal that was so powerful that it almost knocked her sideways. The breath caught in her throat and she found that she was staring up at him while her thoughts tumbled around as though they had been tossed into a spin drier turned to full speed.

'You too,' was all she could think of saying. 'Where did you learn to throw a snowball?'

'Boarding school. Captain of the cricket team. I was their fast bowler.' He rang the doorbell but he didn't take his eyes from her face. 'Did you think that I was so pampered that I wouldn't have been able to retaliate?' he taunted softly.

'Yes.' Her mouth felt as though it was stuffed with cotton wool. Pampered? Yes, of course he was…and yet a less pampered man it would have been hard to find. How did that make sense?

'Where did *you* learn to throw a shot like that? You hit me from thirty metres away. Through thick snow and poor visibility.'

Aggie blinked in an attempt to gather her scattered wits, but she still heard herself say, with complete honesty, 'We grew up with snow in winter. We learned to build snowmen and have snowball fights and there were always lots of kids around because we were raised in a children's home.'

Deafening silence greeted this remark. She hadn't planned on saying that, but out it had come, and she could have kicked herself. Thankfully she was spared the agony of his contempt by the door being pulled open and they were ushered inside by a short, jolly woman in her sixties who beamed at them as though they were much expected long-lost friends, even though it was nearly ten and she had probably been sound asleep.

Of course there was room for them! Business was never good in winter…just the one room let to a long-standing resident who worked nearby during the week…not that there was any likelihood that he would be leaving for his home in Yorkshire at the weekend…not in this snow…had they seen anything like it…?

The jovial patter kept Aggie's turbulent thoughts temporarily at bay. Regrettably, one of the *en suite* rooms was occupied by the long-standing resident who wouldn't be able to return to Yorkshire at the weekend. As she looked brightly between them to see who would opt for the remaining *en suite* bedroom, Aggie smiled innocently at Luiz until he was forced to do the expected and concede to sharing a bathroom.

She could feel him simmering next to her as they were proudly shown the sitting room, where there was 'a wide assortment of channels on the telly because they had recently had cable fitted'. And the small breakfast room where they could have the best breakfast in the village, and also dinner if they would like, although because of the hour she could only run to sandwiches just now...

Aggie branched off into her own, generously proportioned and charming bedroom and nodded blandly when Luiz informed her that he would see her in the sitting room in ten minutes. They both needed something to eat.

There was just time to wash her face, no time at all to unpack or have a bath and get into fresh clothes. Downstairs, Luiz was waiting for her. She heard the rumble of his voice and low laughter as he talked to the landlady. Getting closer, she could make out that he was explaining that they were on their way to visit relatives, that the snow had temporarily cut short their journey. That, yes, public transport would have been more sensible but for the fact that the trains had responded to the bad weather by going on strike. However, what a blessing in disguise, because how else would they have discovered this charming part of the world? And perhaps she could bring them a bottle of wine with their sandwiches...whatever she had to hand would do as long as it was cold...

'So...' Luiz drawled as soon as they had the sitting room to themselves. 'The truth is now all coming out in the wash. Were you ever going to tell me about your background or were you intending to keep that little titbit to yourself until it no longer mattered who knew?'

'I didn't think it was relevant.'

'Do me a favour, Aggie.'

'I'm not ashamed of...' She sighed and ran her fingers through her hair. It was cosy in here and beautifully warm, with an open fire at one end. He had removed his jumper and rolled his sleeves up and her eyes strayed to his arms, sprinkled with dark hair. He had an athlete's body and she had to curb the itch to stare at him. She didn't know where that urge was coming from. Or had it been there from the start?

Wine was brought to them and she felt like she needed some. One really big glass to help her through this conversation...

'You're not ashamed of...? Concealing the truth?'

'I didn't think of it as concealing the truth.'

'Well, forgive me, but it seems a glaring omission.'

'It's not something I talk about.'

'Why not?'

'Why do you think?' She glared at him, realised that the big glass of wine had somehow disappeared in record time and didn't refuse when her wine glass was topped up.

Luiz flushed darkly. It wouldn't do to forget that this was not a date. He wasn't politely delving down conversational avenues as a prelude to sex. Omissions like this mattered, given the circumstances. But those huge blue eyes staring at him with a mixture of uncertainty and accusation were getting to him.

'You tell me.'

'People can be judgemental,' Aggie muttered defensively. 'As soon as you say that you grew up in a children's home, people switch off. You wouldn't understand. How could you? You've always led the kind of life people like us dreamt about. A life of luxury, with family all around you. Even if your sisters were bossy and told you what to do when you were growing up. It's a different world.'

'I'm not without imagination,' Luiz said gruffly.

'But this is just something else that you can hold against us…just another nail in the coffin.'

Yes, it was! But he was still curious to find out about that shady background she had kept to herself. He barely noticed when a platter of sandwiches was placed in front of them, accompanied by an enormous salad, along with another bottle of excellent wine.

'You went to a boarding school. I went to the local comprehensive where people sniggered because I was one of those kids from a children's home. Sports days were a nightmare. Everyone else would have their family there, shouting and yelling them on. I just ran and ran and ran and pretended that there were people there cheering *me* on. Sometimes Gordon or Betsy—the couple who ran the home—would try and come but it was difficult. I could deal with all of that but Mark was always a lot more sensitive.'

'Which is why you're so close now. You said that your parents were dead.'

'They are.' She helped herself to a bit more wine, even though she was unaccustomed to alcohol and was dimly aware that she would probably have a crashing headache the following morning. 'Sort of.'

'Sort of? Don't go coy on me, Aggie. How can people be *sort of* dead?'

Stripped bare of all the half-truths that had somehow been told to him over a period of time, Aggie resigned herself to telling him the unvarnished truth now about their background. He could do whatever he liked with the information, she thought recklessly. He could try to buy them off, could shake his head in disgust at being in the company of someone so far removed from himself. She should never have let her brother and Maria talk her into painting a picture that wasn't completely accurate.

A lot of that had stemmed from her instinctive need to protect Mark, to do what was best for him. She had let herself be swayed by her brother being in love for the first time, by Maria's tactful downplaying of just how protective her family was and why... And she also couldn't deny that Luiz had rubbed her up the wrong way from the very beginning. It hadn't been hard to swerve round the truth, pulling out pieces of it here and there, making sure to nimbly skip over the rest. He was so arrogant. He almost deserved it!

'We never knew our father,' she now admitted grudgingly. 'He disappeared after I was born, and continued showing up off and on, but he finally did a runner when Mum became pregnant with Mark.'

'He did a runner...'

'I'll bet you haven't got a clue what I'm talking about, Luiz.'

'It's hard for me to get my head around the concept of a father abandoning his family,' Luiz admitted.

'You're lucky,' Aggie told him bluntly and Luiz looked at her with dry amusement.

'My life was prescribed,' he found himself saying. 'Often it was not altogether ideal. Carry on.'

Aggie wanted to ask him to expand, to tell her what he meant by a 'prescribed life'. From the outside looking in, all she could see was perfection for him: a united, large family, exempt from all the usual financial headaches, with everyone able to do exactly what they wanted in the knowledge that if they failed there would always be a safety net to catch them.

'What else is there to say? I was nine when Mum died.' She looked away and stared off at the open fire. The past was not a place she revisited with people but she found that she was past resenting what he knew about her. He would never change his mind about the sort of person he imagined she was, but that didn't mean that she had to accept all his accusations without a fight.

'How did she die?'

'Do you care?' Aggie asked, although half-heartedly. 'She was killed in an accident returning from work. She had a job at the local supermarket and she was walking home when she was hit by a drunk-driver. There were no relatives, no one to take us in, and we were placed in a children's home. A wonderful place with a wonderful couple running it who saw us both through our bad times, we couldn't have hoped for a happier upbringing, given the circumstances. So please don't feel sorry for either of us.' The sandwiches were delicious but her appetite had nosedived.

'I'm sorry about your mother.'

'Are you?' But she was instantly ashamed of the bitterness in her voice. 'Thank you. It was a long time ago.' She gave a dry, self-deprecating laugh. 'I expect all this information is academic because you've already made your mind up about us. But you can see why it wouldn't have made for a great opening conversation...especially when I knew from the start that the only reason you'd bothered to ask Maria out with us was so that you could check my brother out.'

Normally, Luiz cared very little about what other people thought of him. It was what made him so straightforward in his approach to tackling difficult situations. He never wasted time beating about the bush. Now, he felt an unaccustomed dart of shame when he thought back to how unapologetic he had been on every occasion he had met them, how direct his questions had been. He had made no attempt to conceal the reason for his sudden interest in his niece. He hadn't been overtly hostile but Aggie, certainly, was sharp enough to have known exactly what his motives were. So could he really blame her if she hadn't launched into a sob story about her deprived background?

Strangely, he felt a tug of admiration for the way she had managed to forge a path for herself through difficult circumstances. It certainly demonstrated the sort of strength of personality he had rarely glimpsed in the opposite sex. He grimaced when he thought of the women he dated. Chloe might be beautiful but she was also colourless and unambitious...just another cover girl born with a silver spoon in her mouth, biding her time at a fairly pointless part-time job until a rich man rescued her from the need to pretend to work at all.

'So where was this home?'

'Lake District,' Aggie replied with a little shrug. She looked into those deep, deep, dark eyes and her mouth went dry.

'Hence you said that they went somewhere that had sentimental meaning for you.'

'Do you remember everything that people say to you?' Aggie asked irritably and he shot her one of those amazing, slow smiles that did strange things to her heart rate.

'It's a blessing and a curse. You blush easily. Do you know that?'

'That's probably because I feel awkward here with you,' Aggie retorted, but on cue she could feel her face going red.

'No idea why.' Luiz pushed himself away from the table and stretched out his legs to one side. He noticed that they had managed to work their way through nearly two bottles of wine. 'We're having a perfectly civilised conversation. Tell me why you decided to move to London.'

'Tell me why *you* did.'

'I took over an empire. The London base needed expanding. I was the obvious choice. I went to school here. I understand the way the people think.'

'But did you *want* to settle here? I mean, it must be a far cry from Brazil.'

'It works for me.'

He continued looking at her as what was left of the sandwiches were cleared away and coffee offered to them. Considering the hour, their landlady was remarkably obliging, waving aside Aggie's apologies for arriving at such an inconvenient time, telling them that business was to be welcomed whatever time it happened to arrive. Beggars couldn't be choosers.

But neither of them wanted coffee. Aggie was so tired that she could barely stand. She was also tipsy; too much wine on an empty stomach.

'I'm going to go outside for a bit,' she said. 'I think I need to get some fresh air.'

'You're going outside in *this* weather?'

'I'm used to it. I grew up with snow.' She stood up and had to steady herself and breathe in deeply.

'I don't care if you grew up running wild in the Himalayas, you're not going outside, and not because I don't think that you can handle the weather. You're not going outside because you've had too much to drink and you'll probably pass out.'

Aggie glared at him and gripped the table. God, her head was swimming, and she knew that she really ought to get to bed, do just as he said. But there was no way that she was going to allow him to dictate her movements on top of everything else.

'Don't tell me what I can and can't do, Luiz Montes!'

He looked at her in silence and then shrugged. 'And do

you intend to go out without a coat, because you're used to the snow?'

'Of course not!'

'Well, that's a relief.' He stood up and shoved his hands in the pockets of his trousers. 'Make sure you have a key to get back in,' he told her. 'I think we've caused our obliging landlady enough inconvenience for one night without having to get her out of bed to let you in because you've decided to take a walk in driving snow.'

Out of the corner of his eye, he saw Mrs Bixby, the landlady, heading towards them like a ship in full sail. But when she began expressing concern about Aggie's decision to step outside for a few minutes, Luiz shook his head ever so slightly.

'I'm sure Agatha is more than capable of taking care of herself,' he told Mrs Bixby. 'But she will need a key to get back in.'

'I expect you want me to thank you,' Aggie hissed, once she was in possession of the front-door key and struggling to get her arms into her coat. Now that she was no longer supporting herself against the dining-room table, her light-headedness was accompanied by a feeling of nausea. She also suspected that her words were a little slurred even though she was taking care to enunciate each and every syllable very carefully.

'Thank me for what?' Luiz walked with her to the front door. 'Your coat's not done up properly.' He pointed to the buttons which she had failed to match up properly, and then he leaned against the wall and watched as she fumbled to try and remedy the oversight.

'Stop staring at me!'

'Just making sure that you're well wrapped up. Would you like to borrow my scarf? No bother for me to run upstairs and get it for you.'

'I'm absolutely fine.' A wave of sickness washed over her as she tilted her head to look him squarely in the face.

Very hurriedly, she let herself out of the house while Luiz turned to Mrs Bixby and grinned. 'I intend to take up residence in the dining room. I'll sit by the window and make sure I keep an eye on her. Don't worry; if she's not back inside in under five minutes, I'll forcibly bring her in myself.'

'Coffee while you wait?'

'Strong, black would be perfect.'

He was still grinning as he manoeuvred a chair so that he could relax back and see her as she stood still in the snow for a few seconds, breathing in deeply from the looks of it, before tramping in circles on the front lawn. He couldn't imagine her leaving the protective circle of light and striking out for an amble in the town. The plain truth was that she had had a little too much to drink. She had been distinctly green round the gills when she had stood up after eating a couple of sandwiches, although that was something she would never have admitted to.

Frankly, Luiz had no time for women who drank, but he could hardly blame her. Neither of them had been aware of how much wine had been consumed. She would probably wake up with a headache in the morning, which would be a nuisance, as he wanted to leave at the crack of dawn, weather permitting. But that was life.

He narrowed his eyes and sat forward as she became bored with her circular tramping and began heading towards the little gate that led out towards the street and the town.

Without waiting for the coffee, he headed for the front door, only pausing on the way to tell Mrs Bixby that he'd let himself back in.

She'd vanished from sight and Luiz cursed fluently

under his breath. Without a coat it was freezing and he was half-running when he saw her staggering up the street with purpose before pausing to lean against a lamp post, head buried in the crook of her elbow.

'Bloody woman,' he muttered under his breath. He picked up speed as much as he could and reached her side just in time to scoop her up as she was about to slide to the ground.

Aggie shrieked.

'Do you intend to wake the entire town?' Luiz began walking as quickly as he could back to the bed and breakfast. Which, in snow that was fast settling, wasn't very quickly at all.

'Put me down!' She pummelled ineffectively at his chest but soon gave up because the activity made her feel even more queasy.

'Now, that has to be the most stupid thing ever to have left your lips.'

'I said put me *down*!'

'If I put you down, you wouldn't be able to get back up. You don't honestly think I missed the fact that you were hanging onto that lamp post for dear life, do you?'

'I don't need rescuing by you!'

'And I don't need to be out here in freezing weather playing the knight in shining armour! Now shut up!'

Aggie was so shocked by that insufferably arrogant command that she shut up.

She wouldn't have admitted it in a million years but it felt good to be carried like this, because her legs had been feeling very wobbly. In fact, she really had been on the point of wanting to sink to the ground just to take the weight off them before he had swept her off her feet.

She felt him nudge the front door open with his foot, which meant that it had been left ajar. It was humiliating to think of Mrs Bixby seeing her like this and she buried herself against Luiz, willing herself to disappear.

'Don't worry,' Luiz murmured drily in her ear. 'Our friendly landlady is nowhere to be seen. I told her to go to bed, that I'd make sure I brought you in in one piece.'

Aggie risked a glance at the empty hall and instructed him to put her down.

'That dumb suggestion again. You're drunk and you need to get to bed, which is what I told you before you decided to prove how stubborn you could be by ignoring my very sound advice.'

'I am not *drunk*. I am *never* drunk.' She was alarmed by a sudden need to hiccup, which she thankfully stifled. 'Furthermore, I am *more than* capable of making my own way upstairs.'

'Okay.' He released her fast enough for her to feel the ground rushing up to meet her and she clutched his jumper with both hands and took a few deep breaths. 'Still want to convince me that you're *more than capable* of making your own way upstairs?'

'I hate you!' Aggie muttered as he swept her back up into his arms.

'You have a tendency to be repetitive,' Luiz murmured, and he didn't have to see her face to know that she was glaring at him. 'And I'm surprised and a little offended that you hate me for rescuing you from almost certainly falling flat on your face in the snow and probably going to sleep. As a teacher, you should know that that is the most dangerous thing that could happen, passing out in the snow. While under the influence of alcohol. Tut, tut, tut. You'd be struck off the responsible-teacher register if they ever found out about that. Definitely not a good example to set for impressionable little children, seeing their teacher the worse for wear...'

'Shut up,' Aggie muttered fiercely.

'Now, let's see. Forgotten which room is yours… Oh, it's coming back to me—the only one left with the *en suite*! Fortuitous, because you might be needing that…'

'Oh be quiet,' Aggie moaned. 'And hurry up! I think I'm going to be sick.'

CHAPTER FOUR

SHE made it to the bathroom in the nick of time and was horribly, shamefully, humiliatingly, wretchedly sick. She hadn't bothered to shut the door and she was too weak to protest when she heard Luiz enter the bathroom behind her.

'Sorry,' she whispered, hearing the flush of the toilet and finding a toothbrush pressed into her hand. While she was busy being sick, he had obviously rummaged through her case and located just the thing she needed.

She shakily cleaned her teeth but lacked the energy to tell him to leave.

Nor could she look at him. She flopped down onto the bed and closed her eyes as he drew the curtains shut, turned off the overhead light and began easing her boots off.

Luiz had never done anything like this before. In fact, he had never been in the presence of a woman quite so violently sick after a bout of excessive drinking and, if someone had told him that one day he would be taking care of such a woman, he would have laughed out loud. Women who were out of control disgusted him. An out-of-control Chloe, shouting hysterically down the phone, sobbing and shrieking and cursing him, had left him cold. He looked at Aggie, who now had her arm covering her face, and wondered why he wasn't disgusted.

He had wet a face cloth; he mopped her forehead and heard her sigh.

'So I guess I should be thanking you,' she said, without moving the hand that lay across her face.

'You could try that,' Luiz agreed.

'How did you know where to find me?'

'I watched you from the dining room. I wasn't going to let you stay out there for longer than five minutes.'

'Because, of course, you know best.'

'Staggering in the dark in driving snow when you've had too much to drink isn't a good idea in anyone's eyes,' Luiz said drily.

'And I don't suppose you'll believe me when I tell you that this is the first time I've ever…ever…done this?'

'I believe you.'

Aggie lowered her protective arm and looked at him. Her eyes felt sore, along with everything else, and she was relieved that the room was only lit by the small lamp on the bedside table.

'You do?'

'It's my fault. I should have said no to that second bottle of wine. In fact, I was barely aware of it being brought.' He shrugged. 'These things happen.'

'But I don't suppose they ever happen to you,' Aggie said with a weak smile. 'I bet you don't drink too much and stagger all over the place and then end up having to be helped up to bed like a baby.'

Luiz laughed. 'No, can't say I remember the last time that happened.'

'And I bet you've never been in the company of a woman who's done that.'

No one would dare behave like that in my presence, was what he could have said, except he was disturbed to find that that would have made him sound like a monster.

'No,' he said flatly. 'And now I'm going to go and get you some painkillers. You're going to need them.'

Aggie yawned and looked at him drowsily. She had a sudden, sharp memory of how it had felt being carried by him. He had lifted her up as though she weighed nothing and his chest against her slight frame had been as hard as steel. He had smelled clean, masculine and woody.

'Yes. Thank you,' she said faintly. 'And once again, I'm so sorry.'

'Stop apologising.' Luiz's tone was abrupt. Was he really so controlling that women edited their personalities just to be with him; sipped their wine but left most of it and said no to dessert because they were afraid that he might pass judgement on them as being greedy or uncontrolled? He had broken off with Chloe and had offered her no explanation other than that she would be 'better off without him'. Strictly speaking, true. But he knew that, in the face of her hysterics, he had been impatient, short tempered and dismissive. He had always taken it as a given that women would go out of their way to please them, just as he had always taken it as a given that he led a life of moving on; that, however hard they tried, one day it would just be time for him to end it.

Aggie bristled at his obvious displeasure at her repeated apology. God, what must he think of her? The starting point of his opinions had been low enough, but they would be a hundred times lower now —except when the starting point was gold-digger, then how much lower could they get?

She was suddenly too tired to give it any more thought. She half-sat up when he approached with a glass of water. She obediently swallowed two tablets and was reassured that she would be right as rain in the morning. More or less.

'Thanks,' Aggie said glumly. 'And please wake me up first thing.'

'Of course.' Luiz frowned, impatient at the sudden burst of unwelcome introspection which had left him questioning himself.

Aggie fell asleep with that frown imprinted on her brain. It was confusing that someone she didn't care about should have any effect on her whatsoever, but he did.

She vaguely thought that things would be back to normal in the morning. She would dislike him. He would stop being three-dimensional and she would cease to be curious about him.

When she groggily came to, her head was thumping, her mouth tasted of cotton wool and Luiz was slumped in a chair he had pulled and positioned next to her bed. He was fully clothed.

For a few seconds, Aggie didn't take it in, then she struggled up and nudged him.

'What are *you* doing here?'

Belatedly she realised that, although the duvet was tucked around her, she was trouserless and jumperless; searing embarrassment flooded through her.

'I couldn't leave you in the state you were in.' Luiz pressed his eyes with his fingers and then raked both hands through his tousled hair before looking at her.

'I wasn't *in a state*. I...yes...I was...sick but then I fell asleep.'

'You were sick again,' Luiz informed her. 'And that's not taking into account raging thirst and demands for more tablets.'

'Oh God.'

'Sadly, God wasn't available, so it was up to me to find my way down to the kitchen for orange juice because you claimed that any more water would make you feel even more sick. I also had to deal with a half-asleep temper tantrum when I refused to double the dose of painkillers…'

Aggie looked at him in horror.

'Then you said that you were hot.'

'I didn't.'

'You threw off the quilt and started undressing.'

Aggie groaned and covered her face with her hands.

'But, gentleman that I am, I made sure you didn't completely strip naked. I undressed you down to the basics and you fell back asleep.'

Luiz watched her small fingers curl around the quilt cover. He imagined she would be going through mental hell but she was too proud to let it show. Had he ever met anyone like her in his life before? He'd almost forgotten the reason she was with him. She seemed to have a talent for running circles round his formidable single-mindedness and it wasn't just now that they had been thrown together. No, it had happened before. Some passing remark he might have made to which she had taken instant offence, dug her heels in and proceeded to argue with him until he'd forgotten the presence of other people.

'Well…thank you for that. I…I'd like to get changed now.' She addressed the wall and the dressing table in front of her, and heard him slap his thighs with his hands and stand up. 'Did you manage to get any sleep at all?'

'None to speak of,' Luiz admitted.

'You must be exhausted.'

'I don't need much sleep.'

'Well, perhaps you should go and grab a few hours before we start on the last leg of this journey.' It would be nice if the ground could do her a favour and open up and swallow her whole.

'No point.'

Aggie looked at him in consternation. 'What do you

mean that there's no point? It would be downright fool-hardy for you to drive without sleep, and I can't share any of the driving with you.'

'We've covered that. There's no point because it's gone two-thirty in the afternoon, it's already dark and the snow's heavier.' Luiz strode towards the window and pulled back the curtains to reveal never-ending skies the colour of lead, barely visible behind dense, relentlessly falling snow. 'It would be madness to try and get anywhere further in weather like this. I've already booked the rooms for at least another night. Might be more.'

'You can't!' Aggie sat up, dismayed. 'I thought I'd be back at work on Monday! I can't just *disappear*. This is the busiest time of the school year!'

'Too bad,' Luiz told her flatly. 'You're stuck. There's no way I intend to turn around and try and get back to London. And, while you're busy worrying about missing a few classes and the Nativity play, spare a thought for me. I didn't think that I'd be covering half the country in driving snow in an attempt to rescue my niece before she does something stupid.'

'Meaning that your job's more important than mine?' Aggie was more comfortable with this: an argument. Much more comfortable than she was with feverishly thinking about him undressing her, taking care of her, putting her to bed and playing the good guy. 'Typical! Why is it that rich people always think that what they do is more impor-tant than what everyone else does?' She glared at him as he stood by the door, impassively watching her.

For one blinding moment, it occurred to her that she was in danger of seeing beyond the obvious differences between them to the man underneath. If she could list all the things she disliked about him on paper, it would be easy to keep her distance and to fill the spaces between them with hostility and resentment. But to do that would be to fall into the trap of being as black-and-white in her opinions as she had accused him of being.

She paled and her heartbeat picked up in nervous confusion. Had he been working his charm on her from the very beginning? When he had drawn grudging laughs from her and held her reluctantly spellbound with stories of his experiences in foreign countries; when he had engaged her interest in politics and world affairs, while Maria and Mark had been loved up and whispering to each other, distracted by some shared joke they couldn't possibly resist. Had she already begun to see beyond the cardboard cut-out she wanted him to be?

And, stuck together in a car with him, here in this bed and breakfast. Would an arrogant, pompous, single-minded creep really have helped her the way he had the night before, not laughing once at her inappropriate behaviour? Keeping watch over her even though it meant that he hadn't got a wink of sleep? She had to drag out the recollection that he had offered her money in return for his niece; that he was going to offer her brother money to clear off; that liking or not liking someone was not something that mattered to him because he was like a juggernaut when it came to getting exactly what he wanted. He had loads of charm when it suited him, but underneath the charm he was ruthless, heartless and emotionless.

She felt a lot calmer once that message had got to her wayward, rebellious brain and imprinted itself there.

'Well?' she persisted scornfully, and Luiz raised his eyebrows wryly.

'I take it you're angling for a fight. Is this because you feel embarrassed about what happened last night? If it is, then there's really no need. Like I said…these things happen.'

'And, like you also said, you've never had this experience in your life before!' Aggie thought that it would help things considerably if he didn't look so damn gorgeous standing there, even though he hadn't slept and should look a wreck. 'You've never fallen down drunk, and I'll bet that none of your girlfriends have either.'

'You're right. I haven't and they haven't.'

'Is that because none of your girlfriends have ever had too much to drink?'

'Maybe they have.' Luiz shrugged. 'But never in my presence. And, by the way, I don't think that my job is any better or worse than yours. I have a very big deal on the cards which is due to close at the beginning of next week. A takeover. People's jobs are relying on the closure of this deal, hence the reason why it's as inconvenient for me to be delayed with this as it is for you.'

'Oh,' Aggie said, flustered.

'So, if you need to get in touch with your school and ask them for a day or so off, then I'm sure it won't be the end of the world. Now, I'm going to have a shower and head downstairs. Mrs Bixby might be able to rustle you up something to eat.'

He closed the door quietly behind him. At the mention of food, Aggie's stomach had started to rumble, but she made sure not to rush her bath, to take her time washing her hair and using the drier which she found in a drawer in the bedroom. She needed to get her thoughts together. There was no doubt that the fast-falling snow would keep them in this town for another night. It wasn't going to be a case of a few hours on the road and then, whatever the outcome, goodbye to Luiz Montes for ever.

She was going to have his company for longer than she had envisaged and she needed to take care not to fall into the trap of being seduced by his charm. It amazed her that common sense and logic didn't seem to be enough to keep her mind on the straight and narrow.

Rooting through her depleted collection of clothes, she pulled out yet more jeans and a jumper under which she stuck on various layers, a vest, a long-sleeved thermal top, another vest over that...

Looking at her reflection in the mirror, she wondered whether it was possible to look frumpier. Her newly washed hair was uncontrollable, curling in an unruly tumble over her shoulders and down her back. She was bare of make-up because there seemed no point in applying any, and anyway she had only brought her mascara and some lip gloss with her. Her clothes were a dowdy mixture of blues and greys. Her only shoes were the boots she had been wearing because she hadn't foreseen anything more extended than one night somewhere and a meal grabbed on the hop, but now she wished that she had packed a little bit more than a skeleton, functional wardrobe.

Luiz was on the phone when she joined him in the sitting room but he snapped shut the mobile and looked at her as she walked towards him.

With all those thick, drab clothes, anyone could be forgiven for thinking that she was shapeless. She wasn't. He had known that from the times he had seen her out, usually wearing dresses in which she looked ill at ease and uncomfortable. But even those dresses had been designed to cover up. Only last night had he realised just how shapely she was, despite the slightness of her frame.

Startled, he felt the stirrings of an arousal at the memory and he abruptly turned away to beckon Mrs Bixby across for a pot of tea.

'Not for me.' Aggie declined the cup put in front of her. 'I've decided that I'm going to go into town, get some fresh air.'

'Fresh air. You seem to be cursed with a desire for fresh air. Isn't that what got you outside last night?'

But she couldn't get annoyed with him because his voice was lazy and teasing. 'This time I'm not falling over myself. Like I told you, I enjoy snow. I wish it snowed more often in London.'

'The city would grind to a standstill. If you're heading out, then I think I'll accompany you.'

Aggie tried to stifle the flutter of panic his suggestion generated. She needed to clear her mind. However much she lectured herself on all the reasons she had for hating him, there was a pernicious thread of stubbornness that just wanted to go its own merry way, reminding her of his sexiness, his intelligence, that unexpected display of consideration the night before. How was she to deal with that stubbornness if he didn't give her a little bit of peace and privacy?

'I actually intended on going on my own,' she said in a polite let-down. 'For a start, it would give you time to work. You always work. I remember you saying that to us once when your mobile phone rang for the third time over dinner and you took the call. Besides, if you have an important deal to close, then maybe you could get a head start on it.'

'It's Saturday. Besides, it would do me good to stretch my legs. Believe it or not, chairs don't make the most comfortable places to sleep.'

'You're not going to let me forget that in a hurry, are you?'

'Would you if you were in my shoes?'

Aggie had the grace to blush.

'No,' Luiz murmured. 'Thought not. Well, at least you're honest enough not to deny it.' He stood up, towering over her while Aggie stuffed her hands in the pockets of her coat and frantically tried to think of ways of dodging him.

And yet, disturbingly, wasn't she just a little pleased that he would be with her? For good or bad, and she couldn't decide which, her senses were heightened whenever he was around. Her heart beat faster, her skin tingled more, her pulse raced faster and every nerve ending in her seemed to vibrate.

Was that nature's way of keeping her on her toes in the face of the enemy?

'You'll need to have something to eat,' was the first thing he said when they were outside, where the brutal cold was like a stinging slap on the face. The snow falling and collecting on the already thick banks on the pavements turned the winter-wonderland scene into a nightmare of having to walk at a snail's pace.

Her coat was not made for this depth of cold and she could feel herself shivering, while in his padded Barbour, fashioned for arctic conditions, he was doubtless as snug as a bug in a rug.

'Stop telling me what to do.'

'And stop being so damned mulish.' Luiz looked down at her. She had rammed her woolly hat low down over her ears and she was cold. He could tell from the way she had hunched up and the way her hands were balled into fists in the pockets of the coat. 'You're cold.'

'It's a cold day. I like it. It felt stuffy inside.'

'I mean, your coat is inadequate. You need something warmer.'

'You're doing it again.' Aggie looked up at him and her breath caught in her throat as their eyes tangled and he didn't look away. 'Behaving,' she said a little breathlessly, 'as though you have all the answers to everything.' She was dismayed to find that, although she was saying the right thing, it was as if she was simply going through the motions while her body was responding in a different manner. 'I've been meaning to buy another coat, but there's hardly ever any need for it in London.'

'You can buy one here.'

'It's a bad time of the year for me,' Aggie muttered. 'Christmas always is.' She eyed the small town approaching with some relief. 'We exchange presents at school… then there's the tree and the food…it all adds up. You wouldn't understand.'

'Try me.'

Aggie hesitated. She wasn't used to confiding. She just wasn't built that way and she especially couldn't see the point in confiding in someone like Luiz Montes, a man who had placed her in an impossible situation, who was merciless in pursuit, who probably didn't have a sympathetic bone in his body.

Except, a little voice said in her head, *he took care of you last night, didn't he? Without a hint of impatience or rancour.*

'When you grow up in a children's home,' she heard herself say, 'even in a great children's home like the one I grew up in, you don't really have any money. Ever. And you don't get brand-new things given to you. Well, not often. On birthdays and at Christmas, Betsy and Gordon did their best to make sure that we all had something new, but most of the time you just make do. Most of my clothes had been worn by someone else before. The toys were all shared. You get into the habit of being very careful with the small amounts of money you get given or earn by doing chores. I still have that habit. We both do. You'll think it silly, but I've had this coat since I was seventeen. It only occurs to me now and again that I should replace it.'

Luiz thought of the women he had wined and dined

over the years. He had never hesitated in spending money on them. None of those relationships might have lasted, but all the women had certainly profited financially from them: jewellery, fur coats, in one instance a car. The memory of it repulsed him.

'That must have been very limiting, being a teenager and not being able to keep up with the latest fashion.'

'You get used to it.' Aggie shrugged. 'Life could have been a lot worse. Look, there's a café. You're right. I should have something to eat. I'm ravenous.' It also felt a little weird to be having this conversation with him.

'You're changing the subject,' he drawled as they began mingling with the shoppers who were out in numbers, undeterred by the snow. 'Is that something else you picked up growing up in a children's home?'

'I don't want to be cross-examined by you.' They were inside the café which was small and warm and busy, but there were spare seats and they grabbed two towards the back. When Aggie removed her gloves, her fingers were pink with cold and she had to keep the coat on for a little longer, just until she warmed up, while two waitresses gravitated, goggle-eyed, to Luiz and towards their table to take their order.

'I could eat everything on the menu.' Aggie sighed, settling for a chicken baguette and a very large coffee. 'That's what having too much to drink does for a girl. I can't apologise enough.'

'And I can't tell you how tedious it is hearing you continually apologise,' Luiz replied irritably. He glanced around him and sprawled back in the chair. 'I thought women enjoyed nothing more than talking about themselves.'

Aggie shot him a jaundiced look and sat back while her baguette, stuffed to bursting, was placed in front of

her. Luiz was having nothing; it should have been a little embarrassing, diving into a foot-long baguette while
he watched her eat, but she didn't care. Her stomach was
rumbling with hunger. And stranded in awful conditions
away from her home turf was having a lowering effect on
her defences.

'I'll bet that really gets on your nerves,' Aggie said between mouthfuls, and Luiz had the grace to flush.

'I tend to go out with women whose conversations fall
a little short of riveting.'

'Then why do you go out with them? Oh yes, I forgot.
Because of the way they look.' She licked some tarragon
mayonnaise from her finger and dipped her eyes, missing
the way he watched, with apparent fascination, that small,
unconsciously sensual gesture. Also missing the way he
sat forward and shifted awkwardly in the chair. 'Why do
you bother to go out with women if they're boring? Don't
you want to settle down and get married? Would you marry
someone who bored you?'

Luiz frowned. 'I'm a busy man. I don't have the time
to complicate my life with a relationship.'

'Relationships don't have to complicate lives. Actually,
I thought they were supposed to make life easier and more
enjoyable. This baguette is delicious; thank you for getting it for me. I suppose we should discuss my contribution to this…this…'

'Why? You wouldn't be here if it weren't for me.'

He drummed his fingers on the table and continued
to look at her. Her hair kept falling across her face as she
leant forward to eat the baguette and, as fast as it fell, she
tucked it behind her ear. There were crumbs by her mouth
and she licked them off as delicately as a cat.

'True.' Aggie sat back, pleasantly full having demol-
ished the baguette, and she sipped some of her coffee, hold-

ing the mug between both her hands. 'So.' She tossed him a challenging look. 'I guess your parents must want you to get married. At least, that's…'

'At least that's what?'

'None of my business.'

'Just say what you were going to say, Aggie. I've seen you half-undressed and ordering me to fetch you orange juice. It's fair to say that we've gone past the usual pleasantries.'

'Maria may have mentioned that everyone's waiting for you to tie the knot.' Aggie stuck her chin up defiantly because if he could pry into her life, whatever his reasons, then why shouldn't she pry into his?

'That's absurd!'

'We don't have to talk about this.'

'There's nothing *to* talk about!' But wasn't that why he found living in London preferable to returning to Brazil— because his mother had a talent for cornering him and pestering him about his private life? He loved his mother very much, but after three futile attempts to match-make him with the daughters of family friends he had had to draw her to one side and tell her that she was wasting her time.

'My parents have their grandchildren, thanks to three of my sisters, and that's just as well, as I have no intention of tying any knots any time soon.' He waited for her response and frowned when none was forthcoming. 'In our family,' he said abruptly, 'the onus of running the business, expanding it, taking it out of Brazil and into the rest of the world, fell on my shoulders. That's just the way it is. It doesn't leave a lot of time for pandering to a woman's needs. Aside from the physical.' He elaborated with a sudden, wolfish smile.

Aggie didn't smile back. It didn't sound like that great a trade-off to her. Yes, lots of power, status, influence and money, but if you didn't have time to enjoy any of that with someone you cared about then what was the point?

She suddenly saw a man whose life had been prescribed from birth. He had inherited an empire and he had never had any choice but to submit to his responsibility. Which, she conceded, wasn't to say that he didn't enjoy what he did. But she imagined that being stuck up there at the very top, where everyone else's hopes and dreams rested on your shoulders, might become a lonely and isolated place.

'Spare me the look of sympathy.' Luiz scowled and looked around for a waitress to bring the bill.

'So what happens when you marry?' she asked in genuine bewilderment, even though she was sensing that the conversation was not one he had any particular desire to continue. In fact, judging from the dark expression on his face, she suspected that he might be annoyed with himself for having said more than he wanted to.

'I have no idea what you mean by that.'

'Will you give over the running of your…er…company to someone else?'

'Why would I do that? It's a family business. No one outside the family will ever have direct control.'

'You're not going to have much time to be a husband, in that case. I mean, if you carry on working all the hours God made.'

'You talk too much.' The bill had arrived. He paid it, leaving a massive tip, and didn't take his eyes from Aggie's face.

She, in turn, could feel her temples begin to throb and her head begin to swim. His eyes drifted down to her full mouth, taking in the perfect, delicate arrangement of her features. Yes, he had looked at her before, had sized her up the first time they had met. But had he looked at her in the past like *this*? There was a powerful, sexual element

to his lazy perusal of her face. Or was she imagining it?
Was it just his way of avoiding the conversation?

Her breasts were tingling and her thoughts were in tur-
moil. Aside from the obvious reasons, this man was not
her type at all. She might appreciate his spectacular good
looks in a detached way but on every other level she had
never had time for men who belonged to the striped-suit
brigade, whose *raison d'être* was to live and die for the
sake of work. She liked them carefree and unconventional
and creative, so why had her body reacted like that just
then—with the unwelcome frisson of a teenager getting
randy on her first date with the guy of her dreams? God,
even worse, was it the first time she had reacted like that?
Or had she contrived to ignore all those tell-tale signs of
a woman looking at a man and imagining?

'Yes. You're right. I do.' Her breathing was shallow,
her pupils dilated.

On a subliminal level, Luiz registered these reactions.
He was intensely physical, and if he didn't engage in soul
searching relationships with women he made up for that
in his capacity to read them and just know when they were
affected by him.

Usually, it was a simple game with a foregone conclusion, and the women who ended up in his bed were women
who understood the rules of the game. He played fair, as
far as he was concerned. He never promised anything, but
he was a lavish and generous lover.

So what, he wondered, was *this* all about? What the
hell was going on?

She was standing up, brushing some crumbs off her
jumper and slinging back on the worn, too-thin coat, pulling the woolly hat low down on her head, wriggling her
fingers into her gloves. She wasn't looking at him. In fact,

she was doing a good job of making sure that she didn't look at him.

Like a predator suddenly on the alert, Luiz could feel something inside him shift gear. He fell in beside her once they were outside and Aggie, nervous for no apparent reason, did what she always did when she was nervous. She began talking, barely pausing to draw breath. She admired the Christmas lights a little too enthusiastically and paused to stand in front of the first shop they came to, apparently lost in wonder at the splendid display of household items and hardware appliances. Her heart was thumping so hard that she was finding it difficult to hold on to her thoughts.

How had they ended up having such an intensely personal conversation? When had she stopped keeping him at a distance? Why had it become so easy to forget all the things she should be hating about him? Was that the power of lust? Did it turn your world on its head and make you lose track of everything that was sensible?

Just admitting to being attracted to him made her feel giddy, and when he told her that they should be getting back because she looked a little white she quickly agreed.

Suddenly this trip seemed a lot more dangerous than it had done before. It was no longer a case of trying to avoid constant sniping. It was a case of trying to maintain it.

CHAPTER FIVE

By the Monday morning—after two evenings spent by Aggie trying to avoid all personal conversation, frantically aware of the way her body was ambushing all her good intentions—the relentless snow was beginning to abate, although not sufficiently for them to begin the last leg of their journey.

The first thing Aggie did was to telephone the school. As luck would have it, it was shut, with just a recorded message informing her that, due to the weather, it would remain shut until further notice. She didn't know if it was still snowing in London, but the temperatures across the country were still sub-zero and she knew from experience that, even if the snow had stopped, sub-zero temperatures would result in frozen roads and pavements, as well as a dangerously frozen playground. This routinely happened once or twice a year, although usually only for a couple of days at most, and Health and Safety were always quick to step in and advise closures.

Then she looked at the pitiful supply of clothes remaining in her bag and said goodbye to all thoughts of saving any money at all for the New Year.

'I need to go back into town,' she told Luiz as soon as she had joined him in the dining room, where Mrs Bixby was busy chatting to the errant guest who had returned the evening before and was complaining bitterly about his chances of doing anything of any use. Salesmen rarely appreciated dire weather.

'More fresh air?'

'I need to buy some stuff.'

'Ah. New coat, by any chance?' Luiz sat back, tilting his chair away from the table so that he could cross his legs.

'I should get another jumper…some jeans, maybe. I didn't think that we would be snowed in when we're not even halfway through this trip.'

Luiz nodded thoughtfully. 'Nor had I. I expect I'll be forced to get some as well.'

'And you're missing your…meetings. You mentioned that deal you needed to get done.'

'I've telephoned my guys in London. They'll cover me in my absence. It's not perfect, but it'll have to do. This evening I'll have a conference call and give them my input. I take it you've called the school?'

'Closed anyway.' She sat back as coffee was brought for them, and chatted for a few minutes with their landlady, who was extremely cheerful at the prospect of having them there longer than anticipated.

'So your school's closed. How fortuitous,' Luiz murmured. 'I've tried calling the hotel where your brother is supposed to be holed up with Maria and the lines are down.'

'So is there any point in continuing?' Aggie looked at him and licked her lips. 'They were only going to be there for a few days. We could get up there and find they've already caught the train back to London.'

'It's a possibility.'

'Is that all you have to say?' Aggie cried in an urgent undertone. '*It's a possibility?* Neither of us can afford to spend time away from our jobs on a possibility!' The thought of her cold, uncomfortable, Luiz-free house beckoned like a port in a storm. She didn't understand why she was feeling what she was, and the sooner she was removed from the discomfort of her situation the better, as far as she was concerned. 'You have important meetings to go to. You told me so yourself. Just think of all those poor people whose livelihoods depend on you closing whatever deal it is you have to close!'

'Why, Aggie, I hadn't appreciated how concerned you were.'

'Don't be sarcastic, Luiz. You're a workaholic. It must be driving you crazy being caught out like this. It would take us the same length of time to return to London as it would to get to the Lake District.'

'Less.'

'Even better!'

'Furthermore, we would probably be driving away from the worst of the weather, rather than into it.'

'Exactly!'

'Which isn't to say that I have any intention of returning to London without having accomplished what I've set out to do. When I start something, I finish it.'

'Even if finishing it makes no sense?'

'This is a pointless conversation,' Luiz said coolly. 'And why the sudden desperation to jump ship?'

'Like I said, I thought I would be away for one night, two at most. I have things to do in London.'

'Tell me what. Your school's closed.'

'There's much more to teaching than standing in front of the children and teaching them. There are lessons to prepare, homework to mark.'

'And naturally you have no computer with you.'

'Of course I haven't.' He wasn't going to give way. She hadn't really expected that he would. She had known that he was the type of man who, once embarked on a certain course, saw it through to the finish. 'I have an old computer. There's no way I could lug that anywhere with me. Not that I thought I'd need it.'

'I'll buy you a laptop.' To Luiz's surprise, it was out before he had had time to think over the suggestion.

'I beg your pardon?'

'Everyone needs a laptop, something they can take with them on the move.' He flushed darkly and raked his fingers through his hair. 'I'm surprised you haven't got one. Surely the school would subsidise you?'

'I have a school computer but I don't take it out of the house. It's not my property.' Aggie was in a daze at his suggestion, but underneath, a slow anger was beginning to build. 'And would the money spent on this act of generosity be deducted from my full and final payment when you throw cash at me and my brother to get us out of the way? Are you keeping a mental tally?'

'Don't be absurd,' Luiz grated. He barely glanced at the food that had been placed in front of him by Mrs Bixby who, sensing an atmosphere, tactfully withdrew.

'Thanks, but I think I'll turn down your kind offer to buy me a computer.' This was how far apart their lives were, Aggie thought. Her body might play tricks on her, make her forget the reality of their situation, but this was the reality. They weren't on a romantic magical-mystery tour and he wasn't the man of her dreams. She was here because he had virtually blackmailed her into going with him and, far from being the man of her dreams, he was cold, single-minded and so warped by his privileged background that it was second nature to him to buy people. He could, so why not? His dealings with the human race were all based on financial transactions. He had girlfriends because they were beautiful and amused him for a while. But what else was there in his life? And did he imagine that there was nothing money couldn't buy?

'Too proud, Aggie?'

'I have no idea what you're talking about.'

'You think I've insulted you by offering to buy you something you need. You're here because of me. You'll probably end up missing work because of me. You'll need to buy clothes because of me.'

'So are you saying that you made a mistake in dragging me along with you?'

'I'm saying nothing of the sort.' Luiz looked at her, frowning with impatience. More and more he was finding it impossible to believe that she could be any kind of gold-digger. What sane opportunist would argue herself out of a free wardrobe? A top-of-the-range laptop computer? 'Of course you had to come with me.' But his voice lacked conviction. 'It's possible you weren't involved in trying to set your brother up with my niece,' he conceded.

'So you *did* make a mistake dragging me along with you.'

'I still intend to make sure that your brother stays away from Maria.'

'Even though you must know that he had no agenda when he got involved with her?'

Luiz didn't say anything and his silence spoke louder than words. Of course, he would never allow Mark to marry his niece. None of his family would. The wealthy remained wealthy because they protected their wealth. They married other wealthy people. That was his world and it was the only world he understood.

It was despicable, so why couldn't she look at him with indifference and contempt? Why did she feel this tremendous physical pull towards him however much her head argued that she shouldn't? It was bewildering and enraging at the same time and Aggie had never felt anything like it before. It was as if a whole set of brand-new emotions had been taken out of a box and now she had no idea how to deal with them.

'You really do come from a completely different world,' Aggie said. 'I think it's very sad that you can't trust anyone.'

'There's a little more to it than that,' Luiz told her, irritated. 'Maria's mother fell in love with an American twenty years ago. That American was Maria's father. There was a shotgun wedding. My sister went straight from her marriage vows to the hospital to deliver her baby. Of course, my parents were concerned, but they knew better than to say anything.'

'Why were they concerned? Because he was an American?'

'Because he was a drifter. Luisa met him when she was on holiday in Mexico. He was a lifeguard at one of the beaches. She was young and he swept her off her feet, or so the story goes. The minute they were married, the demands began. It turned out that Brad James had very expensive tastes. The rolling estate and the cars weren't enough; he wanted a private jet, and then he needed to be bankrolled for ventures that were destined for disaster. Maria knows nothing of this. She only knows that her father was killed in a light-aeroplane crash during one of his flying lessons. Luisa never forgot the mistakes she made.'

'Well, I'm sorry about that. It must have been hard growing up without a father.' She bit into a slice of toast that tasted like cardboard. 'But I don't want anything from you and neither does my brother.'

'You don't want anything from anyone. Am I right?'

Aggie flushed and looked away from those dark, piercing eyes. 'That's right.'

'But I'm afraid I insist on buying you some replacement clothes. Accept the offer in the spirit in which it was intended. If you dislike accepting them to such an extent, you can chuck them in a black bin-bag when you return to London and donate them all to charity.'

'Fine.' Her proud refusal now seemed hollow and churlish. He was being practical. She needed more clothes through no fault of her own. He could afford to buy them for her, so why shouldn't she accept the offer? It made sense. He wasn't to know that she wasn't given to accepting anything from anyone and certainly not charitable donations. Or maybe he had an idea.

At any rate, if he wanted to buy her stuff, then not only would she accept but she would accept with alacrity. It was better, wasn't it, than picking away at generosity, finding fault with it, tearing it to shreds?

With Christmas not far away, the town was once again bustling with shoppers, even though the snow continued falling. There was no convenient department-store but a series of small boutiques.

'I don't usually shop in places like this.' Aggie dithered outside one of the boutiques as Luiz waited for her, his hand resting on the door, ready to push it open. 'It looks expensive. Surely there must be somewhere cheaper?' He dropped his hand and stood back to lean against the shop front.

They had walked into town in silence. It had irritated the hell out of Luiz. Women loved shopping. So what if she had accepted his offer to buy her clothes under duress? The fact was, she was going to be kitted out, and surely she must be just a little bit pleased? If she was, then she was doing a damned good job of hiding it.

'And I've never stayed in a bed and breakfast before the

one we're in now,' Luiz said shortly. 'You're fond of reminding me of all the things I'm ignorant of because I've
been insulated by my background. Well, I'm happy to try
them out. Have you heard me complain once about where
we're staying? Even though you've passed sufficient acid
remarks about me being unable to deal with it because the
only thing I can deal with are five-star hotels.'

'No,' Aggie admitted with painful honesty, while her
face burned. She wanted to cover her ears with her hands
because everything he was saying had a ring of truth about
it.

'So I'm taking it that there are two sets of rules here.
You're allowed to typecast me, whilst making damned
sure that you don't get yourself typecast.'

'I can't help it,' Aggie muttered uncomfortably.

'Well, I suggest you try. So we're going to go into that
shop and you're going to try on whatever clothes you want
and you're going to let me buy whatever clothes you want.
The whole damned shop if it takes your fancy!'

Aggie smiled and then giggled and slanted an upwards
look at him. 'You're crazy.'

In return, Luiz smiled lazily back at her. She didn't
smile enough. At least, not with him. When she did, her
face became radiantly appealing. 'Compliment or not?' he
murmured softly, and Aggie felt the ground sway under
her feet.

'I'm not prepared to commit on that,' she told him
sternly, but the corners of her mouth were still twitching.

'Come on.'

It was just the sort of boutique where the assistants
were trained to be scary. They catered for rich locals and
passing tourists. Aggie was sure that, had she strolled in,
clad in her worn clothes and tired boots, they would have
followed her around the shop, rearranging anything she

happened to take from the shelves and keeping a close eye
just in case she was tempted to make off with something.

With Luiz, however, shopping in an over-priced boutique was something of a different experience. The young
girl who had greeted them at the door, as bug-eyed in
Luiz's presence as the waitress had been on Saturday in
the café, was sidelined and they were personally taken
care of by an older woman who confided that she was the
owner of the shop. Aggie was made to sit on the *chaise
longe*, with Luiz sprawled next to her, as relaxed as if he
owned the place. Items of clothing were brought out and
most were immediately dismissed by him with a casual
wave of the hand.

'I thought *I* was supposed to be choosing my own outfits,' Aggie whispered at one point, guiltily thrilled to
death by this take on the shopping experience.

'I know what would look good on you.'

'I should get some jeans...' She worried her lower lip
and inwardly fretted at the price of the designer jeans
which had been draped over a chair, awaiting inspection.
Belatedly, she added, 'And you don't know what would
look good on me.'

'I know there's room for improvement, judging from the
dismal blacks and greys I've seen you wear in the past.'

Aggie turned to him, hot under the collar and ready
to be self-righteous. And she just didn't know what happened. Rather, she knew *exactly* what happened. Their
eyes clashed. His, dark and amused... Hers, blue and
sparking. Sitting so close to each other on the sofa, she
could breathe him in and she gave a little half-gasp.

She knew he was going to kiss her even before she felt
his cool lips touch hers, and it was as if she had been waiting for this for much longer than a couple of days. It was

as if she had been waiting ever since the very first time they had met.

It was brief, over before it had begun, although when he drew back she found that she was still leaning into him, her mouth parted and her eyes half-closed.

'Bad manners to launch into an argument in a shop,' he murmured, which snapped her out of her trance, though her heart was beating so hard that she could scarcely breathe.

'You kissed me to shut me up?'

'It's one way of stopping an argument in the making.'

Aggie tried and failed to be enraged. Her lips were still tingling and her whole body felt as though it was on fire. That five-second kiss had been as potent as a red-hot branding iron. While she tried hard to conceal how affected she had been by it, he now looked away, the moment already forgotten, his attention back to the shop owner who had emerged with more handfuls of clothing, special items from the stock room at the back.

'Jeans—those three pairs. Those jumpers and that dress...not that one, the one hanging at the back.' He turned to Aggie, whose lips were tightly compressed. 'You look as though you've swallowed a lemon whole.'

'I would appreciate it if you would keep your hands to yourself!' she muttered, flinty-eyed, and Luiz grinned, unperturbed by this show of anger.

'I hadn't realised that my hands had made contact with your body,' he said silkily. 'If they had, you would certainly know about it. Now, be a good girl and try on that lot. Oh, and I want to see how you look in them.'

Aggie, the very last person on earth anyone could label an exhibitionist, decided that she hated parading in front of Luiz. Nevertheless, she couldn't deny the low-level buzz of unsettling excitement threading through her as she walked out in the jeans, the jumpers and various T-shirts in bright colours. He told her to slow down and not run as though she was trying out for a marathon. When she finally arrived at the dress, she held it up and looked at him quizzically.

'A dress?'

'Humour me.'

'I don't wear bright blues.' Nor did she wear silky dresses with plunging necklines that clung to her body like a second skin, lovingly outlining every single curve.

'This is a crazy dress for me to try on in the middle of winter,' she complained, walking towards him in the high heels which the sales assistant had slipped under the door for her. 'When it's snowing outside...'

Luiz could count on the fingers of one hand the times when he had ever been lost for words. He was lost for words now. He had been slouching on the low sofa, his hands lightly clasped on his lap, his long legs stretched out in front of him. Now he sat up straight and ran his eyes slowly up and down the length of her small but incredibly sexy body.

The colour of the dress brought out the amazing aquamarine of her eyes, and the cut of the stretchy, silky fabric left very little to the imagination when it came to revealing the surprising fullness of her breasts, the slenderness of her legs and the flatness of her stomach. He wanted to tell her to go back inside the dressing room and remove her bra so that he could see how the dress looked without two white bra-straps visible on her narrow shoulders.

'We'll have the lot.' His arousal was sudden, fierce and painful and he was damned thankful that he could reach for his coat which he had draped over the back of the chair and position it on his lap. He couldn't take his eyes off her but he knew that the longer he looked, the more uncomfortable he was going to get.

'And we'd better get a move on,' he continued roughly. 'I don't want to be stuck out here in town for much longer.' He watched, mesmerised, at the sway of her rounded bottom as she walked back towards the changing room. 'And we'll have those shoes as well,' he told the shop owner, who couldn't do enough for a customer who had practically bought half the shop, including a summer dress which she had foreseen having to hold in the store room until better weather came along.

'Thank you,' Aggie said once they were outside and holding four bags each. A coat had been one of the purchases. She was wearing it now and, much as she hated to admit it, it felt absolutely great. She hadn't felt a twinge of conscience as she had bid farewell to her old threadbare one in the shop, where it had been left for the shop owner to dispose of.

'Was it as gruelling an experience as you had imagined?' He glanced down and immediately thought of those succulent, rounded breasts and the way the dress had clung to them.

'It was pretty amazing,' Aggie admitted. 'But we were in there way too long. You want to get back. I understand that. I just…have one or two small things I need to get. Maybe we could branch off now? You could go and buy yourself some stuff.'

'You mean you don't want me to parade in front of you?' Luiz murmured, and watched with satisfaction the hectic flush that coloured her cheeks.

He hadn't expected this powerful sexual attraction. He had no idea where it was coming from. He wasn't sure when, exactly, it had been born and it made no sense, because she was no more his type than he, apparently, was hers. She was too argumentative, too mouthy and, hell, hadn't he started this trip with her in the starring role of gold-digger? Yet there was something strangely erotic and forbidden about his attraction, something wildly exciting about the way he knew she looked at him from under her lashes. He got horny just thinking about it.

Problem was…what was he to do with this? Where was he going to go with it?

He surfaced from his uncustomary lapse in concentration to find her telling him something about a detour she wanted him to make.

'Seven…what? What are you talking about?'

'I said that I'd like to stop off at Sevenoaks. It'll be a minor detour and I haven't been back there in over eighteen months.'

'What's Sevenoaks?'

'Haven't you been listening to a word I've been saying?' She assumed that, after the little jaunt in the clothes shop, his mind had now switched back to its primary preoccupation, which was work, and in that mode she might just as well have been saying 'blah, blah, blah'.

'In one ear, out the other,' Luiz drawled, marvelling that he could become so lost in his imagination that he literally hadn't heard a word she had been saying to him.

'Sevenoaks is the home we grew up in,' Aggie repeated. 'Perhaps we could stop off there? It's only a slight detour and it would mean a lot to me. I know you're in a rush to get to Mark's hotel, but a couple of hours wouldn't make a huge difference, would it?'

'We could do that.'

'Right…well…thanks.' Suddenly she felt as though she wouldn't have minded spending the rest of their time in the town with him. In response to that crazy thought, she took a couple of small steps back, just to get out of that spellbinding circle he seemed to project around him, the one which, once entered, wreaked havoc with her thought processes. 'And I'll head off now and see you back at the bed and breakfast.'

'What are you going to buy?' Luiz frowned as he continued to stare down at her. 'I thought we'd covered all essential purchases. Unless there are some slightly less essential ones outstanding? There must be a lingerie shop of sorts somewhere...'

Aggie reacted to that suggestion as though she had been stung. She imagined parading in front of him wearing nothing but a lacy bra and pants and she almost gasped aloud.

'I can get my own underwear—thank you.' She stumbled over the words in her rush to get them out. 'And, no, I wasn't talking about that!'

'What, then?'

'Luiz, it's getting colder out here and I'd really like to get back to the bed and breakfast so...' She took a few more steps back, although her eyes remained locked with his, like stupid, helpless prey mesmerised by an approaching predator.

Luiz nodded, breaking the spell. 'I'll see you back there in...' he glanced at his watch. '...a couple of hours. I have some work to do. Let's make it six-thirty in the dining room. If we're to have any kind of detour, then we're going to have to leave very early in the morning, barring any overnight fall of snow that makes it impossible. So we'll get an early night.'

'Of course,' Aggie returned politely. She was gauging from the tone of his voice that, whatever temporary truces came into effect, nothing would deflect him from his mission. It suddenly seemed wildly inappropriate that she had thrilled to his eyes on her only moments before as she had provided him with his very own fashion show, purchased at great expense. She might have made a great song and dance about her scorn for money, her lack of materialism but, thinking about how she had strutted her stuff to those lazy, watchful eyes, she suddenly felt as though without even realising it she had been bought somehow. And not only that, she had enjoyed the experience.

'And I just want you to know…' Her voice was cooler by several degrees. 'That once we're back in London, I shall make sure that all the stuff you bought for me is returned to you.'

'Not this rubbish again!' Luiz dismissed impatiently. 'I thought we'd gone over all that old ground and you'd finally accepted that it wasn't a mortal insult to allow me to buy you a few essential items of clothing, considering we've been delayed on this trip?'

'Since when is a summer dress *an essential item of clothing*?'

'Climb out of the box, Aggie. So the dress isn't essential. Big deal. Try a little frivolity now and again.' He couldn't help himself. His gaze drifted down to her full lips. It seemed that even when she was getting on his nerves she still contrived to turn him on.

'You think I'm dull!'

'I think this is a ridiculous place to have an ongoing conversation about matters that have already been sorted. Standing in the snow. The last thing either of us need is to succumb to an attack of winter flu.'

With her concerns casually swatted away, and her pride not too gently and very firmly put in its place, Aggie spun round on her heels without a backward glance.

She could imagine his amusement at her contradictory behaviour. One minute she was gracefully accepting his largesse, the next minute she was ranting and railing against it. It made no sense. It was the very opposite of the determined, cool, always sensible person she considered herself to be.

But then, she was realising that in his presence that determined, cool and always sensible person went into hiding.

Annoyed with herself, she did what she had to do in town, including purchasing some very functional underwear, and once back at the bed and breakfast she retreated up to her bedroom with a pot of tea. The landline at the hotel to which they were heading was still down and neither could she make contact with her brother on his mobile.

At this juncture, she should have been wringing her hands in worry at the prospect of the scene that would imminently unfold. She should have been depressed at the thought of Luiz doing his worst and bracing herself for a showdown that might result in her having to pick up the pieces. Her fierce protectiveness of her brother should have kicked in.

Instead, as she settled in the chair by the window with her cup of tea, she found herself thinking of Luiz and remembering the brush of his lips on hers. One fleeting kiss that had galvanised all the nerve-endings in her body.

She found herself looking forward to seeing him downstairs, even though she knew that it was entirely wrong to do so. Fighting the urge to bathe and change as quickly as possible, she took her time instead and arrived in the dining room half an hour after their agreed time.

She paused by the door and gathered herself. Luiz was in the clothes he had presumably bought after they had parted company, a pair of black jeans and a black, round-necked jumper. He had pushed his chair back and in front of him was his laptop, at which he was staring with a slight frown.

He looked every inch the tycoon, controlling his empire from a distance. He was a man who could have any woman he wanted. To look at him was to know that beyond a shadow of a doubt. So why was she getting into such a tizzy at the sight of him? He had kissed her to shut her up, and here she was, reacting as though he had swept her off her feet and transported her to his bed.

Luiz looked up and caught her in the act of staring. He shut his computer and in the space of a few seconds had clocked the new jeans, tighter than her previous ones, and one of the new, more brightly coloured long-sleeved T shirts that clung in a way she probably hadn't noticed. It was warm in the dining room. No need for a thick jumper.

'I hope I'm not interrupting your work,' Aggie said, settling in the chair opposite him. There was a bottle of wine chilling in a bucket next to the table and she eyed it suspiciously. Now was definitely not the time to over-indulge.

'All finished, and you'll be pleased to know that the deal is more or less done and dusted. Jobs saved. Happy employees. A few lucky ones might even get pay rises. What did you buy in town after you left me?'

He poured her some wine and she fiddled with the stem of the glass.

'A few toys,' Aggie confessed. 'Things to take to the home. The children don't get a lot of treats. I thought it would be nice if I brought some with me. I shall wrap them; it'll be hugely exciting for them. 'Course, I couldn't really splash out, but I managed to find a shop with nothing in it over a fiver.'

Luiz watched the animation on her face. This was what the women he dated lacked. They had all been beautiful. In some cases, they had graced the covers of magazines. But, compared to Aggie's mobile, expressive face, theirs seemed in recollection lifeless and empty. Like mannequins. Was it any wonder that he had tired of them so quickly?

'Nothing over a fiver,' he murmured, transfixed by her absorption in what she was saying.

Having pondered the mystery of why he found her so compellingly attractive, Luiz now concluded that it was because she offered more than a pretty face and a sexy body. He had always tired easily of the women he had gone out with. No problem there; he didn't want any of them hanging around for ever. But the fact that Chloe, who had hardly been long-term, could be classified as one of his more enduring relationships was saying to him that his jaded palate needed a change of scene.

Aggie might not conform to what he usually looked for but she certainly represented a change of scene. In every possible way.

'Why are you looking at me like that?' Aggie asked suspiciously.

'I was just thinking about my own excessive Christmases.' He spread his hands in a self-deprecating gesture. 'I am beginning to see why you think I might live in an ivory tower.'

Aggie smiled. 'Coming from you, that's a big admission.'

'Perhaps it's one of the down sides of being born into money.' As admissions went, this was one of his biggest, and he meant it.

'Well, if I'm being perfectly honest...' Aggie leaned towards him, her face warm and appreciative, her defence system instantly defused by a glimpse of the man who could admit to shortcomings. 'I've always thought that pursuing money was a waste of time. 'Course, it's not the be-all and end-all, but I really enjoyed myself in that boutique today.'

'Which bit of it did you enjoy the most?'

'I've never actually sat on a chair and had anyone bring clothes to me for my inspection. Is that how it works with you?'

'I don't have time to sit on chairs while people bring me clothes to inspect,' Luiz said wryly. 'I have a tailor. He has my measurements and will make suits whenever I want them. I also have accounts at the major high-end shops. If I need anything, I just have to ask. There are people there who know the kind of things I want. Did you enjoy modelling the clothes for me?'

'Well…um…' Aggie went bright red. 'That was a first for me as well. I mean, I guess you wanted to see what you were paying for. That sounds awful. It's not what I meant.'

'I know what you meant.' He sipped some of his wine and regarded her thoughtfully over the rim of his glass. 'I would gladly have paid for the privilege of seeing you model those clothes for me,' he murmured. 'Although my guess is that you would have been outraged at any such suggestion. Frankly, it was a bit of a shame that there was any audience at all. Aside from myself, naturally. If it had been just the two of us, I would have insisted you remove your bra when you tried that dress on, for starters.'

Aggie's mouth fell open and she stared at him in disbelieving shock.

'You don't mean that,' she said faintly.

'Of course I do.' He looked surprised that she should disbelieve him.

'Why are you saying these things?'

'I'm saying what I mean. I don't know how it's happened, but I find myself violently attracted to you, and the reason I feel I can tell you this is because I know you feel the same towards me.'

'I do not!'

'Allow me to put that to the test, Aggie.'

This time there was nothing fleeting or gentle about his kiss. It wasn't designed to distract her. It was designed to prove a point, and she was as defenceless against its urgent power as she would have been against a meteor hurtling towards her at full tilt.

There was no rhyme or reason behind her reaction, which was driven purely on blind craving.

With a soft moan of surrender, she reached further towards him and allowed herself to drown in sensations she had never felt before.

'Point proved.' Luiz finally drew back but his hand remained on the side of her face, caressing her hot cheek. 'So the only remaining question is what we intend to do about this...'

CHAPTER SIX

AGGIE couldn't get to sleep. Luiz's softly spoken words kept rolling around in her mind. He had completely dropped the subject over dinner but the electricity had crackled between them and the atmosphere had been thick with unspoken thoughts of them in bed together.

Had she been that transparent all along? When had he realised that she was attracted to him? She had been at pains to keep that shameful truth to herself and she cringed to think how casually he had dropped it into the conversation as a given.

He was a highly sexual man and he would have no trouble in seeing sex between them as just the natural outcome of mutual attraction. He wouldn't be riddled with anxiety and he wouldn't feel as though he was abandoning his self-respect. For him, whatever the reasons for their trip, a sexual relationship between them would always be a separate issue which he would be able to compartmentalise. He was accustomed to relationships that didn't overlap into other areas of his life.

At a little after one, she realised that it was pointless trying to force herself to go to sleep.

She pulled on the dressing gown that had been supplied and was hanging on a hook on the bathroom door, shoved her feet in her bedroom slippers and headed for the door.

One big disadvantage of somewhere as small as this was that there was no room-service for those times when sleep was elusive and a glass of milk was urgently needed. Mrs Bixby had kindly pointed out where drinks could be made after hours and had told them both that they were free to use the kitchen as their own.

Aggie took her time pottering in the kitchen. A cup of hot chocolate seemed a better idea than a glass of milk and it was a diversion to turn her mind to something other than turbulent thoughts of Luiz.

She tried without success to stifle her flush of pleasure at his admission that he had been looking at her.

Caught up between the stern lectures she was giving herself about the craziness of his proposal, like uninvited guests at a birthday party were all sorts of troublesome questions, such as when exactly had he been looking at her and how often…?

None of that mattered, she told herself as she headed back up the stairs with the cup of hot chocolate. What mattered, what was *really* important, was that they get this trip over with as soon as possible and, whatever the outcome, she would then be able to get back to her normal life with its safe, normal routine. One thing that had been gained in the process was that he no longer suspected her of profiteering and she thought that he had probably dropped his suspicions of her brother as well. He still saw it as his duty to intervene in a relationship he thought was unacceptable, but at least there would be no accusations of opportunism.

However, when Aggie tried to remember her safe, normal routine before all these complications had arisen, she found herself thinking about Luiz. His dark, sexy face superimposed itself and squashed her attempts to find comfort in thinking about the kids at the school and what they would be getting up to in the run up to Christmas.

She didn't expect to see the object of her fevered thoughts at the top of the stairs. She was staring down into the mug of hot chocolate, willing it not to spill, when she looked up and there he was. Not exactly at the top of the stairs, but in the shadowy half-light on the landing, just outside one of the bedrooms, with just a towel round his waist and another hand towel slung over his neck.

Aggie blinked furiously to clear her vision and when the vision remained intact she made a strangled, inarticulate noise and froze as he strolled towards her.

'What are you doing here?' she asked in an accusing gasp as he reached to relieve her of the mug, which threatened to fall because her hands were trembling so much.

'I could ask *you* the same question.'

'I...I was thirsty.'

Luiz didn't answer. There were only five rooms on the floor and, if he hadn't known already, it wouldn't have been hard to guess which was hers because it was the only one with a light on. It shone through the gap under the door like a beacon and he beelined towards it so that she found herself with no choice but to follow him on unsteady legs.

The sight of his broad, bronzed back, those wide, powerful shoulders, made her feel faint. Her breasts ached. Her whole body was in the process of reminding her of the futility of denying the sexual attraction he had coolly pointed out hours earlier, the one she had spent the last few restless hours shooting down in flames.

He was in no rush. While her nerves continued to shred and unravel, he seemed as cool as a cucumber, standing back with a little bow to allow her to brush past him into the bedroom, where she abruptly came to a halt and stopped before he could infiltrate himself any further.

'Good night.'

Her cheeks were burning and she couldn't look him in

the eye but she could imagine the little mocking smile on his mouth at her hoarse dismissal.

'So you couldn't sleep. I'm not sure if a hot drink helps with that. I have a feeling that's an old wives' tale…' Luiz ignored her good-night, although he didn't proceed into the bedroom. It was sheer coincidence that he had bumped into her on the landing, *pure bloody coincidence,* but didn't fate work in mysterious ways? The laws of attraction… wasn't that what they called it? He remembered some girl-friend waffling on about that years ago while he had listened politely and wondered whether she had taken leave of her senses. Yet here it was at work, because he had been thinking about the woman standing wide-eyed in front of him and had decided to cool his thoughts down with a shower, only to find her practically outside his bedroom door. Never did he imagine that he would thank providence for the basic provisions of a bed and breakfast with only two *en suites.*

'I was thirsty, I told you.'

'I was having trouble sleeping too,' Luiz said frankly, his dark eyes roving over her slight frame. Even at this un-godly hour, she still managed to look good. No make-up, hair all over the place but still bloody good. Good enough to ravish. Good enough to lift and carry straight off to that king-sized bed behind her.

He felt his erection push up, hard as steel, and his breath quickened.

Aggie cleared her throat and said something polite along the lines of, 'oh dear, that's a shame,' at which Luiz grinned and held out the mug so that she could take it.

'Would you like to know why?'

'I'm not really interested.'

'Aren't you?' Whatever she might say, Luiz had his answer in that fractional pause before she predictably shook her head.

He hadn't been off the mark with her. She wanted him as much as he wanted her. He could always tell these things. His mouth curved in lazy satisfaction as he played with the idea of eliminating the talking and just...kissing her. Just plunging his hands into that tangled blonde hair, pulling her towards him so that she could have proof of just how much he was turned on, kissing her until she begged him not to stop. He could feel her alertness and it hit him that he hadn't been turned on by any woman to this extent before in his life.

He had spent the past couple of hours with his computer discarded next to him on the bed while he had stared up at the ceiling, hands folded behind his head, thinking of her. He had made his intentions clear and then dropped the matter in the expectation that, once the seed was planted, it would take root and grow.

'I want you,' he murmured huskily. 'I can't make myself any clearer, and if you want to touch you can feel the proof for yourself.'

Aggie's heart was thudding so hard that she could barely think straight.

'And I suppose you always get what you want?' She stuck her disobedient hands behind her back.

'You tell me. Will I?'

Aggie took a deep breath and risked looking at him even though those dark, fabulous eyes brought on a drowning sensation.

'No.'

For a few seconds, Luiz thought that he had heard incorrectly. Had she just turned him down? Women never said no to him. Why would they? Without a trace of vanity, he knew exactly what he brought to the table when it came to the opposite sex.

'No,' he tried out that monosyllable and watched as she glanced down with a little nod.

'What do you mean, *no*?' he asked in genuine bafflement.

Aggie's whole body strained to be touched by him and the power of that yearning shocked and frightened her.

'I mean you've got it wrong,' she mumbled.

'I can feel what you're feeling,' he said roughly. 'There's something between us. A chemistry. Neither of us was asking for this but it's there.'

'Yes, well, that doesn't matter.' Aggie looked at him with clear-eyed resolve.

'What do you mean, *that doesn't matter*?'

'We're on opposite sides of the fence, Luiz.'

'How many times do I have to reassure you that I have conceded that you were innocent of the accusations I originally made?'

'That's an important fence but there are others. You belong to a dynasty. You might think it's fun to step outside the line for a while, but I'm not a toy that you can pick up and then discard when you're through with it.'

'I never implied that you were.' Luiz thought that, as toys went, she was one he would dearly love to play with.

'I may not be rich and I may have come from a foster home, but it doesn't mean that I don't have principles.'

'And if I implied that you didn't, then I apologise.'

'And it doesn't mean that I'm weak either!' Aggie barrelled through his apology because, now that she had gathered momentum, she knew that it was in her interests to capitalise on it.

'Where are you going with that?' Luiz had the strangest feeling of having lost control.

'I'm not going to just *give in* to the fact that, yes, you're an attractive enough man and we happen to be sharing the same space...'

'I honestly can't believe I'm hearing this.'

'Yes, well, it's not my fault that you've lived such a charmed life that you've always got everything you wanted at the snap of a finger.'

Luiz looked down into those aquamarine eyes that could make a grown man go weak at the knees and shook his head in genuine incomprehension. Yes, okay, so maybe he had had a charmed life and maybe he had always got what he wanted, but this was crazy! The atmosphere between them was tangible and electric... What was wrong with two consenting adults giving in to what they both clearly wanted, whether she was brave enough to admit that or not?

'So...' Aggie took a couple of steps towards the door and placed her hand firmly on the door knob. As a support, it was wonderful because her legs felt like jelly. 'If you don't mind, I'm very tired and I really would like to get to bed now.'

She didn't dare meet his eyes, not quite, but lowering them was equally hazardous because she was then forced to stare at his chest with its dark hair that looked so aggressively, dangerously *un-English*; at his flat, brown nipples and at the clearly defined ripple of muscle and sinew.

Luiz realised that he was being dismissed and he straightened, all the time telling himself that the woman, as far as he was concerned, was now history. He had never been rejected before, at least not that he could remember, and he would naturally accept the reality that he was being rejected now, very politely but very firmly rejected. He had never chased any woman and he should have stuck with that format.

'Of course,' he said coldly, reaching to hold both ends of the towel over his shoulders with either hand.

Immediately, Aggie felt his cool withdrawal and hated it.

'I'll...er...see you tomorrow morning. What time do you want to leave?' This time she did look him squarely in the face. 'And will you still be taking that detour to...you know? I'd understand if you just want to get to our destination as quickly as possible...' But she would miss seeing Gordon and Betsy and all the kids; would miss seeing how everything was. Opportunities to visit like this were so rare. Frankly non-existent.

'And you question *my* motives?'

'What are you talking about?' It was Aggie's turn to be puzzled and taken aback at the harsh, scathing contempt in his voice.

'You have just made me out to be a guy who can't control his baser instincts—yet I have to question your choice of men because you seem to lump me into the category as the sort of man who gives his word on something only to retract it if it's no longer convenient!'

Hot colour flared in her cheeks and her mouth fell open.

'I never said...'

'Of course you did! Well, I told you that I would make that detour so that you could visit your friends at your foster home and I intend to keep my promise. I may be many things, but I am honourable.'

With that he left, and Aggie fell against the closed door, like a puppet whose strings had been suddenly severed. Every bone in her body was limp and she remained there for a few minutes, breathing heavily and trying not to think about what had just taken place. Which, of course, was impossible. She could still breathe in his scent and feel his disturbing presence around her.

So he had made a pass at her, she thought, trying desperately to reduce it to terms she could grasp. Men had made passes at her before. She was choosy, accustomed to brushing them aside without a second thought.

But this man…

He got to her. He roused her. He made her aware of her sexuality and made her curious to have it explored. Even with all those drawbacks, all those huge, gaping differences between them…

But it was good that she had turned him down, she told herself. He had been open and upfront with her, which naturally she appreciated. Fall into bed because they were attracted to one another? Lots of other women would have grabbed the opportunity; Aggie knew that. Not only was he drop-dead gorgeous, but there was something innately persuasive and unbearably sexy about him. His arrogance, on the one hand, left her cold but on the other it was mesmeric.

Fortunately, she reasoned as she slipped back between the sheets and closed her eyes, she was strong enough to maintain her wits! That strength was something of which she could justifiably be proud. Yes, she might very well be attracted to him, but she had resisted the temptation to just give in.

With the lights out, the cup of hot chocolate forgotten and sleep even more elusive than it had been before she had headed down to the kitchen, Aggie wondered about those other women who had given in. He always got what he wanted. What had he wanted? And why on earth would he be attracted to a woman like her? She was pretty enough, but he could certainly get far prettier without the hassle of having any of them question him or argue with him or stubbornly refuse to back down.

Aggie was forced to conclude that there might be truth in the saying that a change was as good as a rest.

She was different, and he had assumed that he could just reach out and pluck her like fruit from a tree, so that he could sample her before tossing her aside to return to the other varieties of fruit with which he was familiar.

It was more troubling to think of her own motivations, because she was far more serious when it came to relationships. So why was she attracted to him? Was there some part of her, hitherto undiscovered, that really was all about the physical? Some hidden part of her, free of restraint, principles and good judgement, that she had never known existed?

More to the point, how on earth were they going to get along now that this disturbing ingredient had been placed in the mix? Would he be cool and distant towards her because she had turned him down?

Aggie knew that she shouldn't really care but she found that she did. Having seen glimpses of his charm, his intelligence, his sense of humour, she couldn't bear the thought of having to deal with his coolness.

She found that she need not have worried. At least, not as much as she had. She arrived for breakfast the following morning to find him chatting to Mrs Bixby. Although his expression was unreadable when he looked across to where she was standing a little nervously by the door, he greeted her without any rancour or hostility, drawing her into the conversation he had been having with the older woman. Something about the sights they could take in *en route*, which also involved convoluted anecdotes about Mrs Bixby's various relatives who lived there. She seemed to have hordes of family members.

Luiz looked at her not looking at him, deliberately keeping her face turned away so that she could pour all her energy into focusing on Mrs Bixby.

He had managed to staunch his immediate reaction to her dismissal of him. He had left her room enraged and baffled at the unpleasant novelty of having been beaten back. The rage and bafflement had been contained, as he had known they would be, because however uncharacteristic his behaviour had been in that moment, he was still a man who was capable of extreme self-control. He would have to shrug her off with the philosophical approach of you win a few, you lose a few. And, if he had never lost any, then this was as good a time as any to discover what it felt like. With a woman who was, in the bigger picture, an insignificant and temporary visitor to his life.

Outside, the snow had abated. Aggie had called the school, vaguely explained and then apologised for her absence. She hadn't felt all that much better when she had been told that there was nothing to rush back for because the term was nearly over.

'You know what it's like here,' the principal had chuckled. 'All play and not much work with just a week to go before the holidays. If you have family problems, then don't feel guilty about taking some time off to sort them out.'

Aggie did feel guilty, though, because the 'family problems' were a sluggish mix of her own problems which she was trying to fight a way through and it felt deceitful to give the impression that they were any more widespread than that.

She looked surreptitiously at Luiz and wondered what was going through his head. His deep, sexy voice wafted around her and made her feel a little giddy, as though she was standing on a high wire, looking a long way down.

Eventually, Mrs Bixby left and Luiz asked politely in a friendly voice whether she was packed and ready to go.

'We might as well take advantage of the break in the weather,' he said, tossing his serviette onto his plate and pushing his chair back. 'It's not going to last. If you go and bring your bag down, I'll settle up and meet you by reception.'

So this was how it was going to be, Aggie thought. She knew that she should have been pleased. Pleased that he was being normal. Pleased that there would not be an atmosphere between them. Almost as though nothing had happened at all, as though in the early hours of the morning she hadn't bumped into him on the landing, he hadn't strolled into her room wearing nothing but a couple of towels and he certainly hadn't told her that he wanted her. It could all have been a dream because there was nothing in his expression or in the tone of his voice to suggest otherwise.

There was genuine warmth in Mrs Bixby's hugs as she waved them off, and finally Aggie twisted back around in her seat and waited for something. Something to be said. Some indication that they had crossed a line. But nothing.

He asked for the address to the foster home and allowed her to programme the satnav, although her fingers fumbled and it took ages before the address was keyed in and their course plotted.

It would take roughly a few hours. Conditions were going to worsen slightly the further north they went. They had been lucky to have found such a pleasant place to stay a couple of nights but they couldn't risk having to stop again and make do.

Luiz chatted amiably and Aggie was horrified to find that she hated it. Only now was she aware of that spark of electricity that had sizzled between them because it was gone.

When the conversation faltered, he eventually tuned in to the local radio station and they drove without speaking, which gave her plenty of time alone with her thoughts.

In fact, she was barely aware of the motorway giving way to roads, then to streets, and she was shocked when he switched off the radio, stopped the car and said,

'We seem to be here.'

For the first time since they had started on this uncomfortable trip, Luiz was treated to a smile of such spontaneous delight and pleasure that it took his breath away. He grimly wondered whether there was relief in that smile, relief that she was to be spared more of his company. Whether she was attracted to him or not, she had made it perfectly clear that her fundamental antipathy towards him rendered any physical attraction null and void.

'It's been *such* a long time since I was here,' she breathed fervently, hands clasped on her lap. 'I just want to sit here for a little while and breathe it in.'

Luiz thought that anyone would be forgiven for thinking that she was a prodigal daughter, returned to her rightful palatial home. Instead, what he saw was an averagely spacious pebble-dashed house with neat gardens on either side of a gravel drive. There was an assortment of outside toys on the grass and the windows of one of the rooms downstairs appeared to have drawings tacked to them. There were trees at the back but the foliage was sparse and unexciting.

'Same bus,' she said fondly, drawing his attention to a battered vehicle parked at the side. 'Betsy's always complained about it but I think she likes its unpredictability.'

'It's not what I imagined.'

'What did you imagine?'

'It seems small to house a tribe of children and teenagers.'

'There are only ever ten children at any one time and it's bigger at the back. You'll see. There's a conservatory—a double conservatory, where Betsy and Gordon can relax in the evenings while the older ones do their homework. They were always very hot on us doing our homework.' She turned to him and rested her hand on his forearm. 'You don't have to come in if you don't want to. I mean, the village is only a short drive away, and you can always go there for a coffee or something. You have my mobile number. You can call me when you get fed up and I'll come.'

'Not ashamed of me, by any chance, are you?' His voice was mild but there was an edge to it that took her aback.

'Of course I'm not! I was…just thinking of you. I know you're not used to this…er…sort of thing.'

'Stop stereotyping me!' Luiz gritted his teeth and she recoiled as though she had been slapped.

He hadn't complained once when they had been at the bed and breakfast. In fact, he had seemed sincerely impressed with everything about it, and had been the soul of charm to Mrs Bixby. Aggie was suddenly ashamed at the label she had casually dropped on his shoulders and she knew that, whatever his circumstances of birth, and however little he was accustomed to roughing it, he didn't deserve to be shoved in a box. If she did that, then it was about *her* hang-ups and not his.

'I'm sorry,' she said quickly, and he acknowledged the apology with a curt nod.

'Take your time,' he told her. 'I'll bring that bag in and don't rush. I'll watch from the sidelines. I've just spent the last few hours driving. I can do without another bout of it so that I can while away some time in a café.'

But he allowed her half an hour to relax in familiar surroundings without him around. He turned his mind to work, although it was difficult to concentrate when he was half-thinking of the drive ahead, half-thinking of her, wondering what it must feel like to be reunited with her pseudo-family. He had thought that she had stopped seeing him as a one-dimensional cardboard cut-out, but she hadn't, and could he blame her? He had stormed into her life like a bull in a china shop, had made his agenda clear from the beginning, had pronounced upon the problem and produced his financial solution for sorting it out. In short, he had lived down to all her expectations of someone with money and privilege.

He had never given a passing thought in the past as to how he dealt with other people. He had always been supremely confident of his abilities, his power and the reach of his influence. As the only son from a family whose wealth was bottomless, he had accepted the weight of responsibility for taking over his family's vast business concerns, adding to them with his own. Alongside that, however, were all the advantages that came with money—including, he reluctantly conceded, an attitude that might or might not be interpreted as arrogant and overbearing.

It was something that had never been brought to his notice, but then again he was surrounded by people who feared and respected him. Would they ever point out anything that might be seen as criticism?

Agatha Collins had no such qualms. She was in a league of her own. She didn't hold back when it came to pointing out the things she disliked about him although, he mused, she was as quick to apologise if she thought she had been unfair as she was to heap criticism when she thought she had a point. He had found himself in the company of someone who spoke her mind and damned the consequences.

On that thought, he slung his long body out of the car, collected the bag of presents which she had bought the day before and which he could see, as he idly peered into the bag, she had wrapped in very bright, jolly Christmas paper.

The door was pulled open before he had time to hit the

buzzer and he experienced a few seconds of complete dis-
orientation. Sensory overload.

Noise; chaos; children; lots of laughter; the smell of
food; colour everywhere in the form of paintings on the
walls; coats hanging along the wall; shoes and wellies
stacked by the side of the door. Somewhere roundabout
mid-thigh area, a small dark-haired boy with enormous
brown eyes, an earnest face and chocolate smeared round
his mouth stared up at him, announced his name—and also
announced that he knew who *he* was, because Aggie had
said it would be him, which was why Betsy had allowed
him to open the door, because they were *never* allowed
to open the door. All of this was said without pause while
the noise died down and various other children of varying
sizes approached and stared at him.

Luiz had never felt so scrutinised in his life before, nor
so lost for something to say. Being the focus of attention
of a dozen, unblinking children's eyes induced immediate seizure of his vocal chords. Always ready with words,
he cleared his throat and was immensely relieved when
Aggie emerged from a room at the back, accompanied by
a woman in her early seventies, tall, stern-looking with
grey hair pulled back in a bun. When she smiled, though,
her face radiated warmth and he could see from the reaction of the kids that they adored her.

'You look hassled,' Aggie whispered when introduc-
tions had been made. He was assured by Betsy that pan-
demonium was not usual in the house but she was being
lenient, as it was Christmas, and that he must come and
have something to eat, and he needn't fear that there would
be any food throwing at the table.

'Hassled? I'm never hassled.' He slid his eyes across
to her and raised his eyebrows. 'Overwhelmed might be
a better word.'

Aggie laughed, relaxed and happy. 'It's healthy to be overwhelmed every so often.'

'Thanks. I'll bear that in mind.' He was finding it difficult to drag his eyes away from her laughing face. 'Busy place.'

'Always. And Betsy is going to insist on showing you around, I'm afraid. She's very proud of what she's done with the house.'

They had passed several rooms and were heading towards the back of the house where he could see a huge conservatory that opened out onto masses of land with a small copse at the back, which he imagined would be heaven for the kids here when it was summer and they could go outside.

'We won't be here long,' she promised. 'There's a little present-giving Christmas party. It's been brought forward as I'm here. I hope you don't mind.'

'Why should I?' Luiz asked shortly. It irked him immensely that, even though he had mentally decided to write her off, he still couldn't manage to kill off what she did to his libido. It was also intensely frustrating that he was engaging in an unhealthy tussle with feelings of jealousy. Everyone and everything in this place had the power to put a smile on her face. The kind of smile which she had shown him on rare occasions only.

He didn't understand this confused flux of emotion and he didn't like it. He enjoyed being in control of his life and of everything that happened around him. Agatha Collins was very firmly out of his control. If she were any other woman, she would have been flattered at his interest in her, and she wouldn't have hesitated to come to bed with him. It had been a simple, and in his eyes foolproof, proposition.

To have been knocked back was galling enough, but to have been knocked back only to find himself getting back to his feet and bracing himself for another onslaught on her defences bordered on unacceptable.

'I thought you might be bored,' Aggie admitted, flushing guiltily as his face darkened. 'Also...'

'Also what?'

'I know you're angry with me.'

'Why would I be angry with you?' Luiz asked coldly.

'Because I turned you down and I know I must have... You must have found that... Well, I guess I dented your ego.'

'You want me. I want you. I proposed we do something about that and you decided that you didn't want to. There's no question of my pride being dented.'

'I just can't approach sex in such a cold-blooded way.' Aggie was ashamed that after her show of will power she was now backtracking to a place from which she could offer up an explanation. 'You move in and out of women and...'

'And you're not a toy to be picked up and discarded when the novelty's worn off. I think you already made that clear.'

'So that's the only reason why I feel a little uncomfortable about asking you to put yourself out now.'

'Well, don't. Enjoy yourself. The end of the journey is just round the corner.'

CHAPTER SEVEN

'WE'RE never going to make it to Sharrow Bay tonight.'

They had been driving for a little under an hour and Luiz looked across to Aggie with a frown.

'Depends on how much more the weather deteriorates.'

'Yes, well, I don't see the point of taking risks on the roads. I mean, it's not as though Mark and Maria are going anywhere. Not in these conditions. We spent a lot longer than I anticipated at Sevenoaks and I apologise about that.'

Aggie didn't know how to get through the impenetrable barrier that Luiz had erected around himself. He had smiled, charmed and chatted with everyone at the home and had done so without a flicker of tension, but underneath she could feel his coolness towards her. It was like an invisible force field keeping her out and she hated it.

'I hope you didn't find it too much of a chore.' She tried again to revive a conversation that threatened to go in the same direction as the last few she had initiated—slap, bang into a brick wall of Luiz's disinterest.

Her pride, her dignity and her sense of moral self-righteousness at having rightly turned down a proposal for no-strings sex for a day or two had disintegrated, leaving in its wake the disturbing realisation that she had made a terrible mistake. Why hadn't she taken what was on offer? Since when did sex have to lead to a serious commitment? There was no tenderness, and he would never whisper sweet nothings in her ear, but the power of the sexual pull he had over her cut right through all of those shortcomings.

Why shouldn't she be greedy for once in her life and just take without bothering about consequences and without asking herself whether she was doing the wrong thing or the right thing?

She had had three relationships in her life and on paper they had all looked as though they would go somewhere. They had been free-spirited, fun-loving, creative guys, nothing at all like Luiz. They had enjoyed going to clubs, attending protest marches and doing things on impulse.

And what had come of them? She had grown bored with behaviour that had ended up seeming juvenile and irresponsible. She had become fed up with the fact that plans were never made, with Saturdays spent lying in bed because none of them had ever shown any restraint when it came to drinking—and if she had tried to intervene she had been shouted down as a bore. With all of them, she had come to dread the aimlessness that she had initially found appealing. There had always come a point when hopping on the back of a motorbike and just riding where the wind took them had felt like a waste of time.

Luiz was so much the opposite. His self-control was formidable. She wondered whether he had ever done anything spontaneous in his life. Probably not. But despite that, or maybe because of it, her desire for him was liberated from the usual considerations. Why hadn't she seen that at the time? She had shot him down as the sort of person who could have relationships with women purely for sex, as if the only relationships worth considering were ones where you spent your time plumbing each other's depths. Except she had tried those and none of them had worked out.

'The kids loved you,' she persevered. 'And so did Betsy and Gordon. I guess it must have been quite an eye-opener, visiting a place like that. I'm thinking that your background couldn't have been more different.'

Like a jigsaw puzzle where the pieces slowly began to fit together, Luiz was seeing the background picture that had made Aggie the woman she had become. It was frustrating and novel to find himself in a position of wanting to chip away at the surface of a woman and dig deeper. She was suspicious, proud, defensive and fiercely independent. She had had to be.

'There's a hotel up ahead, by the way, just in case you agree with me that we need to stop. Next town along...' With every passing minute of silence from him, Aggie could feel her chances of breaking through that barrier slipping further and further out of reach.

'Is there? How do you know?' With her childhood home behind them, she was no longer the laughing, carefree person she had been there. Luiz could feel the tension radiating out of her, and if it were up to him he would risk the snow and plough on. The mission he had undertaken obviously had to reach a conclusion, but the cold-blooded determination that had initially fuelled him had gone. In its place was weary resignation for an unpleasant task ahead.

Aggie's heart picked up speed. How did she know about the hotel? Because she had checked it on the computer Betsy kept in the office. Because she had looked at Luiz as he had stood with his arms folded at the back of the room, watching Christmas presents being given out, and she had known that, however arrogant and ruthless he could be, he was also capable of generosity and understanding. He could easily have turned down her request for that detour. He was missing work, and the faster he could wrap up the business with Mark and his niece, the better for him. Yet not only had he put himself out but he had taken the experience in his stride. He had shown interest in everything Betsy and Gordon had had to say and had interacted with the kids who had been fascinated by the handsome, sophisticated stranger in their midst.

She had been proud of him and had wanted him so intensely that it physically hurt.

'I saw a sign for it a little way back.' She crossed her fingers behind her back at that excusable white lie. 'And I vaguely remember Betsy mentioning ages ago that there was a new fancy hotel being built near here, to capture the tourist trade. It's booming in this part of the world, you know.'

'I didn't see any sign.'

'It was small. You probably missed it. You're concentrating on driving.'

'Wouldn't you rather just plough on? Get where we're heading? If we stick it out for another hour, we should be there, more or less.'

'I'd rather not, if you don't mind.' It suddenly occurred to her that the offer he had extended had now been withdrawn. He wasn't the sort of man who chased women. Having done so with her, he wasn't the sort of man who would carry on in the face of rejection. Did she want to risk her pride by throwing herself at him, when he now just wanted to get this whole trip over and done with so that he could return to his life?

'I have a bit of a headache coming on, actually. I think it must be all the excitement of today—seeing Gordon and Betsy, the children. Gordon isn't well. She only told me when we were about to leave. He's had some heart problems. I worry about what Betsy will do if something happens to him.'

'Okay. Where's the turning?'

'Are you sure? You've already put yourself out enough as it is.' Aggie held her breath. If he showed even a second's reluctance, then she would abandon her stupid plan; she would just accept that she had missed her chance; she would tell herself that it was for the best and squash any inclination to wonder...

'The turning?'

'I'll direct you.'

He didn't ask how she just happened to know the full address of the hotel, including the post code, in case they got lost and needed to use his satnav. After fifteen minutes of slow driving, they finally saw a sign—a real sign this time—and Aggie breathed a sigh of relief when they swung into the courtyard of a small but very elegant country house. Under the falling snow, it was a picture-postcard scene.

A few cars were in the courtyard, but it was obvious that business was as quiet here as it had been at Mrs Bixby's bed and breakfast. How many other people were slowly wending their way north by car in disastrous driving conditions? Only a few lunatics.

Her nerves gathered pace as they were checked in.

'Since this was my suggestion...' She turned to him as they walked towards the winding staircase that led to the first floor and up to their bedrooms. 'I insist on picking up the tab.'

'Have you got the money to pick up the tab?' Luiz asked. 'There's no point suggesting something if you can't carry it out.'

'I might not be rich but I'm not completely broke!' Nerves made her lash out at him. It wasn't the best strategy for enticing him into her bed. 'I'm doing this all wrong,' she muttered, half to herself.

'Doing what all wrong?' Luiz stopped and looked down at her.

'You're nothing like the guys I've been out with.'

'I don't think that standing halfway up the stairs in a hotel is the place for a soul-searching conversation about the men you've slept with.' He turned on his heels and began heading upstairs.

'I don't like you being like this with me!' Aggie caught up with him and tugged the sleeve of his jumper until he turned around and looked at her with impatience.

'Aggie, why don't we just go to our rooms, take some time out and meet in an hour for dinner? This has already turned into a never-ending journey. I've been away from work for too long. I have things on my mind. I don't feel inclined to get wrapped up in a hysterical, emotional conversation with you now.'

Luiz was finding it impossible to deal with his crazy obsession with her. He wondered if he was going stir crazy. Was being cooped up with her doing something to his self-control? It had not even crossed his mind, when he had made a pass at her, that she would turn him down. Was that why he had watched her with Betsy and Gordon and all those kids and the only thing he could think was how much he wanted to get her into his bed? Was he so arrogant, in the end, that he couldn't accept that any woman should say no to him?

The uneasy swirl of unfamiliar emotions had left him edgy and short-tempered. He would have liked to dismiss her from his mind the way he had always been able to dismiss all the inconveniences that life had occasionally thrown at him. He had always been good at that. Ruthlessness had always served him well. That and the knowledge that it was pointless getting sidetracked by things that were out of your control. Aggie sidetracked him and the last thing he needed was an involved conversation that would get neither of them anywhere. Womanly chats were things he avoided like the plague.

'I'm not being hysterical.' Aggie took a deep breath. If she backed away now, she would never do what she felt she had to do. Falling into bed with Luiz might be something she would never have contemplated in a month of Sundays, but then again she had never had to cope with a sexual attraction that was ripping her principles to shreds.

She had come to the conclusion that, whilst she knew it was crazy to sleep with a guy whose attitude towards women she found unnerving and amoral, not to sleep with him would leave her with regrets she would never be able to put behind her. And, if she was going to sleep with him, then she intended to have some control over the whole messy situation.

A lifetime of independence would not be washed away in a five-minute decision.

'I just want to talk to you. I want to clear the air.'

'There's nothing to clear, Aggie. I've done what you asked me to do, and I'm pleased you seemed to have had a good time seeing all your old friends, but now it's time to move on.'

'I may have made a mistake.'

'What are you talking about?'

'Can we discuss this upstairs? In your room? Or we could always go back downstairs to the sitting room. It's quiet there.'

'If you don't mind me changing while you speak, then follow me to my room, by all means.' He turned his back on her and headed up.

'So…' Once inside the bedroom, Luiz began pulling off his sweater which he flung on a chair by the window. Their bags had been brought up and deposited in their separate rooms and he began rummaging through his for some clothes.

'I never wanted to make this trip with you,' Aggie began falteringly, and Luiz stilled and turned to look at her.

'If this is going to be another twenty minutes of recriminations, then let me tell you straight away that I'm not in the mood.' But, even as he spoke, he was seeing her tumble of fair hair and the slender contours of her body encased in a pair of the new jeans and deep burgundy jumper that was close-fitted and a lot sexier than the baggy jumpers she seemed to have stockpiled. Once again, his unruly lack of physical control made him grit his teeth in frustration. 'I'm also not in the mood to hear you make a song and dance about paying your own way.'

'I wasn't going to.' She pressed her back against the closed door.

'Then what was it you wanted to tell me?'

'I've never met anyone like you before.'

'I think,' Luiz said drily, 'you may have mentioned that to me in the past—and not in a good way—so unless you have something else to add to the mix then I suggest you go and freshen up.'

'What I mean is, I never thought I could be attracted to someone like you.'

'I don't do these kinds of conversations, Aggie. Post mortems on a relationship are bad enough; post mortems on a non-relationship are a complete non-starter. Now, I'm going to have a shower.' He began unbuttoning his shirt.

Aggie felt the thrill of sudden, reckless excitement and a desperate urgency to get through to him. Despite or maybe because of her background she had never been a risk taker. From a young age, she had felt responsible for Mark and she had also gathered, very early on, that the road to success wasn't about taking risks. It was about putting in the hard work; risk taking was for people who had safety nets to fall into. She had never had one.

Even in her relationships, she had never strayed from what her head told her she should be drawn to. So they hadn't worked out. At no point, she now realised, had she ever concluded that maybe she should have sat back and taken stock of what her head had been telling her.

Luiz, so different from anyone she had ever known, who had entered her life in the most dubious of circumstances, had sent her into a crazy tailspin. She had found herself in terrifying new territory where nothing made sense and she had reacted by lashing out.

Before he could become completely bored with her circuitous conversation, Aggie drew in a deep breath. 'You made a pass at me and I'm sorry I turned you down.'

Luiz, about to pull off his shirt, allowed his arms to drop to his sides and looked at her through narrowed eyes. 'I'm not with you,' he said slowly.

Aggie propelled herself away from the safety of the door and walked towards him. Every step closer set up a tempo in her body that made her perspire with nervous tension.

'I always thought,' she told him huskily, 'that I could never make love to a guy unless I really liked him.'

'And the boyfriends you've had?'

'I really liked them. To start with. And please don't make it sound as though I've slept around; I haven't. I've just always placed a lot of importance on compatibility.'

'We all make mistakes.' At no point did it occur to Luiz that he would turn her away. The strength of his attraction was too overwhelming. He didn't get it, but he knew himself well enough to realise that it was something that needed sating. 'But the compatibility angle obviously didn't play out with you,' he couldn't help adding with some satisfaction.

'No, it didn't,' Aggie admitted ruefully. She sneaked a glance at him and shivered. He was just so gorgeous. Was it any wonder her will power was sapped? She would never have made a play for him. She would never have considered herself to be in the category of women he might be attracted to. It occurred to her that he only wanted her because she was different from the women he dated, but none of that seemed to matter, and she wasn't going to try and fight it.

'What happened?' Luiz strolled towards the king-sized four-poster bed and flopped down on it, his hands linked behind his head. His unbuttoned shirt opened to reveal a tantalising expanse of bronzed, muscular chest. This was the pose of the conqueror waiting for his concubine, and it thrilled her.

Aggie shrugged. 'They were free spirits. I liked it to start with. But I guess I'm not much of a free spirit.'

'No. You're not.' He gave her a slow, lingering smile that made her toes curl. 'Are you going to continue standing there or are you going to join me?' He patted the space next to him on the bed and Aggie's heart descended very rapidly in the direction of her feet.

She inched her way towards the bed and laughed when he sat forward and yanked her towards him. Her laughter felt like an unspoken release of all her defences. She was letting go of her resentment in the face of something bigger.

'What do you mean?' Heart beating a mile a minute, she collapsed next to him and felt the warmth of his body next to her. It generated a series of intensely physical reactions that left her breathless and gasping.

'So you're not impressed by money. But a free spirit would have taken what I offered—the computer, the extensive wardrobe; would have factored them in as gifts to be appreciated and moved on. You rejected the computer out of hand and agonised over the wardrobe. The only reason you accepted was because you had no more clothes and I had to talk you into seeing the sense behind the offer. And you still tell me you're going to return them all to me when we get back to London. You criticise me for wanting control but you fall victim to the very same tendency.'

'We're not alike at all.' They were both on their sides, fully clothed, staring at one another. There was something very erotic about the experience, because underneath the excitement of discovery lurked like a thrilling present concealed with wrapping paper.

'Money separates us,' Luiz said wryly. 'But in some areas I've discovered that we're remarkably similar. Would this conversation benefit from us being naked, do you think?'

Aggie released a small, treacherous moan and he delivered a rampantly satisfied smile in response. Then he stood up and held out one hand. 'I'm going to run a bath,' he murmured. 'Your room's next to mine. Why don't you go and get some clothes...?'

'It feels weird,' Aggie confided. 'I've never approached an intimate situation like this.'

'But then this is an intimate situation neither of us expected,' Luiz murmured. 'And that in itself is a first for me.'

'What do you mean?'

'It never fails to surprise me just how turned on I get for you.'

'Because I'm nothing like the women you've gone out with?'

'Because you're nothing like the women I've gone out with,' Luiz agreed.

Aggie knew that she should be offended by that, but

then who would she be kidding? He was nothing like the guys she had gone out with. Mutual physical attraction had barrelled through everything and changed the parameters. Maybe that was why it felt so dangerously exciting.

'You're a lot more independent and I find that a turn on.' He softly ran his fingers along her side. He couldn't wait for her to be naked but this leisurely approach was intoxicating. 'You're not a slave to fashion and you're fond of arguing.'

Aggie conceded privately that all three of those things represented a change for him, but a change that he would rapidly tire of. Since she wasn't in it for the long haul, since she too was stepping outside the box, there was no harm in that, although she was uneasily aware of a barely acknowledged disappointment floating aimlessly inside her.

'You like your women submissive,' she said with a little laugh.

'Generally speaking, it's worked in the past.'

'And I like my guys to be creative, not to be ruled by money.'

'And yet, mysteriously, your creative paupers have all bitten the dust.' Luiz found, to his bemusement, that he didn't care for the thought of any other man in her life. It was puzzling, because he had never been the possessive type. In fact, in the past women who had tried to stir up a non-existent jealousy gene by referring to past lovers had succeeded in doing the opposite.

'They haven't been paupers,' Aggie laughed. 'Neither of them. They've just been indifferent to money.'

'And in the end they bored you.'

'I'm beginning to wish I'd never mentioned that,' Aggie said, though only half-joking. 'And if they bored me,' she felt obliged to elaborate, 'it was because they turned out to be boring people, not because they were indifferent to money.' She wriggled off the bed and stood up. 'Perhaps I'll have a bath in my own bathroom...'

Luiz frowned, propping himself up on one elbow. 'Second thoughts?' His voice was neutral but his eyes had cooled.

'No.' Aggie tilted her chin to look at him. 'I don't play games like that.'

'Good.' He felt himself relax. To have been rejected once bordered on the unthinkable. To be rejected twice would have been beyond the pale. 'Then what games do you play? Because I think I can help you out there...'

The promise behind those softly spoken words sent a shiver up her spine and it was still there when she returned to his bedroom a few minutes later. She had not been lying when she had confessed that she had never approached sex like this before. Stripped of all romantic mystique and airy-fairy expectations that it would lead somewhere, this was physical contact reduced to its most concentrated form.

The bath had been run. Aggie could smell the fragrance of jasmine bath oil. The steam in the enormous bathroom did nothing whatsoever to diminish the impact of Luiz, who had stripped out of his clothes and was wearing a towel around his waist.

Outside, the snow continued to fall. In her room, she had taken a few seconds to stare out of the window and absorb the fact that Mark and Maria, and the mission upon which they had embarked only a few days previously, couldn't have been further from her mind. When exactly had she lost track of the reason why she was here in the first place? It was as though she had opened the wardrobe door to find herself stepping into Narnia, reality left behind for a brief window in time.

She could barely remember the routine of her day-today existence. The school, the staff room, the kids getting ready for their Nativity play.

Was Luiz right? She had always fancied herself as a free-spirited person and yet she felt as though this was the first impulsive thing she had ever done in her life. She had thought him freakishly controlled, a power-hungry tycoon addicted to mastering everything and everyone around him, while she—well, she was completely different. Maybe the only difference really was the fact that he was rich and she wasn't, that he had grown up with privilege while she had had to fight her way out of her background, burying herself in studies that could provide her with opportunities.

'Now, what I'd like…' Luiz drawled, and Aggie blinked herself back to the present, 'is to do what I was fantasising about when you did your little catwalk in that shop for me. Instead of showing me how you look with clothes on, show me how you look with them off.'

He sauntered out of the bathroom and lay back down on the bed, just as he had before.

Aggie realised in some part of her that, whilst this should not feel right, it did. She would never have believed it possible for either of them to set aside their personal differences and meet on this plane. Certainly, she would never have believed it of herself, but before she could begin nurturing any doubts about the radical decision she had made she told herself that everyone deserves some time out, and this was her time out. In a day or two, it would be nothing more than a wicked memory of the one and only time she had truly strayed from the path she had laid out for herself.

She watched, fascinated and tingling all over, shocked as he drew back the towel which had been modestly covering him, and revealed his arousal. She nearly fainted when he gently held it in one hand.

Luiz grinned at her. 'So easy to make you blush,' he murmured. Then he fell silent and watched as she began removing her clothes, at first with self-conscious, fumbling fingers, then with more confidence as she revelled in the sight of his darkened, openly appreciative gaze.

'Come here,' he rasped roughly, before she could remove the final strips of clothing. 'I'm finding it hard to wait.'

Aggie sighed and flung her head back as his big hands curved over her breasts, thinly sheathed in a lacy bra. Their mouths met in an explosive kiss, a greedy, hungry kiss, so that they gasped as they surfaced for air and then resumed their kissing as if neither could get enough of the other. Her nipples were tender and sensitive and she moaned when he rolled his thumb over one stiffened peak, seeking and finding it through the lacy gaps in the bra.

She was melting. Freeing a hand from the tangle of his black hair, she shakily pulled off the panties which were damp, proof of her own out-of-control libido.

Luiz was going crazy with *wanting* her. He could hardly bear the brief separation of their bodies as she unclasped her bra from the back and pulled it off.

Her nipples were big, circular discs, clearly defined, pouting temptingly at him. He realised that he had been fantasising about this moment perhaps from the very first time he had laid eyes on her. He had not allowed himself to see her in a sexual way, not when he had been busy working out how to disengage her and her brother from his niece and the family fortune. But enforced time together had whittled away his self-control. It had allowed the seeds of attraction to take root and flourish.

'You have the face of an angel,' he breathed huskily as he rolled her on top of him. 'And the body of a siren.'

'I'm not sure about that.' Aggie gazed down at him. 'Aren't sirens supposed to be voluptuous?'

'God, you're beautiful...' His hands could almost span her waist and he eased her down so that he could take one of those delicate breasts to his mouth and suckle on the hot, throbbing tip. He loved the way she arched her body back, offering herself to him—and even more he loved the way he could sense her spiralling out of control, her fists clenched as she tried to control the waves of sensation washing over her.

He smoothed his hand along the inside of her thigh and she wriggled to accommodate his questing finger. She shuddered when that finger dipped into her honeyed moistness and began stroking her. With her body under sensual attack on two fronts as he continued to worship her breast with his mouth and tease the wet, receptive bud of her femininity with his finger, she could bear it no longer. She flipped off him and lay on her back, breathing heavily and then curling onto her side as he laughed softly next to her.

'Too much?' he asked, and she sighed on a moan.

'Not fair. It's your turn now to feel like you're about to fall off the edge.'

'What makes you think I'm not already there?'

It transpired that he wasn't. In fact, it transpired that he didn't have a clue what being close to the edge was all about. He had foolishly been confusing it with simply *being turned on*.

For an excruciatingly long period of time, she demonstrated what being close to the edge was all about. She touched him and tasted him until he thought he had died and gone to heaven.

Their bodies seemed to merge and become one. She touched him and he touched her, from her breasts, down to her flat belly with its little mole just above her belly button, and then at last to the most intimate part of her.

He peeled apart her delicate folds and dipped his tongue just there until she squirmed with pleasure, her fingers tangled in his hair, her eyes shut and her whole body thrust back to receive the ministrations of his mouth.

He lazily feasted on her silky-sweet moistness until she was begging him to stop. Lost in the moment, he could have stayed there for ever with her legs around him and her body bucking under his mouth.

He finally thrust into her only after he was wearing protection. Putting it on, he found that his hands were shaking. He kicked off the last slither of duvet that remained on the bed and she opened up to him like a flower, her rhythm and movements matching his so that they were moving as one.

Aggie didn't think that she had ever felt so united and in tune with another human being in her life before. Her body was slippery, coated in a fine film of perspiration. His was too.

They climaxed and it was like soaring high above the earth. And then, quietening, they subsided gently back down. She rolled onto her side and looked at him with pleasure.

'That was…'

'Momentous? Beyond description?' God, this was nothing like what he had felt before! Could good sex do this to a man? Make him feel like he could fly? They had only just finished making love and he couldn't wait to take her again. Did that make sense? He had made love to any number of beautiful women before but he had never felt like this. He had never felt as though he was in possession of an insatiable appetite, had never wanted to switch the light on so that he could just *look*…

'I want to take you again, but first…' Luiz felt an urgent need to set a few facts straight, to reassure himself that this feeling of being out of control, carried away by a current against which he seemed to be powerless, was just a temporary situation. 'You know this isn't going to go anywhere, don't you?' He brushed her hair away from her face so that he could look her directly in the eye. So this might be the wrong time and the wrong place to say this, but it had to be said. He had to clear the air. 'I wouldn't want you to think…'

'Shh. I don't think anything.' Aggie smiled bravely while a series of pathways began connecting in her brain. This man she loathed, to whom she was desperately attracted, was a man who could make her laugh even though she had found him overbearing and arrogant, the same man who had slowly filled her head and her heart. It was why she was here now. In bed with him. She hadn't suddenly become a woman with no morals who thought it was fine to jump into bed on the basis of sexual attraction. No. That had been a little piece of fiction she had sold herself because the truth staring her in the face had been unacceptable.

'I'm not about to start making demands. You and I, we're not suited and we never will be. But we're attracted to one another. That's all. So, why don't we just have some fun? Because we both know that tomorrow it all comes to an end.'

CHAPTER EIGHT

AGGIE spent the night in her own bedroom. Drunk with love-making, she had made sure to tiptoe along the corridor at a little after two in the morning. It was important to remind herself that this was not a normal relationship. It had boundaries and Luiz had made sure to remind her of that the night before. She wasn't about to over step any of them.

She heard the beeping of her phone the following morning and woke to find a series of messages from her brother, all asking her to give him a call.

Panicked, Aggie sat up and dialled his mobile with shaking fingers. She was ashamed to admit that her brother had barely registered on her radar over the past few hours. In fact, she guiltily realised that she had been too focused on herself for longer than that to spare much thought for Mark.

She got through to him almost immediately. The conversation, on her end, barely covered a sentence or two. Down the other end of the line, Mark did all the talking and at the end of ten minutes Aggie ended the call, shell-shocked.

Everything was about to change now, and for a few seconds she resented her brother's intrusion into the little bubble she had built for herself. She checked the time on her phone. Luiz had tried to pull her back into bed with him before she had left in the early hours of the morning, but Aggie had resisted. Luiz was a man who always got what he wanted and rarely paused to consider the costs. He wanted her and would see nothing wrong in having her, whenever and wherever. He was good when it came to detaching and, once their time together was over, he would instantly break off and walk away. Aggie knew that she would not be able to, so putting some distance between them, if not sharing a room for the night could be termed putting distance between them, was essential.

So they had agreed to meet for breakfast at nine. Plenty of time to check the weather and for Luiz to catch up with emails. It was now a little after eight, and Aggie was glad for the time in which she could have a bath and think about what her brother had told her.

Luiz was waiting for her in the dining room, where a pot of coffee was already on the table and two menus, one of which he was scanning, although he put it down as she hovered for a few seconds in the doorway.

She was in a pair of faded jeans and a blue jumper, her hair tied back. She looked like a very sexy schoolgirl, and all at once he felt himself stir into lusty arousal. He hadn't been able to get enough of her the night before. In fact, he recalled asking her at one point whether she was too sore for him to touch her again down there. He leaned back in the chair and shot her a sexy half-smile as she walked towards him.

'You should have stayed with me,' were his first words of greeting. 'You would have made an unbeatable wake-up call.'

Aggie slipped into the chair opposite and helped herself to some coffee. Mark and his news were at the top of her mind but it was something she would lead up to carefully.

'You said you wanted to get some work done before you came down to breakfast. I wouldn't have wanted to interrupt you.'

'I'm good at multi-tasking. You'd be surprised how much work I can get through when there's someone between my legs paying attention to…'

'Shh!' She went bright red and Luiz laughed, entertained at her prurience.

'You get my drift, though?'

'Is that the kind of wake-up call you're accustomed to?' She held the cup between her hands and looked at him over the rim. She had kept her voice light but underneath she could feel jealousy swirling through her veins, unwelcome and inappropriate.

'The only wake-up calls I'm accustomed to are the ones that come from alarm clocks.' He hadn't thought about it, but women sleeping in his bed didn't happen.

'You mean you've never had a night with a woman in your bed? What about holidays?'

'I don't do holidays with women.'

Aggie gazed at him in surprise.

'It's not that unusual,' Luiz muttered, shooting her a brooding look from under his lashes. 'I'm a busy man. I don't have time for the demands of a woman on holiday.'

'How on earth do you ever relax?'

'I return to Brazil. My holidays are there.' He shrugged. 'I used to go on holidays with a couple of my pals. The occasional weekend. Usually skiing. Those have dried up over the past few years.'

'Your holidays were with your guy friends?'

'How did we end up having this conversation?' He raked his fingers through his dark hair in a gesture that she had come to recognise as one of frustration.

If this was about sex and nothing more—and he had

made it clear that for him it was—then Aggie knew she should steer clear of in-depth conversations. He wouldn't welcome them. She fancied that it had always been his way of avoiding the commitment of a full-blown relationship, his way of keeping women at a safe distance. If you didn't have any kind of revealing conversation with someone, then it was unlikely that anyone would ever get close to you. Her curiosity felt like a treacherous step in dangerous waters.

'There's nothing wrong with talking to one another.' She glanced down at the menu and made noises about scrambled eggs and toast.

'Guys don't need attention to be lavished on them,' Luiz said abruptly. 'We're all experienced skiers. We do the black runs, relax for a couple of hours in the evening. Good exercise. No one complaining about not being entertained.'

'I can't imagine anyone having the nerve to complain to you,' Aggie remarked, and Luiz relaxed.

'You'd be surprised, although women complaining fades into insignificance when set alongside your remarkable talent for arguing with me. Not that I don't like it. It's your passionate nature. Your *extremely* passionate nature.'

'Plus those chalet girls can be very attractive if you decide you miss the entertainment of females...'

Luiz laughed, his dark eyes roaming appreciatively over her face. 'When I go skiing, I ski. The last thing I've ever wanted is any kind of involvement in those brief windows of leisure time I get round to snatching for myself.'

'And those brief windows have dried up?'

'My father hasn't been well,' Luiz heard himself say. It was a surprising admission and not one he could remember making to anyone. Only he and his mother knew the real state of his father's health. Like him, his father didn't appreciate fuss and he knew that his daughters would fuss around him. He was also the primary figurehead for the family's vast empire. Many of the older clients would react badly to any hint that Alfredo Montes was not in the prime of good health. Whilst for years Luiz had concentrated on his own business concerns, he had been obliged to take a much more active role in his father's various companies over the past few years, slowly building confidence for the day when his father could fully retire.

'I'm sorry.' She reached out and covered his hand with hers. 'What's wrong with him?'

'Forget I said anything.'

'Why? Is it…terminal?'

Luiz hesitated. 'He had a stroke a few years ago and never made a full recovery. He can still function, but not in the way he used to. His memory isn't what it used to be, nor are his levels of concentration. He's been forced into semi-retirement. No one is aware of his health issues aside from me and my mother.'

'So…you've been overseeing his affairs so that he can slow down?'

'It's not a big deal.' He beckoned across a waitress, closing down the conversation while Aggie fitted that background information about him into the bigger picture she was unconsciously building.

Luiz Montes was a workaholic who had found himself in a situation where he couldn't afford to stand still. He had no time for holidays and even less for the clutter of a relationship. But, even into that relentless lifestyle, he had managed to fit in this tortuous trip on behalf of his sister. It proclaimed family loyalty and a generosity of spirit that she had not given him credit for.

'There's something you need to know,' she said, changing the subject. 'Mark finally got through to me this morning. In fact, last night. I left my phone in the bedroom and didn't check it before I went to sleep. I woke up this morning to find missed calls and text messages for me to call him.'

'And?'

'They're not in the Lake District after all. They're in Las Vegas.'

'So they did it. They tied the knot, the bloody fools.' Luiz didn't feel the rage he had expected. He was still dwelling on the uncustomary lapse in judgement that had allowed him to confide in her. He had never felt the need to pour his heart and soul out to anyone. Indeed, he had always viewed such tendencies as weaknesses, but strangely sharing that secret had had a liberating effect. Enough to smooth over any anger he knew he should have been feeling at his niece doing something as stupid as getting married when she was still a child herself.

'I never said that.' Aggie grinned and he raised his eyebrows enquiringly.

'Share the joke? Because I'm not seeing anything funny from where I'm sitting.' But he could feel himself just going through the motions.

'Well, for a start, they haven't got married.'

Luiz looked at her in silence. 'Come again?'

'Your sister was obviously worried for no good reason. Okay, maybe Maria confided that she loved my brother. Maybe she indulged in a bit of girlish wishful thinking, but that was as far as it went. There was never any plan to run away and get married in the dead of night.'

'So we've spent the past few days on a fool's errand? What the hell are they doing in *Las Vegas*?' Less than a week ago, he would have made a sarcastic comment about the funding for such a trip, but then less than a week ago he hadn't been marooned with this woman in the middle of nowhere. Right at this moment in time, he really couldn't give a damn who had paid for what or who was ripping whom off.

He found himself thinking of that foster home—the atmosphere of cheeriness despite the old furnishings and the obvious lack of luxuries. He thought of Aggie's dingy rented house. Both those things should have hit him as evidence of people not out to take what they could get.

'Mark's over the moon.' Aggie rested her chin in the palm of her hand and looked at Luiz with shining eyes. 'He got a call when they'd only just left London. He said that he was going to call me but then he knew that he wasn't expected back for a few days and he didn't want to say anything just in case nothing came of it. But through a friend of a friend of a friend, a record producer got to hear one of his demos and flew them both over so that they could hear some more. He's got a recording contract!'

'Well, I'll be damned.'

'So…' Aggie sat back to allow a plate of eggs and toast to be put in front of her. 'There's no point carrying on any further.'

'No, there isn't.'

'You'll be relieved, I bet. You can get back to your work, although I'm going to preach at you now and tell you that it's not healthy to work the hours you do, even if you feel you have no choice.'

'You're probably right.'

'I mean, you need to be able to enjoy leisure time as much as you enjoy working time. Sorry? What did you say?'

Luiz shrugged. 'When we get back to London.' He hadn't intended on having any kind of relationship with her, but after last night he couldn't foresee relinquishing it just yet. 'A slight reduction in the workload wouldn't hurt. It's the Christmas season. People are kicking back. It's not as frenetic in the business world as it usually is.'

'So you're going to take a holiday?' Aggie's heart did a sudden, painful flip. 'Will you be going to Brazil, then?'

'I can't leave the country just yet.'

'I thought you said that you were going to have a break.'

'Which isn't to say that I'm suddenly going to drop out of sight. There are a couple of deals that need work, meetings I can't get out of.' He pushed his plate away and sat back to look at her steadily. 'We need to talk about... us. This.'

'I know. It wasn't the wisest move in the world. Neither of us anticipated that...that...'

'That we wouldn't be able to keep our hands off one another?'

How easy it was for him to think about it purely in terms of sex, Aggie thought. While *she* could only think of it in terms of falling in love. She wondered how many women before her had made the same mistake of bucking the guidelines he set and falling in love with him. Had his last girlfriend been guilty of that sin?

'The circumstances were peculiar,' Aggie said, keen to be as light-hearted about what happened between them as he was. 'It's a fact that people can behave out of character when they're thrown into a situation they're not accustomed to. I mean, none of this would have happened if we hadn't...found ourselves snowbound on this trip.'

'Wouldn't it?' His dark eyes swept thoughtfully over her flushed face.

'What do you mean?'

'I like to think I'm honest enough not to underestimate this attraction I feel for you. I noticed you the first time I saw you and it wasn't just as a potential gold-digger. I think I was sexually attracted to you from the beginning.

Maybe I would never have done anything about it but I wouldn't bet on that.'

'*I* didn't notice you!'

'Liar.'

'I didn't,' Aggie insisted with a touch of desperation. 'I mean, I just thought you were Maria's arrogant uncle who had only appeared on the scene to warn us off. I didn't even like you!'

'Who's talking about like or dislike? That's quite different from sexual attraction. Which brings me back to my starting point. We'll head back down to London as soon as we've finished breakfast, and when we get to London I want to know what your plans are. Because I'm not ready to give this up just yet. In fact, I would say that I'm just getting started…'

Just yet. Didn't that say it all? But at least he wasn't trying to disguise the full extent of his interest in her; at least he wasn't pretending that they were anything but two ships passing in the night, dropping anchor for a while before moving on their separate journeys.

When Aggie thought of her last boyfriend, he had been fond of planning ahead, discussing where they would go on holiday in five years' time. She had fancied herself in love, but like an illness it had passed quickly and soon after she had realised that what she had really loved was the feeling of permanence that had been promised.

Luiz wasn't promising permanence. In fact, he wasn't even promising anything longer than a couple of weeks or a couple of months.

'You're looking for another notch on your bedpost?' Aggie said lightly and he frowned at her.

'I'm not that kind of man and if you don't think I've been honest with you, then I can only repeat what I've said. I'm not looking for a committed relationship, but neither do I work my way through women because I have a little black book I want to fill. If you really think that, then we're not on the same page, and whatever we did last night will remain a one-time memory.'

'I shouldn't have said that, but Luiz, you can't really blame me, can you? I mean, have you ever had a relationship that you thought might be going somewhere?'

'I've never sought it. On the other hand, I don't use women. Why are we discussing this, Aggie? Neither of us sees any kind of future in this. I thought we'd covered that.' He looked at her narrowly. 'We *have* covered that, haven't we? I mean, you haven't suddenly decided that you're looking for a long-term relationship, have you? Because, I repeat, it's never going to happen.'

'I'm aware of that,' Aggie snapped. 'And, believe me, I'm not on the hunt for anything permanent either.'

'Then what's the problem? Why the sudden atmosphere?' He allowed a few seconds of thoughtful silence during which time she tried to think of something suitably dismissive to say. 'I never asked,' he said slowly. 'But I assumed that when you slept with me there was no one else in your life…'

Aggie's blue eyes were wide with confusion as she returned his gaze, then comprehension filtered through and confusion turned to anger.

'That's a horrible thing to say.' She felt tears prick the back of her eyes and she hurriedly stared down at her plate.

Luiz shook his head, shame-faced and yet wanting to tell her that, horrible it might be, but it wouldn't be the first time a woman had slept with him while still involved with another man. Some women enjoyed hedging their bets. Naturally, once he was involved, all other men were instantly dropped, but from instances like that he had developed a healthy dose of suspicion when it came to the opposite sex.

But, hell, he couldn't lump Aggie into the same category as other women. She was in a league of her own.

Cheeks flushed, Aggie flung down her napkin and stood up. 'If we're leaving, I need to go upstairs and get my packing done.'

'Aggie...' Luiz vaulted to his feet and followed her as she stormed out of the dining room towards the staircase. He grabbed her by her arm and pulled her towards him.

'It doesn't matter.'

'It *matters*. I...I apologise for what I said.'

'You're so suspicious of everyone! What kind of world do you live in, Luiz Montes? You're suspicious of gold-diggers, opportunists, women who want to take advantage of you...'

'It's ingrained, and I'm not saying that it's a good thing.' But it was something he had never questioned before. He looked at her, confused, frowning. 'I want to carry on seeing you when we get back to London,' he said roughly.

'And you've laid down so many guidelines about what that entails!' Aggie sighed and shook her head. This was so bad for her, yet even while one part of her brain acknowledged that there was another part that couldn't contemplate giving him up without a backward glance. Even standing this close to him was already doing things to her, making her heart beat faster and turning her bones to jelly.

'I'm just attempting to be as honest as I can.'

'And you don't have to worry that I'm going to do anything stupid!' She looked at him fiercely. If only he knew how stupid she had already been, he would run a mile. But, just as she had jumped in feet first to sleep with him and damn the consequences, she was going to carry on sleeping with him, taking what she could get like an addict too scared of quitting until it was forced upon them.

She wasn't proud of herself but, like him, she was honest.

Luiz half-closed his eyes with relief. He only realised that he had been holding his breath when he expelled it slowly. 'The drive back will be a lot easier,' he said briskly. His hand on her arm turned to a soft caress that sent shivers racing up and down her spine.

'And are you still going to…talk to Mark when they get back from London? Warn him off Maria?'

Luiz realised that he hadn't given that any thought at all. 'They're not getting married. Crisis defused.' He looked at her and grinned reluctantly. 'Okay. I've had other things on my mind. I hadn't given any thought to what was going to happen next in this little saga. Now I'm thinking about it and realising that Luisa can have whatever mother-to-daughter chat she thinks she needs to have. I'm removing myself from the situation.'

'I'm glad.'

She smiled and all Luiz could think was that he was chuffed that he had been responsible for putting that smile on her face.

Once, he would not have been able to see beyond the fact that any relationship where the levels of wealth were so disproportionately unbalanced was doomed to failure, if not worse. Once the financial inequality would have been enough for him to continue his pursuit, to do everything within his power to remove Aggie's brother from any position from which he could exert influence over his niece. Things had subtly changed.

'So,' she said softly. 'I'm going to go and pack and I'll see you back here in half an hour or so?'

Luiz nodded and she didn't ask for any details of what

would happen next. Of course, they would return to her house, but then what? Would they date one another or was that too romantic a notion for him? Would he wine and dine her, the way he wined and dined the other women he went out with? She was sure that he was generous when it came to the materialistic side of any relationship he was in. What he lacked in emotional giving, he would more than make up for in financial generosity. He was, after all, the man who had suggested buying her a laptop computer because she happened not to possess one. And this before they had become lovers.

But, if he had his ground rules, then she had hers. She would not allow him to buy anything for her nor would she expect any lavish meals out or expensive seats at the opera or the theatre. If his approach to what they had was to put all his cards on the table, then she would have to make sure that she put some of her own cards on the table as well.

As if predicating for a quick journey back to London, as opposed to the tortuous one they had embarked upon when they had set off, the snow had finally dwindled to no more than some soft, light flurries.

The atmosphere was heavy with the thrill of what lay ahead. Aggie was conscious of every movement of his hands on the steering wheel. She sneaked glances at his profile and marvelled at the sexy perfection of his face. When she closed her eyes, she imagined being alone with him in a room, submitting to his caresses.

Making small talk just felt like part of an elaborate dance between them. He was planning on visiting his family in Brazil over the Christmas period. She asked him about where he lived. She found that she had an insatiable appetite for finding out all the details of his background. Having broken ground with his confidences about his father, he talked about him, about the stroke and the effect it had had on him. He described his country in ways that brought it alive. She felt as though there were a million things she wanted to hear about him.

Mark and Maria would not be returning to the country for a few days yet, and as they approached the outskirts of London he said in a lazy drawl that already expected agreement to his proposal, 'I don't think you should carry on living in that dump.'

Aggie laughed, amused.

'I'm not kidding. I can't have you living there.'

'Where would you have me living, Luiz?'

'Kensington has some decent property. I could get you somewhere.'

'Thanks, but I think we've already covered the problem of rent in London and how expensive it is.'

'You misunderstand me. When I say that I could get you somewhere, I mean I could *buy* you somewhere.'

Aggie's mouth dropped open and she looked at him in astonishment and disbelief.

'Well?' Luiz prompted, when there was silence following this remark.

'You can't just go and *buy somewhere* for a woman you happen to be sleeping with, Luiz.'

'Why not?'

'Because it's not right.'

'I want you to live somewhere halfway decent. I have the money to turn that wish into reality. What could be more right?'

'And just for the sake of argument, what would happen with this halfway decent house when we broke up?'

Luiz frowned, not liking the way that sounded. He knew he was the one who'd laid down that rule, but was there really any need to underline it and stick three exclamation marks after it for good measure?

'You'd keep it, naturally. I never give a woman gifts and then take them away from her when the relationship goes sour.'

'You've had way too much your own way for too long,' Aggie told him. It was hardly surprising. He had grown up with money and it had always been second nature to indulge his women with gifts. 'I'm not going to accept a house from you. Or a flat, or whatever. I'm perfectly happy where I am.'

'You're not,' Luiz contradicted bluntly. 'No one could be perfectly happy in that hovel. The closest anyone could get to feeling anything about that place is that it's a roof over your head.'

'I don't want anything from you.' After the great open spaces of up north, the business of London felt like four walls pressing down on her.

That was not what Luiz wanted to hear, because for once he *wanted* to give her things. He wanted to see that smile on her face and know that he was responsible for putting it there.

'Actually,' Aggie continued thoughtfully, 'I think we should just enjoy whatever we have. I don't want you giving me any presents or taking me to expensive places.'

'I don't do home-cooked meals in front of the television.'

'And I don't do lavish meals out. Now and again, it's nice to go somewhere for dinner, but it's nice not to as well.' Aggie knew that she was treading on thin ice here. Any threat of domesticity would have him running a mile, but how much should she sacrifice for the sake of love and lust?

'I'm not into all that stuff,' she said. 'I don't wear jewels and I don't have expensive tastes.'

'Why are you so difficult?'

'I didn't realise I was.'

'From a practical point of view, your house is going to be a little cramped with your brother there and my niece popping her head in every three minutes. I'm not spending time at your place with the four of us sitting on a sagging sofa, watching television while my car gets broken into outside.'

Aggie laughed aloud. 'That's a very weak argument for getting your own way.'

'Well, you can't blame a guy for trying.'

But he wished to God he had tried a little harder when they finally arrived back at her dismal house in west London. Snow had turned to slush and seemed to have infused the area with a layer of unappealing grey.

Aggie looked at him as he reviewed the house with an expression of thinly concealed disgust and she smiled. He was so spoiled, so used to getting everything he wanted. It was true that he had not complained once at any of the discomforts he had had to endure on their little trip, at least at any of the things which in his rarefied world would have counted as discomforts. But it would be getting on his nerves that he couldn't sort this one out. Especially when he had a point. Mr Cholmsey couldn't have created a less appealing abode to rent if he had tried.

She wondered how she could have forgotten the state of disrepair it was in.

'You could at least come back with me to my apartment,' Luiz said, lounging against the wall in the hallway as Aggie dumped her bag on the ground. 'Indulge yourself, Aggie.' His voice was as smooth as chocolate and as tempting. 'There's nothing wrong with wanting to relax in a place where the central heating doesn't sound like a car backfiring every two minutes.'

Aggie looked helplessly at him, caught up in a moment of indecision. He bent to kiss her, a sweet, delicate kiss as he tasted her mouth, not touching her anywhere else, in fact hardly moving from his indolent pose against the wall.

'Not fair,' she murmured.

'I want to get you into my bath,' Luiz murmured softly. 'My very big, very clean bath, a bath that can easily fit the both of us. And then afterwards I want you in my bed, my extra-wide and extra-long king-sized bed with clean linen. And if you're really intent on us doing the telly thing, you can switch on the television in my bedroom; it's as big as a cinema screen. But before that, I want to make love to you in comfort, and then when we're both spent I want to send out for a meal from my guy at the Savoy. No need for you to dress up or go out, just the two of us. He does an excellent chocolate mousse for dessert. I'd really like to have it flavoured with a bit of you...'

'You win,' Aggie said on a sigh of pure pleasure. She reached up and pulled him down to her and in the end they found themselves clinging to one another as they wended an unsteady path up to her bedroom.

Despite Luiz's adamant proclamations that he wanted to have her in his house, she was so damned delectable that he couldn't resist.

Her top was off by the time they hit the top of the stairs. By the bedroom door, her bra was draped over the banister and she had wriggled out of her jeans just as they both collapsed onto the bed which, far from being king-sized, was only slightly bigger than a single.

'I've been wanting to do this from the second we got into my car to drive back to London,' Luiz growled, in a manner that was decidedly un-cool. 'In fact, I was very tempted to book us into a room in the first hotel we came to just so that I could do this. I don't know what it is about you, but the second I'm near you I turn into a caveman.'

Aggie decided that she liked the sound of that. She lay back and watched as he rid himself of his clothes. This was frantic sex, two slippery bodies entwined. Leisurely foreplay would have to wait, he told her, he just needed to feel himself inside her, hot and wet and waiting for him.

Luiz could say things that drove her wild, and he drove her wild now as he huskily told her just how she made him feel when they were having sex.

Every graphic description made her wetter and more turned on and when he entered her she was so close to the edge that she had to grit her teeth together to hold herself back.

His movements were deep, his shaft big and power-ful, taking her higher and higher until she cried out as she climaxed. Her nails dug into his shoulder blades and she arched back, her head tilted back, her eyes closed, her nostrils slightly flared.

She was the most beautiful creature Luiz had ever laid eyes on. He felt himself explode inside her and by then it was too late. He couldn't hold it back. He certainly couldn't retrieve the results of his ferocious orgasm and he col-lapsed next to her with a groan.

'I didn't use protection.' He was still coming down from a high but his voice was harshly self-admonishing, bitterly angry for his oversight. He looked at her, then sat up, legs over the side of the bed, head in his hands, and cursed si-lently under his breath.

'It's okay,' Aggie said quickly. Well, if she hadn't got the message that this was a man who didn't want to set-tle down, then she was getting it now loud and clear. Not only did he not want to settle down, but the mere thought of a pregnancy was enough to turn him white with horror.

'I'm safe.'

Luiz exhaled with relief and lay back down next to her. 'Hell, I've never made that mistake in my life before. I don't know what happened.' But he did. He had lost control. This was not the man he was. He didn't lose control.

Looking at him, Aggie could see the disgust on his face that he could ever have been stupid enough, *human* enough to make a slip-up.

For all the ways he could get under her skin, she reminded herself that Luiz Montes was not available for anything other than a casual affair. She might love him but she should look for nothing more than unrequited love.

CHAPTER NINE

'WHAT'S wrong?' Luiz looked at Aggie across the width of the table in the small chain restaurant where he had just been subjected to a distinctly mediocre pizza and some even more mediocre wine.

'Nothing's wrong.' But Aggie couldn't meet his eyes. He had a way of looking at her. It made her feel as though he could see down to the bottom of her soul, as though he could dredge up things she wanted to keep to herself.

The past month had been the most amazing time of her life. She had had the last week at school, where the snow had lingered for a few days until finally all that had been left were the remains of two snowmen which the children had built.

Luiz had visited her twice at school. The first time he had just shown up. All the other teachers had been agog. The children had stared. Aggie had felt embarrassed, but embarrassed in a proud way. Everyone, all her friends at the school, would be wondering how she had managed to grab the attention of someone like Luiz, even if they didn't come right out and say it. And, frankly, Aggie still wondered how she had managed to achieve that. She didn't think that she could ever fail to get a kick just looking at him and when those dark, fabulous eyes rested on her she didn't think that she could ever fail to melt.

He had returned to Brazil for a few days over Christmas. Aggie had decided that it would be a good time to get her act together and use his absence to start building a protective shell around her, but the very second she had seen him again she had fallen straight back into the bottomless hole from which she had intended to start climbing out.

She felt as though she was on a rollercoaster. Her whole system was fired up when he was around and there wasn't a single second when she didn't want to be in his company, although at the back of her mind she knew that the rollercoaster ride would end and when it did she would be left dazed and shaken and turned inside out.

'It's this place!' Luiz flung his napkin on his half-eaten pizza and sat back in his chair.

'What?'

'Why are you too proud to accept my invitations to restaurants where the food is at least edible?'

Aggie looked at him, momentarily distracted by the brooding sulkiness on his dark face. He looked ridiculously out of place here. So tall, striking and exotic, surrounded by families with chattering kids and teenagers. But she hadn't wanted to go anywhere intimate with him. She had wanted somewhere bright, loud and impersonal.

'You've taken me to loads of expensive restaurants,' she reminded him. 'I could start listing them if you'd like.'

Luiz waved his hand dismissively. Something was wrong and he didn't like it. He had grown accustomed to her effervescence, to her teasing, to the way she made him feel as though the only satisfactory end to his day was when he saw her. Right now she was subdued, her bright-blue eyes clouded, and he didn't like the fact that he couldn't reach her.

'We need to get the bill and clear out of here,' he growled, signalling to a waitress, who appeared so quickly that Aggie thought she might have been hanging around waiting for him to call her across. 'I can think of better things to do than sit here with cold, congealing food on our plates, waiting for our tempers to deteriorate.'

'No!'

'What do you mean, *no?*' Luiz narrowed his eyes on her flushed face. Her gaze skittered away and she licked her lips nervously. The thought of her not wanting to head back to his place as fast as they could suddenly filled him with a sense of cold dread.

'I mean, it's still early.' Aggie dragged the sentence out while she frantically tried to think of how she would say what she had to say. 'Plus it's a Saturday. Everyone's out having fun.'

'Well, let's go have some fun somewhere else.' He leaned towards her and shot her a wolfish grin. 'Making love doesn't have to be confined to a bedroom. A change of scenery would work for me too...'

'A change of scenery?' Aggie asked faintly. She giddily lost herself in his persuasive, sexy, slow smile. He had come directly to her house, straight from the office, and he was still in his work clothes: a dark grey, hand-tailored suit. The tie would be bunched up in the pocket of his jacket, which he had slung over the back of the chair along with his coat, and he had rolled up the sleeves of his shirt. He looked every inch the billionaire businessman and once again she was swept away on an incredulous wave of not knowing how he could possibly be attracted to her.

And yet there were times, and lots of them, when they seemed like two halves of the same coin. Aggie had grown fond of recalling those times. Half of her knew that it was just wishful thinking on her part, a burning desire to see him relating to her in more than just an insatiably sexual capacity, but there was no harm in dreaming, was there?

'I'm losing you again.' Luiz ran his fingers through his hair and looked at her with an impatient shake of his head. 'Come on. We're getting out of here. I've had enough of this cheap and cheerful family eaterie. There's more to a Saturday night than this.'

He stood up and waited as she scrambled to her feet. It was still cold outside, but without the bite of before Christmas, when it had hurt just being outdoors. Aggie knew she should have stayed put inside the warm, noisy, crowded restaurant but coward that she was, she wanted to leave as much as he did.

Once she would have been more than satisfied with a meal out at the local pizzeria but now she could see that it could hardly be called a dining experience. It was a place to grab something or to bring kids where they could make as much mess as they wanted without staff getting annoyed.

'We could go back to my house,' Aggie said reluctantly as Luiz swung his arm over her shoulders and reached out to hail a cab with the other.

He touched her as though it was the most natural thing in the world. It was just something else she had relegated to her wishful-thinking cupboard. *If he can be so relaxed with me, surely there's more to what we have than sex…?*

Except not once had he ever hinted at what that something else might be. He never spoke of a future and she knew that he was careful not to give her any ideas. He had warned her at the beginning of their relationship that he wasn't into permanence and he had assumed that the warning held good.

He didn't love her. She was a temporary part of his life and he enjoyed her and she had given him no indication that it was any different for her.

'And where's your brother?'

'He might be there with Maria. I don't know. As you

know, he leaves for America on Monday. I think he was planning on cooking something special for them.'

'So your suggestion is we return to that dump where we'll be fighting for space alongside your brother and my niece, interrupting their final, presumably romantic meal together. Unless, of course, we hurry up to your unheated bedroom where we can squash into your tiny bed and make love as noiselessly as possible.'

Luiz loathed her house but he had given up trying to persuade her to move out to something bigger, more comfortable and paid for by him. She had dug her heels in and refused to budge, but the upshot was that they spent very little time there. In fact, the more Aggie saw her house through his eyes, the more dissatisfied she was with it.

'There's no need to be difficult!' Aggie snapped, pulling away to stare up at him. 'Why do you always have to get your own way?'

'If I always got my own way then explain why we've just spent an hour and a half in a place where the food is average and the noise levels are high enough to give people migraines. What the hell is going on, Aggie? I didn't meet you so that I could battle my way through a bad mood!'

'I can't always be sunshine and light, Luiz!'

They stared at each other. Aggie was hardly aware of the approach of a black cab until she was being hustled into it. She heard Luiz curtly give his address and sighed with frustration, because the last place she wanted to be with him was at his apartment.

'Now...' He turned to face her and extended his arm along the back of the seat. 'Talk to me. Tell me what's going on.' His eyes drifted to the mutinous set of her mouth and he wanted to do nothing more than kiss it back into smiling submission. He wasn't normally given to issuing invitations to women to talk. He was a man of action and his preferred choice, when faced with a woman who clearly *wanted to talk*, was to bury all chat between the sheets. But Aggie, he had to concede, was different. If he suggested burying the chat between the sheets, she would probably round on him with the full force of her feisty, outspoken, brazenly argumentative personality.

'We do need to talk,' she admitted quietly, and she felt him go still next to her.

'Well, I'm all ears.'

'Not here. We might as well wait till we get to your place, although I would have preferred to have this conversation in the restaurant.'

'You mean where we would hardly have been able to hear one another?'

'What I have to say…people around would have made it easier.'

Luiz was getting a nasty, unsettled feeling in the pit of his stomach. She had turned him down once. It was something he hadn't forgotten. This sounded very much like a second let-down and he wasn't about to let that happen. Pride slammed into him with the force of a sledgehammer.

'I'm getting the message that this *talk* of yours has to do with us?'

Aggie nodded miserably. This *talk* was something she had rehearsed in her head for the past four hours and yet she was no closer to knowing where she would begin.

'What's there to talk about?' Luiz drawled grimly. 'We've already covered this subject. I'm not looking for commitment. Nor, you told me, were you. We understand one another. We're on the same page.'

'Sometimes things change.'

'Are you telling me that you're no longer satisfied with what we've got? That after a handful of weeks you're looking for something more?' Luiz refused to contemplate having his wings clipped. He especially didn't care for the thought of having anyone try to clip them on his behalf. Was she about to issue him with some kind of ultimatum? Promise more if he wanted to carry on seeing her, sleeping with her? Just thinking about it outraged him. Other women might have dropped hints—grown misty-eyed in front of jewellers, introduced him to friends with babies—but none of them had ever actually given him a stark choice and he was getting the feeling that that was precisely what Aggie was thinking of doing.

Aggie clenched her fists on her lap. The tone of his voice was like a slap in the face. Did he really think that she had been stupid enough to misunderstand his very clear ground rules?

'What if I were?' she asked, curious to see where this conversation would take them, already predicting its final, painful destination and willing it masochistically on herself.

'Then I'd question whether you weren't wondering if being married to a rich man might be more financially lucrative than dating him!'

Every muscle in Aggie's body tensed and she looked at him astounded, hurt and horrified.

'How could you *say* that?'

Luiz scowled and looked away. He fully deserved that reprimand. He could scarcely credit that he had actually accused her of having a financial agenda. She had proved to be one of the least materialistic women he had ever met. But, hell, the thought of her walking out on him had sparked something in him he could barely understand.

'I apologise,' he said roughly. 'That was below the belt.'

'But do you honestly believe it?' Aggie was driven to know whether this man she loved so much could think so little of her that he actually thought she might try and con him into commitment.

'No. I don't.'

She breathed a sigh of relief because she would never have been able to live with that.

'Then why did you say it?'

'Look, I don't know what this is about, but I'm not interested in playing games. And I won't have my hand forced. Not by you. Not by anybody.'

'Because you don't need anyone? The great Luiz Montes doesn't need anything or anyone!'

'And tell me, what's wrong with that?' He was baffled by her. Why the hell was she spoiling for a fight? And why had she suddenly decided that she wanted more than what they had? Things had been pretty damn good between them. Better than good. He fought down the temptation to explode.

'I don't want to have this argument with you,' Aggie said, glancing towards the taxi driver who was maintaining a discreet disinterest. He probably heard this kind of thing all the time.

'And I don't want to argue with you,' Luiz confirmed smoothly. 'So why don't we pretend none of it happened?' There was one way of stalling any further confrontation. He pulled her towards him and curled his hands into her soft hair.

Aggie's protesting hands against his chest curved into an aching caress. As his tongue delved to explore her mouth, she felt her body come alive. Her nipples tightened in the lace bra, pushing forward in a painful need to be suckled and touched. Her skin burned and the wetness between her legs was an agonising reminder of how this man could get to her. No matter that there was talking to be done. No matter that making love was not what she wanted to do.

'Now, isn't that better?' he murmured with satisfaction. 'I'd carry on, my darling, but I wouldn't want to shock our cab driver.'

As if to undermine that statement, he curved his hand over one full breast and slowly massaged it until she had to stop herself from crying out.

Ever since they had begun seeing one another, her wardrobe had undergone a subtle transformation. The uninspiring clothes she had worn had been replaced by a selection of brighter, more figure-hugging outfits.

'You're wearing a bra,' he chided softly into her ear. 'You know I hate that.'

'You can't always get what you want, Luiz.'

'But it's what we *both* want, isn't it? I get to touch you without the boring business of having to get rid of a bra and you get to be touched without the boring business of having to get rid of a bra. It's a win-win situation. Still, I guess sometimes it adds a little spice to the mix if I have to work my way through layers of clothes...'

'Stop it, Luiz!'

'Tell me you don't like what I'm doing.' He had shimmied his hand underneath the tight, striped jumper and had pulled down her bra to free one plump mound.

This was the way to stifle an argument, he thought. Maybe he had misread the whole thing. Maybe she hadn't been upping the ante. Maybe what she wanted to talk about had been altogether more prosaic. Luiz didn't know and he had no intention of revisiting the topic.

With a rueful sigh, he released her as the taxi slowed, moving into the crescent. He neatly pulled down the jumper, straightening it. 'Perhaps just as well that we're here,' he confessed with a wicked glint in his dark eyes.

'Going all the way in the back seat of a black cab would really be taking things a step too far. I think when we get round to public performing we'll have to think carefully where to begin...'

Aggie had had no intention of performing with him on any level, never mind in public. She shifted in the seat. When she should have been as cool as she could, she was hot and flustered and having to push thoughts of him taking her in his hallway out of her head.

The house which had once filled her with awe she now appreciated in a distinctly less gob-smacked way. She still loved the beautiful *objets d'art*, but there were few personal touches which made her think that money could buy some things, but not others. It could buy beauty but not necessarily atmosphere. In fact, going out with Luiz had made her distinctly less cowed at the impressive things money could buy and a lot less daunted by the people who possessed it.

'So.' Luiz discarded his coat and jacket as soon as they were through the door. 'Shall we finish what we started? No need to go upstairs. If you go right into the kitchen and sit on one of the stools, I'll demonstrate how handy I can be with food. I guarantee I'll be a damn sight more imaginative with ingredients than that restaurant tonight was.'

'Luiz.' She was shaking as she placed her hand firmly on his chest. No giving in this time.

'Good God, woman! Tell me you don't want to start talking again.' He pushed his hands under her coat to cup her rounded buttocks, pulling her against him so that she could feel his arousal pushing through his trousers, as hard as a rod of iron. 'And, if you want to talk, then let's talk in bed.'

'Bed's not a good idea,' Aggie said shakily.

'Who says I want good ideas?'

'I'd like a cup of coffee.'

Luiz gave in with a groan of pure frustration. He banged his fist on the wall, shielded his head in the crook of his arm and then glanced at her with rueful resignation.

'Okay. You win. But take it from me, talking is never a very good idea.'

How true, Aggie thought. From his point of view, it would certainly not herald anything he wanted to hear.

She marvelled that in a few hours life could change so dramatically.

She had been poring over the school calendar and working out what lessons she should think about setting when something in her head had suddenly clicked.

She had seen the calendar and the concept of dates had begun to flicker. Dates of when she had last seen her period. She had never paid a great deal of attention to her menstrual cycle. It happened roughly on time. What more was there to say about it?

Her hands had been shaking when, a little over an hour later, she had taken that home-pregnancy test. She had already thought of a thousand reasons why she was silly to be concerned. For a start, Luiz was obsessive about contraception. Aside from that one little slip-up, he had been scrupulous.

Within minutes she had discovered how one little slip-up could change the course of someone's life.

She was pregnant by a man who didn't love her, had warned her off involvement and had certainly never expressed any desire to have children. In the face of all those stark realities, she had briefly contemplated not telling him. Just breaking off the relationship; disappearing. Disappearing, she had reasoned for a few wild, disoriented moments, would not be difficult to do. She hated the house and her brother was soon to leave London to embark upon the next exciting phase of his life. She could ditch everything and return up north, find something there. Luiz would not pursue her and he would never know that he had fathered a child.

The thought didn't last long. He would find out; of course he would. Maria would tell him. And, aside from that, how could she deprive a man of his own child? Even a child he hadn't wanted?

'What I'm going to say will shock you,' Aggie told him as soon as they were sitting down in his living room, with a respectable distance between them.

Luiz, for the first time in his life, was prey to fear. It ripped through him, strangling his vocal chords, making him break out in a fine film of perspiration.

'You're not…ill, are you?'

Aggie looked at him with surprise. 'No. I'm not,' she asserted firmly. He had visibly blanched and she knew why. Of course, he would be remembering his own father's illness, which he had spoken to her about in more depth over the time they had been together.

'Then what is it?'

'There's no easy way to tell you so I'm going to come right out and say it. I'm pregnant.'

Luiz froze. For a few seconds, he wondered whether he had heard correctly but he was not a man given to flights of imagination and the expression on her face was sufficient to tell him that she wasn't joking.

'You can't be,' he said eventually.

Aggie's eyes slid away from his. Whenever she had thought of being pregnant, it had been within a rosy scenario involving a man she loved who loved her back. Never had she envisaged breaking the news to a man who looked as though she had detonated a bomb in his front room.

'I'm afraid I can be, and I am.'

'I was careful!'

'There was that one time.' Against her better judgement—for she had hardly expected her news to be met with whoops of joy—she could feel a slow anger begin to burn inside her.

'You told me that there was no risk.'

'I'm sorry. I made a mistake.'

Luiz didn't say anything. He stood up and walked restively towards the floor-to-ceiling window to stare outside. The possibility of fatherhood was not one that had ever occurred to him. It was something that lay in the future. Way down the line. Possibly never. But she was carrying his baby inside her.

Aggie miserably looked at him, turned away from her and staring out of the window. Doubtless he was thinking about his life which now lay in ruins. If ever there was a man who was crushed under the weight of bad news, then he was that man.

'You decided to tell me this in a *pizzeria*?' Luiz spun round and walked towards her. He leaned over, bracing himself on either side of her, and Aggie shrank back into the chair.

'I didn't want…*this*!' she cried.

'This *what*?'

'I knew how you'd react and I thought it would be more…more…civilised if I told you somewhere out in the open!'

'What did you think I would do?'

'We need to discuss this like adults and we're not going to get anywhere when you're standing over me like this, threatening me!'

'God, how the hell did this happen?' Luiz returned to the sofa and collapsed onto it.

It felt to Aggie as though everything they had shared

had shattered under the blow of this pregnancy. Which just went to show how fragile it had all been from the very start. Not made to last and not fashioned to withstand any knocks—although, in fairness, a pregnancy couldn't really be called a knock. More like an earthquake, shaking everything from the foundations up.

'Stupid question.' He pressed his thumbs to his eyes and then leaned forward to look at her, his hands resting loosely on his thighs. 'Of course I know how it happened, and you're right. We have to talk about it. Hell, what's there to talk about? We'll have to get married. What choice do we have?'

'Get married? That's not what I want!' she threw at him, fighting to contain her anger because he was just doing what, in his misguided way, he construed as the decent thing. 'Do you really think I told you about this because I wanted you to marry me?'

'What does it matter? My family would be bitterly disappointed to think I had fathered a child and allowed it to be born out of wedlock.'

What a wonderful marriage proposal, Aggie thought with a touch of hysteria: *you're pregnant; we'd better get married or risk the wrath of my traditional family.*

'I don't think so,' Aggie said gently.

'What does that mean?'

'It means that I can't accept your generous marriage proposal.'

'Don't be crazy. Of course you can!'

'I have no intention of marrying someone just because I happen to be having his baby. Luiz, a pregnancy is not the right reason to be married to someone.' She could tell from the expression on his face that he was utterly taken aback that his offer had been rejected. 'I'm sorry if your parents would find it unacceptable for you to have a child

out of wedlock, but I'm not going to marry you so that
your parents can avoid disappointment.'

'That's not the only reason!'

'Well, what are the others?' She could quell the faint
hope that he would say those three words she wanted to
hear. That he loved her. He could expand on that. She
wouldn't stop him. He could tell her that he couldn't live
without her.

'It's better for a child to have both parents on hand. I
am a rich man. I don't intend that any child of mine will
go wanting. Two reasons and there's more!' Why, Luiz
thought, was she being difficult? She had just brought his
entire world crashing down around him and he had risen
admirably to the occasion! Couldn't she see that?

'A child can have both parents on hand without them
being married,' Aggie pointed out. 'I'm not going to deprive you of the opportunity to see him or her whenever
you want, and of course I understand that you will want
to assist financially. I would never dream of stopping you
from doing that.' She lowered her eyes and nervously fiddled with her fingers.

There was something else that would have to be discussed. Would they continue to see one another? Part of
her craved their ongoing relationship and the strength and
support she would get from it. Another part realised that
it would be foolhardy to carry on as though nothing had
happened, as though a rapidly expanding stomach wasn't
proof that their lives had changed for ever. She wouldn't
marry him. She couldn't allow him to ruin his life for
the sake of a gesture born from obligation. She hated the
thought of what would happen as cold reality set in and
he realised that he was stuck with her for good. He would
end up hating and resenting her. He would seek solace in

the arms of other women. He might even, one day, find a
woman to truly love.

'And there's something else,' she said quietly. 'I don't
think it's appropriate that we continue...seeing one another.'

'What?' Luiz exploded, his body alive with anger and
bewilderment.

'Stop shouting!'

'Then don't give me a reason to shout!'

They stared at each other in silence. Aggie's heart was
pounding inside her. 'What we have was never going to
go the full distance. We both knew that. You were very
clear on that.'

'Whoa! Before you get carried away with the preaching,
answer me this one thing. Do we or do we not have fun
when we're together?' Luiz felt as though he had started
the evening with clear skies and calm seas, only to discover that a force-ten hurricane had been waiting just over
the horizon. Not only had he found himself with a baby on
the way, but on top of that here she was, informing him
that she no longer wanted to have anything to do with
him. A growing sense of panicked desperation made him
feel slightly ill.

'That's not the point!'

'Then what the hell is? You're not making any sense,
Aggie! I've offered to do the right thing by you and you
act as though I've insulted you. You rumble on about a
child not being a good enough reason for us to be married.
I don't get it! Not only is a child a bloody good reason to
get married, but here's the added bonus—we're good together! But that's not enough for you! Now, you're talking
about walking away from this relationship!'

'We're friends at the moment and that's how I'd like
our relationship to stay for the sake of our child, Luiz.'

'We're more than just friends, damn it!'

'We're friends with benefits.'

'I can't believe I'm hearing this!' He slashed the air with his hand in a gesture of frustration, incredulity and impatience. His face was dark with anger and those beautiful eyes that could turn her hot and cold were flat with accusation.

In this sort of mood, withstanding him was like trying to swim up a waterfall. Aggie wanted to fly to him and just let him decide what happened next. She knew it would be a mistake. If they carried on seeing one another and reached the point where, inevitably, he became fed up and bored, their relationship thereafter would be one of bitterness and discomfort. Couldn't he see long-term? For a man who could predict trends and work out the bigger picture when it came to business, he was hopelessly inadequate in doing the same when it came to his private life. He lived purely for the moment. Right now he was living purely for the moment with her and he wasn't quite ready for it to end. Right now, his solution to their situation was to put a ring on her finger, thereby appeasing family and promoting his sense of responsibility. He just didn't think ahead.

Aggie knew, deep down, that if she didn't love him she would have accepted that marriage proposal. She would not have invested her emotions in a hopeless situation. She would have been able to see their union as an arrangement that made sense and would have been thankful that he was standing by her. Was it any wonder that he was now looking at her as though she had taken leave of her senses?

'I don't want us to carry on, waiting until the physical side of things runs out of steam and you start looking somewhere else,' she told him bluntly. 'I don't want to become so disillusioned with you that I resent you being in my life. It wouldn't be a good background for a child.'

'Who says the physical side would run out of steam?'

'It always has for you! Hasn't it? Unless…I'm different? Unless what you feel for me is…different?'

Suddenly feeling cornered, Luiz fell back on the habits of a lifetime of not yielding to leading questions. 'You're having my baby. Of course you're different.'

'I'm beginning to feel tired, Luiz.' Aggie wondered why she continued to hope for words that weren't going to come. 'And you've had a shock. I think we both need to take a little time out to think about things, and when we next meet we can discuss the practicalities.'

'The practicalities…?' Luiz was finding it hard to get a grip on events.

'You've been nagging me to move out of that house.' Aggie smiled wryly. 'I guess that might be something on the list to discuss.' She stood up to head for her coat and he stilled her with his hand.

'I don't want you going back to that place tonight. Or ever. It's disgusting. You have my baby to consider now.'

'And that's the word, Luiz—*discuss*. Which doesn't mean you tell me what you want me to do and I obey.'

She began putting on her coat while Luiz watched with the feeling that she was slipping through his fingers.

'You're making a mistake,' he ground out, barring her exit and staring down at her.

'I think,' Aggie said sadly, 'the mistakes have already been made.'

CHAPTER TEN

Luiz looked at the pile of reports lying on his desk eagerly awaiting his attention and swivelled his chair round to face the expanse of glass that overlooked the busy London streets several stories below.

It was another one of those amazing spring days: blue, cloudless skies, a hint of a breeze. It did nothing to improve his concentration levels. Or his mood, for that matter. Frankly, his mood was in urgent need of improvement ever since Aggie had announced her pregnancy over two months ago.

For the first week, he had remained convinced that she would come to her senses and accept his offer of marriage. He had argued for it from a number of fronts. He had demanded that she give him more good reasons why she couldn't see it from his point of view. It had been as successful as beating his head against a brick wall. It had seemed to him, in his ever-increasing frustration, that the harder he tried to push the faster she retreated, so he had dropped the subject and they had discussed all those practicalities she had talked about.

At least there she had listened to what he had to say and agreed with pretty much everything. At least her pride wasn't going to let her get in the way of accepting the massively generous financial help he had insisted on providing, although she had stopped short of letting him buy her the house of her dreams.

'When I move into my dream house,' she had told him, her mouth set in a stubborn line, 'I don't want to know that it's been bought for me as part of a package deal because I happen to be pregnant.'

But she had moved out of the hovel two weeks previously, into a small, modern box in a pleasant part of London close to her job. The job which she insisted she would carry on doing until she no longer could, despite his protests that there was no need, that she had to look after herself.

'I'm more than happy to accept financial help as far as the baby is concerned,' she had told him firmly. 'But there's no need for you to lump me in the same bracket.'

'You're the mother of my child. Of course I'm going to make sure that you get all the money you need.'

'I'm not going to be dependent on you, Luiz. I intend to carry on working until I have the baby and then I shall take it up again as soon as I feel the baby is old enough for a nursery. The hours are good at the school and there are all the holidays. It's a brilliant job to have if you've got a family.'

Luiz loathed the thought of that just as he loathed the fact that she had managed to shut him out of her life. They communicated, and there were no raised voices, but she had withdrawn from him and it grated on him, made him ill-tempered at work, incapable of concentrating.

And now something else had descended to prey on his mind. It was a thought that had formulated a week ago when she had mentioned in passing that she would be going to the spring party which all the teachers had every year.

Somehow, he had contrived to ignore the fact that she had a social life outside him. Reminded of it, he had quizzed her on what her fellow teachers were like, and had discovered that they weren't all female and they weren't all middle-aged. They enjoyed an active social life. The teaching community was close-knit, with many teachers from different schools socialising out of work.

'You're pregnant,' he had informed her. 'Parties are a no-go area.'

'Don't worry. I won't be drinking,' she had laughed, and right then he had had a worrying thought.

She had turned down his marriage proposal, had put their relationship on a formal basis, and was this because she just wanted to make sure that she wasn't tied down? Had he been sidelined because at the back of her mind, baby or no baby, she wanted to make sure that she could return to an active social life? One that involved other men, the sort of men she was normally drawn to? He had been an aberration. Was she eager to resume relationships with one of those creative types who weren't mired in work and driven by ambition?

Luiz thought of the reports waiting on his desk and smiled sardonically. If only she knew... No one could accuse him of being mired in work now, or driven by ambition. Having a bomb detonate in his life had certainly compelled him to discover the invaluable art of delegation! If only his mother could see him now, she would be overjoyed that work was no longer the centre of his universe.

A call interrupted the familiar downward trend of his thoughts and he took it on the second ring.

He listened, scribbled something on a piece of paper and stood up.

For the first time in weeks, he felt as though he was finally doing something; finally, for better or for worse, trying to stop a runaway train, which was what his life had become.

Over the weeks, his secretary had grown so accustomed to her boss's moody unpredictability—a change from the man whose life had previously been so highly organised—that she nodded without question when he told her that he would be going out and wasn't sure when he would be back. She had stopped pointing out meetings that required his presence. Her brain now moved into another gear, the one which had her immediately working out who would replace him.

Luiz called his driver on his way down. Aggie would be at school. He tried to picture her expression when he showed up. It distracted him from more tumultuous thoughts—thoughts of her having his child and then re-discovering a single life; thoughts of her getting involved with another man; thoughts of that other man bringing up his, Luiz's, child as his own while Luiz was relegated to playing second fiddle. The occasional father.

Having never suffered the trials and tribulations of a fertile imagination, he found that he had more than made up for the lifelong omission. Now, his imagination seemed to be a monstrous thing released from a holding pen in which it had been imprisoned for its entire life, and now it was making up for lost time.

It was a situation that Luiz could not allow to continue but, as the car wound its way through traffic that was as dense as treacle, he was gripped by a strange sense of panic. He had spent all of his adult life knowing where he was going, knowing how he was going to get there. Recently, the signposts had been removed and the road was no longer a straight one forward. Instead, it curved in all directions and he had no idea where he would end up. He just knew the person he wanted to find at its destination.

'Can't you go a little faster?' he demanded, and cursed silently when his driver shot him a jaundiced look in the rear-view mirror before pointing out that they hadn't yet invented a car that could fly—although, when and if they ever did, he was sure that Mr Montes would be the first to own one.

They made it to the school just as the bell sounded for lunch and Aggie was heading to the staff room. She had been blessed with an absence of morning sickness but she felt tired a lot of the time.

And it was such a struggle maintaining a distance from Luiz. Whenever she heard that deep, dark drawl down the end of the telephone, asking her how her day had been, insisting she tell him everything she had done, telling her about what he had done, she wanted nothing more than to take back everything she had said about not wanting him in her life. He phoned a lot. He visited a lot. He treated her like a piece of delicate china, and when she told him not to he shrugged his shoulders ruefully and informed her that he couldn't help being a dinosaur when it came to stuff like that.

She had thought when she had delivered her speech to him all those weeks ago that he would quickly come to terms with the fact that he would not be shackled to her for the wrong reasons. She had thought that he would soon begin to thank her for letting him off the hook, that he would begin to relish his freedom. An over-developed sense of responsibility was something that wouldn't last very long. He didn't love her. It would be easy for him to cut the strings once he had been given permission to do so.

But he wasn't making it easy for her to get over him. Or to move on.

She had now moved from the dump, as he had continued to call it, and was happy enough in the small, modern house he had provided for her. She was still in her job and had insisted that she would carry on working before and after the baby was born, but there were times when she longed to be away from London with its noise, pollution and traffic.

And, aside from those natural doubts, she was plagued by worries about how things would unravel over time.

She couldn't envisage ever seeing him without being affected. Having been so convinced that she was doing the right thing in refusing to marry him, having prided herself on her cool ability to look at the bigger picture, she found herself riddled with angst that she might have made the wrong decision.

She stared with desolation at the sandwich she had brought in with her and was about to bite into it when... there he was.

Amid the chaos of children running in the corridors and teachers moving around the school stopping to tell them off, Luiz was suddenly in front of her, lounging against the door to the staff room.

'I know you don't like me coming here,' Luiz greeted her as he strolled towards her desk. He wondered whether she should be eating more than just a sandwich for her lunch but refrained from asking.

'You always cause such a commotion,' Aggie said honestly. 'What do you want, anyway? I have a lot of work to do during my lunch hour. I can't take time out.'

As always, she had to fight the temptation to touch him. It was as though, whenever she saw him, her brain sent signals to her fingers, making them restive at remembered pleasures. He always looked so good! Too good. His hair had grown and he hadn't bothered to cut it and the slight extra length suited him, made him even more outrageously sexy. Now he had perched on the side of her table and she had to drag her eyes away from the taut pull of his trousers over his muscular thighs.

Luiz watched as she looked away, eager for him to leave, annoyed that he had shown up at her workplace. Tough. He couldn't carry on as he had. He was going crazy. There were things he needed to say to her and, the further she floated away from him, the more redundant his words would become.

Teachers were drifting in now, released from their classes by the bell, and Luiz couldn't stop himself from glancing at them, trying to see whether any of the men might be contenders for Aggie. There were three guys so far, all in their thirties from the looks of it, but surely none of them would appeal to her?

Once, he would have been arrogantly certain of his seductive power over her. Unfortunately, he was a lot less confident on that score, and he scowled at the thought that some skinny guy with ginger hair might become his replacement.

'You look tired,' Luiz said abruptly.

'Have you come here to do a spot check on me? I wish you'd stop clucking over me like a mother hen, Luiz. I told you I can take care of myself and I can.'

'I haven't come here to do a spot check on you.'

'Then why are you here?' She risked a look at him and was surprised at the hesitation on his face.

'I want to take you somewhere. I… There are things I need to…talk to you about.'

Instinctively, Aggie knew that whatever he wanted to talk about would not involve finances, the baby or her health—all of which were subjects he covered in great detail in his frequent visits—whilst, without even being aware of it, continuing to charm her with witty anecdotes of what he was up to and the people he met. So what, she wondered nervously, could be important enough for him to interrupt her working day and to put such a hesitant expression on his usually confident face?

All at once her imagination took flight. There was no doubt that he was getting over her. He had completely stopped mentioning marriage. In fact, she hadn't heard a word on the subject for weeks. He visited a lot and phoned a lot but she knew that that was because of the baby she was carrying. He was an 'all or nothing' man. Having never contemplated the thought of fatherhood, he had had it foisted upon him and had reacted by embracing it with an enthusiasm that was so typical of his personality. He did nothing in half-measures.

As the woman who happened to be carrying his child, she was swept up in the tidal wave of his enthusiasm. But already she could see the signs of a man who no longer viewed her with the untrammelled lust he once had. He could see her so often and speak to her so often because she had become *a friend*. She no longer stirred his passion.

Aggie knew that she should have been happy about this because it was precisely what she had told him, at the beginning, was necessary for their relationship to survive on a long-term basis. Friendship and not lust would be the key to the sort of amicable union they would need to be good parents to their child.

Where he had taken that on board, however, she was still struggling and now she couldn't think what he might want to talk to her about that had necessitated a random visit to the school.

Could it be that he had found someone else? That would account for the shadow of uncertainty on his face. Luiz was not an uncertain man. Fear gripped her, turning her complexion chalky white. She could think of no other reason for him to be here and to want to *have a talk* with her. A talk that was so urgent it couldn't wait. He intended to brace her for the news before she heard about it via the grapevine, for her brother would surely find out and impart the information to her.

'Is it about…financial stuff?' she asked, clinging to the hope that he would say yes.

'It's nothing to do with money, or with any practicalities, Aggie. My car's outside.'

Aggie nodded but her body was numb all over as she gathered her things, her bag, her lightweight jacket and followed him to where his car was parked on a single yellow line outside the school.

'Where are we going? I have to be back at school by one-thirty.'

'You might have to call and tell them that you'll be later.'

'Why? What can you have to say that can't be said closer to the school? There's a café just down that street ahead. Let's go there and get this little talk of yours over and done with.'

'It's not that easy, I'm afraid.'

She noticed that the hesitation was back and it chilled her once again to the core.

'I'm stronger than you think,' she said, bracing herself. 'I can handle whatever you have to tell me. You don't need to get me to some fancy restaurant to break the news.'

'We're not going to a fancy restaurant. I know you well enough by now not to make the mistake of taking you somewhere fancy unless you have at least an hour to get ready in advance.'

'It's not my fault I still get a little nervous at some of those places you've taken me to. I don't feel comfortable being surrounded by celebrities!'

'And it's what I like about you,' Luiz murmured. That, along with all the thousands of other little quirks which should have shown him by now the significance of what he felt for her. He had always counted himself as a pretty shrewd guy and yet, with her, he had been as thick as the village idiot.

'It is?' Aggie shamefully grasped that barely audible compliment.

'I want to show you something.' The traffic was free-flowing and they were driving quickly out of London now, heading towards the motorway. For a while, Aggie's mind went into freefall as she recollected the last time she had been in a car heading out of London. His car. Except then, the snow had been falling thick and fast and little had she known that she had been heading towards a life-changing destiny. If, at the time, she had been in possession of a crystal ball, would she have looked into it and backed away from sleeping with him? The answer, of course, was no. For better or for worse she had thought at the time, and she still thought so now, even though the better had lasted for precious little time.

'What?' Aggie pressed anxiously.

'You'll have to wait and see.'

'Where are we going?'

'Berkshire. Close enough. We'll be there shortly.'

Aggie fell silent but her mind continued playing with a range of ever-changing worst-case scenarios, yet she couldn't imagine what he could possibly have to show her outside London. She hadn't thought there was much out-side the city that interested him although, to be fair, when-ever he spoke of his time spent on that fateful journey, his voice held a certain affection for the places they had seen.

She was still trying to work things out when the car eventually pulled up in front of a sprawling field and he reached across to push open the door for her.

'What…what are we doing here?' She looked at him in

bewilderment and he urged her out, leading her across the grass verge and into the field which, having been reached via a series of twisting, small lanes, seemed to be surrounded by nothing. It was amazing, considering they were still so close to London.

'Do you like it?' Luiz gazed down at her as she mulled over his question.

'It's a field, Luiz. It's peaceful.'

'You don't like me buying you things,' he murmured roughly. 'You have no idea how hard it is for me to resist it but you've made me see that there are other ways of expressing...what I feel for you. Hell, Aggie. I don't know if I'm telling you this the way I should. I'm no good at... things like this—talking about feelings.'

Aggie stared up at his perfect face, shadowed with doubt and strangely vulnerable. 'What are you trying to say?'

'Something I should have said a long time ago.' He looked down at her and shuffled awkwardly. 'Except I barely recognised it myself, until you turned me away. Aggie, I've been going crazy. Thinking about you. Wanting you. Wondering how I'm going to get through life without you. I don't know if I've left it too late, but I can't live without you. I need you.'

Buffeted in all directions by wonderful waves of hope, Aggie could only continue to stare. She was finding it hard to make the necessary connections. Caution was pleading with her not to jump to conclusions but the look in his eyes was filling her with burgeoning, breathless excitement.

Luiz stared into those perfect blue eyes and took strength from them.

'I don't know what you feel for me,' he said huskily. 'I turned you on but that wasn't enough. When it came to women, I wasn't used to dealing in any other currency aside from sex. How was I to know that what I felt for you went far beyond lust?'

'When you say *far beyond...*'

'I don't know when I fell in love with you, but I did and, fool that I am, it's been a realisation that's been long in coming. I can only hope not too long. Look, Aggie...' He raked long fingers through his hair and shook his head in the manner of someone trying hard to marshal his thoughts into coherent sentences. 'I'm taking the biggest gamble of my life here, and hoping that I haven't blown all my chances with you. I love you and...I want to marry you. We were happy once, we had fun. You may not love me now, but I swear to God I have enough love for the two of us and one day you'll come to...'

'Shh.' She placed a finger over his beautiful mouth. 'Don't say another word.' Tears trembled, glazing over her eyes. 'I turned down your marriage proposal because I couldn't cope with the thought that the man I was...*am*... desperately in love with had only proposed because he thought it was the thing he should do. I couldn't face the thought of a reluctant, resentful husband. It would have meant my heart breaking every day we were together and that's why I turned you down.' She removed her finger and tiptoed to lightly kiss his lips.

'You'll marry me?'

Aggie smiled broadly and fell into him, reaching up to link her hands behind his neck. 'It's been agony seeing you and talking to you,' she confessed. 'I kept wondering if I had done the right thing.'

'Well, it's good to hear that I wasn't the only one suffering.'

'So you brought me all the way out here to tell me that you love me?'

'To show you this field and hope that it could be my strongest argument to win you back.'

'What do you mean?'

'Like I said.' Luiz, with his arm around her shoulders, turned her so that they were both looking at the same sprawling vista of grass and trees. 'I know you don't like me buying you things so I bought this for us. Both of us.'

'You bought...this field?'

'Thirty acres of land with planning permission to build. There are strict guidelines on what we can build but we can design it together. This was going to be my last attempt to prove to you that I was no longer the arrogant guy you once couldn't stand, that I could think out of the box, that I was worth the gamble.'

'My darling.' Aggie turned to him. 'I love you so much.' There was so much more she wanted to say but she was so happy, so filled with joy that she could hardly speak.

* * * * *

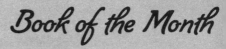

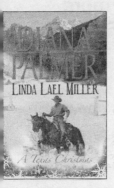

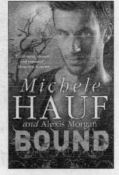

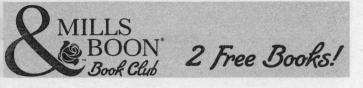

MILLS & BOON Book Club

2 Free Books!

Get your free books now at
www.millsandboon.co.uk/freebookoffer

Or fill in the form below and post it back to us

THE MILLS & BOON® BOOK CLUB™—HERE'S HOW IT WORKS: Accepting your free books places you under no obligation to buy anything. You may keep the books and return the despatch note marked 'Cancel'. If we do not hear from you, about a month later we'll send you 4 brand-new stories from the Modern™ series priced at £3.49* each. There is no extra charge for post and packaging. You may cancel at any time, otherwise we will send you 4 stories a month which you may purchase or return to us—the choice is yours. *Terms and prices subject to change without notice. Offer valid in UK only. Applicants must be 18 or over. Offer expires 31st January 2013. **For full terms and conditions, please go to www.millsandboon.co.uk/freebookoffer**

Mrs/Miss/Ms/Mr (please circle)
_____

First Name
_____

Surname
_____

Address
_____

_____

_____ Postcode _____

E-mail
_____

Send this completed page to: Mills & Boon Book Club, Free Book Offer, FREEPOST NAT 10298, Richmond, Surrey, TW9 1BR

Find out more at
www.millsandboon.co.uk/freebookoffer

Visit us Online

0712/P2YEA